MAGIKAL RECKONING

ALX CHAN YEE

Content/Trigger Warning List

Explicit sexual content, Sucidal Ideation, Blood/graphic torture, Mentions of disordered eating, Image issues, SA mention (not explicit), Mental health issues, Family problems (i.e. generational trauma), Alcohol and drug use, Vomit, Slight body shaming (not explicit), Body dysmorphia, Toxic relationships, Mentions of slight substance addiction/dependency (not explicit)

Magikal Reckoning
Book 2
Cover Design: kiajaelyn.com
Edited by: Jude Baet and Quinton Li

FIRST EDITION: FEBRUARY 2025

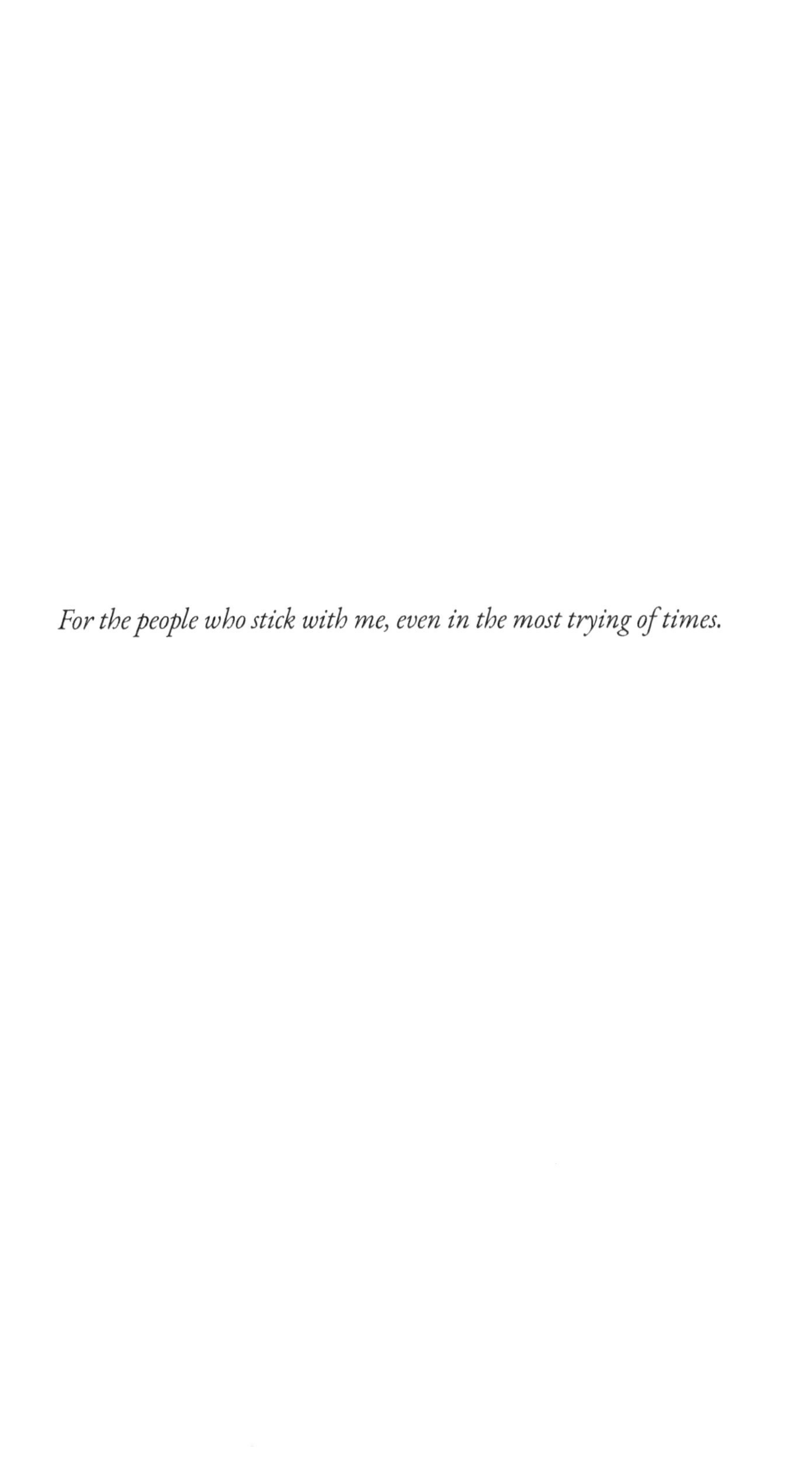

For the people who stick with me, even in the most trying of times.

Legend
Settlements
Estate/House
Border

House of Smoldris
HEARTHIS
WINDWYR
AQUATIUS
Shopping Center
House of Chauvet
House of Oris
ENTHAR
Market
Aeon Estate
Shopping Center

House of Zephys
Shopping Center
Inn
MINDAE
Market
Lake Mindae
Nexus Estate
Phantom Tower
Darkened Forest
IFAERIS

A Pronunciation Guide
POSSIBLE SPOILERS! READ AT YOUR
OWN RISK!

NAMES:

DISARIS: De-sare-is
AEON: A-yawn
ORIS: Or-ehs
CHAUVET: Show-vay
SMOLDRIS: Smol-dress
ZEPHYS: Zeh-phees

LAND/AREAS:

IFAERIS: If-fur-is
CREATURELANDS: Cree-ture Lands
SEARUCKS: See-rooks
MAGIK COVE: Mah-gik Cove
GIGANTIA: Jeye-gan-teeah
HUMAN LANDS: Hue-man Lands
MINDAE: Min-day
ENTHAR: Ehn-thar
AQUATIUS: Ah-kway-shus
HEARTHIS: Har-this
WINDWYRD: Wind-word
LAZIPEUS: Lah-zeh-!s

BLOODLINES:

AIRLIUS: Air-lee-us
FLAMELING: Flame-leen
ROKUS: Rock-us
WATERIEVER: Water-reever
SPIRITUS: Spirit-ous

OTHER:

OKKARING: Ah-ker-een
LASIALIC: Luh-zye-lack
VALSKULL: Vahl-skuhll

Prologue

Arabella

Knives and stones will shatter your bones, but words might be what kills me.

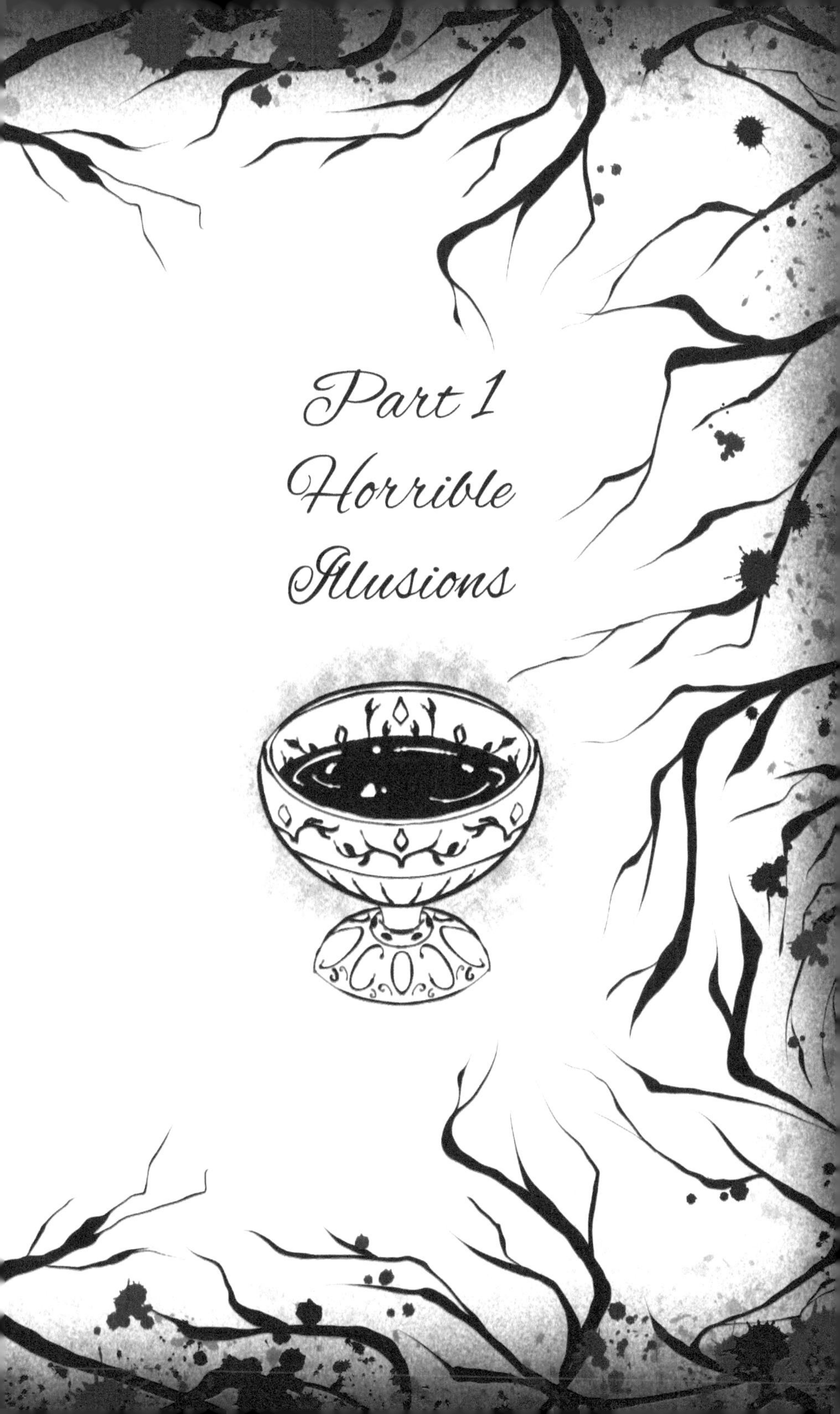

Part 1
Horrible
Illusions

I

Two Months of Nothing

Luka

The room was bone-chilling. Filled with Cassius' shadows and fear coming from the common fae in front of us. He knew what was in his future. There was no hope for him.

Neither of us cared. We entered Phantom Tower with one goal in mind, and that was to gather as much information as we could from those who served Adonis. Unfortunately for this Fae, I lost any patience I had when it came to extracting information from each prisoner.

None captured gave us reliable answers. We were fed nothing but trembles or silence. This one, called Alistair, had the poor luck of being the last Fae we planned on speaking to for the day.

He wasn't interesting by any means. Starting by spewing hatred and disdain for the Disaris family.

That is, until we used our methods.

We began with light torture, drowning him using cloth and water, moving to strangulation from shadows, and finally, wrapping magik to constrict his heart. Tight enough to feel like death, but not so much he couldn't plead for mercy.

The fear in his eyes was nothing in comparison to what I felt. It didn't come close to anything I wanted to do to those involved with Adonis and Delphi. These Fae could spit all the hatred they had for my kind or the rule of the Elemental Fae, but their anger would never touch mine.

I had become too kind. Lacked foresight from my openness and did not allow myself to see possible threats that could harm Arabella on the night she was taken.

Sweat trickled from Alistair's forehead, the liquids from his body dripping into the bucket we used to pour over the cloth covering his face.

He was sobbing, voice hoarse from the screaming. "Please. PLEASE! I told you all I know. Would you not show mercy the same way the witch would?"

Cassius and I glanced at each other, and I sent a curt nod in agreement.

"You are fortunate that it is us handling this matter and not Arabella," Cassius comments. Chuckling. "While you may think us the cruel ones for doing this to you, you are wrong. It is she who would kill you."

Alistair tensed.

"Where could Adonis have taken Arabella?" I asked again. The sight of his clenched jaw and sealed lips only heightened the impatient anger that was frantic within me. "You were one of those controlled by the stone's power. You were taken by them. Where were you held?"

I was losing my control. Cassius glared at me, a hint that I needed to steady myself.

"Do you not think if I knew where I was being held, I would have told you by now? Instead of allowing you to drown me with blood-infused water?" Alistair bit out. He pathetically struggled in his chair,

metal beginning to cut into his skin, before giving up and snapping his head to Cassius. "Even if I did know, the witchling is getting a far better treatment with King Adonis than I with the damned shadow prince. Why would I say something that would take her from such a well-deserved life?"

Every scream and plea became muddled when pouring more liquid. Barely comprehensible under the drenched cloth. I reached for Arabella's dagger, ready to stab iron through his heart, while I paced back and forth by the door. Only a select few knew of her abduction outside the grounds of Nexus.

"What an interesting choice of words. A mishap on your part for referring to me only as a prince, I'm sure." Cassius' voice was calm. No hesitation as his shadow slit a line down the center of Alistair's chest.

From by the door, after collecting myself, I spoke, grabbing Alistair's attention. "You know, there is a chance that we would show you mercy for your lack of knowledge."

Alistair's body immediately loosened, shoulders sagging. Cassius removed the cloth from his face, forcing the Fae to look at me, with the king's shadow pressing into his cheeks.

Slowly stalking closer, I bent my body down so that I was eye level with the common fae. "But being that Arabella is not here due to your 'king' taking her, I will act accordingly." I twisted my fingers, forcing the Fae's tongue out with magik. "You see, she would be kind enough to kill you immediately. I am not her."

He looked at Cassius, a final petition for the king to save him. Little good that would do for him. Before he could choke out another sound, I used Arabella's dagger, slicing out the organ.

I can't bring myself to leave the bed. Kabir is pounding on my door for the third time within the hour, reminding me to meet in the council room. Everything feels like it's falling apart, cutting me one thread at a time. I don't sleep much. Memories of Alastair and others haunt my mind too often to rest.

It's been routine for the past two months. Hold a weekly meeting, concluding with it ultimately resulting in nothing. I've become tired of it.

The first hour after we discovered Adonis and Ari missing, we searched the grounds for any trace of magik. It turned futile when we realized she had taken them hours before the guards found the Disaris son missing. We tried other strategies, such as questioning those who were captured from the battle, but when half of those imprisoned were under the control of the Stone of Elestial and the other half barely knew of Adonis' plan–outside of an uprising or their meetings–that led us no further than the day they were taken.

Two months of interrogating, searching the lands, and attempting other methods, and we have nothing to show for it.

Cassius has matured, though not by much, with his speech being garrulous most times. I've resettled into my unlikable self, but I don't know how much longer I can remain with a level head. It's nearing cruel irony that the universe would bring me back into the world just to rip me from the woman I love.

Seeking a distraction, I find myself in the shower in hopes of putting my mind at bay. I hate entertaining the possibility that Delphi would kill Ari. Delphi may have always been a selfish and prideful witch, but she would not take Ari if she didn't assume it would give her leverage. If it *were* purely for revenge for what Arabella did to Adonis' arm, Delphi would have sent fractures of Arabella to us.

But instead, she hasn't so much as sent a note or indication that she has done anything to Arabella. Never mind given a hint as to what she wants from the king.

The meeting was meant to start ten minutes ago. As if already presumed, the High King cannot be bothered to be punctual.

Oftentimes, I am at odds with Cassius. The few moments we are not, I find that we share many similarities in our thought processes. However, while he chooses to act without forethought, I carefully plan out my actions. I thought that after we had gotten past the issue of who Arabella decided on, we could move on and be cordial. Now I see that, without her here, there is nothing but arguments during this stressful time.

I suppose the most important thing we can agree on is that we intend to bring Ari back. But even *that* is something I have trouble believing we have in common lately.

Though the two of us constantly bicker, his family does what they can to welcome my stay. I exist to them as a charitable act for Ari. She regards them greatly, so I have taken it upon myself to become convivial these months. She would worry about how much I fail to interact with others.

Since many here have similar personalities to mine and Ari's friends, it's not horribly arduous. The Aeon twins frequently invite me to join them for drinks in order to take the edge off from their cousin's behavior. Nearly all times, I have declined, my seneschal duties taking up most of my schedule.

"But Delphi's a witch," Dyana says over everyone speaking as Cassius enters the room. "Why can't we just try another way to locate her? I'm sure there's another tracking spell we could use. Maybe Luka just doesn't know of it."

I abstain from speaking. Attempting to track her had already been unsuccessful. If such magik *did* exist to pinpoint a person rather than an object, I don't know of it.

"Dyana," Celeste stops their cousin while raising a thick eyebrow in her direction. "I think if there were another spell to track her, Luka would have cast it by now. Right, Luka?"

"Yes," I respond. Posed assumptions mean nothing when none in the court have a significant understanding of how magik works. Of course, I would give *some* leniency, as many books about magik in Ifaeris may be outdated, but I have yet to see any of them in the libraries doing research.

One by one, each member offers up more suggestions. All get the same rejecting response from the king.

"Maybe I'm stating the obvious, but it seems like there's a solution that no one has brought up yet," Xavier mutters to his brother. While he is the first to make quips, his stature shifts whenever we are in this room. The bright copper-haired Fae takes this as seriously as the rest of us.

Esme studies him, all of us waiting in response. "What do you suppose we've left out?"

"The tracker," he responds. "Cassius, you told Monty and me that you kept those earrings on her. Why not use it to track her?"

The king's lips thin. His eyes are exhausted, despite having had a full night's rest. "I removed the tracker from her the day before Luka's return."

"You did?" Monty asks.

"Why?" Xavier says in tandem.

"I had a lapse in judgment and listened to the two of you," Cassius snaps with a sour tone. "It was you who called me selfish for keeping a device that tracked her every movement tied to her."

Esme scoffs and rolls her eyes, a hand combing through the little hair she's allowed herself to grow without cutting. "Great. The one fucking time he decides to take our word about his selfish actions."

Cassius turns to his sister, a vexed, sharp look on his face. "I'd have much rather remained selfish in my desires, had I known she would be taken."

Celeste attempts to give more suggestions to their brother, offering up their powers, which he dismisses as if what they said came out of a child. They disregard the king's doubt, defending themself. "I just mean that with the power to manipulate others' emotions, I can ease the Fae enough to feel comfortable giving you answers."

"You speak as if we have not exhausted every attempt to find her. If you are so sure the common fae would offer you answers, I suggest leading the questionings where they spew nothing but loathing towards us." Cassius takes a drink from the glass of Fae wine that sits in front of his person. Smiles when tilting his head towards his sister. "Or you can do your best at attempting to torture for answers, though you do not have the stomach for it."

Maude's face quickly hardens. Of all the siblings, she's typically the first to call out her brother's remarks. "Why do you have to say things that make you so unlikable? I know you're angry, but it doesn't give you a right to speak to us like this."

The air fills with hostility. Something that Celeste constantly works to dismantle with their powers, driving themself to the point of exhaustion.

"As much as we want to find Arabella, you still have a kingdom to run. Your priority is firstly to them," Atticus states with firmness in his voice. The voice of someone who has been in close contact with the common fae. Though Cassius leers at his brother's words, he refuses to rescind them. "My son is freshly born. Do you not wish him to grow up in a better Ifaeris than that which exists? You are the High King of the Fae. Finding Adonis and Delphi is of the utmost importance if we do not wish to be fighting a battle on all fronts. Your duty is to your people."

"My duty is to those loyal to me," Cassius returns, a cavalier attitude in his statement, which quickly turns to a more pleasant demeanor when the former queen sits. "I would think I've done well for our kingdom, despite losing enough."

"You're not the only one who lost her!" I shout, pushing myself from my chair and slamming my hands onto the table. The way that lately, he has done nothing to demonstrate the urgency of finding Ari has steadily been building resentment in me. I am tired of his mismatched reasoning when it comes to finding her.

The room goes silent. Glances flicker between myself and the king, some avoiding moving their focus from the table. Tension rises so high that Celeste does not attempt to mitigate it.

A fleeting moment passes by, neither Cassius nor I uttering a word to alleviate the scathing anger firing in each other's direction.

While I have become friendly with these Fae, no one in the room can relate to how I've felt these past months. The only one who would be able to understand me in the slightest is Cassius, but he is just as unwilling to speak to me about her as I am with him.

Pain is something I've formed a familiar bond with. It's something my life has been defined by. I once thought I knew it best when I could not meet the standards of what was expected of me. But not knowing whether Arabella is dead or alive? Her life being in the hands of the person who hates her most in the world? It's something I cannot bear. Pain is much worse than how most depict it. Full of anguish as your body works to destroy itself from the inside out because nothing will ever quite fill the void. It's when the morsel of morality you have is stripped from you, leaving your chest to mutilate as it descends into a pit you are unsure has an end.

If this is anything like what she felt when I had died, I would do everything in my power to make amends for it.

"We have given countless suggestions, all of which you've rejected without so much as giving a second thought to them. You have spoken about how vital it is to find Arabella, but you refuse to follow through on the search. I'm beginning to wonder if you're prolonging this out of fear that her return would scorn us both."

He blinks. Sits down. There's honesty in what I say. It's not beneficial to place the blame on each other, but my acknowledgment is what he has been refusing to confront. Neither of us have said so, but we both know that finding Ari means the likelihood of anger she would release.

"I think we should go back to discussing Delphi being Magik," Dyana says awkwardly. Our attention turns to her while she sits in the corner, playing with her sharpened nails. "If she's a witch, surely someone is bound to know her activities. The sea has not, but friends perhaps?"

The Mermaid's right. If anyone knows of Delphi's whereabouts, it would likely be her friends. I'm unsure how helpful they would be in giving up answers, being that they would all rather have me die again than divulge details on the witch.

"I don't think that is a possibility," I answer.

Atticus uncrosses his burly arms from the other side of the table, curiosity speaking through his knitted eyebrows. His long, jerboa-like tail is typically hidden inside his clothing, but with the exhaustion of his newborn, he has not bothered to keep it tucked away. "And why is that?"

Hesitant, I know that I owe an answer. I should think of some other reasoning that is just as feasible, but I am far too depleted to do so.

"Well?" Cassius asks impatiently.

"Arabella told me we needed to wait before I made a reappearance to the Magiks." I sit back down, drawing in a long breath, fully aware that this isn't the answer they hoped for. "She wasn't sure how long I would have and thought it best not to get others comfortable with me if my life wouldn't last."

"I don't mean to be brash, but you've been alive for a while now," Monty counters with a delicate tone in his voice. He tries not to overstep his bounds, not wanting to be insensitive to both my and Ari's wishes.

"I think, while it is admirable to fulfill her requests, enough time has gone by, and we don't have the luxury to waste more," Esme agrees, adding to what her cousin had to say.

Both are right. The longer I hold myself from seeking aid from Magiks, the more I too am prolonging Ari's return. It would be just as hypocritical to keep from doing so after chastising Cassius.

"Delphi has many friends," I admit to them. "The ones that she considers herself closest to are children of the Magikal leaders. Leaders who presume me dead. If I were to appear, I would immediately be taken to the Council of the Coven and experimented on or killed before I had the chance to ask about her."

This is true. Magik regarding life and death is not something to be taken lightly. Taking into account everything that is taught in school, as well as having knowledge of the top Magikal elite, I have never come across a record of someone being revived from death. My new life is something unnatural.

"Then we go to *your* friends first," Xavier suggests. "I'm sure they would–"

Esme interrupts her cousin, speaking over him. "Bella said that you and her share a group of friends. A group I know Cassius has met. If he meets with them and explains everything, he can take you without causing suspicion among the Magik Coven."

I ponder this, weighing out both options and all other outcomes. "Delphi's friends do not like Arabella, me, or those we surround ourselves with just as much as Delphi. If our friends attempt to contact those within Delphi's circle, they'll be met with the same brooding attitude that the common fae give you. And if I were spotted by any Magik other than our friends, the ramifications would be the same as presenting ourselves straight to the Council."

"What better option do we have?" Xavier asks.

"By now, those in charge of Magik have to have an idea what is happening, would they not?" Atticus questions.

Maude turns to her brother. "Brother, you know that many Magiks live across the Human Lands. They are not contained to one land as we are. I'm sure their leaders have some idea about the whereabouts of other Magiks, but unless it's causing enough trouble for them to be involved, I doubt they'd know."

"One of theirs is partly responsible for the killings and taking of our people," Cassius utters.

"And up until two months ago, you were unaware that Delphi was included," I retort. His ignorance of Magikal politics should have been rectified long ago. Neither the executives nor the Council leaders of the Coven have deemed this important enough if they have not responded to Cassius by now.

Xavier snaps his head to me in defense. "We suspected–"

"Suspicion does not equate to fact," I remind him. While the intentions are well-meaning, high emotions have caused all to speak rashly. "My father is of high rank among the Coven. If my time shadowing him has taught me anything, it is that without cause to act, they will remain idle. If the Council can prove that Adonis is involved, they will have reason to direct the deaths to a family civil war."

There are things I have yet to tell the Fae family. They are well aware that I know Delphi and that she is of Magik, but what they do not know is how deeply the history goes between me and her. None are aware that Delphi was my girlfriend, let alone the reasoning behind the contempt Delphi holds for Ari. Delphi's resentment goes far beyond me, but it is paramount that Cassius is aware of this information, being that we both hold Ari in the same regard. Before giving this information to the family, I must tell Cassius first.

"Do no other ways exist where we can plead our case to your

leaders without risking your life or ours?" Celeste wonders. Their hands go to their nose, exasperation passing through.

"I don't think going to my friends first is a horrendous idea," I say. "Whether Cassius approves of this or not, someone should go to them. They love Ari. They'll do anything to protect her."

There is an agreement between everyone at the table. Regardless of whether this results in little information, I would send someone to see the people who know Ari and myself best. Others who know Delphi's character and tendencies.

"We would need a course of action if this is what we are deciding," Cassius chimes in.

"Before we move further on that, Cassius, there's something I need to speak with you regarding Delphi." His eyes widen, silently nagging me to finish. "Alone."

He blinks with a dip of his head. Looking at the rest of his family, he speaks. "Out."

After shutting the charcoal doors, he sits back at the head of the table, resting his head on a hand. "Now, what about Delphi did you need to discuss with me without the listening ears of my family?"

II

Blast from the Past

Arabella

I couldn't breathe. The guy I was in love with just told me that if his ex-girlfriend came back to him, he'd leave me for her, and my response was that it would be okay? It's my birthday for fuck's sake, and I'm supposed to be spending my party surrounded by my friends, but instead, I was being taken into a corner by my supposed 'boyfriend' to tell me how much he hates all of them.

Love was something I told him I didn't want. I didn't want to fall if he was going to use me for sex. He promised me before that that's not what this was, but followed by saying rancid somethings like, "Things in life are only temporary".

I became everything he wanted me to be, and I still wasn't enough.

"Ara?" he asked softly, brushing his hand along my arm, trying to grab my attention. "You're not saying anything."

The feel of his touch stung. Like pressing ice to my skin covered in salt. I snapped from my thoughts, taking my hand from his. "Sorry, I was thinking." It's so dark that I'm not sure how well he could see my reactions. Still, I gave him a sulky smile, hoping he wouldn't pay attention to it. "You know, sometimes I get tired of going around with you on this."

He looked at me, light from the other room illuminating his unsuspecting face.

"We go in circles. Have you noticed?" I muttered. "I'm too clingy for you, but then I can't have any guy friends." Fury swashed through me. Not only for his actions, but for him treating me like a joke. Like he viewed me as disposable and some pathetic girl who would run back to him the second he wanted me.

What's worse was that he was right. Because this was the fifth time I've done it.

He stroked my hair, planting a kiss on my temple and scooting closer to me on the couch until his arm wrapped around my shoulder. "Maybe I just don't like my girlfriend talking to other men."

My entire demeanor changed from contained sadness to sadistic irony. Whiplash. "Girlfriend? Up until tonight, you refused to acknowledge me as something worth being exclusive with. You get mad when men flirt with me, knowing damn well that it isn't just men that do it. You get pissed because you only take men as a serious threat to whatever the hell our relationship is."

"Don't do this right now," he complained in annoyance. "You're better than to ruin this."

I could have gone into mania. I didn't care if I would cause a scene at my own birthday. Full, unbridled rage had been festering inside of me for so long. I only wanted him to want me. "I'm never going to be enough for you, am I?"

Even in the poorly lit room, I could sense befuddlement in his energy. He may not have been Magik, but he had the ability of making me stay with him, no matter how many times I tried to leave. "If you don't want me in your life, why'd you invite me tonight? Why'd you introduce me to all your friends?"

"I just–"

"You won't leave 'cause you know whatever mistakes I make, you're a good enough person to stay."

He's right.

Gods, I hated that he was.

A hand went to the back of my neck, bringing me closer to his lips.

Something's wrong. This isn't how it happened. He left my house after he said that. He went to cheat on me with his ex-girlfriend. He never kissed me.

I hear her accent before I can see her face. "You figured out you were in a scenario a lot faster this time. I was hoping to prolong this a bit more." Delphi walks out from the corner, a wolf-like grin on her face as she pushes back her brown hair. "I had other ideas in mind."

The surroundings of the party, my house, everything felt so real. It all looks exactly the same way that it did when this happened. I've been reliving some of the worst months of my life, and there was nothing I could do but be under the influence of Delphi's magik.

With one blink, I'm back in the torture room. The two of us are alone with a table full of punishment instruments, a small, empty wooden table, a fireplace, and a makeshift throne of stone that Delphi sits on when she speaks to me.

"How long was I gone this time?" I ask tightly, my chains loud when I move.

"The entirety of your relationship with Grant, so I'd say about four months." She smiles with a heavy breath, her balance imperfect as she stalks to place the wide goblet full of her blood and other ingredients on the table near the throne.

My eyes roll before returning to stare back at her. Then a sigh. "I know how long I was reliving. I meant here. How long were you in my mind?"

"Oh, that. We were gone for about four hours," she says, crossing her thin legs. Each time she does this, there's an excitement in her. She becomes more energetic while draining all of my energy, though there are remnants of exhaustion emanating on her face from the taxing use that this magik can take. Even then, it is not nearly as much as I would expect.

I wonder how practiced in this magik she is.

"Your mind is exhausting," she mocks. "It's riddled with self-doubt and love for things you'll never reach."

She laughs, passing a piece of fruit to me. It's old and mostly eaten. Barely anything but the core remains.

"You stayed in a relationship with Grant while knowing all the things he already did to you," she continues. "Your desperation never ceases to surprise me."

The physical pain she caused me was nothing in comparison to this. I would be chained by my limbs, spread like a starfish as Delphi dragged knives along my stomach, only to heal my scars as if they didn't exist. There were times she starved me, drowned my head in barrels of water, choked me until I went unconscious. Eventually, I became numb to the physical trauma.

I endured that for about a month before Delphi decided on torturing me alone and making me relive memories or some twisted scenario she would come up with. Each time that she's in my mind, I battle her for the chance to go without these torturing conscious transfers. Each time, I lose. And I swear that every time I'm gone, she steals bits of my magik.

There's no rhyme or reason why she and Adonis do this. I don't understand what torturing will do for them. I offer nothing that would gain them authority. They're just ripping apart my body one thing at a time until Cassius gives them whatever it is Delphi wants.

"Your friends think you're on some important mission with the king, and your parents think you're on a trip with your friends where there's no signal. That should end the relentless messages from your mom for at least a week," she says with a gleam in her hooded, seraphinite eyes, tossing my phone to a table beside her.

I miss my parents and their texts.

"Holding me hostage does nothing for your power, you know," I return. In hopes partly that she would stop, but more so that she would send me back to the locked room I'm held in.

My words are met with displeasure, my throat closing up and my body caving in on itself.

Delphi thrives off of it. Off my torture.

If the gods do exist, I wonder what I did to deserve any of this. Have I played a role in my own misery?

The sharp, painted nails of my old friend collide as she holds her hands together, close to her lips. "Maybe. But your misery is half my fun. Haven't you wondered why the Fae and Luka haven't come to claim you yet?"

In all honesty, I do. I have to have been gone for months now, but I have no sure sense of time.

Outside of Delphi and Adonis, the only other living creature I've spoken to is the Troll that occasionally comes to bathe me. When I was in Phantom Tower, I had the voices of other prisoners, Kabir, and the girls. Here, I have the echoing of my own.

Flames–the same color as mine–light from her fingertips. It burns through the paper of the valskull joint, with Delphi taking an inhale. Her hair may be tied behind her head, but I so badly wish an ember from the joint would set her on fire.

"Maybe the reason they haven't come for you is 'cause you're useless to them now," she mocks. "Or maybe they realized their lives are better off without you in them. I know that's what I've learned."

"Why don't you just go back to torturing me with your toys?"

Delphi leaves her throne while carrying the goblet, her footsteps echoing through the large room with nothing to muddle the sound. Her finger grasps under my chin as she bends down, her nail pressing into my skin before she circles the rim with her fingers. "Because it doesn't nearly elicit the same reaction that emotionally tormenting you does. And you took ruling from me."

I feel woozy, and when I open my eyes, I'm nine. My mom is helping me adjust my Halloween costume, but all I feel is sadness that I don't look like her.

"You look so pretty," she compliments with a wide smile directed towards my direction. "Suck in your stomach for the pictures, sweetheart."

My older brother, Jericho, stands next to me in a superhero costume, cape and all. Unlike him, I am dressed like a princess from the books in the library, wearing one of my older skating competition costumes.

Mom already told me I couldn't dress like a witch if I wanted to keep the secret that I have powers.

No one in my other school believed me, but after I accidentally knocked my classmate off the swing for calling me annoying, the teasing stopped.

When dad drove my brother and me home that day, my brother was angrier than usual. Sometimes, he gets mad when I use my powers because he didn't get any. And that night, when mom came home, she and dad fought. He said no one would've known about my powers, but she insisted I change schools and made a rule that I could only learn magik if she's the one teaching me. Then, during recess a few weeks ago, while my friends and I were in the middle of playing tetherball, I was called into the principal's office over the speaker and was told I'd be switching schools.

I didn't want to go to a different school. I *still* don't want to be at this new school. All my friends are at the one I had to leave. What if my friends find a new best friend and forget all about me?

It hasn't even been a week since I transferred, and I already hate it here.

Sucking in my stomach the best I can, I hold my breath, making my head hurt in the process. "Mom," I whine, "why do I always have to suck in my stomach?"

She looks down, her head tilting to a side with her lips slightly pursed like she's disappointed with me. "You want to look good, don't you? You want to be as pretty as all your other friends, right?" I nod. "Then you have to suck it in. And remember not to eat more than two pieces of candy tonight."

"But why doesn't kuya have to do that?"

"Your brother doesn't need to try as hard to be healthy like you do," she responds while her hands go to my back, straightening my posture. "Honey, you know I love you, but no boy will want a girl who has bad eating habits."

I don't get what a boy has to do with me eating candy, but if it makes my mom happy, I'll do what she says. The comment that no one would want me if I look like this hurts, but it's more for my health than anything.

My mind begins to find clarity. *I'm not nine. I haven't been to my house other than the holidays in years.*

Suddenly, my mind is blank, and in a blink, I'm fifteen and on my way home from school for the winter. Juju flew home to Chicago, so I'm stuck with no one but my family for the next two weeks.

My parents are yelling, both at each other and me. They're arguing over the expenses of school and boarding. Saying things about how we can't afford it and how the money could go towards something useful, like college.

"Why are we still spending thousands of dollars for some school to teach her what you can?" my dad yells.

Mom, who's sitting on the passenger's side, is hitting her hand against her head. "She nearly burned the house down during the years I tried to teach her. Unless you want her to burn all we have, we *need* to keep her at this school!"

"It's been a year and a half of this, Sasha! She's learned enough to control her powers. The only reason I agreed to be taken in was 'cause you promised me she wouldn't be taught magik." My father grips the steering wheel, keeping his focus in front of him. "I took her in 'cause you promised it would keep Jericho safe."

"I never asked for her to be like this either," my mom shouts back.

Instantly, I feel guilty. My parents really do buy me things when I ask. They pay for my clothes and makeup and send me to an extremely expensive school where many students here live in completely different tax brackets than my family does. But the feeling of anger is far in front of the guilt. I never asked for them to take me in. I didn't ask to be born. They adopted *me*, and now I constantly feel terrible for a choice that *they* made. To them, I'd never be part of their family. They will never consider me a Reyes.

Nearing tears, I look at kuya, who says nothing to keep him from getting in trouble. He instead scrolls through his phone while turning up the music he's listening to. My brother's the lucky one. He stays away at college for most of the year. Mom and dad still come to visit me.

"Dad?" I croak out with strain in my voice.

He glances back partially, hands gripped firmly on the steering wheel. "You should be grateful we do any of this for you. I never wanted you."

I can't take it. His roaring words are too much. My emotions shoot up like they're about to explode out of me. I unlock the door, opening it and leaping out of the moving car. I run and run until I can find a place to hide. With the speed the car's going and the direction I've jumped, I have enough time to hide in safety before they can catch up to me.

A terrible decision, but I don't care. If they don't want me, running away should be all they dream for. They'll have less expenses, and they won't have to deal with my attitude. If I happen to die, there's no losing.

I keep going until I find a trash can to crouch behind. Our car passes me three times before the sun begins to disappear. There's nowhere to go. I have no place to stay. So I cry. My parents never wanted me. I'm alone.

I'm always alone.

"So sad," a voice says, *tsking* from around me. "You were so young, and even then you knew that you were worthless."

No. This is something I never shared with anyone, other than Luka and Juju.

She's here.

"Delphi," I hiss.

She flicks her hand, and I'm in my dorm. Juju is out of town, and my parents stand in front of me, rage and humiliation violently thrown in their words. This time, I'm fully conscious. Delphi *wants* me to go through the movements and emotions of this memory.

Yet I'm unable to break myself from the exact movements, emotions, and words I said on this day.

"You know I'm always proud of you, but I thought we were past this," my mother chastises, crossing her arms and throwing the letter I excitedly showed them minutes ago.

My letter of acceptance into Lazipeus, one of the top Magik universities in the world, is mangled on the floor. I thought they would be more pleased since I would be getting a full scholarship, but no, they would rather berate and lecture me.

Dad brings his hand to his forehead in shame, refusing to look at me. "I thought we agreed that you'd drop magik and go to a human college like your brother?"

"Why can't you just be more like Jericho?" mom questions. Louder. Angrier. "He's respectful and doesn't only speak to us when he needs money. I don't have to yell at him nearly as much as you."

Every time I'm around them, all I feel is ostracized, even if they don't mean to do it. If I stay away, I'm pushing them out, but when I'm with them, I need to be the idealized version of their daughter. My relationship with my parents is one contradiction after the next.

For once, I need to find a backbone. I have to stand my ground. "Oh my gods. Have you ever thought I never wanted to be like kuya? You give him all this credit for the bare minimum and raise us in completely different ways. If he was actually born with magikal powers, I'm sure you wouldn't give a fuck about me going to Lazipeus."

A throbbing pain shoots through my cheeks, and it registers that my dad hit me. His hand raises again as I back into my closet, screaming for him to get away from me. Our family only works when we're far apart.

He tries to apologize, grabbing my raised arms that protect my face to pull me into a hug.

"You're so ungrateful," mom continues to lecture. "I do everything for our family, and you treat me like I'm nothing more than a bank. You're only nice to me when you want something, and I give in every time because I want to make you happy. You have no idea how lucky you are."

Pools of liquid stab at my eyes, trickling, despite how hard I fight against it.

She grabs my box of makeup from my desk. One weighed down by products overstuffed into the train case. In a slamming movement, the case is thrown onto my laptop, likely shattering the screen. "Your dad and I are going to die one day, and we don't even know if you'll take care of us. 'Cause I'm sure whenever you leave, we'll never see you again, and you're just going to let us die in an old people's home. Why can't you ever do something for me? For your family? All we asked was that you go to a proper college so you could get a good job."

I can't help the laugh I let out, like a maniac who has nothing to lose while crying. "I don't even have a legal transcript past eighth grade. No regular college would take me."

Yes, in our schooling, we're also taught similar subjects as humans, but emphasis on magik takes precedence. And it's not like my parents put me through human school during the regular year and had me take magik courses during the summer. My magik, prior to being properly taught, was too uncontrollable for that. But then, I know my parents can easily bring up the fact that all Magiks can request a fake certificate that confirms we have a high school education.

Picking up the shreds of my acceptance letter from the ground, I put them on my desk. "You both just want me to do well in your field of work or ones you never achieved. If you don't want to pay for college, fine. I'll find a way to make it work. But if you wanna start treating me the same way you treat kuya, *the way you claim you do*, you'll let me go."

"I know plenty of your cousins who have the same background as you and made it just fine with humans," dad says. I swear he finds shame in me for not excelling in every world I exist in. He takes another look at me, eyes narrowing in disappointment. "Oh, would you cut it out? You think any of us had it easy growing up? Gods, your generation is so soft. It's like none of you can handle the truth."

Neither I nor my mother say another word. Mom just grabs the keys to the car, motioning for the three of us to leave my room and go to dinner.

On the car ride to the restaurant, I fall asleep, only to wake up in Delphi's bed. I'm hyperventilating. Shaking. The pillowcase wet from my eyes.

"Baby," she says with a groggy voice, arm reaching out to me and brushing my chest unintentionally. "What happened? Why are you whimpering?"

My head's killing me. The white from the walls is too loud, and I feel like I'm about to vomit.

I feel like I just relived my entire life and then some. "What am I doing in your bed?" I ask frantically. "Why am I not in chains?"

She laughs, turning to face me. "Chains? Wow, you *really* drank too much last night, didn't you?"

Drank? Last night?

"Last night I was with you?" I question, unsure if this is another lie. She nods groggily against her pillow. The cotton sheets aren't as smooth against me as satin or silk. "But what about Luka? And Cassius? Are they still in Ifaeris?"

Eyes widening, she grabs the water on the floor next to her bed, making sure I drink it. "Luka, as in my ex who constantly lied to me? You've never met him." I open my mouth to speak, but she stops me before I can get a word in. "And who's Cassius? What were you dreaming about?"

"You were torturing me. We stopped talking, and years went by. You hated me for dating Luka, and then he died. I met Cassius, the High King of the Fae, and he made me their queen." Everything I say is rushed without a pause. Like I'm short on time and have to explain everything before something else happens.

Her brows knit, suspecting eyes scanning me to search for a hint of a joke.

All of this happened. I swear it did.

"Queen of the Fae?" she laughs. "The Fae are myths. Or maybe extinct. I can't remember. And I'd never leave you. You're my best friend. You'd never date Luka after the things he said to me."

This has to be wrong. Luka never did anything that Delphi said he did. She twisted everything to turn people against him and victimized herself. None of it was true.

I've never been so confused. I need to know more.

"So what *did* happen?"

"You were ranting about how much you hated Grant to some guy at the club, and just when you were about to go home with him, I dragged you to my flat." She twists her fingers, magiking away the migraine pounding in my head. "You were absolutely hammered, and I wasn't letting you go with some tosser."

Still feeling like I'm losing my mind, I admit, "But you hate me. You said I made your life unbearable."

Sitting up, she pats my arm, bringing me up with her. The tips of her fingers trail my thigh before settling in the middle. "When did I say all of this?"

I try to recall when. The details become hazy in my mind, and my eyes dart around the room to remember any bit of information from the previous night.

"In spring. Like two years ago."

"Ara, two years ago, you were seventeen, and neither of us were at Lazipeus. You just had a nightmare."

I know this is a lie. I just turned twenty-two. But there's no proof that anything I'm saying happened. Even the tattoo above my ankle has disappeared. Like the past years have erased from existence.

Looking down, I now know I'm right. This is another mind game.

"You're lying," I assert. Her apartment bedroom was never this clean or organized. There should be more clothing everywhere with the carpet stained. "We're still in the chamber you torture me in, aren't we?"

She doesn't hesitate to lie, but the sound of her name is being called over and over, the voice familiar.

"Adonis." I smile.

Delphi frowns, touching the top of my forehead, forcing my eyes shut. As I open them, we're back in the stone room, coolness of air hitting me from the opened door.

A glared grimace whips in Adonis' direction. Delphi looks like she's ready to rip him apart. "What have I told you about interrupting me when I'm in here?"

"I'm sorry, my sweet. I only thought to bring you dinner." There's an apologetic tone to him with sincerity on his face. Adonis, with a crooked grin and adoring attitude towards Delphi, brings the tray of food to her. Upon doing so, she snatches it from his hand, setting it on the table next to the knives.

Something that I quickly noticed between the two of them is that Delphi is the sadistic one. I have an inkling that she's the one who curated all the plans against Ifaeris, allowing Adonis to believe that it was he who made them all.

Delphi summons the tray to float to the armrest of her throne, walking towards it to sit. "Since you interrupted me when I was about to break her, you can be in charge of bathing and feeding her tonight." She stuffs a potato chunk into her mouth, emphasizing her chewing to remind me of the food she has that I do not. "Maybe with the two of you gone, I'll take a visit to the little lands of Ifaeris and seek out those lovers of hers."

As the water for the bath heats, Adonis hands me my food. It may be nothing but a slice of bread and a few pieces of meat with water, but it's more than I have gotten most days here.

I chew as slowly as I can, attempting to savor it for as long as possible. At first, I thought I could do with the little food they gave me, since malnourishment isn't a new concept to my body, but as the days turned into weeks and weeks into months, I could barely handle it. Not eating out of personal volition versus being starved, I now know, feels completely different.

Clothes fall to the floor, my body completely stripped. If I had more strength, I'd find a will to be timid that Adonis is seeing my naked body. But I need a bath, and I can't bring myself to care, especially not when he's seen me in this state before.

As I sit in the tub of my filth, washing my body, the shirtless Fae lathers my hair with product. Unlike in Ifaeris, where my chains had been removed in the bathing room, these are always secure when I am here.

"Thank you," I say to Adonis.

"What for?"

"I know it's you that always gives me an extra piece of food whenever the Troll delivers it."

Adonis isn't talented at hiding his generosity. He tries to find ways to deny it, but none of the other creatures are allowed to have unsupervised access to me. It's only the Troll, Delphi, and him.

Maybe I'm wearing him down. Sometimes I can't tell, but other days, Adonis looks more exhausted when carrying out Delphi's orders than his original eagerness.

I flick water towards him before I sink into the tub, laying myself on my back and staring at the ceiling. "Come on. I know you're as arrogant as Ezra was, but you aren't as bad as you think you are."

"You mistake me for being a decent Fae. That is not who I have become to be."

At least he's finally talking.

"You were the one who warned me about Delphi," I remind him. He huffs, rejecting my theory completely. It doesn't matter. I know that it was him. His lack of words answers me well enough.

"I suppose I have spoken to you of many things." He takes a small pail of water from the side, running it through my hair to wash out the product.

Smiling, I know I'm right. "You knew Delphi wrote the note, and it was you who said that she was closer to me than I thought." Now finished with my hair, he moves to sit beside the tub to face me, his slightly bulky body wet from the water. "You meant that she was close to me 'cause we're both Magik. Didn't you?"

His head angles down. He has tighter curls than Cassius.

I move through the water, the edge of the tub pressing against my chest as I lean towards him. "You warned me to go. You basically hinted to leave with Luka before something worse would happen."

"What are you insinuating, witch?" he asks, voice sharper than a blade. The expression on his face exposes that, despite the little kindness he has shown me, he still resents me for cutting off his arm. I don't regret it. We needed to take him for answers and to put an end to the slaughter of the Fae.

"Nothing," I say, deciding against an argument. "I just think there's a bigger reason that you were so willing to warn me."

Rather than denying it, he stands, reaching for the towel and handing it to me to dry off, then turning around so as not to view my nakedness. Fae may be comfortable with nudity, but I still am not. I stare at the scales on his back before he turns around to clasp the buttons of my shirt at my shoulders. They're the picture of small, protective plates of a pangolin, the texture of which I am curious about.

As we walk into the room that I am to be locked in nightly, Adonis hands me a bottle of water that he must have snuck into his pocket. Many of the things on this floor have either been magiked or built to cater to the height of creatures around my size. The locks on the bars, the shorter handles, everything. All are meant to be within reach of Delphi or Adonis.

When alone, I lay in my bed, staring at the stars out the barred window. A tightness locks my throat at my mind's suggestion that maybe Delphi is right, and no one's coming for me. Maybe I'll spend my final days unable to distinguish what's reality and what's Delphi's mind games. The only hope I *do* have is that with the amount I'm being fed, combined with the emotional exhaustion, life won't last much longer.

During my whole relationship with Delphi, I questioned where I stood. I'd question what was true every time she acted like I was her girlfriend before she'd turn around and make it seem like we were only friends. This confusion on what's actually real feels like a rewind of before.

Sometimes, I talk aloud to myself at night. Just to hear another voice. But even then, that voice inevitably reverts to the same rhetoric that Delphi spews. It parrots that I'm worthless and undeserving of anything other than the worst of what I've been put through. I have grown accustomed to believing this in my head, but hearing it being emphasized so often from someone I once placed on a pedestal debilitates me.

No matter how small I feel, I refuse to show that to anyone here. I'll never allow her to know that I'm broken.

I look down at my arms to the only scars that have remained unhealed since being here, laughing at their purpose. I wonder what would happen if I cut too deep or in a different way.

Grabbing the glass shard from inside my pillowcase, I slice my inner forearm. A way to track what my reality truly is.

III

Unwanted Responsibilities

Cassius

It is taking a long while for Luka to piece together what he needs to say. He's hesitant. Mistrustful, definitely. I grow bored of his prolonging, resting upon my hand until he decides to confess his knowledge.

Finally, he says, "Has Ari ever spoken to you about Delphi or their history?"

"No." Throughout our time together, Arabella hardly revealed anything of her past, save her family. "Most of our company resided in arguments. Similar to yours and mine." I pause, recollecting such moments with her. "She hid whatever wasn't necessary to our partnership. And I doubt any of us three would have thought another Magik to be involved."

There was not one who would have assumed a Magik to be connected to the disappearances of the Fae. None but my father, who I presume is mocking my ignorance in the afterlife.

"Delphi knew Arabella," Luka murmurs. Hopelessness sinks his face deeper than a weight thrown to sea. "She knew all of us."

I wait for him to continue, to tell me how all their lives intersected with Delphi's, but he refrains from doing so. He stops for me to form questions that would better fit his answers.

"Am I to assume she also knows all of your Wand group of friends?" I ask.

Luka lets out an airy bit of laughter. "The Wands group chat? Yes, Delphi knew them." A short bit of silence passes, almost as if he finds difficulty in explaining this. "It's not only them that Delphi knows. She also knows Arabella's other friends." He pauses once more, letting out a grumbled huff. "Delphi and I used to be romantically involved."

This information is far from that which I would have guessed. Delphi not only engages with my father's other spawn, but she is an old lover of Luka's. It should not surprise me that he would love another capable of such atrocities, yet at the telling of this, my eyebrow raises.

"And you assume she has taken Arabella due to anger with you?" I wonder.

"It's not out of the question. Delphi and I were in a relationship for months prior to me attending Lazipeus. By the beginning of what was her third year in university, she followed me and, in the process, befriended Arabella."

Hearing Luka speak of this confounds me greatly. It's a waste of a mortal life to carry such animosity over something so transient. Too much energy that could be spent elsewhere.

As if there could not be another shocking revelation, another leaves his mouth. "I wasn't aware they were friends until I fell in love with Ari. After that, Delphi would harass the two of us and keep tabs on everything we did. She would find ways to make Ari feel worse about herself. Doing what she and her new friends could to tear the two of us apart."

"You are what broke apart their friendship?"

His head shakes slightly, eyebrows crossing as if what I ask has an obvious answer. "Their relationship was over long before Ari met me. I would argue that their friendship was never strong to begin with."

"And your friends? They do not like Delphi as well?"

"Those who knew me growing up didn't like Delphi when we dated. They always assumed she had an ulterior motive and that she never wanted me. They would constantly suggest she was just obsessed with something else that I had."

"Were they correct?"

"With the way she treated Arabella..." His voice trails off, a pause halting him. "They were."

There's more I want to ask about Delphi. Her objectives. What she did to both him and Arabella. All things which Arabella would ask in my stead if this were an interrogation.

Instead, I ask, "What was she like?"

"Delphi?"

"*Mmm.*"

Luka's face becomes dejected. "She's not a well-intentioned witch. She draws you in and makes you rely on her, only to weaponize it. You become convinced that she's trying to help, but she just has a superiority complex that prioritizes self-gain."

"What would Delphi have to gain by being friends with Arabella? There was no way to use Arabella to get to you."

"She had a friend."

Confusion in my mind releases from my face as I look at him. "Why would Arabella befriend someone such as her?"

"When you move to a completely different country and have no one, it's not difficult to see why Ari had sympathy for Delphi." He studies my every reaction to his words. "I know she probably hasn't shown this much in the time you've known her, but Ari is kind. Sometimes, too kind. When she and Delphi were friends, Delphi took advantage of that."

"What did she do to her?" I ask, an unduly snippiness heightened in my voice.

"It is not my place to say," he states. "What I can say, is that Ari wasn't in a good place when she was friends with Delphi. She was always willing to let things that Delphi said go without addressing, even if it meant ignoring her emotions."

"If it is relevant to the safety of Arabella, I'd think it important for you to speak on their relationship."

Refusing to divulge any further details, he remains unyielding in his words. "Ari's relationship with Delphi is hers to tell. If she did not feel the need to share it with you, I won't do it for her."

"Her relationship with Delphi may be the very reason she was taken!" Our words overlap, my voice echoing from the volume.

He rises from his chair, marching towards the door, turning back but once. "I have told you all that you need to know about their relationship. If you want to press on that matter, ask Ari yourself when we find her."

At the end of his statement, he shuts the door.

Directly behind him, I am about to leave but am met with my sister's lover, Gideon. His hand is raised, fist clenched and prepared to knock. "King Cassius, I have much to discuss with you if you are able." Without permission, he gives a shallow bow and saunters into the room.

Such formalities for a common fae who enters without expressed consent.

"Proceed."

Across from me, Gideon takes a seat, the two of us sitting at the end of the table and near the door, the common fae holding a stiff posture. "As I am sure you're aware, some common fae have taken issue with the punishments of their loved ones."

"The punishments have been generous. I would think their families would prefer their loved ones alive and imprisoned for a small time, rather than their execution." His face of righteousness does not falter at my words. I close my eyes, taking slow breaths to keep from frustration overtaking me. "They went against the crown. Their sentences are more than fair."

"Yes, well, others don't see it that way. And with the news circulating that Adonis is of Spiritus blood, it will not take long for the common fae to rally against you again."

I consider his words. The common fae had sought loyalty to Adonis when they believed him to fight for their cause. Knowledge of him being of Spiritus blood and bringing about the deaths of their kin has tarnished their faith in him, the same as their faith in the other Elementals.

Gideon's eyebrows turn inward, a frown deepening. Stress from a previous war has caused lines of frustration to make themselves better seen by the eyes, flashing a reminder that he is not of Elemental blood. "Those who still adore Adonis believe him a martyr."

"He was not killed," I correct.

His eyes roll while his head turns to the side, his expression out of view. Then he sighs, the heavily implied reasoning being due to my lack of care. "Rumors care not of the truth. What they do believe, is that he was the first person in nearly a century who was willing to put an end to the poor treatment from the Elemental rulership. Regardless if you've won over some as king, many continue to blame the deaths on both the lower courts' rulers and Arabella."

These are all pieces of information I am well aware of. I do not need the lover of my sister explaining it to me. Rubbing my fingers across my forehead, I take a beat before facing Gideon. His disgruntled nature and rugged appearance would surely beat me in a battle of the physical.

"Have you another reason for coming?" I question. "I know you have more to deliver than gossip my sister has passed along from her time among the town."

"Many common fae know of my relationship with Maude and think me a spy for you." His body shifts while pausing. Hesitating as if frightened to relay his next statement. "None of them are truly aware of the reasoning behind Arabella's disappearance. There are theories of her to have been sent away due to your uninterest, but there are others who believe she is well guarded. So when you do find Arabella, make sure she is safe. They plan on killing her first as retribution for the crimes of your father."

Rage boils from inside of me. "What do you withhold?" I ask.

"Like I said, the common fae no longer trust me, but what I *have* heard from those that do, is that the other Elemental rulers have been conspiring against you."

There are moments when I would have thought Elementals conspiring against the crown an entertaining feat to watch, but that was when I was prince. Without my father here to blame—or my brother, for that matter—I am left with years of political negligence catching up.

"In what way?"

"They believe you're incapable of being a good or kind king and have no knowledge on how to properly converse with rulers, both here and in foreign lands."

Those under this impression may have a point in their favor, though I would never grant them an agreement aloud. My eyes narrow, observing the body language of the man in front of me. "And you believe their assumptions accurate?"

He lifts his legs, dropping his feet on the table and leaning back, arms behind his head, ultimately disturbing the fineness that is the polished table. "Does it matter if I do?"

An amused grin forms on my face. "I suppose not."

"Servants say they heard many of the other Elementals' desire to depart from the rulership of the Spiritus bloodline." His face turns sour. Mocking, as a chortling huff exits from his nose. "They assume themselves capable of ruling over their own land, answering to no one but themselves."

Against my attempt to restrain it, laughter bursts out of me. "While my father may have been a poor leader to his people, the treatment of the common fae falls under the responsibility of the other rulers. And they have only added to the common fae's hardships."

I leave my seat, striding towards the head of the table to grab my chalice. "While I appreciate your findings, I need time to deliberate with my court before I decide what should be done."

Displeasing sounds of the chair pushing against the floor screech through the room. I think the wood ought to have broken off the bottom legs with the grating noise that echoes, perhaps splintering into something more useful as weapons. The half-haired Fae is red in the cheeks, flushed with vexation that I care not of.

"You are the king now. I urge you not to make the mistakes of those before you, Your Majesty," Gideon says before moving from where he stands and out the door.

A carriage pulls Luka and myself to the House of Smoldris. The crimson bricks that are used for the foundation of many structures in Hearthis are hardly vibrant without the sun to light them.

Small Sprites, tending to the many fountains, fly around, their songs of joy faintly heard, with flowing cloths of red variations covering their bodies. There are a few young Dryads near the trees, shooting arrows for target practice.

Lady Fatima, the only one of the other Elemental rulers who understands the destruction that Adonis can create, is kind enough to host a dinner for us and the lower courts' rulers. I have informed her prior that I had been made aware of their plans to leave the Spiritus rule and section off their lands into their own rulership. She attempted to deny it, of course, only to admit that she did not strongly agree with the others' decision.

The first to welcome Luka and myself are the rulers of this land. They meet us at the entrance of their home, their frocks of peach matching–Pyrros' jewelry of silver corresponding to the aging streaks of gray in his hair, which reaches the middle of his torso. Both grace us with pleasantries as we are led to the dining hall, where I find that Luka and I are the last to arrive.

Gleeful conversations immediately come to a halt, smiles dropping as I step into the room. The large dining area is vast in decor, many of the walls filled with art of the previous Smoldris bloodline's kin. Rose metal covers the framing of pathway openings, while the seats have intricately burned designs.

As I catch a better view of others in the room, I come to a pitiful conclusion. I realize that I may not be in clothing as charming as the other rulers.

My mind troubles itself with attires that I could have worn instead. Even the Enthar rulers are dressed more opulent than I am.

"King Cassius," Lady Jiya, mother of Harrison, greets with a bow. "How are you, child?"

Taking her arm, I return her courtesy with a kiss lightly placed on the hand. "I wish I could say that all is well, but considering the circumstances in which we are meeting, I would not attempt to alter my words. Not even for civility."

The Fae with hair black, compared to her son's golden, releases a breath of amusement. "You never were one to attempt falsehoods to me. Even as a boy."

Jiya leaves, flocking to her wife's side, both speaking to one of the servants.

My attention is then pulled to Cassandra, mother of Lady Theodosia, counsel to her daughter in her decisions ruling over Aquatius. Her gown of sea green carries sleeves fitted just above her elbow. "My king." She bows, a tight, imitated smile of Lady Jiya plastered on her face. "If you have come with the goal of deterring us from our decision, you may as well take your leave now."

"Now, now," Fatima reprimands. Her tone is as bright as her ruby hair, her face as scalding as my mother's. "Can we not enjoy a meal together before we delve into politics?"

Luka stands behind me, saying nothing since his greeting to the head of the manor upon our entrance.

All in the room take a seat, eating while small, unimportant discussions are being had between some. Sweet glazings of meats, executed to the finest of cooking, burst with flavor in each bite. It is so enjoyable, I can easily ignore the glares of Lord Tanzin and Lady Vaela which fire towards myself. Korine truly adopted the expressions of her parents.

The rulers of Enthar once liked me. I was in their favor until their daughter deceived them into believing that it was I who disposed of her heart, rather than admitting guilt. I suppose I could have amended our relationship once the two of us became acquainted once more, but it held no significance when the two assumed me to remain a prince, never giving their daughter the title of a queen.

"Your Majesty," Tanzin mocks in a dismissive tone. Taking the knife, he slices the meat on his plate thinly enough to swallow in a speedy manner. "There are many grievances that you are now responsible for. How long do you propose that you will requite the Fae with favors and pleasantries instead of punishment?"

"Tanzin!" Fatima berates. "We are eating a fine meal. Your inquiries can wait."

Tanzin lets out a grumbled sound, ignoring her requests. His hand grips one of his forks so firmly, he turns it into dust. "We have gathered to discuss the common fae. I've waited long enough to speak my thoughts!"

"You must forgo any disrespect on the tip of your tongue," I command without a care of what he has to say in response. Addressing all surrounding the table, I look at each of them. "If you wish to depart the rule of the Spiritus bloodline, you are free to do so and risk the repercussions of the lands. I would just like to remind you that any issues will henceforth fall under your responsibility."

Those at the table stay quiet. Servants who have left us to each other's company, I assume, are listening to our conversation behind the door. I have known these Fae well throughout my life. I was raised with two of their children. So, I am highly aware of how each of them act in times of politics.

No longer can I remain the prince that the Fae assumed incompetent and vicious. I have to do what it takes, play whatever role, when presenting as a leader. I must be the king that would earn enough respect for the Elementals to side against Delphi.

"You desire to rule over your own land and claim that the Spiritus leadership has caused death to your people. To your family." I look sorrowfully to both Fatima and Cassandra for a sympathetic moment. "But you cannot accuse me of wrongdoings when it was you and my father who allowed the deaths of the common fae to go on for so long."

Those at the table exchange glances, their hushed thoughts loud as I pause my speech. Expressions, just as the light atmosphere has molded, have turned rotten and spoiled. None at the table offer a rebuttal. They are all patiently observing, perhaps with a gleam of higher regard than they initially thought me to have.

"I am sure you have heard talk that Adonis has escaped, and that much is true. The significance of the matter is that there is, in fact, a witch who aided Adonis in the revolution against our bloodlines." The way I am presenting myself seems to be flourishing their confidence in my false skills. "In escaping, both had also taken Arabella."

"The witch?" Tanzin hollers. He laughs until he is choking on his tongue, wiping tears from two of his five eyes. With skin slightly warmer than mine, his face does not take long to color to that of a ripened tomato. "A witch has taken one of their own as vengeance against us? Why do they suppose we would care? Just because the king has taken a liking to her, does not mean the whole of us would mind if her head was returned back to us with nothing else."

Luka remains firm in his seat, fist clenched around the meat knife. The level of restraint that binds him is impressive.

Neither of us speak on Arabella being the queen. Outside of my brother, another threat against the crown may break out if the Fae were to know the truth.

"She is a creature more lowly than humans. Perhaps a bit more dangerous, but easily killable if murdered by her own kind. I would enjoy tasting her meat cooked," he taunts further, emphasizing his statement by sticking a bloodied piece of deer into his mouth.

Jumping on the table, Luka knocks Tanzin with his chair to the ground and hovers over his plump body, stabbing the cutting utensil into the floor a hair away from the Fae's left antler. Using his free fist, Luka bludgers Tanzin's face. An act not entirely uncharacteristic of him to be so hasty in the name of Arabella.

Cries and voices toppling over each other argue. Cassandra is screaming for Luka to get off of the Elemental, the other rulers are condemning me for bringing a sorcerer to tonight's events, and I am doing my best to keep from laughing.

"That is it!" Fatima yells. Her hands flatten in front of her, and up shoots the temperature of my body. Faces of open mouths and high-pitched sounds screech against the air from others. "Now I said we are going to have supper together without violence. If you are unwilling to abide by the rules of my land, I request that you leave."

Jiya watches me, regret in her eyes. Her youth is deceiving, an age older than every in this room by nearly a millennium. "King Cassius, I know that my son aided you in battle. And while we are aware of your feelings towards the witch, if her taking means peace, why shouldn't we seize that opportunity?"

"I do not give a damn what it is you want at the moment. Until we find Arabella and those truly behind the deaths and disappearances of our kind, there is no more a chance of the common fae returning." I pull Luka from where he traps Tanzin, signaling that it is best we take our leave. "I ask that you trust I will do right by our people, even if my father had not. If your decision to break apart remains unwavering, it will result in another battle in which we waste what little Fae blood our kind has left. It will do your rulership well to have patience."

After thanking Fatima and Pyrros for the wonderful meal, Luka and I depart. Remains of optimism are being trampled beneath the wheels of the carriage while the two of us sit in silence during the long ride back to Nexus.

Perhaps it was a gamble to expect this night to have gone well. Or to think that the others would aid us without much debate.

IV

Homoerotic Friendships

Arabella

She's lying. I know Delphi's lying. She didn't see Luka and Cassius saying they'd leave me here to die. They wouldn't give up on me. I know they wouldn't.

The sound of laughter explodes from Delphi, eyes locked and full of amusement. "You think I'm trying to trick you again, but I'm not. Adonis told me himself that he snuck into your precious palace and heard it."

No. They wouldn't.

"*Oh, I see.* You don't *want* to believe me." She uncrosses her legs, stepping towards me. All I can focus on is my erratic heartbeat that's risen to my ears. "See for yourself." With a vial of her blood, she pours it into the goblet.

My eyes open, and I'm in a shadowed corner of the throne room, where Adonis had supposedly been lurking. No one is in the room except Cassius and three feminine Fae I don't know, all just as drunk and kissing the exposed skin of his body. I'm not sure whether the stomach acid that's climbing up will come out or if I'm going to snap their necks. My fists are clenched, but there's nothing I can do. I'm powerless in both a literal and metaphorical sense.

The women look so different from me. They're so much thinner in comparison, and Cassius is looking at them in a way he's never looked at me.

Is there something wrong with my body? I wonder this while glancing at everything I wish I could physically change about myself. These thoughts have lessened over the years, but they never completely go away. Especially not when one of your biggest fears is displayed right in front of you.

Luka enters through the door, full of more vivacity than I've seen in him in a long time. His stare goes to Cassius, then the women. I think he's about to say something in my defense–maybe something as disastrous as the stormy gray of his eyes–but all that comes from him is a light breath of chuckling.

Behind him is Gavin, standing at the door and observing the room for danger.

Clearly, he didn't do a good job if he didn't see Adonis behind this statue's shadow.

"You were supposed to examine and speak to the common fae today," Luka says, shaking his head.

Cassius offers wine, dripping some on himself, one of the Fae women more than happy to clean it. *With her tongue.*

"I *am* examining the common fae."

"The imprisoned ones," Luka clarifies.

On instinct, I move from the corner, stopping on the scarlet rug that leads from the door to the thrones themselves.

"What are you doing?" Delphi scolds, chasing after me and pulling my clothing from the back.

Her strength inferiority against my size does nothing to keep me from walking closer, despite my weakened state. I spin back to her, looking down at my temporarily free hands. "You said this was a memory from Adonis, right? So everything we do won't change the memory unless we want it to. That's what you've been doing in my mind. What I do doesn't matter when I can't be seen."

"You may go," Cassius says.

Anxiety and hope hit me, possibly containing the naive idea that he can see me, but instead, I realize he is dismissing the women from the room.

The three scurry down the stairs, walking through Delphi and me as if we are as intangible as mist.

Luka waits until the doors are closed, taking the glass from Cassius' hand and placing it on the tray to the table closest to the angled window. "Shouldn't we be searching for Adonis? Instead, you're surrounding yourself with alcohol, sugar, and women."

"There's not been a single Fae that has gone missing or been found dead since his escape. I propose that is enough to end the search."

But what about me? Or those still missing?

The king swings his feet, resting them on the empty throne. "Are you perhaps more interested in finding Adonis when his capture means a unification with Arabella?"

Without hesitation, Luka makes an exhaled sound, disputing his accusation and deeming it absurd. "I'm suggesting we put an end to your brother's reign and find Delphi. I will bring her to the Council and be done with this."

"And what of Arabella?" Cassius asks, face twisted with his expression lifted.

"Knowing Delphi and the methods Adonis used on the Elementals, Arabella is likely dead. She's become collateral damage."

Hustling up the stairs, I stand between the two, looking for any indication of a ploy. Some proof that they're saying this because they know Adonis is here and need to trick him.

Fae cannot tell lies.

I can feel my heart in my chest as my throat stings with a burning sensation. But now is no time for tears or irrational emotions caused by something that's likely another fake scenario produced by Delphi.

And yet, I still feel the urge to give in.

The Fae rises from the throne, striding closer to Luka. "And if she is alive?"

"She was damaged before she was taken by Delphi," Luka confesses. I reach for him, to feel him. "If she's alive, she is nothing more than a shattered mirror. She's useless and a danger to everyone." He walks down with Cassius, stopping at the bottom of the stairs. They seem friendlier with each other than before. Maybe I *am* the problem. Maybe people have a better life without me in it, and I hold them back.

Cassius walks until Gavin opens the door, his voice echoing from the hallway. "Until there is evidence of the two wreaking havoc among Ifaeris once more, you are free to enjoy the luxuries of the lands as the king's seneschal."

I close my eyes, and we're back in Delphi's torture room. She clicks her tongue, kneeling to face me on the ground. "You see? All you are is a burden on everyone. You rely on everyone to pick up the shit that you cause."

"And you would know what giving up on someone who loved you looks like, wouldn't you?" I mutter with heavy sarcasm. My glare doesn't cut nearly the way I want it to, but it does enough for Delphi's face to tighten.

Fabric from her jeans brushes against my skin, hitting my still-healing cuts of the day. She magiks water from the side of the table, hovering the barrel over me before slowly emptying it onto my head for what feels like minutes. "Of all people, I know what it's like to deal with your incessant problems."

The point of her boot digs into my chest, knocking me over

and putting me on my back. She lowers herself over me, one foot crushing my stomach like an anvil. In almost every possible way, Delphi's found a way to target and wound me.

I yank the chains, bringing my hands to my shoulder, taking her down in the process. A loud *thud* echoes through the room, anger in her exhale. I know I'll regret doing that, but the look on her face is worth whatever pain she would bring upon me.

Instead of immediately cursing me, she grabs me by the back of my head, forcing me into a kneeling position. She takes the little blood I've drawn from her, mixing it into the goblet and circling the rim until it makes a high-pitched note.

That's when I can feel my lids falling.

My door flings open, and Delphi rages in while wearing a scorned face with a mouth ready to unleash itself. I haven't spoken to her since May, when she decided I wasn't good enough to be her friend.

"You're dating Luka?" she shouts.

Delphi has no right to be angry with me. She's the one who ended our friendship. She's the one who said our friendship was unhealthy. There is no reason for her to be mad at me for having sex with Luka. Not after everything that Vi, Gray, and Damien told me about their relationship.

A chair is pulled out by my magik for her to sit, but she doesn't take my offer. This isn't a relationship I expected would ever be repaired after all was said, but now I question if our friendship was ever something she held to the same level that I did.

"First of all, we aren't dating. We've had sex *maybe* three times since I met him. And second, I didn't think you'd care since you left to join that group that we used to hate." I try to present myself as calm and unbothered. This is supposed to be a new school year, yet my past keeps coming up. Despite how hard I try to convince myself that Delphi doesn't care, I keep catching different ways she keeps tabs on me.

She lets out a grunt of frustration, her arms crossed and voice louder. "You're still dating my ex! You don't do that!"

"I didn't even know it was the same Luka until two weeks ago," I argue. My hands are becoming more expressive than my voice, though even that is raised to match Delphi's energy. "You never showed me what he looked like in the nine months you called me your 'best friend'. How was I supposed to know it was the same one?"

Huffed breaths leave her mouth while she rolls her eyes. Her body loosens, appearing more annoyed than irate. "I don't think there are many British Lukas that attend our uni."

Maybe that's true. I may not have known it was the same Luka, but it shouldn't have taken me so long to realize it was the one that Delphi would vent about.

None of that matters. When comparing everything she said about him to the experiences that Vi, Damien, Gray, and Luka had, it was no time before I realized Delphi twisted everything in her stories. And after factoring in the months nearing the end of our friendship, all the things she said to me that I never spoke out about, I didn't hesitate to believe their side.

Part of me wonders if she's only mad about their breakup because their relationship offered her family bigger name recognition.

"You don't even sound sincere in your guilt. You're just trying to manipulate me into forgiving and feeling sorry for you," she accuses. Her small lips somehow look even thinner. "You're a shit friend, and more than just my family saw that in you."

It's ironic. I'm not apologizing, and I don't realize that I'm snickering. But there's something twisting in me. "We stopped being friends the second you joined your little cult, and we both know it."

Our argument is one that's been building. Somehow, I've known this fight was coming, despite us having cut contact months ago.

I take a deep breath to keep myself from saying something I know I'll regret. "You've been waiting for a better friend group since we met, and you got it. Congrats." Another grounding breath. "As for Luka, I'm allowed to fuck him if I want since it's clear you never really viewed me as a friend. I'm done with you and this conversation." I open the door with my magik, swinging it harder than I mean it to, the knob hitting into the wall. "Get out."

She doesn't.

She stays where she is, facing me as the light hits her fair skin. "I remember this."

In that same sentence, I become conscious of everything. It's as if she now possesses her body in my memory.

Tugging us back to reality, both our bodies fall flat on the floor from our kneeled positions, Adonis helping Delphi, while I struggle to lift myself to sit.

"That was the day you put the final knife in my back as my friend," Delphi scorns.

Adonis' face drops, shocked eyes darting with a tilted head. To him, a bond between the two of us is impossible to have ever occurred. "You two were *friends*?"

"Oh, did your girlfriend not tell you?" I ask, smiling. The Fae's eyes hop between the two of us. He really has no idea. "We were *best* friends."

"I wouldn't call us best friends," Delphi counters. "You're making things up again."

My brows lift at the roll of my eyes. "Silly me. How could I forget the homoerotic aspect where you'd treat me like we were together, to the point where people genuinely thought we were? Or how you quickly abandoned me when you had the opportunity to up your status."

"Oh, let's not develop a superiority complex." She moves to the weapons table, fingers hovering on the spiked baton. "Even now, you've somehow become the queen of creatures that hate you."

Until she had said this, I forgot that I admitted to becoming queen when she tried convincing me everything had been a bad dream. That none of it was real, and she was still my friend.

I'm struck by the weapon, spikes stuck in the side of my arm. Delphi rips out the baton while I curl in pain on my side. I bite down on my teeth, keeping me from screaming. But it doesn't stop the tears that fall from the corner of my eye. Or the whines of pain.

I hate her.

Who was once my closest friend has become the one thing she used to swear she was against. The woman in front of me is no longer the witch that I would make snide jokes with and laugh with over nothing. I've seen her slowly transform into my worst nightmare, using everything I love and hate against me.

She heals the wounds of torture, only to strike me multiple times. Each time is done in rounds with different weapons. From knives, to whips, to ones that are unknown to me, the pain from each is no more pleasant than the others.

Through each blow, I wonder if Cassius and Luka are looking for me. I wonder if they care.

After what feels like hours, with my mind wandering to different places, Delphi finally stops and laughs. "You could never be happy in our friendship. You made me miserable and depended on me for your happiness 'cause you were too busy playing victim to ever take care of your own issues. *That's* why our friendship ended and why you deserve what comes to you now."

"Oh please," I bark. "The reason we stopped being friends

was 'cause you preyed on the fact I was insecure and needed your reassurance." There's too much adrenaline from the pain to keep me from holding back. My blood is dripping down my body. It hurts to breathe. "And when you found people at school to inflate your ego with their status, you dropped me."

Adonis stands beside the throne, watching our interaction but showing no reaction. It's strange to have someone so similar in appearance to your lover bear witness to your torture.

He's a lot like Cassius in some ways. Smug. Craving the love he never received.

Delphi hits me harder. This time with her fist. "Don't act so tough now. We both know what you do when you're alone in your room." She looks down, yanking up my left arm. "Did you think I wouldn't notice these?"

My head is pounding. Worse with the clacking sound of her steps as she heads to her throne. The endorphins are wearing off, and I can feel myself becoming too weak to breathe. "You think I'm pathetic, but you're just mad I got to live the life you wanted. I get a better relationship with Luka. *And* I became High Queen of the Fae while you did nothing but use Adonis."

Her body became rigid, eyes filled with nothing but wrath from her desires crushed. "You should have killed yourself." She's so loud that Adonis too is aghast. My mouth feels sewn shut as her fist clenches. "You've given me something to think about, Ara. Take her to her cell."

In a way, Delphi sending me back to my room exposes that I cut deeply enough to want me out of her sight. Her hand releases when the blood rushing to my head begins dropping me to the floor, and I can open my mouth again, gasping for air.

Adonis drags me up by my arm to push me in front of him and towards the door. All I see are black stars as I walk, everything feeling dizzy. Taking in deep breaths, I try to contain the nausea hitting me, but it's no use. I feel the stomach acid rising, vomit spewing beside the door's entrance. I wipe my mouth with the skin of my arms as Adonis nudges me forward, but it's physically too difficult to move.

The barely plump cushion of the mattress in the cell is the first thing I feel when I open my eyes. My head snaps around the room, where I see Adonis sitting against the barred door, idly reading something.

I don't even remember fainting.

"You're here," I remark with suspicion.

If Delphi thinks putting him in here to play guard is another form of torture, I don't understand it. I've enjoyed talking with him. Or, at least, I enjoy it more than when I'm with her.

He smiles, bringing the tray of food to my bedside and sitting beside it. "We still have to ensure you're alive."

"Why? Delphi already showed me the memory of Cas and Luka not caring whether I'm dead or alive." Putting the food down, I lean in towards him, making eye contact. "Unless, of course, you admit that it wasn't *really* your memory she showed me."

Adonis refuses to confess that Delphi had been lying to me. Silent while avoiding eye contact, taking time to formulate his next words as carefully as he can. "If she says it to be true, then it is her truth to show."

My face scrunches, annoyed by the way that Fae cannot lie yet constantly having to deal with their ability to twist anything into the truth.

"I'm thankful for you sometimes," I admit, my food now gone, with Adonis still in my company.

"Sometimes?" he asks, closing his book.

And I realize that it's my journal.

I take it from him, setting it down so he's forced to address me.

"You gave me this journal," I say, though it's more of an assumption. In honesty, I still haven't confirmed if he was the one who actually gave it to me.

"I did not hand this to you."

"You can twist your words all you want, but I know it's from you. Even if it was the Troll who gave it to me."

"Yes, well, Delphi had shown me kindness, so I suppose I should extend such grace unto you," he returns. Disbelief nearly leaves my mouth before he continues. "Are you aware that she was the first person to care for me since the death of my aunt and uncle?"

Changing the subject is useless, but I suppose collecting information from him may be useful. I say nothing in response, just shaking my head and allowing for him to go on.

He looks at the notebook, tossing it aside. "For years, I sought to find my father. I always wanted retribution for what he did to me." My eyes run from his gaze, but he never stops looking at me. "Oh, yes. I knew I was his son. I attempted to forget all he did, but I would still have terrorizing dreams of him. I would be reminded of him with every pat my uncle congratulated me with."

"You knew for years and still waited this long to get revenge?" I'm beyond lost. He had decades to exact his plan. Why now? Why with Delphi?

"I denied for a long while that my nightmares were true." His fingers crack, holding off what he is about to say. "That is, until I was fifteen and asked my uncle one day about my mother. I knew I wasn't their child. I look nothing like their image."

There's something vulnerable in the way he's speaking to me. From how he hesitates and the inability to look at me as he speaks, I'm sure no one else knows of this story. Except possibly Delphi.

I sit against the wall, under the window, and straighten my legs. "What did he say?"

"To spare you the details involving the mistreatment by my father, I shall skip that." He moves so that he sits against the wall next to my bed, adjacent to where I sit. "My uncle told me about the death of my mother. He told me of Helena's plan to hide me in the Human Lands when my father sent for my death. She was looking at it as an act of mercy, which I suppose it was since my father granted them permission to reside within the Human Lands."

Adonis' face changes. It deflates from a stone emptiness into something more bittersweet. "Being raised by an aunt and uncle who wanted a child seems far better than to be raised by a man who will never love you. Or one that would beat you for simply being the spawn of his wife."

His story is one I had been told by Helena, but to hear the pain this brought Adonis personally feels different. Seeing the kid who never recovered from the actions of his father is something no one should endure.

Regardless if he was told this at fifteen or at thirty, both must seem like a blink in the eyes for someone with an extended lifespan. It's infinitely smaller when the Elemental Fae are immortal.

"Years after their deaths, I found my father. I would watch him from the shadows with loathing in my very essence. The more I saw how he treated the common fae, the more I realized how pitiful of a ruler he was. There were even times I thought perhaps he saw me. But he assumed me dead, paying no mind if his eyes played tricks on him. I suppose we'll never know now, will we?"

I should feel disgusted with the humor. Knowing that Elliot carried his own grief had made me pity him, but with how he treated his children and the Fae, I can't help but laugh internally at Adonis' question. "You said you hated your father, but why not seek him alone? Why kill other Fae?"

He shrugs with shoulders slumped over. "I first spied on my father, plotting retribution against him and other Elementals for what they had done to cause my mother's death, but when I saw my sisters living a life of childhood innocence, I turned bitter. It was something I never had the opportunity to have. They were living a life I deserved to be part of. Why did they care for each other and never..."

He doesn't need to finish the sentence.

My mouth parts, jaw unclenching. I suck in a sharp inhale before closing my mouth again. What I say has to be worded well, unless I want to return to having no one but Delphi to speak with when she plays in my mind.

"Adonis," I tread with caution, "they didn't know you existed. You can't expect people who don't know of you to look for you."

Crossing his arms, he resents my statement, still assuming himself to be in the right.

"If you were so upset about what happened to your mother, wouldn't you hate Magiks just like your dad did?" I shift my position, sitting cross-legged and putting the weight on my arms for support. "Why partner yourself with someone who'll just toss you aside when she gets what she wants?"

He pushes himself up, towering over me from across the bed. "You speak too disrespectfully for someone in your position."

It takes a bit to lift myself, struggling with the weight of my chains. His height is just one forehead above me. That advantage aside, I stare him in the eyes, refusing to back down. "You said before that I'm powerful, and now you know I'm the High Queen. I get you're still hurt by what your father did, but if you'd just align yourself with us and return me, you might be welcomed into the family."

"Delphi is the only one to have my best interest at heart!" he roars. But he doesn't hit me. He moves farther away, stomps towards the door. "Perhaps she is right in saying you are full of nothing but deception." He slams the cell in a huff, leaving me alone with nothing. Inside, he has to know that I'm right. I think he suspects it. He just hasn't brought himself to admit it.

The journal is not returned to me. Adonis had stashed it inside of his jacket before he left. My single plea is that he is kinder than he assumes himself to be and will keep it from Delphi.

V

Another Day, Another Note

Luka

"I do want to address a final concern before you leave," the advisor says. "Lord Tanzin and Lady Vaela would like to know why the common fae need not pay as many Zips towards their homes."

Nearly two hours ago, the Aeon twins accompanied me to Enthar in order to meet with the rulers' advisor and discuss the finalized requirements of Zip distribution, which Cassius has decreed. Other than the rulers of Hearthis, the lower courts' rulers rarely meet with me on account of me being a sorcerer. In their place, they send their advisors.

"The common fae deserve to afford the places they live in," I tell the Fae. "Prince Atticus already builds housing for those without as many Zips. I'm sure the Enthar rulers can do without such a large profit if it means the Fae they rule over will live better lives."

The advisor says nothing, holding a cordial decorum with a stiff jaw, presumably wishing I were not the king's seneschal. "Correctly assumed, sir. But it bears asking why we cannot fund something more sensible, such as herbal care."

Both rulers of Enthar live in gluttony, taking from those they govern over without any sense of their folly and only occasionally caring for the common fae if it puts the rulers in lethal danger. The real root of this concern lies in why the rulers will no longer be collecting the amount that they are accustomed to.

Socializing isn't particularly my favorite pastime, but the political sphere is something my parents prepared me for, so I assume it to have paid off in some sense.

"The last time you and I came to discuss funds, you relayed their request and asked that three hundred and fifty thousand Silver Zips be given towards funding education for your herbalists. A trade that King Cassius accepted in exchange that your better healers not strictly be reserved for the rulers, but instead be distributed throughout all lands."

"Forgive any possible impertinence," he starts in an attempt to persuade me, "but if our healers and educators are such assets, why does the king not want the primary focus to be on them? Can funds not be redistributed towards another area?"

Of all the advisors I meet with, the one from Enthar is the most direct. Something which is commendable and keeps from our meetings from dragging on, though his energy is hostile when we make arrangements. He encourages that no deceit transpires between the two of us, yet he uses more passive words in place of his aggression when given an answer that does not work in favor of both him and those he serves.

However, my job does not solely require me to coddle fragile egos. At times, perhaps it is necessary, but after the maddening written correspondence with the Enthar rulers, I have no patience for this Fae's attempt at conning the crown.

"King Cassius' decision is final," I say, rising to my feet. Begin my exit with my hands behind me. "I will not listen to any other argument. Either those in charge of Enthar's finances can find a better way to redistribute it, or exposure of the Rokus bloodline's selfishness may be at risk."

Upon the end of the meeting and exiting Oris grounds, Monty pardons himself rather than taking the carriage back to Nexus with us. He claims to have private matters to attend to, though according to his brother, the matter in question is a Fae by the name of Daraja.

"It wouldn't come as a surprise if he's lost faith in searching for her," I say as the long-haired twin and I walk up the stairs and into the palace.

Being unable to speak to my friends is not without its difficulties. The reminder that I miss them becomes heavier whenever Xavier joins me while I complete my responsibilities. His energy reminds me of both Ari's lack of filter and Grayson's unsolicited comments. He will babble on like an unintelligent imbecile with nothing but crudeness in all he says.

Xavier denies my statement before I can go on, shaking his head. "If you've lived with him in your life as long as I have, you'd know that Cassius does care for her." In a flickering look, I see doubt. Uncertainty in his claim. "But I will admit, Cassius does grow bored of things easily, and that has well extended past clothing and statement pieces."

"Meaning?" I push, demanding an answer. If Cassius no longer harbors romantic emotions towards Ari, it's something that is no business of mine. However, to completely disregard her life is inexcusable. Especially when he now knows of the hatred Delphi has towards Ari.

I refuse to let Ari become a side thought. Refuse to let her be something that Cassius casts off due to taking effort he doesn't care to put in.

"Cassius has admirers, many of whom I doubt care about Ara." Xavier clenches his jaw, sucking in his cheeks and making a noise when he opens his mouth. "If he fell to the same Fae he once was, his thoughts are not of Arabella's care."

His statement of his cousin's history completely contradicts his defense. Curious to make sense of this, I ask, "Didn't you say you believe him to care for Arabella?"

The Fae waits, taking his time to answer while we make our way towards my room.

"He does. He was never really tolerable to us until he met Ara. And I wouldn't question him agreeing to horrible terms or tearing apart the kingdom if it meant her return, but caring for her changes nothing of his past and how easily bored he grows of something."

Staying silent, I desist from debating further. If Cassius cares, he does not show it, at least not to any of us.

I open my door, allowing the two of us to enter so that I may hang my blazer before traveling into the flat land of Mindae. My closet is full of clothing precisely identical to those at my house next to the university. The tailors are skilled in interpreting our style based on the few things answered when asked. From long-sleeved button-downs to overcoats and slacks, it is as if they delivered my personal wardrobe here.

Xavier, in a long, mahogany waistcoat, leans against my wall, crossing his arms and mindlessly tapping his tongue in rhythm. "You know, Cassius has done everything that he could do as a prince, but I think he forgets that he is *king* now."

Cassius utilized his power well before he gave up on locating Ari. Each time he spoke to the prisoners in Phantom Tower, he applied intel that Maude supplied him.

However, with the way he had become crowned, I cannot blame him for being unknowledgeable on how to use his new political status. From what Ari has told me, how Cassius presents himself as king is partially rooted in mimicking what he learned from his father, with the help of his family. And when observing the way I have seen him solve issues within Ifaeris, he now mimics the decisions that Ari herself would make.

"Speaking of admirers," Xavier says cheerily. He grabs something that lies on my pillow. "It would seem you have one of your own."

He hands me the item. A handwritten note.

It's from Delphi.

Panic surges within me. It's the first time in a long while that I feel hope resurfacing. "We need to find Cassius."

The two of us run through the hallway, pounding on Cassius' door at the end of the east wing.

"Cassius!" I shout. More knocking. "If you do not open the door, I'll break it down."

The door pulls open, with the king standing groggily. He looks as if he recently woke up, his unclothed body supporting this. "What of importance could possibly have your fists waking me this early?"

"It's nearing mid-afternoon," Xavier returns, snorting.

Disregarding the condescending comment, Cassius drags himself back into his room, covering himself with a silken, black flat sheet.

"Delphi left a note." I reach out my hand, Cassius grabbing the paper from me, which drops the fabric that wraps around him. "It says Arabella is alive and that Delphi's willing to make a trade."

Cassius is stunned, crumpling the note and throwing it into the trash. "Gather the Royal Court. We will discuss as a whole."

In the council room, we all gather. Spread around the same table we have sat at for months. The difference this time is that we finally have a way to track Ari.

Whether it is blind yearning that keeps me in this state or a small blessing, I am grateful.

For all the art and decor that is hung around the palace, this room is the most bare of all. Archways of light beam into the room from the clear windows, with a singular chandelier hanging over the middle of the table. The only art in this room is a mural on the wall behind the king's chair, pillars interrupting sections of the piece.

Kabir also joins us, taking a seat next to me. His face is tired. Eyes heavy and appearing in likeness to someone in mourning.

I don't know the Fae well, but he is someone who cares for the safety of Ari. It was he who asked that she find safety the day I arrived. The Fae who killed any who neared my girlfriend during battle.

His reaction since Ari's taking stretches past that of a guard on duty. Melancholy is equally distributed between him and the others in this room.

"You wouldn't be sitting in this room if you were just another guard," I say. "Why is Arabella so important to you?"

He sighs, dropping his head and taking a moment before facing me. "Lady Arabella was not only someone whom I was originally tasked with protecting, but she was my friend." Glancing at the empty spot that Arabella sat in the last time she was here, his eyes fall. "And I failed her."

"Do not speak of her as if she is already dead when the note says otherwise," Cassius says, dryly aggravated, entering the room.

"We don't know if that note is true," Atticus interjects, Disaris blue eyes pointed at his brother.

Attention redirects itself to him, stunned at his candor. He doesn't add to what he said.

Esme speaks up, but what she says holds no sway over my

decision. Not meeting with Delphi is out of the question. If I would be the only one to carry Ari back, I would do so without hesitation.

The family continues their contention, none able to get a word in over the other. Celeste's soft-spoken voice manages to overpower all, their power calming the rest in the room so that they may be heard. "Atticus is right. What if this is another trick? It isn't the first time a note has been sent to negotiate."

"Cassius, you're the king," Monty says, words spoken meticulously so as not to invoke the king's temper. "You must consider the fact that Delphi has the capability to tell lies."

I don't speak. In part because he makes a point about Delphi holding the power to lie, but mainly because whatever I say will be told to Cassius regardless. I assume that perhaps my quiet would keep me from being dragged into the arguments of the court of kin. What I have to say wouldn't matter. I would be meeting Delphi at the ruins in Enthar, with or without the approval of the king.

"Luka, I ask that you share any thoughts you have," Cassius prompts from down the table. He leans forward, hands held in front of him. "You are the only one of us to know Delphi and her actions. Do you think her note untrue?"

I knew on instinct when reading the letter that it was true. She has nothing to gain in this situation by lying. She knows that Ari is worth more alive than dead. Though the question remains: How much left of Arabella is alive?

"As someone who has known Delphi for years, she will do anything if it presents an advantage."

Dyana sticks her arm towards me, golden specks in her white eyes glowing brighter. "See? If Luka's saying she would do anything, doesn't that prove she would lie about Bella being alive?"

"Just because I said she would do anything does not mean I believe her dead."

No one speaks. It's quiet for the duration of over thirty seconds.

Others here regard Delphi's honesty with absolute doubt, which I admit, I do as well. The difference being I cannot afford to be right.

"While both *do* crave power and control, Arabella is clever and has her own ways of going about things, whereas Delphi never cared who she hurt," I explain. "If it gives her the attention of others, she would do it. She does not take risks. Arabella is alive."

My statement earns a nod from Cassius. To him, my word is irrefutable.

He darts his eyes to everyone at the table, scanning for an objection to what I've revealed. His hands remove themselves from the table, dips below what I can see. "It is decided then. I will meet with Delphi to make the trade."

"I'm going with you," I affirm.

Cassius waves me off. "I figured as much."

"I will also join you," Kabir states without thought. It should be one of the crown's knights to come along instead, though that is just as risky. My attendance is already a problem in accordance with the demands of the letter.

"No," Cassius says. "You're to stay here and do your duty to protect Nexus as Head Guard."

"Then I'm going in his place," Xavier declares.

"Would anyone else enjoy my refusal? The witch's words clearly stated for me to go alone. I would not think the rest of you to fall into such thoughtless volunteering."

At the king's statement, no one dares speak out against him.

The coachman who drives the carriage to our destination is the only other to join Cassius and me. Though Cassius' siblings thought it pointless to have us transported by this medium, the king proved once again that he is far more intelligent than what others expect of him.

Okkaring would be the most efficient transportation in the case that Ari needed a healer, but if she is with minimal energy, that could possibly drain the last of what she has. It's better that we take all the precautions necessary since we don't know the state she will be in.

My eyes squeeze shut, fantasizing of what it will be like to have her in my arms again. I imagine the press of her skin as she clings to me. The excitement in her eyes. She would feel the comfort of safety.

Then, my mind drifts to her smile. Her kiss. The way she wraps herself around me when she is tired. I think about the face she makes when she is completely intoxicated. As if we are the only two people in existence.

Suddenly, I am aware of my leg bouncing. Whether it be from the anticipation of seeing my love or the fear of what it is Delphi will ask of us, the thoughts crash at once, bringing my body into a forceful shutdown.

If Delphi is lying about this, if this is some elaborate scheme to take power from the king, there would be no force strong enough to keep me from scouring the depths and finding her. I would stop at nothing to conjure new ways of torturing her.

I would never stop. Not even when she pleads for death.

Then my heart drops.

If Delphi is sadistic enough to follow through on what she wrote in her note those months ago, Ari wouldn't be returning to us the same. She will likely put on a hardened face, acting as if nothing is wrong, but it would be a lie.

Arabella is nothing if not someone who refuses to wear her heart on her sleeve.

Pressing my head back to the cushion of the seats, I stop

allowing myself to partake in these invasive thoughts. They are exaggerations. My greatest fears manifested from the pits of my mind. But I cannot stop myself from drowning in them.

We don't know what Delphi wants from Cassius. She offered a trade but made no indication what it is she wants in exchange for Ari.

Arabella is alive. If you want her returned, join me alone on Wednesday at noon at the ruins in Enthar.

I obsess about the frustratingly vague wording of the note. It promises her alive, yes, but it doesn't say to what degree. Arabella could be starved. She could be brought to us, nearing death. Or my worst thought yet: she could be perfectly well, just for Delphi to kill her in front of us.

Nervousness fills me as I think of Ari's thoughts at the sight of us. Will she be happy that we came to her rescue? Angry and insisting that she does not need saving? Or will she be furious for taking so long to find her, thinking us unintelligent? Who knows what type of venom she has been injecting into Ari's mind?

In a way, this is my fault. I should have shielded Ari more from the wrath of Delphi during our time as a couple at school.

The confidence I had that Delphi no longer would care about my existence after gaining the social idolization from others was blind. When putting together the bitterness of Delphi and the power of her friends who watched our every move, there was hardly a way to steer clear of them. Not when my friends and I had run in similar social circles as theirs.

Hardly did I know the awful comments they made in hopes of relapsing Ari's confidence. She thought it better to combat feelings by herself rather than to be open about what hurt her. If I found a more permanent way to keep Delphi from Ari, perhaps she would be safe.

Without Delphi interfering and thrusting herself on me at the party all those months ago, Ari would have never been upset. She would have never kept me away. And I never would have been killed.

In my heart, I have always known that only two people are capable of shredding the last bit of happiness I have.

Ari would tell me that this isn't my burden to bear. That I can't control the actions of others. But this torment? This agony that breaks me every night? I fear that Arabella will come to hate Cassius and me.

I'm so trapped in my mind that Cassius' words drown out. Anxiety creeps its way into my pulse, speeding to something I can hardly breathe from. I only feel his tap next to me, and on reflex, I chop his arm, lunging up from my spot and choking him. The sound of air knocking from his windpipe and his hands pushing my face pulls me from my thoughts.

I am grateful.

I am suffocating.

Immediately, I'm staring as he nervously laughs at my reaction, motioning for me to claim the seat across his. "I understand."

Relaxing, I sit. Damask patterning is embedded into the soft padding of the seats of this mode of transportation, royal curtains open and giving a complete view of the outside world around us. I have no idea how much time has passed since we departed and have gone over the many knolls. The one clue I have that we are in Enthar is the buildings made of basalt. That, and the abundance of Banyan trees.

"How long have you trained?" asks Cassius. I can't quite understand what it is he's asking. "You appear similar to my build while clothed, but once shirtless, you are much more toned. And although your arms are certainly not as large as the guards', they still exhibit muscle."

I almost laugh. *Almost.* "I exercise daily. When I wasn't in classes or with Ari and our friends, my free time was spent at a gym." I glance at him. The king is leaner in size and just barely shorter than me. "What about you? I wouldn't expect you to carry the strength that you do."

"Fae are stronger than most average mortals. However, Atticus carries abnormal strength from his ability. He sets his mind to lift something, and with the strength of multiple spirits, they aid in lifting him."

Curiosity drifts slightly through my thoughts. "But other Fae all have a natural strength that is above mortals?"

"Most *average* mortals, yes," he corrects.

The carriage falls quiet again. The only sound I hear is the galloping of the horses and occasional reins snapping together.

"Delphi," Cassius says.

I peer out the window, assuming that he means she is near.

"No." His body shifts, angling it towards me. "You spoke of being romantically involved with her. What is the tale behind that?"

Huffing, I force myself to think back to our disagreeable time together. A period I have not thought much of in detail since I broke up with her. "It's not a long one to tell."

I'm sent a look from the king. It's nearly as if he is telling me that we have time.

"I met her at a party that my older cousin was hosting. It was a gathering during the middle of the term for all the first year students at the university. My family was staying at my uncle's manor because my father had business to attend to. No one was home besides us, and the music was too loud to focus on my studies, so I made my way downstairs."

It's off-putting to think about. That one small decision had paved out a path for me and completely changed what I expected my future to be.

Cassius shifts his position. Leans his back against the door and fully directs his attention at me, with legs propped by the cushions.

"I was still deciding where I would attend university at that time, so I walked around to observe the students there. And that's when I met Delphi." I glide a hand through my hair, recalling every last detail from that night. The party was overcrowded. Full of bodies grinding on each other. "She was pouncing around while drunk and came up to me, saying she was trying to find the best kisser at the party. I was far from sober, so I kissed her."

The king clears his throat. It's evident he is uncomfortable at the thought that I once shared a bed with the witch holding Ari hostage.

Against my need to forget I ever touched her, I go on. "We dated for months before I could no longer handle the fact we shared nothing of interest. It shouldn't have gone on for so long, but my family thought our relationship would be beneficial. They admired her ambition."

"This was years before she met Arabella?"

"Over a year preceding their meeting, yes. I chose to attend Lazipeus, not only for their prestige, but it's also where those I grew up with were planning on attending." A smile quickly grows wide on my face. "It also helped that it would get me out of Delphi's clutches and was nowhere near our estates in New York and England."

One side of his mouth twitches upward, snorting. "You were wrong."

I look directly into his eyes, slightly chuckling. "Evidently."

"How is it she befriended Arabella if she did not attend the schooling that you did?"

"Delphi is a year above me. She sent her papers to transfer to Lazipeus the year after the end of my first, claiming the university had a better education." I pull my sleeves to my elbows. The heat does not agree with my choice of clothing. "For some time, it was nothing of significance. Rumors of her contempt spread to my friends, who would help me in avoiding her. And the summer before my third year, something changed."

Cassius stays silent as he thinks, tilting his head just slightly in question. "That was when you met Arabella, I presume?"

Momentarily, I am in my most blissful memories. I nod my head, closing my eyes and grinning. "It was Grayson's twenty-first birthday. He knew Juliette from a course they took the previous spring semester and asked if he could invite both Ari and Juli. None of us cared, so we told him yes."

What we did not know was that it would be the start of our friend group. Others in the group were also unaware that I knew of Ari since our first class together our first year of university. I never approached her then, and she claimed not to remember me when we were introduced.

"Ari and I got into a disagreement at that party," I say, the quarrel becoming fresh in my mind. Her words calling me pretentious.

She viewed our argument as flirting.

"Then, weeks later, I found myself leaving her house and agreeing to never speak of it." I laugh at the absurdity. I think even then, we knew it was a lie as we agreed. "And that one time turned into months."

His eyes grow wide as he studies my face with suspicion. "She confessed her feelings for you with no complications?"

"Oh no," I remark with joyful clarity and an ironic snicker. "It took months until she finally admitted she liked me. And those months were filled with endless confrontations and harsh words–sometimes followed by okkaring into one of our rooms."

There were times we didn't bother to okkar to a bedroom at all.

I choose not to tell him this.

"Eventually, there was a point when the two of us weren't speaking to each other for over a week. It annoyed every last bit of patience everyone had with us." My eyes roll at thinking back to the dissonance of that time. "So when we and our friends hosted a party, Damien locked us inside a closet until we spoke to each other. Then, after about twenty minutes of hostility and silence, she expressed regret for alienating me."

The carriage stops, and without a minute passing, the coachman opens the door. Cassius is led out first, myself following before we take off towards the ruins.

Delphi is not here when we reach the old Oris manor. The only creatures that lurk are the animals and insects within the trees.

Cassius' face molds into solemnity. It's unusual to see him without the playful demeanor that he holds, even in anger.

He beckons for me to move to him. Patting my back, he whispers, "She will be here."

Inexplicably, a sense of uneasiness sends a chill to my body. I trust that Ari will be present, though I still feel a sense of dread at the knowledge of her being brought by two people who despise her.

Shoes hitting stone turn my attention behind me. Before my eyes is Arabella. She is pale and hunched, appearing sickly. While her skin is lighter than those on her father's side of the family, she has never reached a level of fairness lighter than my skin's complexion. Never reached a color nearing Cassius'.

She lifts her head up, looking between me and the king. Her eyes linger, then widen, swelling with brief softness and disregarding her misery as she tries to run to us.

She doesn't make it.

VI

Blind Delusions

Arabella

The Troll, whom I call Mohawk since I still don't know his name, is poking me with something sharp. "Get up," he commands. "Lady Delphi commands that you are to be bathed."

Typically, Mohawk mutters to himself in a language I don't understand, but he speaks English whenever he deals with me, Delphi, or Adonis.

I rub my eyes, groaning from being forced awake after having *just* fallen asleep. "I took a bath two days ago. Why is she letting me again so soon?"

"That is not for you to know. You are to be brought out today." He pulls me by my arm, forcing me up.

"Do you know where?"

He stays silent, bringing me to the bathing room, where an already-filled tub is waiting for me. There, Mohawk unbuttons the clasps at the top of my shoulders, parting the shirt I wear in two.

The water is hot, nearing a boiling temperature. I should

have figured that Delphi wouldn't give me a privilege without counterbalancing it.

Outside of the window is a bleak view, but the sounds of night distract me before settling into the water. Other than my cell window, this is the only place I'm able to view the world. It's not much, but it's real and reminds me that there's life other than those I am constrained to.

"Can I at least have your name? You've seen me naked enough times," I joke. It's much harder to get him to speak. At least with Kabir, I could annoy him into talking. With Mohawk, he doesn't care. I'd assume it's due to the fact his life rests at the power of Delphi's hands, but then, so does mine. And I receive the worst of her lashings.

His focus is glued to his task. To wash me as quickly as he can. "You are being taken to Enthar."

Holy shit.

Holy shit.

Immediately, he regrets his words, inhaling sharply and pressing the cloth too harshly into my skin. Ten seconds of nothing pass between us. "I must leave. You will be retrieved momentarily."

He exits, shutting the door and isolating me with my thoughts.

I lift my feet, resting them on the tub's edge, while my head leans back, staring at the ceiling until my eyes fall shut.

Some days–most days–I'll allow myself to think of Cassius and Luka. The water is warm enough that, if I try hard enough, I can imagine it's their touch on my skin.

It's poison to my thoughts, but worse when I snap back to reality.

Because when I open my eyes, there's no one there but me, naked in a steel bathtub. There are no sounds but the splash of my body moving the water. I'm utterly alone and without supervision.

If I'm being taken to Enthar, that means Delphi's bringing me to Cassius and Luka. That, or she's finally planning on killing me.

The thought consumes me. Of being back at Nexus. With Cassius. With Luka.

But what could they have possibly offered her in my exchange? I'm the queen, yes, but my being here renders me powerless. Whatever they have to offer her, it should be thought out. Delphi wouldn't pass on the opportunity to keep me under her control unless she has something better planned in her favor.

The past months have been the worst of my life. I've said nothing, *done nothing*, to Delphi since the day she came into my house and scorned me about Luka.

For all I know, I wouldn't be returning to Nexus. Just because I am to be brought to Enthar, it doesn't mean that I would be going home with Luka and Cassius. I don't know if a deal's been made or if I am a bargaining tool for Delphi. While both want the crown, Delphi is unpredictable and obviously the dominant between her and Adonis.

Fear grows deeper inside of me, weaving its roots through my skeleton at the thought of Cassius working with Delphi. Whatever deal he may have struck with her, there's no possibility of it ending positively. My return can't be worth the chaos that would arise.

I feel like I'm going insane, and this is exactly what she wants. Delphi has made me relive the worst points of my life and created scenarios that never happened, and all of them felt just as painful as if I were brought back to those exact points in time.

Everything feels real and simultaneously not. My breath is shuddering, and I realize there are tears from my face joining the water I bathe in.

If this is another scenario, another way for Delphi to keep me questioning what reality is true, I don't know if I'll survive this time. Having me question myself aside, the thought of being brought back safely is too good to fathom. I refuse to believe this is anything other than a means to torture me. I'd much rather believe that than be ultimately heartbroken when I open my eyes and am back in Delphi's room of purgatory.

As if on cue, Delphi bursts through the door, staring down at me as I wipe my face. She's not smiling, which is suspicious when my pain is precisely what she wants.

"We were supposed to leave five minutes ago, and you're sitting here crying?" She throws me a towel, allowing me to dry myself.

I'm only able to put on the underwear and pants she provides for me, begrudgingly looking at her for help with my shirt.

"I didn't know we were on a schedule," I respond. She ties the strings around my neck. A halter top that crops at my waist, above my belly button. "If you wanna blame my sulking on anyone, blame the Troll. He left me after saying we were going to Enthar."

"I see," she says. Her hair is parted off-center, the line not entirely straight. Fitting for someone so unstable. "I will deal with him later."

Guilt corners my mind at my passing of blame. I doubt Delphi would give him a fair understanding for his slip-up.

Adonis joins us in the bathroom, and the two hold me, each linking an arm with mine. Their grip squeezes too tight, but at once, before I have the chance to say anything, we're pulled from our place to the ruins of the Oris' old home.

I'm so weak from the starvation and dehydration that I think I might vomit again.

As I finally get the strength to stand straighter, I see two figures. But for a short amount of time, the bright sunlight forces everything unviewable, rendering me unable to take in more of their features.

When my eyes finally adjust, I process my two lovers. This feels real, too real for me to believe.

I don't care.

If this is Delphi trying to break me, I don't care. If this is a false reality, it doesn't matter. I'm looking at the two I've been waiting to see for months. And they're looking back at me.

They can see me.

Relief floods my body. A need knocks at my chest to be in their arms. If this is fake or true, I don't dare overthink it. I only care if the touch from them *feels* real.

Cassius looks as ostentatious as he always does. The only difference is now the sides of his hair are trimmed much shorter, with the top of his hair falling forward. I forgot how purely black his hair is when compared to mine. It's the same shade as ink droplets staining fine parchment. He never fails to wear something so extravagant, whether it be for a revel thrown in his honor or a negotiation between him and the witch who orchestrated his people's death.

He dresses like he's trying to justify that he is worthy of his title. His clothes are regal, the deep cherry color of his shirt emphasizing the raw dough of his skin. Similarly, his eye makeup is the shimmery color of rosewood, contoured by black eyeliner close to his eyelashes. While he stands still, the accessory I can't help but pay the most attention to is the crown he wears. The golden one I had given him for his birthday.

Luka too looks dressed as he normally would. Casual with the sleeves of his white button-up shirt pulled up but formal attire nonetheless. His hair perfectly complements the sunlight dancing off the strands that are a tad warmer than the brightness of this time of day. I could kiss the two of them for looking in such a way that practically makes me forget what's happening.

I run to them, a smile on my face, but I don't make it very far. Delphi chokes me with her magik, and I'm on my knees, clenching my fists, reaching an arm up for mercy.

This cut from my relief is what I should have anticipated. I feel as helpless as my first week when she filled every inch of my body with physical anguish. My optimism is being torn from me all over again.

"Enough!" Cassius shouts. I'm released from Delphi's hold on me and am brought up by Adonis while the king steps next to Luka. "Now, you asked us to meet you here with the promise that Arabella is alive, and yet you were delayed in your arrival. Never mind punishing the witch before our eyes."

Her smile is nefarious. Not sent to anyone specific, yet I still feel as if I am on the receiving end of it. "Apologies. Your witch dawdled for too long."

I'm petrified. Scared and anxious when thinking of all the things she's going to do. Thinking of the endless possibilities she has in mind, in hopes of stealing what she believes she is owed from this universe.

Delphi shoves me forward, and instantly, I am back on the ground. Debris and rubble from stone still inconsistently scatter around the ruins, with nature growing between cracks and crevices. And when looking up, Luka is offering his outstretched hand.

I cling to him as I'm pulled up. Holding on as if he's my last breath of life. Like he's the only thing keeping me tethered to this plane and not drifting away to a dark place that I fear awaits me.

"Hi, love. I've got you."

He doesn't let go. Only holds me tighter as he kisses the top of my head before resting his chin in its place. His smell of bergamot, sandalwood, and lavender brings comfort to me. There's something both gentle and tightly tense about his hold. Whatever it is, no matter if my torturer is just steps away, I finally feel safe.

Eyes going to Cassius, he glares at me in anger. Almost as if he is displeased at my sight. Or maybe he's angry I made no attempt to reach for him first. He steps in front of the two of us, standing less than five paces from Delphi, neither of the two breaking eye contact.

"You see that Arabella is even unharmed," she speaks first, pointing her head in my direction.

"You and I have a different understanding of what unharmed means," Cassius replies with jarring mockery.

After the things I've seen conjured by Delphi in my mind, it still saddens me to hear him sound so uncaring. But I can't be angry with him over what he did in a scenario which I'm now sure Delphi had curated to torment me.

"She is one missed meal away from collapsing to her death," Luka scorns.

"But she's not *dead*," replies Delphi.

Luka's arms around me stiffen, locking me in my place. He is slightly shaking, though I doubt it's noticeable from sight alone. And despite not glancing down to see them, I know the color in his hands has become white. "You call this," he pauses, referencing my state, voice strained, "alive? She can barely hold herself up!"

I'm completely mortified. Not just for being presented to them in the condition I'm in, but for also not arguing. The two of them shouldn't be the ones defending me from Delphi.

Cassius waves his hand, ordering Luka's silence.

My body wiggles, signaling for my boyfriend to loosen his grip on me. There's an initial stiffness in him before realizing that I'm not leaving.

While moments of fraught silence pass through the five of us, I hear my heartbeat echoing. Panicking that at any given second, Delphi will snap her fingers, and I'll return to her and Adonis' side, okkaring out of reach of Cassius and Luka.

"I've held up my end of what was promised," Delphi says. Her eyes hone in directly on me, her mouth quirked at the corners. "Now, where is my payment?"

The High King scoffs at her demand. With the privilege he's lived off of his whole life, I doubt he's used to being commanded in such a way, outside of his father. "You have brought Arabella here, true." One of his hands rises, and I can't be sure what he does with it. "What is it you say you want in exchange?"

"Isn't it obvious?" Delphi points to Cassius' head, nail directly in line of the piece he wears. "I want your crown."

No.

There's a pause. No one's saying anything, and I can't believe that Cassius would even consider this. He'd give up the whole kingdom just to have me returned.

On the one hand, I find it endearing that he would sacrifice a kingdom in my honor. On the other, as queen, I'm irritated that he would be this irrational without thinking of the consequences that would ensue. He risks not only those we rule over, but his family as well.

Cassius laughs. "She *is* one of many fine mortals whom the Fae wish dead. But she is only one witch. If rulership is what you desire, I suggest a trade."

I don't think anyone knows what he's planning with this. What other trade can he possibly offer Delphi that is equal to the crown?

Whatever it is he offers, he does so for the both of us. That thought is what makes me nervous most of all. But I remain quiet, trusting that he won't make such an irresponsible decision.

He turns around, walking towards me and stroking my face with his thumb. There's no show of care or indication of worry. Instead, his face is hardened. Studying me. And like a lovesick idiot, my eyes glance down to his hand, eliciting an involuntary smile from my lips.

Delphi makes a sound of disgust. "If you're done, can we get back to our deal?"

Again, Cassius leaves me to return his focus to her.

I hate it. She can't, for longer than thirty seconds, let me enjoy the feeling of peace.

"I will not offer you the crown," Cassius says. My chest relaxes, relief instantly filling my lungs. "Instead, in exchange for a small portion of land to rule over, I request that you return any remaining Fae who you keep locked away. You would have the same command that each Elemental ruler does. However, you will still be under my rulership."

"Ara and my people in exchange for a measly plot of land?" She snorts. I'm convinced she won't make the trade. She has too much leverage. "Your Majesty, I know you don't know much about the politics of being a leader, but this is not ideal."

"I did not reveal my terms," Cassius responds. "I offer you the land in exchange for *their* freedom. I said nothing about Arabella's."

My stomach drops.

He can't be serious.

Delphi's eyes narrow, fascinated with what Cassius offers. Her mouth is spread wider than I've ever seen it. "You would give Arabella up in exchange for your people? I'm intrigued."

"It will take approximately a week to arrange this with the other Elementals post sending word. But in exchange for this, you are not to unjustly take other Fae. Furthermore, you are not to cause outrage amongst the other rulers. Those who choose to remain under your rule are free to do so."

Adonis, still unmoved from where we first okkared, seems indecisive on the matter. "Delphi," he says, taking one step closer. "Should we not take time to consider other–"

"And what about Arabella?" she questions, completely ignoring and speaking over Adonis. "What am I supposed to do with her?"

Cassius lifts his hand in dismissal. He looks like all the horrendous things people say about him. "Whatever it is you feel best suits her. If it pleases you, I offer Luka in promise that you no longer kill those who detest you. I've heard the two of you share a history."

I should be angry. Furious with the words that just came out of his mouth, but all I can do is remain stuck in place. Distraught with a driving force of a million different thoughts and emotions colliding at once. After everything he's said, *everything he's promised*, he would do this.

It makes no sense, yet I'm not surprised. This is the same Fae that I once knew to be nothing but selfish and cruel. I was told he cared about nothing except himself, and I thought that maybe I was wrong. I got to know him. I let my guard down, and it only led me back to the worst person I have ever known.

I care. Maybe that's my fault.

"What?" My voice cracks, barely above a whisper. There are a plethora of words in existence, but this is all I can muster without curling down or falling.

The coward doesn't have the decency to face me. He takes her hand, kissing its back and lingering for longer than he's touched me this whole time. "If it is power you crave, let me be the one to give it to you. Thereafter, I expect a vow that you refrain from using the Stone of Elestial."

This is why it took so long for them to find me. Luka may have done all that he could, but Cassius did not. The king spent months finding ways to keep me away. And now, I'm offered up without remorse. Speechless, as he kisses the cheek of the woman who's kept me prisoner.

My throat goes tight, my heart completely without function.

While my mouth can find ways to keep silent, my face often cannot.

A solid shadow in the shape of a sharp blade comes close to my neck as Cassius turns to me, its edge tracing down until it slightly pierces right by my collarbone. I'm bleeding, but not for long. Delphi's already using her magik to heal the opening.

I can feel the heat on my face. The frozenness of my body. But worst, I feel the sting of rage emanating from me.

Adonis takes the spare chained cuffs he had brought with us, and I wonder if the two of them had planned to take Luka and me back regardless of whatever deal was made.

Luka is unquestionably loyal to me. He doesn't resist, instead offering an unpleasant smile and holding his hands out for Adonis to place shackles on him. Only he would be this courteous and outwardly composed while likely contemplating murder.

I shouldn't. I know I shouldn't, but I can't keep myself from looking back. I try searching for a glimmer that Cassius feels an ounce of regret, but when it processes, I feel disappointment when seeing that his face is unmoved, grinning even. So I opt for the next best thing. I muster all the anger I feel and show it on my face. If this is the choice he's decided on, he would look into my eyes and be forced to see the unfolding of his actions. "You've become your father."

At my words, Adonis and Delphi take Luka and me back to the cell I'm held in. I'm unfocused on everything else. It feels like everything is happening around me, and I'm at a standstill.

The two don't say a word when standing in the cell. Delphi just looks at us, using magik to force Luka onto the ground. She smirks to herself like she's won, and we're her trophy prisoners. Her allowing Luka and me to stay together might be the kindest thing she has done.

Laughing at the outcome of today, Delphi moves closer to me, patting my cheek with light slaps. "Even when given the opportunity, those you thought cared about you will give up. Just remember that, Ara."

Though Adonis had a lot to say when I last spoke with him,

he barely says a word when Delphi is around. She treats him less as her boyfriend, and more like someone who is hopelessly following around their crush that will never reciprocate those same feelings.

Everyone can see he's growing despondent from this. He's become detached. More brainwashed than the Fae that were under his every command.

"Gather those from Ifaeris and have them brought to the courtyard," Delphi commands.

He nods, making haste and swiftly rushing away.

She is directly behind, shutting the cell as she exits, bars clanking against the frame and pulling me back into my body. I don't know what to think. Luka tries to say something, but nothing comes out. He opens his arms but realizes that holding me would be nearly impossible. I duck from under the chains between the cuffs and stand between the space of his body and rusting metal. It feels like he's cradling me as we struggle to fall back onto the mattress.

This is the first time that I hope Delphi will snap me to my right mind. To have me close my eyes and open them to being stranded in a room with only her. I blink and blink and hold down my eyes, counting to ten, but nothing works. This is real. This is happening.

Cassius betrayed me.

And I want him dead.

Part 2
Separation

VII

A Bloody Hell

Luka

There aren't enough words in any language to describe the outrage I feel towards Cassius. I should have guessed long ago that he stopped caring for Ari, and any barrage of questions he had in regard to my past was a ploy to use for his personal agenda.

If this is for a newfound respect from his subjects that he hopes to attain, I'm more than sure this will suffice to earn their approval. What happens to us onward is his doing.

There has to be some way to escape. The walls are exceptionally plain. We're in a bare room with one window, which overlooks the outside world. Gauging from the explicitly large size of the cell alone, I can assume we are in Gigantia. The dingy space has stone covering every surface, aside from the metal bars that open as a door. There are no voices coming from neighboring cells. No one to converse with.

A lonely, lonely experience to have endured for months.

It has been silent for an extended period of time, the only sounds coming from birds in the distance. Something that should not be possible when I have gone this long without seeing Ari. She hasn't spoken a word in the hours that we have been alone. Hasn't touched the food that was delivered at dawn, despite me urging her to eat it.

She just sits adjacent to me with a blank expression, reaching for me to touch her in any way.

It's unlike her. While she has grown comfortable with my physical affection, this is nearly overcompensating. I am deeply concerned over what has been done to her, which would call for the reminder that I am here. Not that it matters, of course. What's important is that I am with her.

I attempt to get her to eat. To talk. Anything that can break her from the trance that she is in. Her eyes are glassy, tears welling along the line of her lower lashes, refusing to fall. Showing any vulnerability, especially in front of others she cares about, is something she locks so far inside her that I've wondered many times if she would ever allow herself to face them. She hates to do so but does her best to be open with those she holds closest. I, of course, cannot condemn her when she is the only one I can trust with my deepest secrets.

"Talk to me, my love," I whisper, tightening my hand on hers. Her eyes blink, finally making eye contact with me. "You need to show me that you're still here."

She says nothing, communicating with a few more blinks and rising to get the tray of food, which has carved imprints into the softer foods from barely sliding under the door.

Unsurprisingly, she eats less than half of what is on the tray, offering me the rest. I hate it. I want to break her open and start the fire that burns inside her. "You need to eat, Arabella."

Still reluctant, she takes the fork and stabs it back into the meat—eating but insistently offering the food every few bites she takes. She is so adamant in her ability to care for me. For everyone she loves, but particularly me at this moment. She attributes her kindness to basic decency, failing to realize how selfish the average person is. Here we are, hours into our capture, and her worry is to make sure that I am not hungry when she has undergone a long period of isolation. No contact, other than the witch who disparaged her trust.

I am begging at this point, trying to get a reaction that evokes any emotion, which would allow her to let go of whatever she is holding in. She is so far gone that I don't even know where to begin when sifting through my ideas, which ensure Delphi and Adonis be paid back in full for what they have done.

After every attempt failing, I've reached my last tactic. Something that I know is efficient enough to get a response from her.

As Ari sets down her finished food, she crawls back to my side, laying her head in my lap. I grimace at my clothes covered in grime from the floor, the fabric torn from when it had been caught on the bars as Adonis had shoved us in. "I hope I'm given a fresh set of clothing after they so rudely sullied mine."

"Seriously?" Ari turns her head, eyebrows rising. She lifts her torso slightly so that she is able to view my eyes. "We're in a building, captured by your ex, and you're worried about how you'll look in front of her?"

"You sound jealous," I respond lightly. "And captured or not, my clothing is filthy."

A smile forms ever so small on her lips as she amusedly scoffs and rolls her eyes. "You're lucky I'm weak right now, or I'd strangle you."

"But not weak enough to threaten me."

"Never." Her body completely lifts, placing her head on my shoulder but keeping her hands between her thighs.

"I don't crave validation," I remind her before taking her hand to kiss it. "You are the only one whose opinion matters to me, Blossom."

I can't see it, but I feel her smile. I feel the way her cheeks widen, pushing lightly against my clothing. She shifts around, her right hand lightly brushing my left as she sits herself against the wall, perpendicular to where I am. Though I can see no visible evidence, I know the torment that Delphi is capable of. Whatever Ari has experienced, it is infinitely more than what anyone could survive living through.

Her legs rest over mine, and as she moves, I'm given a clear view of her lifeless face. I have never seen her so drained of color. So close to the brink of collapse. Her body has narrowly changed, but it appears exceedingly frail.

"You know," she rasps, "I probably wouldn't have survived without thinking you were looking for me." She pauses as if contemplating whether to say something. "You didn't stop looking for me?"

A panic seizes my entire being. During our time apart, there hadn't been a single moment where I was not searching for her. Hoping to find a way to bring her back.

"I would have slaughtered every living creature in existence if it meant finding you." Still, she remains unsure. My declaration, while concise, is failing to surmount the doubt she has invited in. "I would have searched for you until my last breath."

"Sometimes, Delphi would convince me that you never wanted to find me. Everything she did, none of it compared to the realities where she made me believe you didn't care." Ari's voice croaks partly, strangling a breath to continue. She wipes her hand to her eyes, doing anything she can to hide her emotions. "I think that was enough torture for her to take pleasure in. She'd revel in the pain she could cause without so much as physically harming me."

My mouth parts from shock. It would suit Delphi's personality to torture in a way far more damaging than physical pain. Ari's knee lurches, and I realize that, unknowingly, my hands have touched her skin through the holes in the black jeans that she wears.

She can deduce her reveal of information has stopped my thoughts in their tracks. My hand is suddenly filled with hers, replacing the emptiness of space with her touch. "But I was wrong. You're here. And somehow, we'll get out of this. If anything, I can annoy her to death." She laughs out lightly, a slight grin appearing on her face. Her way of pushing through anything she has been put through her whole life. "Won't be the first time I've done that to her."

"Or maybe we would be loud enough to warrant relocating us farther from her grasp."

Her mouth opens, a hand slapping over her mouth. It's a slower reaction with the chain weighing her down.

"Really? Here?" She looks down. "In shackles?"

I smile to myself at the sight of a true glimpse of life peeking from her. Normally, I would not utter something so crude in a situation such as this, but I had known before saying it that the comment would amuse Ari. She kisses me. Hard. Showing more drive than when she was taking care of her own needs by eating. I love the way that she is completely open with me.

Unprecedented footsteps knock my attention into place. Ari turns and lets out a breathy giggle, all while I curse whatever power that may be for taking this from me.

Creatures of all types walk past, varying from heights to features, all ancient texts of different cultures' mythology written by humans holding a truth. One by one, from left to right, they pass our cell. Few appear to be smaller and of a fluorescent skin tone, differing in colors from blue to green or even purple, while others look of crossed hybrids between humans and other creatures. A small Pixie with wings, transparent with reflective colors, appears before us.

There are Fae that appear beaten, a few with eyes swollen, the crust from dried blood keeping them shut. Darker colors than their skin cloud along their torsos and faces, some creatures only able to drag themselves, some holding the limp bodies of other Fae that I'm not sure are dead. Though a few peek in, most march forward, relieved from being held hostage. Based on the diffraction, the distant sounds of the footsteps indicate they come from corners farther down.

Then, a Troll stops. He lingers at our cell, making eye contact with Ari. An acute pain shoots through my chest, and I think that I may be dying from a collapsed lung. Perhaps a heart attack. Prospects that he is coming to commit an act of loyalty for Delphi crowd into my thoughts.

Instead of my fears coming to fruition, his gaze holds on us two, mouthing a quick apology to Ari. She, in response, sends a subtle nod as if she accepts his apology. Forgiveness that is not deserved.

Sensing my tension, Ari lightly presses her lips to mine, pulling me from my thoughts and spreading a grin across my face.

Just then, the cell is opened, and there stands one of the men who I have been impatiently waiting to serve justice to. My bit of a smile is immediately wiped from my face. Adonis remains unmoved, eyes darting between the two of us before settling on Ari. He stalks closer, never taking his sights off the woman I love.

My feet take me to him slower than I'd want, my body bending forward before pushing my shoulder from under Adonis and into his chest. I can hear the air leave the Fae's mouth when pushing him farther into the wall. Both my hands rise, pinning around the sides of his neck. His height is shorter than all of his brothers', Ezra included. The chain chokes him as I bring a knee to his groin, knocking him into my body, my hand going to his throat.

Ari is yelling, but I can't hear her over the rage that has been set off. Adonis' face has become purple, turning closer and closer to a shade of blue. He's reaching up, grasping the air in an attempt to breathe.

I lean in close to his ear. Reminding him, "I don't need my magik to strangle the air out of you."

Hands grab me from behind, releasing my grip on the Fae. For a brief moment, he is able to catch his breath. A moment short-lived before I bring Adonis to the ground, taking my fist and pounding it into his face in sporadic timing. Grabbing his hair to repeatedly slam his head into the stone. Hard enough to draw blood, punches strong enough to cause his skin to tear, and hopefully, a chronic wound.

His lack of an arm gives me an advantage. Without a prosthetic, if I keep his one working arm pinned, he cannot harm me. With the cuffs suppressing my magik, the two of us are on an even match.

Ari yells again, attempting to push me off him. "Luka, can you fucking stop! Adonis is the nice one."

"You need to talk to more people, Blossom. It's clear you've had to resort to scraps of a barrel. If you think I would willingly spare his life, you're wrong." I keep one knee weighted on Adonis, locking his arm to the stone. He flashes his teeth, spitting blood up and refusing to show signs of surrendering. "There are few people I care about in this abomination of a world. Arabella is one of them. You're the reason she is here." My fist meets his face again, pounding his head to the side.

With a kick, Ari knocks me off of Adonis. I fall over, her knees quickly spread on both sides of me. After a breath of bitterness, when looking at her face, I realize there is a chance her kindness may very well have a reason that I should hear.

"You can't kill him," she manages with a hoarse voice. One quick glance at Adonis hardens her face. "At least not now. He's been generous... ish. And one arm or not, he still has his Elemental ability. Plus, Delphi could easily kill you. Without our magik and it just being the two of us, we're defenseless."

In all my time with her, Ari has never sounded so defeated. However, this does not sound like pessimism. Neither is it her showing kindness. She may be doing this for a reason that is just as smart and calculative as always. To her, showing him mercy may be our best way to freedom.

One loud snort breaks the tense silence. All our heads whip in the same direction, and there waits Delphi, leaning on the side of the opened bars with an entertained look plastered on her face. "Oh no, please continue. I'd love a show."

"Of course you'd enjoy your ex and boyfriend killing each other, you demented, fucking narcissist," Ari insults with a deadly glare in her eyes. It's a glare so direct, I can assess how fast her brain has flipped to return herself from showing any morsel of fragility.

Delphi's mouth widens with the cock of her head. In that single action, it answers in favor of Ari's statement.

"You're here because?" I snap.

"I only came to see what was taking Adonis so long to fetch Ara, but I see he was preoccupied with being bloodied by a psychopath."

A smile reaches my face. It could have been a compliment coming from her.

Ari's mouth is clenched, jaw locked, with restraint holding herself from speaking words that would earn her something abhorrent in pain. "You don't get to call anyone a psychopath when you've done nothing but kill and torture for the better half of a year." Her head tilts up at me to where I am sitting up. "Especially not Luka."

When I dated Delphi, there was no one there to defend me from her accusations of my character. Hearing Ari, the words she says to take my side, to shield me from the name-calling that Delphi does, is truly something I will never grow tired of.

Delphi makes a hummed noise, sharp with pondering undertones. I'm unable to move from my place, Delphi's magik keeping me still with one hand, while her other takes Ari's arm and pulls her out of the cell.

One final, smug glance is tossed in my direction by Delphi before the door slams, screeching from the rusting metal reverberating after its closure.

There is undoubtedly malevolence embedded in her genetics. Maybe she wasn't loved enough as a child by her parents. Or perhaps it's the fact that her stepmother never gave her nearly as much as her stepsister. Regardless, my actions may have inadvertently caused a harsher punishment than what was already planned for Ari.

I don't know when, but at some point, I've fallen asleep and have only awoken due to the sound of the cell shutting. One look outside the window, and the sight of twilight gleams my vision. Hours must have passed. The only source of light in the room comes from what little sun there is left, which creates shadows from the bars of the window.

Ari makes her way over to me, impassive with an expression cold. Vacant almost. She weans away from my touch as I attempt to hold her. Her eyes are swollen, body flushed and wearing something entirely different than when she was taken. When attempting to ask her what happened, she flinches back. To her, the reminder that my very presence here may be painful enough.

"Did she hurt you?" is the only thing I can voice without misdirecting my scathing anger. There is silence as Ari lays herself beside me with her face away from mine. I keep myself calm, steady enough that I don't touch her in a way that would cause a worse impact.

A lengthy stretch of time passes before she exhales loudly. She scoots closer to me, and when maneuvering, I feel the heat of her cheek on my hand. There are two drops that wet the tips of my fingers as I touch her face. She's crying. This entire time while lying down, she's been crying, unbeknownst to me.

I grasp her as closely as I am able without the chain becoming an uncomfortable nuisance. Muted quiet between the two of us would not be alarming on any other occasion when she is overwhelmed or, conversely, comfortable enough to go without speaking. But in this silence, I find my thoughts traveling to horrible places.

"You're too patient with me." She breathes from her nose, congested and voice barely audible. Her small, shuddered breathing circles my hearing. "I've been nothing but a mess since you met me, and I don't deserve it. I'll never be worthy of the kindness you show to me."

That's why you pulled away from me?

Everything done earlier this day, it has been reset to nothing. She's been hollowed out from the progress made. The reignition of the strong attitude that courses through her has been snuffed out. Her words are closer to the conversation we had before we officially dedicated ourselves to the other.

Careful to avoid further regression, I sheepishly press my lips to the back of her neck. "Love isn't something you have to be worthy of to receive. You deserve to be shown it the same way you do to others. Every thought of denial that you have, it's implanted by Delphi. I know you don't want her to have that control over you."

While I am fortunate to have her back, she is adjusting to being in the company of another. She is reacquainting with someone who will assure her that it is okay to be unguarded in their presence. Something we both desperately need after the length of separation.

"But she's right," she argues, struggling as she turns to face me. "I'm not easy to love. Look at what loving me's gotten us into."

A sigh escapes me. Not from being annoyed–though it is a factor–but because Ari views her pain as a reflection of her true character. She doesn't see the honor that it is to love her. "You have to stop trying to dictate my feelings for you. I never wanted you because you were easy to love." Abruptly, she freezes, her emotions seeping through. I lift myself, ensuring she sees me and the sincerity in my words. She is the only one in the world who can make me understand love and heartbreak. "I want you because for once in my life, I feel a sense of safety. I always find myself seeking the comfort of your presence. Every thought, every little moment I have spent with you, cannot be traded for anything. Loneliness becomes an insignificant word at the thought of you. No one knows me or would have given me the chance that you have. And when I hold you, I can't ever imagine leaving." I plant a soft kiss on her lips, remaining there as she breathes in my words.

"I love you."

"Don't ever let Delphi warp your mind into forgetting how I feel about you," I remind her, returning to my previous position.

"So what was dealing with Cassius like without me?" she wonders, completely switching the topic. Hints of charm and anger are suggested, both squandered under the cracks from her voice.

I'm stunned this is a topic she's prepared to speak about. After Cassius' betrayal, I had assumed his name to be stricken from any conversation we might have. But therein lies my misunderstanding. It's not him that she specifically wants to discuss. Instead, she is questioning me to divert her attention. She seeks the gossip of the palace. She wants to know exactly what everyone has been doing during her absence. Most importantly, she misses her friends and needs to hear about life beyond these walls.

"The past months were spent with his family in constant confrontations and impasses. A meeting wouldn't go by without one of them holding Cassius accountable for his mistakes. He wouldn't bother to hear anyone's ideas, and–"

"The common fae," she interrupts. "What do the common fae think about me and Adonis disappearing?"

I shut my lips, taking a cautious beat to think on how to form this using the best wording possible. I'm unsure of exactly what she is not ready to hear. "They don't know about you being taken. Most of them are either grateful that Cassius caught Adonis and live in blissful ignorance or are infuriated that Adonis is imprisoned. Some even think he's escaped."

"He has," she remarks, as if that much is not obvious.

The air feels dithering, Ari delaying a question from fear of the topic itself. I've yet to tell her of the good things that Cassius has done.

I can't tell if she's fallen asleep or thinking. Only at the exaggerated sound from her breath am I aware she is still awake. "What were *you* doing in my absence?" she asks.

My mouth smiles so wide that it renders me speechless. I'm full of so much comfort that I stand, reaching a hand towards her. I pull her up from the bed, kissing her with much more ferocity.

"I had duties as seneschal, consisting of advising Cassius while also overseeing communications between him and the lower courts' rulers. And on days when I chose to spar with Kabir as a different form of exercise, he would tell me interesting stories of *your* training with him."

She snorts sharply, her shoulders jolting up in lightness. "Oh, I bet he also said how he's surprised I didn't die in battle with my half-decent form."

My hand brushes over the buttons on her shoulder as I take her arm, guiding us to the high-rising window to view the sky. A picture of befuddlement stays on her, questioning why I would take her from the cushion of the mattress to a sky that she can peer at nightly.

"You see that star that's three left from the constellation? It's your birthday present," I say, directing her the best that I can. She turns her head to the window and back to me, eyebrows furrowed. "Well, more selfishly, the present was for me. I bought the star and named it after you. That way, when I peered into the night sky, I would see you, even if it is nearly six light-years away."

Her eyes open wide, arms wrapping around and embracing me the best she can. The chains push tightly into my torso, but I don't care.

Then, for a time, she is quiet with her back melted into my chest. She views the stars that are dotting the dark sky, and I sense her fatigue as her head begins drifting to the side.

"Are you tired?" I don't wait for her to answer before leading us back to the mattress.

She shakes her head, the weight of it falling onto the pillow with a face looking at mine. "If you just woke up, I'll stay up with you until you sleep."

Her body twists, shifting around with her back turned to me. It's quiet again for minutes, heavy breathing coming from Ari.

"Love?" I call. My hand lightly skims her arm. "Are you still awake?"

"I'm just resting my eyes," she mumbles. Just as she says every time before she begins to snore.

VIII

Misinterpreted Viewpoints

Cassius

Arabella is smart, but an even more talented actress. The feigned pain in her eyes when she left with Delphi could have tricked anyone. Her choice of wording had been deliberate. Surely she knows that I would not make such a move without thinking to be as astute as she. Though forgiveness is sparse in her nature, I am sure she is well understanding of what I have planned.

There was not a scar on her. Arabella can endure another week if they had not touched her. Even so, I can admit the very real brokenness in her when the three okkared to the land of Enthar. I saw the light in her eyes when viewing us and the horrid pain that I felt watching her leave with Delphi.

Perhaps I was too flippant in my decision to send off Luka, but upon seeing Arabella, my theory that she required someone to share in her misery was confirmed. She needed a companion so that she would not be alone. But primarily, it had been of utmost importance that Luka be taken with them. Both for the saving of the common fae and for the safety of the two.

Inside Phantom Tower, I descend the stairs towards those who have committed lesser offenses. After freeing prisoners who were confined here under my father's reasonless sentencing, their cells have become occupied by those whom Delphi had kept under her control. These Fae were not in the sane of mind when committing their acts of treason. For that, I've granted the privilege of a lesser stay in the tower.

Upon their arrival after retrieving them, most were perplexed by their actions. A few were relieved to be free of the witch, though many had much to say about my claim to the crown.

I follow behind Kabir down the hall until he opens the door to a cell with a woman rocking back and forth in the corner. According to my Head Guard, she has not eaten in her days since being chained. She has not spoken nor bathed, only moving from her corner to the door to shout for her child.

"Ria, is it?" I ask, making no effort to stand near her. She stills but does not turn around. Nothing more than a disapproving grunt leaves her at my voice. "I've heard you have yet to eat. Starvation is a poor way to succumb to death after being freed from Delphi."

She keeps from a response. It may have paid me better use to ask another imprisoned, but Ria has someone who I can bring that she longs for.

Nearer, I stalk. Not so close to touch her, but close enough to where my words can be heard from a faint mutter. I can smell her odor from the distance, gagging with my face turned. "If you don't wish to see your child, then I will not press on the matter."

At this, her head whips, her body slamming to the ground right after. "You have my son?" she hisses. "I knew your family was capable of stooping to such levels, but to see the king actively put a mere faeling in peril for his own political gain..."

"My motives are far different than those which my father had. I come to you with an offer."

She examines her surroundings. Peering around the area, glancing to Kabir outside the barred cell, and understandably, her eyes carefully scan me for any sign of trickery. "You offer me my freedom for information on your witch."

A chuckle escapes me. I would be foolish to allow one piece of information to grant freedom to the common fae. Not when I already know the location of the two Magiks whom I intend on bringing back to their rightful place of living. "What right have you for freedom? I offer you a chance at speaking to your child."

Her mouth opens, gratitude surging through her expression.

"If," I clarify, "you tell me all that you were aware of prior to being controlled by Adonis and his lover."

"We were not aware of much," she admits. Her posture squares towards me, presenting herself in a more open state. And in it, I see her tail moving behind her. "Many of us were sent into the Human Lands to retrieve information. But, due to being manipulated by their accursed stone, the details of our experiences are a haze. Delphi had us watch your witch's friends. We would spy and report if there were ever meetings between each other."

Ria cannot lie, but that does not mean she is bound from telling an untruth by omission. However, from the way she speaks so desperately for the chance of seeing her son, I doubt she is keeping anything from me.

Sheepishly, she looks at me with pleading eyes, holding her knees between her arms. "If you are asking how you can contact her friends, I can bring you to them."

"I will not jeopardize Arabella and Luka, nor their loved ones' safety, for your taste of freedom. If you harm them, I will ensure both you *and* your son face the repercussions of your actions."

"Then go to them yourself."

I have been to Arabella's residence only once. I did not take in the details of the land well enough to envision it for okkaring. If I am to succeed in finding Arabella and Luka, retrieving them from the hands of Delphi and my brother, Magiks would prove essential.

"I have not been to all their homes," I reply. I recall Arabella saying that she lives in Los Angeles, but navigating the Human Lands would prove strenuous without the assistance of someone familiar with the land. Not only that, but I have the least bit of understanding where I would find her friends if they live among the hidden Magikal world. "Might you be so kind as to give their locations?"

She snorts. "I only have the exact address of your witch's house. I can give that to you."

I call to Kabir, demanding paper and a quill, and he rushes off instantly, returning in seconds with the materials in each hand. Then, after giving everything to the prisoner, she scribbles down a number followed by a name.

"You've done a kindness for your king," I tell Ria when Kabir and I take the paper and writing medium from her. "I will see to it that your son has the chance of seeing his mother alive."

An exchange has been made. For her aid, I am bound to follow through with my promise.

My siblings and mother are waiting for me inside the council room, watching me intently until I take my seat.

"Well?" Cel asks impatiently. "Are we getting them now?"

"No," I respond. "I was given the address to Arabella's home in the Human Lands. If we want to rescue the two, we will firstly need their Magik friends."

Helena purses her lips, considering every angle of this idea. "And how will you collect each individual Magik if you do not know where they reside?"

"Arabella lives with another," I inform. Running my hand through my hair, I carefully think on how to go about this without repercussions. As a former High Queen, Helena knows exactly the weight of each decision I have to make. It is why she is so critical of everything I do as king. She worries for the consequences of my actions. "Juliette will be able to contact the rest of her friends, and from then forward, I can okkar the group to Nexus. We have plenty of spare chambers for them to stay in."

"That we do," Helena says, though I do not think that is her primary concern. "But after retrieving Arabella and Luka, how will you go about achieving the trust of the common fae with Adonis and Delphi still free?"

"Having Arabella and Luka at our side will fare better than capturing the other two. With the Magiks involved, we are guaranteed to hold the advantage. When I made the trade, Adonis hardly got a word in, and when he did, Delphi spoke over him. The Magiks know Delphi the best and will be our greatest chance of overtaking her. Bringing about their end requires finding her weakness."

Mother looks at me, impressed with how I lay out the assets of those involved.

Atticus, with clear worry showing, sits perfectly still. "Cassius, would going to the Human Lands and explaining to Arabella's friends that she was taken be the smartest option? If they find out you deliberately let Delphi keep her when you had the chance to free her, they may hex you."

Maude lets out a hum, agreeing with our brother.

"We have run low on options, and I refuse to allow Arabella and Luka to be imprisoned for longer than I promised."

"I don't think that Atticus is suggesting your plan is bad," Maude says to me. "Just that going at it alone is a bad proposal."

I give a nod, taking what she says into consideration. We have days to make our final decision, but I would rather have the Magiks here, where we are able to both explain and formulate a better course of action. "They will understand if I can explain–"

"And what if they don't?" Xavier interrupts, standing at the door as his siblings enter the room. "What if, when hearing of what you did, you're met with hostility?"

Monty sits, claiming the seat next to Cel, with Dyana sitting across from them.

"Cassius," Monty says, "while we have chided you mercilessly, the people who have known her for years won't be as forgiving."

"You have the benefit of us being your family," Esme agrees. Her hands clasp together, elbows on the table. "These are Magiks that have only met you once."

"You told us yourself that some had trouble taking a liking to you because of the impression that Bella had given them originally," Dyana elaborates.

Xavier takes a chair from the end of the table, dragging it across the floor, the teakwood lightly screeching. He places it next to Helena, him sitting closer to me than anyone at the table. "Listen, you're worried for Ara. We all are. You're scared and upset and taking it out on everyone. But, regardless of how much you claim to know she's okay, you ought to know by now that she can't be."

"You do not know what you speak," I return. "She is resilient to all forms of torture and can handle herself."

"She doesn't need to be resilient. She needs to be *safe*."

The table is at an awkward standstill. We are sitting in silence with no one to speak after what Xavier says.

Moments of nothing pass before Cel smacks their lips together, making a popping noise and forcing our attention on them. I am instantly relieved, the tension in the air ceasing. They smile, confirming that they have once more used their abilities to mollify the table.

"I'm open to suggestions if anyone is willing to give them," I say to the bodies full of blank stares.

"You might not know your way through the Human Lands, but I do," Esme declares after a long while of nothing spoken. Our mother looks at her in dismay, though not shocked. "I can okkar us to Los Angeles, and we can find a ride to her house. Once we're there, you can speak to Juliette, and we'll figure the rest out."

Suspicious of my sister's motives, I say, "You offer me your guidance when your only job is to give counsel."

"I do this because you need all the help any are willing to spare. And if Arabella is not here to keep you under control soon, I may hit you myself," she quips, but her face immediately turns demure when she notices I do not find this entertaining.

While it is true that Esme frequently returns to the Human Lands, I can see no other reason for her to accompany me unless it involves meeting her female lover. Matters of the Fae affect Esme very little, due to her fascination with human culture.

Strange creatures humans are. They are all too dull and uninspiring, with their restrictions and lying being a language their bodies know well before they can put their tongue to speech.

Esme's face drops down, sucking in a breath before facing me again. "At the end of the day, this is my friend, and this situation with Delphi involves our kingdom. I refuse to let some power-hungry witch destroy the people I have grown up around."

An understanding is reached between the two of us. I nod, dismissing the rest of my family from the room.

"Allow me some time to get ready," Esme requests. She blathers on about searching for currency and changing her attire. It reminds me that I may once more be in need of the leather gloves and must search for the uninteresting clothing that Arabella had purchased for me.

The two of us hurry up the stairs, my sister explaining the time difference and importance of allowing her to speak to humans in order not to draw suspicion.

Inside my room, I fall onto my bed, preparing for the worst of what Arabella's friends have to say to me yet.

"You asked me to gather all of Ara's closest friends here, just for you to drop the news that you let her and our other best friend get kidnapped by the worst bitch alive?" Juliette screams over the others. She throws her arms, restraining herself from using any magik on me.

The feeling of pride I had originally carried once removing my shoes in Arabella's home has washed away.

I attempt to explain. "If I may–"

"No. You may not." Juliette glares at me, her face blooming to a deep red, departing with the other Magiks.

In the kitchen, the Magiks have huddled together in a circle, whispering over their revulsion with me. There is debate between the group, wondering what their best course of action may be.

Finally, I hear Grayson whisper a little too loudly, "What if we killed him after? Problem solved, right?"

Their assumption that my hearing is the same as theirs is evident, though they are not very far from my eyesight to begin with.

"I do not think that is the best idea," I interject, simpering. My hand immediately rubs at the base of the back of my neck.

My sister has yet to come to my aid during this difficult time. She sits on a chair, separate from the group, watching this spectacle as she types on her phone. If she cares to help me in the Human Lands as she had claimed, she ought to have stepped in by now.

"You not only came to my house *uninvited* without Arabella, but then you tell us Luka is alive, *and* Delphi has both of them?"

Juliette returns to her scolding. She is shouting, disbelief and rage heating with every punctuated word while her friends spread themselves around the common area.

Violette interjects, overtaking the anger of the group. "And now you have the fucking audacity to ask for *our* help to save this land of yours, which caused all this in the first place?"

"This is much more than my kingdom," I argue. And that is true. This is about Luka as well. About Arabella.

Damien–relaxed on the couch with a sullen face–frowns deeper while keeping one arm on the thigh of Violette. "I don't know. If Luka's been alive for over two and a half months, why choose to tell us now?"

"I was unaware you did not know of his re-existence until a short time ago."

Grayson glowers at me, with an arm wrapped around Juliette's wider waist. He appears as if he is ready to throw his fist or use his magik. A fatal enough result to rupture every bodily function of mine. Perhaps this is what it is to face the consequences of my actions.

"I ask you to aid me in retrieving both of your friends. Assist me in the saving of my kingdom and people." I have more dignity, but if they demanded it of me, I would kneel or bow for their agreement. "I am sure I cannot carry this on without your help. It is what your friends would want."

"Don't say this is what they'd want!" Evie barks with ferociousness. She has spoken nothing thus far, but to speak on the beliefs of others is clearly something she does not stand for. I'm quite positive that she, though the smallest, has the harshest words to belittle any. "I don't give a fuck if they were the ones to kill your dad themselves! You shouldn't have let Delphi take them."

A witch with bronze skin named Reyna glares at me, her russet eyes fantasizing my death, wearing uninspiring attire that depicts her as a guard. She has brown hair falling to her side, her plump lips frowning. "You let my fucking sister get taken hostage, and you *still* think she'd wanna save your kingdom? After the multiple times you treated her like shit."

Rather than defending myself from the impression that the witch holds of me, I reply with, "You're no sister of Arabella's."

"Are you serious? That's your response?" Grayson says with a mocking sneer.

"She has spoken only of a brother, mother, and father," I reply, shrugging.

Damien steps to me, his height just over mine. "Haven't you heard not all families are blood?" He huffs, darting his eyes to the other Magiks in the room.

"Maybe the two of them never saw the Fae as worthy enough of that kinda trust," Amber mutters. How little she knows that I am aware of how highly Arabella regards them.

"Cassius came to tell you the truth," my sister retorts, standing from where she sat.

Amber steps back, her lips curling inward when sitting down between Reyna and Evie.

Reyna crosses her legs, rolling her eyes at Esme's statement. "Not like your kind can lie anyway."

"All true," Esme admits, unwavering from her place next to me. "But he wants not only to save your friends, but to keep his people from being ruled over by Delphi."

Juliette snorts, her emotions displaying both entertainment and disgust. "Gods, people can barely stand to be in a room *with* her. Imagine putting her in charge of an entire kingdom."

"Her company's punishment enough. I think if she were queen, it would likely start a war," Violette jokes, voice raspier than her friends'.

"Which circles back to the fact," Grayson says, refocusing

everyone's anger towards me, "that no one hates Ara as much as Delphi. So why the *hell* would you give her up?"

At this very moment, I fear for my life and am grateful none in this room are aware of the effect that iron holds on us. "I assure you there is more than what this seems. Arabella was unscathed when first appearing to me, save the color drained from her skin. I saw no marks of harm visible on her."

"No marks that were visible?" Damien voices loudly, pulling from Violette. "Did you forget that scars are easily erasable with magik? Or that there are things that cut her much deeper than knives? Haven't you once thought about the emotional damage Delphi could have caused Ara?"

To that, I am speechless. Every word has been stolen from my vocabulary, and I am silenced.

"I don't care about what you wanted or if you had good intentions. *Our friends could be dead 'cause of you,*" Damien blames.

His words should not affect me so. It is what I expected, and yet when all blame is sprawled in front of me, I'm struck with my own oversight.

My sister looks at everyone in the room. Her glare is as silencing and deadly as Helena's. "You can blame my brother if you want, but Arabella and Luka are still with Delphi. While your talents as Magik are useful, it is not impossible to go without them."

After a long while of none responding, Juliette says, "Delphi *was* barely seen with her friends since Luka's funeral." She is fiddling with her nails, picking at a piece of dead skin that hangs.

Perhaps she is unaware of how disgusting her action of nervousness is.

Damien recalls this, relaxing his body and putting an arm around Violette, his other hand curling under his chin. A height difference large. "Which means she was probably gone because of this. Even *we* noticed when she stopped coming to parties with her friends."

"So, why do you need all of us?" Evie asks, motioning for my attention with a hand.

"Yeah," Amber says. Her round, brown eyes narrow, suspicious in my motives. "Doubt you need seven Magiks to help with your escape plan."

"Arabella will likely need reacquainting with social interactions, and she trusts you. You all know Delphi far better than I, meaning that you have a higher chance of understanding her motives and abilities."

Reyna stands, matching my eye level the same way that Dyana does with our differing heights. "And we're all supposed to go with you to this Fae land?"

"Yes," Esme responds. "This is why I came along. So that we can share the taxing burden of okkaring all of you."

"I'm up for it," Evie says, drawing closer and motioning to her friends. "I still owe that group for trying to get me expelled, so at least *one of them* will face consequences."

Everyone stands, holding each other as we clump into an irregular shape. Right before we okkar, Grayson sends me a scowl, muttering, "We're doing this for them, not you."

Once back at Nexus, I explain the bedchamber arrangements. I have Isaak, Kabir, and Gavin escort them to their respective rooms, allowing myself peace from flaring scowls. Esme realizes my exhaustion and leaves me to my own devices. A pity, really, that no one cares to join me.

Uncertainty sneaks its way into my mind. There is no way to know for sure where my choices will lead, nor if this will work.

VIX

Neverending Betrayal

Arabella

My chest is falling in on itself. I've lost all ability to breathe, and I feel like I'm choking. All that comes out is the occasional, sharp-pitched noise whenever I try to get in a breath.

Somehow, in the past days with Luka here, Delphi's managed to increase my torture to an extreme measure. I thought she had found enough ways to target my insecurities and worst memories, but all of what she did before was child's play. Each day, Luka and I are alternately taken from each other. Him being here brings another form of suffering that's been previously untouched by Delphi.

Here, in the chamber where I'm held during my time away from Luka, I'm living a multitude of painful storylines. I have *maybe* five to ten seconds as a break between each scenario before my mind is wiped blank, and I'm transported into 'memories' that Delphi curates for her entertainment.

I'm so terrified that one day I'm going to open my eyes, and this will all be the worst nightmare of my life. That all these months that I've lived will have been some illusion, and I'll wake up in a cold sweat, alone in my bed. With Luka dead and none of this being real. That reality might be worse than all the other ones.

"Stop," I plead with Delphi. It's been hours since I was brought in here. My body is trembling, but I do my best to keep from revealing my despair and drained energy.

In my relapse of a beg, Delphi's face grows more wicked. "Why would I? You were always the most tolerable when you looked to me for security."

Her hand goes under my chin, cupping me at the bottom of my cheeks and leaning my whole gravity towards her. I can't move my head much, and shaking it only tightens her grip while she scans me up and down.

"You haven't said anything about Cassius giving you up so quickly," she mocks, allowing no time for a response before removing her hand, causing my body to flop onto the ground from the lack of support. She walks so fast that by the time I lift myself onto my knees, she's reached her throne.

Her fingers dance around the indents of the rock, tracing over the carved whirls. With the twirl of her fingers, my knees scrape across the rough and raw texture of the floor, digging abrasions into my skin. The corner of her lip quirks, her eyes twisting into darkness.

"You claim I never gave a shit about you. But that Fae? He uses you for his desire to cause pain." She touches my temples with her stiletto nails. They're freshly manicured and sharp.

Blood is still fresh in the goblet.

My eyes roll towards the inside of my head, and I feel my body being shifted into the council room at Nexus with intense speed.

Without others in the room, I sit next to a 'memory' of Delphi's past self, her leaning into her chair more comfortably, with legs spread wide apart as she impatiently waits for Cassius to respond to her. Both are sitting across from each other in the exact positions he and I sat the day he told me about the missing Fae.

Cassius sits in a blue vest that secures in the middle of his torso. Under it, he wears a white shirt with a cravat that is much more simple in design than the vest.

In contrast, Delphi is in a thinly-strapped orchid shirt and light-washed denim jeans. Her long hair freely falls over her chest, the seat next to her hanging a black mini backpack.

"You wish to return Arabella to me?" he says with a questioning face, a brow raised.

"For a trade," she replies. "Her life must mean *something* to you. She's worthless to me, but I can be persuaded with compensation."

"*Ha!*" he laughs without taking any time to consider her offer.

It burns. Like dripping alcohol into an open wound you didn't know was there. His betrayal of sending me back with Delphi hurt at the time, but now, seeing this fuels my hatred past the point of full.

I try to tell myself that this is another thing that Delphi's forcing me to believe until I beg her to kill me, but I've turned to ribbons from the past year, and I know that she would want my death to be more satisfying.

"You are foolish to assume her position is not without replacement," Cassius chimes. "Arabella rots even the most unsuspecting parts of my mind."

With each word he says, another part of me cracks. Soon, I would be nothing but a piece of broken glass. Or something more explosive.

Delphi surveys him, puzzled. Her hand moves from her forearm onto the table, elbows spread. "You don't want her?"

Cassius grins with all the maliciousness I now know him capable of. His eyes show no hesitation or feeling at Delphi's question. Like

I'm nothing to him. "For certain pleasures, she is, of course, more than adequate. But that does not involve the ears of your own."

"Why the sudden change of heart?"

He shrugs, and time feels suspended. He's yet to deny me. "Her presence, I've learned, sometimes comes with much more grief than it does good. Perhaps if she had never entered my life, I would be free to live as I wished. I would never have to deal with incessant ramblings and emotional outbursts of unwarranted anger."

Our eyes meet, though he can't see me, and my heart sinks. The beat freezes, transforming into full-fledged heartbreak. But I regret it. I regret things I said to him in my anger. But more so, I'm embarrassed that I had fallen so hard that it made me blind to the Fae everyone in the lands told me that he is.

"You strive for power," Cassius says. "So, might I offer you something that not even *you* can deny?"

Delphi listens with intrigue, her body pressed against the table as if waiting to strike down the first offer made. And it's clear that she never informed Adonis of her plans to meet with his brother. "And what is that, Your Majesty?"

"I offer you land in exchange for the common fae's return."

His expression is entirely inscrutable.

"That's it? Not for Arabella?" Both her arms and legs cross, sitting back against the chair while eyeing the king with radiant glee. "What if I want more?"

His head shifts slightly, never backing from her stare. He sees her challenge and intends on championing. "Well, I'd rather see that you were properly handled for your crimes, so I suppose this is a compromise for the both of us."

"That's your only condition?" she asks again for clarification.

His lips part to speak. There's more.

Of course there's something more.

"Allow me to finalize this bargain with Arabella present. I will bring Luka along to oversee it all so that she may see us both. This will devastate her in more ways than one."

Now, Delphi is full-on smiling as if her lips could curve from one ear to the other. "I'll agree, but on *my* condition that you can't request for Arabella once our deal is made."

"I did not intend on doing so."

There's a smug look on his face, and I can't tell if he's proud of how quickly he has learned to make these decisions or if it's from the natural, arrogant mien that Fae carry. I would assume it's the former, but I can't be sure. Though, something is suspicious in everything he has said. The exact word choices.

My eyes close, and when I open them, my face is wet from crying. The room's odor is rancid. Both ripe and sour. I'm not sure if that's from my nose breathing in my tears or Delphi's personality circulating into the air.

She leans low enough so that she's facing me, wearing a look without sympathy. "You see? This was the plan from the start. He never once bargained to save you."

Why though? Trade me for a trick, fine, but Luka was unnecessary. Did the two disagree to such an extent that sending Luka away provided a demonstration of his power?

"Was Luka part of the deal?"

"No, that was a pleasant surprise," she replies with a lightness in her voice.

For a suspicious reason, Delphi offers a hand. She may be half a foot shorter, but the cut of her words makes her stand well above me. "And now, there's nothing for you in those Fae lands. Cassius finally saw through your selfishness like I did years ago. You wonder why everyone in your life leaves you. This is why. *You* are the problem. Everything you do just ruins their life."

I've gone completely mute. I can't find it in myself to fight anymore. There's no retort, no witty comeback to spit at her. All

I can do is stand there, feeling emotionless as my shoulders drop from the shock of it all.

My heart's jumped into my throat, and I'm so nauseous that I think I'm going to die. Forget the fact that Delphi kicked me from her life when she made new friends. Forget the fact that when she did that, all her new friends joined in on making my life worse. Grudges aside, my rage reminds me there's truth in what she says.

I *am* what ruins people's lives.

I hate that even when I act like I don't care, I desperately crave approval. I base myself off it. But no one can ever know these thoughts. There's so much more I can be.

As we walk back, Adonis stands ready at my room's door–if you can call it that. He waits and listens carefully as Delphi instructs him to bring me to bathe, voicing that we're done for the day.

Throughout the whole process, Adonis asks about the things Delphi did to me. It's become our little tradition whenever he would speak to me. If he wasn't in the room to see my torture, I'd inform him of what Delphi did when we were alone.

What started as a way to guilt-trip him into pitying and releasing me, turned into him genuinely caring and showing worry whenever Delphi went too far by his standards.

As the two of us return, Delphi is waiting, hair oily to match her face's complexion. She takes a bronze key that clings to her side, opening up the barred door and allowing me to join Luka, who's sitting against the wall in loose pants and a white V-neck shirt.

I speed to him. My body is so exhausted, and my head throbs harshly enough that I don't stop myself from flopping onto the mattress, ready to sleep off today.

Flipping onto my back, my head turns to Luka, who looks down at me with concern. His hand glides its way to mine, interlocking our fingers and squeezing my hand until I close my fingers.

"Enjoy each other while you can," Delphi's voice sings. I haven't heard the clang of the door shutting, so she must still be inside the room. "It won't be long until we return to Ifaeris, and I separate the two of you."

Luka's face turns terrifying when tilting his face in her direction. Outside of our friends, everyone assumes he is callous, but in the way that the slightest movement on his face could mean life or death.

I think people are wrong. He's much more than his father's son. More than the cold-hearted man that his dad trained him to be. However, even I can't deny the things that he's done.

"Don't forget to tell Luka how you spent your day," Delphi reminds me. "You can tell him of the memory. Or just how you got those shallow scars."

Glares can't freeze time. But if it could, Luka's would stop all of eternity. He softly lets go of me, and I push myself up, darting my stare between the two of them, who are staring at each other like they're in combat where their looks are deadlier than any weapon.

As if he's overpowered her, he says, "You're just as insufferable at a grown age as you were years ago. Have you ever thought that your complete inability to register you have the personality of a splattered carcass is why no one could ever love you?"

My mouth drops open before I clamp my lips down on each other, sucking them into my mouth. The action makes no sense, being that his issue isn't with me.

"*Why I could never love you,*" he finishes.

And there's the final earth-shattering blow.

Adonis' posture straightens, while Delphi remains unaffected by his words. A battle of exchanges between Delphi and Luka, and the only ones recognizing the harm of what's said are me and the Fae.

"I'd be careful of what I said if I were you," Delphi warns. I don't doubt that his words have an effect on her, but they may not be for the reason that he intended.

"Why? Should I fear the magik you wield?" Luka remarks sarcastically.

Please don't hurt him.

Delphi's cocky face returns, arms crossing over her chest. "You should. But I'd also think you'd show more appreciation to the person who returned you to this world."

"Wait, what?" I blurt, my mind hollow.

"Goodnight." Delphi shuts the door, handing the key to Adonis and turning off the light, leaving the three of us in darkness.

It shouldn't be possible. I should have figured it was her who brought Luka back, but the thought has never occurred. If Delphi's the one who did this, she's created a form of restricted magik that tampers with life and death. She's a threat to every creature that crosses her.

"Is it true?" I ask Adonis, who stands on the other side, his silhouette barely visible without any light, aside from the moon, to illuminate him.

"Yes," he responds delicately.

"I will give you thirty seconds to remove yourself from my presence before I find a way to free myself from these chains and decapitate you." Fury, both in and out of Luka's eyes, shoots. A reminder to me that he holds more energy than I do with the less time he's spent here.

I don't say anything to stop him. I know he's probably capable of doing everything he said. So instead, I pull myself up, walking to the bars standing between us and Adonis. "How did Delphi do it? And don't throw that Fae bullshit where you tell me half-truths and keep out information."

Adonis is still difficult to see. My eyes are squinting until a light from the hallway turns back on, the Fae's presence fully lit as he returns. "I wasn't in the room when Luka was brought back. I only returned after a meeting with my most entrusted followers to find the unconscious sorcerer with a murmuring heartbeat."

"You have to know something," I push further.

"I only know that throughout our time recruiting Fae to join us, Delphi acquired a magnitude of knowledge that now makes her nearly unstoppable."

To avoid a confrontation that betters no one, I sigh. Questions badger my thoughts, nearly leaving my mouth, all of which I know cannot be answered by Adonis. "I've told you the things she's done to me. Hell, you've seen it. You can't tell me you still think you're equals."

I hear the movement of Luka's steps approaching behind me, likely ready to follow through on the promise he made not minutes ago. Turning so that my back is parallel to the cold touch of the rusty bars, I cautiously say, "Wait."

"You don't honestly expect me to show him mercy again," Luka rebukes in disbelief. I keep quiet, not responding. "This Fae–their whole land–they've caused you nothing but suffering, and you want to keep me from righting this wrong?"

"Luka," I warn, my eyes widening. I'm both shivering and on the verge of sweating because I know that I can't overpower him. Not when I'm reminded he's able to carry well over my body weight when he does any of his weight training.

His steps fall back two paces, just enough for him to scan my face. "Ask me anything, love. Anything in the world, and I'll get it for you." Adjusting his focus, he angles to the Fae behind me, staring with untrusting aggravation narrowed shortly before returning his eyes to mine. "But I can only give it to you if we are free. Allow me to kill him in return."

"Are you aware of Delphi's family's ranking within the Magik community?" Adonis interrupts, pulling the two of us in his direction.

Luka walks until he is inches away from Adonis, his hands a finger away from the bars. "It isn't Delphi whose family is of high rank."

"It's her friends. Her family's only somewhat renowned 'cause they befriend a few Magiks in the Coven," I finish. Her family isn't completely unknown in elite lower circles, but hers isn't nearly as acquainted with the rich as Luka's.

Adonis takes in a breath, with brows twitching. "Regardless, her connections are what allowed her access to spell books, which were locked away from the general public of Magik." He paces back and forth around the opening, debating something that I have no intention of asking about.

Finally making a decision, he takes another key from his pocket, walking towards us. The Fae makes a motion, stretching his arm and motioning for us to do the same. When we do, he takes the key, inserting it in each cuff that locks our wrists, which drops the chains from the cuffs themselves.

I feel a vague sense of memory clouding me. I'm reminded of the mornings when Kabir would unchain me, allowing me to shower in Phantom Tower.

"I do not condone everything she does," Adonis states in passing, leaving Luka and me to our own company.

The two of us go to the mattress, neither of us saying a word. I'm not even undressing myself before Luka wraps his arms around me to pull me in. It's more peaceful than what I've felt in days.

Reaching my hands inside his shirt, I feel the muscles of his body on my fingertips. They skim up and down his back a few times before settling on descending, tugging on the hem of his shirt and trying to lift it off his body.

"Ari, are you sure?" He's gentle as he pushes me away far enough to angle his head down to mine. "Your body must be exhausted."

"I'll survive." I don't think either of us want to think about the fact that Delphi's the one to have brought him back. "Need you."

He strips from his shirt, pulling the clothing from the back and over his head. Air seems to have gotten lost trying to find its way to my lungs when his body reveals itself. Flawless in all possible ways of existence.

"Lay down, love."

So I do it.

Kisses of protective comfort move from my lips down to my neck, parting my legs wider with his hands as his body sets itself onto me. The taste of him reminds me of everything I never expected to have in life but was lucky enough to. Like two cursed tragedies that cancel each other out into tranquil bliss. A shard of happiness from the pile of wreckage.

As he runs a hand through my hair, the other skims up to unsnap my shirt from my shoulders. Without a razor, shadows of hair lightly shade Luka's face, though only a hint of stubble brushes against my skin. I've never particularly been a fan of facial hair, but my gods, even this slight alteration of his appearance doesn't change how attractive he is.

I'm burning up and dizzy, all my blood directing itself to my head. Yet, I refuse to stop. My desire far outweighs my lack of energy.

Whenever Luka touches me, it's like I'm falling in love with him over and over and over again. When we have sex, I feel a specific sense of love. He's the first person to ever love me for me, instead of making me feel like my only value is for others' sexual gratification. I'm never used just for my body. I never have to think that this is all I can ever offer someone in exchange for their affection. With him, I never feel the need to pause the moment. He feels like home.

Luka is my constant reminder that I am meant for more than

settling. He makes loving him the easiest thing in the world. It's as natural as breathing to me.

In a movement faster than I can react to, he pins my arms above my head, grinding himself onto me. Then, his hands are at my waist while his lips feather down my naked torso. When he gets to my lower stomach, his head lifts, pulling my shorts down to my ankles. My skin is nearly free, but not completely. His fingers glide into my underwear, thumb moving around my clit while dragging his lips back up my body.

When he gets to my chest, he sucks on my nipple, a hand going to the other and pinching before massaging it.

It knocks me into a state of insecurity.

I wonder if I'll ever love my body instead of only growing to accept it.

That sense of wondering doesn't last long. His lips that have once touched every part of me are rooted in love. When his mouth and fingers move, I'm so lost in his actions that I can't remember anything else.

Moving from my chest, he goes to my arms, starting from my shoulder and making his way down. Just below the end of my upper arm, he stops. I feel his mouth pause. Feel his hair brushing my skin as he puts distance between us.

White pales his expression when he looks up at me, clouds gathering in his gaze. His fingers trace over the horizontal scars that cover my forearm. "What are these from?"

His voice is raised, but not exactly yelling at me. I'm too terrified to tell him the truth.

The absence of him on top of me is hitting harder than it should.

"Were these from Delphi?" he asks as if trying to extract vital information.

There's a drumming in my ear, and all the words I can think to explain myself escape my brain. I can't explain it to Luka without him becoming more perturbed than he already is.

On my back, I am frozen in place. Unable to move. Unable to lie.

"Please," I utter, both to myself and him. The word is but a silent prayer to the universe to get him to stop asking.

When I manage to gain feeling in my body again, I push myself against the wall that's perpendicular to the one he sits against.

I can't lie to him. If I tried, he'd figure it out. Because he knows me.

X

Admissions and Assurance

Luka

These cuffs are the only things keeping me from okkaring out of this room and searching this building for Delphi. Adonis made a miscalculated error by removing our restrictions.

Seeing Arabella in this state causes me high levels of distress. It's significantly more upsetting in my mixture of emotions when she sits away from me. She has been unresponsive for minutes, looking at me like I find her hideous. As if her body is now somehow defaced and ruined.

After several more minutes of stillness, she says, "It wasn't Delphi."

That admission leaves Adonis as culprit. Her refusal to elaborate only confirms this as she shies away from the topic, crossing her arms around her bare chest and bringing her knees into a curl.

"Mahal," she says, scooting closer to me until she is between my legs, her back pressed to my torso, "Delphi tortured me. I don't know what she's done to you because you don't talk about it, but she did unspeakable things to me."

When I am taken away and left alone with Delphi, she tortures me with unconventional methods. She doesn't harm me or cast hexes but instead sits there in silence, studying me before taunting. Session after session, when I express that Ari tells me nothing of what she's endured, Delphi gladly returns with examples, detailing things she would do to my girlfriend. It's more sadistic than any infliction of pain she could ever perform.

My eyes carefully observe every muscle movement against me. I have no doubt that Ari chooses this position so that I cannot read her expressions.

"Tell me what you need, Blossom." I know that my words fall to nothing in her mind as I ask this, but it will not stop me from wanting to help her in any way that she needs.

"Seriously, I'm fine." Her body shakes once to insist on her state, but I know well that she would lie about this if it means not depending on others.

"You're not. You say that, *you always say that*, but not once has that ever proven true." My hand combs her hair, running it through the strands that drip droplets of water down her back. "Why do you dismiss your pain but fuss over everyone else? I want to take care of you too, love."

She switches positions, opting for wrapping her legs around my waist and nuzzling her cheek pressed between my chest and shoulder. I listen as she explains the worst of the mental strain she has endured. Say nothing as she lists the torture that began physically before shifting to the mental manipulation of her psyche. I do my best to hold myself properly. No matter how difficult it is to hear this, I was not the one suffering.

Ari unwinds herself from my torso with uneasy trepidation, pushing herself so that she can face me directly. Her voice cracks, splinters in her tone when asking, "What did she do to *you*?"

"She would spend time projecting your torture onto a wall

before leaving me alone with my thoughts." Starvation, physical hexing, anything remotely similar to my past, are all things I have faced here with little issue. But recalling those few accounts of torture, the agony in Ari's screams, it's so difficult that I can't find any words to describe the feeling it brought me. "I was forced to watch while she showed me how she peeled your skin."

I can't find it in me to continue.

"Gods," she remarks, her tone a breathy sigh. "Delphi's a lot of things, but I can't deny her ability to get us where we're most vulnerable." Her eyes tentatively lower from her focal point to my lips, staring at me as if I'm something she wants to sink her teeth into.

"Love," I say, stopping her before she can do anything. "Is this *really* what you need?"

Ari collides her mouth with mine, three drops of water from her hair wetting the two of us. Air from ironic laughter leaves her between each demolishing kiss. "Probably not. For all I know, this could be another one of Delphi's simulations." I can feel the breath coming from her lips, which are barely apart from mine. "I don't know what's real anymore. But I want you."

"I'm real," I affirm, my heart soaring.

Each kiss is prolonged as I lay her on her back, lips trailing down her body while I eagerly await to taste her.

"I will spend every day for the rest of our lives together reminding you of that fact. That this?" I purr, holding myself by my knees before dropping down to her thigh and lightly biting down. "This is real. I am completely yours."

My hands reach up, pulling the thin fabric which covers the place I want to be in most. I tug until it's at her ankles, replacing where the cloth had been with my mouth.

Seeing how her body reacts in pleasure from this angle, her back arching from my touch, it's something that slams me to the earth's crust. A number of beings she could have fallen in love with, and she chooses me.

I love her.

My knees could fracture at any given second, burying me into her wetness, and it would be a position I would happily remain.

For seconds, she stiffens from my touch that grazes her stomach on its way to her breasts. Her obvious self-consciousness is waging a fight against her thoughts of desire, unsure of which feeling is more dominant.

"Love, speak to me."

"I'm fine," she shoots off. From her position, she lifts onto her elbows and stares at me. "I need you inside me."

She is the ocean, and I am the shore, the two of us destined to crash.

My head dips, swallowing her with every intention of drawing out her pleasure. Nothing but addiction and intensity can best describe my need for her. I am but a man who would commit sacrilegious acts against the gods in her name. My tongue flicks around her clit, my fingers diving inside the divine that is her cunt.

Her hands grip my hair, attempting to pull me back. Laughable that she thinks that will slow me. She writhes beneath me, whimpering and crying out for a need to come. My mouth responds, sucking harsher while my tongue savors her, capturing the taste that I have longed for throughout my life.

Lifting my head, I crawl up until I am gazing into her eyes. They're difficult to see with such little light, but they engulf me. She's a manifestation of everything good in this world.

"Your whimpers are so cute," I tease. "I bet you missed this, didn't you?"

Ari's head returns from its thrown-back position. Her face is that of a vengeful woman, raging and frustrated for stealing her pleasure from her. She glares, hands pushing me away and guiding my body until she is on top of me. Knowing I can make her desire me to this degree, it drives me to absurdity.

She drives me to absurdity.

While her bare cunt grinds on me through my bottoms, I am guiding her by the waist. My body is in full distress until I am inside of her. She tugs down the clothing, undressing me to nothing, where my cock is waiting to take her.

Teasing the head of my length, her tongue tantalizingly drags across the slit. I shudder from under her, my hand reaching her head and thrusting into her mouth as she glides herself down.

The sound of her gagging and enjoying herself while her head works with my strength is exhilaration I've only known with her. My hand eases from her head, giving her absolute freedom around me.

Hollowed cheeks being used to her advantage, she returns to her movements, taking me as deeply as she can while her hand takes whatever she cannot fit. The last time I had her, it was full of loving sweetness. We were unified, clinging to each other as a reminder that we are inseparable. This time, though, we tease and hold each other with desire.

"I might've missed this," she rasps, crawling so that she hovers above me, leaning down towards my ear. "But I bet you missed my mouth more."

The touch of her breasts slides along my chest, her cunt gliding against my length. Torturously so.

"I missed more than just your mouth, love."

"Then fuck me."

Her challenges are nothing but expected. An act disguising her desperation for me. She is an impulse that I will never find the strength to stay away from.

I switch our positions again, putting her onto her back and nudging my cock into her.

"Are you sure you can take it after all this time?" I tease.

Her feet push into me, guiding my length deeper and exhaling a moan of pleasure. A moan so perfect that it inclines me to capture her with my lips.

An arm shoots around my neck, pulling me closer. She inhales me with all the pent-up energy she has saved for this very occasion, grinning while looking at me. "Do *you* remember how to fuck me?"

My hand goes around her throat, pressing into her skin. A smile never leaves as her eyes roll back briefly, returning to make contact with mine. They narrow at me. A warning to tell me this is the last act I would commit before diminishing to nothing. Little does she know that before her, I will always be nothing.

"Tell me how I should fuck you then," I hum into her ear. I'm weak around her. More than she will ever realize. My hips move in a rhythmic pattern. Slow enough to appreciate the feel of her, but not so slow that I'm driving myself mad.

The movement fails to please her in the way she desires. I'm glared at with discontent, my girlfriend shifting her hips to create a friction faster than I am going. The two of us are crazed. The difference is that one of us has to maintain composure.

Just as my thrusts become harder, she brings me back down. Her tongue glides from my neck up to my ear. Nibbling at the lobe of my skin, she says softly, "I want you to fuck me like I'm yours."

At the seduction in her voice, I have lost all sense of self. My cock is pulsing, my hand moving and supporting me while I pump into her.

"So beautiful," I sigh into the air, one hand tracing down to her clit. "So good at taking me."

The warmth of her cunt hugging me tightly emits a groan. It ignites me with the surging demand that I steal her lips until they are plumped so fully that there would be no question who did it. I want to erase every word she was forced to defend herself with and replace them with nothing but my name.

Her nails pierce into my back, raking across and gripping while I drive into her at a pace that makes my cock throb.

"How many times did you touch yourself when thinking of me?" I thrust back into her, my pace much slower.

"I–" she whines out the moment I suck on her neck. Right on the sensitive area that weakens her.

"I bet your thoughts were filled by me, weren't they?"

"Yes," she murmurs in a low, soft sound.

Her noises are melodic as she evades from releasing a cry louder than a minimally audible whisper.

I suck on her bottom lip as my hand briefly kneads her breast before returning to her clit. Simply touching her rewrites who I am. I would do anything to ensure that she is happy. "Louder, love. Or I'd think you were embarrassed of me."

She pants with the movement of her head, her mouth parted open and eyelids glued shut. Her moans are louder with her coming release, her body rolling itself.

"*Love. Fuck. That's it.*"

The sounds of our bodies slapping against each other penetrate the air, overpowering the noise of other creatures below these floors. Every movement is driven. Every thought, filled with understanding each other. No one in the universe can compare to Ari in any way.

Her hands roam around the mattress, each breath moaning. "Luka- *Please.*"

My cock plunges into her, lips moving around her between each of my thrusts. At her side, my left hand is fisting the sheets that cover the mattress.

"No need to whine, Blossom. I'm not stopping," I croon into her skin before marking her.

Heat boils at the base of my stomach. I am dangerously close to my orgasm, but it should be her who comes first. My love. The other half of my soul.

Thumb twirling in rhythm, it speeds at a complementary movement with my cock that pushes inside her. The clenching of her cunt turns my mind into a mushy fiber with thoughts incomprehensible.

Curses seem to be the only words I'm able to remember.

Her hands are gripping the pillow below her head, breath heavy and high-pitched sounds leaving her. My teeth bite down, and I feel the bar of her jewelry.

"Mahal, gods–"

I can't trust myself to go at the pressure I would like. If I could have her the way that I want, neither of us would know any other motor function when we finished.

Every time she loses herself around me, becoming so tranced that she only finds herself in joy, I am unhinged. Her pleasure is just as much mine as it is hers.

I'm narrowly focused. Aware of nothing besides my drive to fill her cunt with so much of my cum that it leaks onto the softness of her thighs.

Under me, Ari is whimpering, voice croaking and forming half words that bleed into only sounds.

"That's it, love. Come for me."

My words are the encouragement she needs to shake around me. She moans out in pleasure, arching closer to my body. Her eyes cross, rolling to the back of her head, my lips pressing to hers.

I continue my thrusting, taking my hand from her clit and fucking her through her orgasm as she squeezes my cock tighter, pulling me towards my own.

Ari bites her lip, letting out one single moan as a result of the constant that is our bodies.

"Need-" She gasps. "Come-" Another sharp breath. "*Fuck. Inside.*"

Chuckling, my lips travel to her breasts, pressing to anything I've left untouched. My left hand travels to her right, twining them together as I lift it above her head. "Blossom, I can't do anything to you if you refuse to form a sufficient sentence."

Her chest is heaving, bouncing up with every thrust. "Come in me," she pants, struggling through her words, half of them unfinished.

Gods, she is going to be the death of me.

She rolls her hips, my thrusting becoming faster in response. Then, in a string of litanies, her name passes multiple times through my lips as I fill her.

When pulling myself from her, I admire the way she lies there, her legs giving out and slumping onto the mattress. Every night she has been sleeping beside me, but the restrictions of chains had been a bothersome reminder in the back of my mind.

She is the most beautiful creature in the universe.

My lips go to her shoulders, peppering loving kisses as our heart rates and bodies settle. Nothing needs to be voiced when our actions say everything that is needed.

I lay on my back, she on hers, while we hold hands for several minutes. Eventually, she maneuvers herself to lay half of her body on top of me, her hair scattered.

"I did it to myself," she whispers, throwing her arm around my chest and placing the other under her head. My fingers find themselves brushing through the strands, which have become tangled, pushing it from her face. "The scars on my arm. They were from me."

A thorny sensation pricks my skin at her confession. Denial is the best word to describe this. Yes, that's what this is. Denial.

Air releases from me, a significant amount of time feeling as if it has passed before finally finishing. Ari jabs into my chest and sides with two fingers, testing for a response.

My hand moves on top of hers, interweaving our fingers in each other's. Ari hisses a curse in a hushed tone, shrieking from the sudden movement. "I thought you fell asleep. Did you hear what I said? About the scars?"

"You didn't," reject. My arms around her hold her close, wrapping tighter until she taps my biceps.

There are two deep breaths before her body relaxes again. "Mahal, I did. Delphi didn't force me, and I didn't know she knew about me doing this to myself."

"Why?" I ask, the word coming out more as a stern yell.

The backs of her palms rise up and down my torso before breaking us apart and putting distance between our bodies. She shuns away, moving herself to the bed's edge and staring outside of the cell. "You wouldn't understand."

"I can try." I turn to my side, reaching my right arm out and snaking it across her body, pulling us closer.

She takes a moment to herself. Sighs out in trepidation. "I wasn't sure what reality was real, and when I found a broken shard under the mattress, I started cutting myself. Delphi would heal me after every time she tortured me, but the cuts were something she never touched. It's why I thought she never knew about them."

I become a vest, tightening with each word that wants nothing more than to protect a body from any infliction of pain. "You did this so that when she invaded your mind, you knew what wasn't real," I comment, pausing for confirmation.

"Yeah." Some time passes, Ari too stiff and her voice too soft. "Also, I think Cassius is coming for us."

"What makes you say that?"

"Delphi showed me something about him, and all his responses were too specific. I'm not a hundred percent sure if it was real or accurate, but she looked too happy for it not to have been."

He must have spoken swiftly when responding.

When Ari is with Delphi, similar thoughts and questions have proposed that his exchange held a trick. Now that the initial shock is no longer present, the ruse has become much easier to see. When Ari and I are together, there have been pauses and silence when I have thought to bring this up, but she often returns despondent—eyes glossy, with thoughts far away and unwilling to speak for hours.

Things I want to say must remain unspoken.

"You may be right."

I hear her tongue click. Feel as her body shifts. "I can't be sure though. Maybe I'm just trying to justify it."

More silence. More distance.

XI

A Surprising Roommate

Luka

Sleep had overtaken me before Ari had the ability to close her eyes. In fact, as I feel her shifting around–my body still pressed against the wall–I'm not sure that she's gotten any sleep at all.

Her rapid movement is what forces my eyes to lazily open. Immediately, I see Adonis in the cell, the whites of his eyes completely red. It isn't bloodshot, but instead appears bloody due to a popped blood vessel, which must have caused a hemorrhage.

His hair is messier than it had been in battle. The curls puff in multiple directions, the same way they would when waking up in the morning. His lip is cut and swollen, the rest of his beige complexion bruised enough to cover large sections of the skin that I can see.

Arabella isn't aware that I have woken. While my body acquaints itself with a new day, I believe my eyes have hallucinated him. But how wrong I am when I make eye contact with the Fae, and he, on instant, drops his eyes to the ground.

My arm yanks from under my head, shooting up and darting towards the Fae.

He doesn't take his eyes off me while I kick him onto his back, refusing to fight back.

"Why did Delphi send you in here?" I ask, taking my left fist and driving it into his already-beaten face.

It only takes seconds before I feel the thin flat sheet from the bed wrapped around me. I'm pulled back slightly, the force barely moving my body. At the fabric digging harshly into my skin, I realize that Ari and I are still without clothes. While Adonis sits in clothing similar to mine, ours are scattered around the mattress.

I put on both my underwear and pants, throwing Ari her shorts and buttoning the shoulders of her shirt. The two of us finish collecting ourselves, sitting on the mattress while staring at Adonis for too long without an explanation–me eyeing him, her trying to understand.

"Adonis, really," she says, blinking a few times, "why *are* you here?" Whether it is from her feeling of sympathy towards him or a larger plan, there is a level of trust between the two that I refuse to acknowledge.

The Fae shows no emotion that would hint at him being a spy for Delphi. He takes a gulp, shame creeping on his face. "Do you recall your words about Delphi casting me aside when she acquired a better opportunity?"

"Uh-huh."

"It would seem that being a queen alone is better than having me continue to believe that I am in charge," he replies, air of resentment from her manipulation exhaling from his nose. Though I speak more formally than my friends, I would have thought Adonis to have a more common vocabulary, being that he was raised mainly in the Human Lands for decades.

"Delphi did all that?" Ari asks, her hand moving in a circle, gesturing to the state of his body.

Adonis stills, dragging himself closer to us but continuing to stare at me as though he is scanning for his safety. Neither a confirmation nor denial. "She saw that I left the light on when she checked on you in the dawn's quiet. But she said it wasn't until she saw your clothing on the ground and caught sight of your chains that she was confident enough to send for my punishment."

While he tells his story, I notice the cuff on his wrist. It doesn't hold a chain, being that there is no other place to connect it to, other than his ankles.

Moving his hand through his hair, his fingers catch themselves in a knot. After being unable to detangle the bonded strands, he gives up on it entirely, letting out a defeated sigh. "I thought she was putting on the cuff for more intimate activities–"

"Get to the point," I cut off. The story is going through details which have no importance.

"I meant to tell the full truth," he responds.

Face still stuck in twisted disgust, Ari glances off to the side. "No, Luka's right. That's disgusting, Adi."

Adonis jerks his head to Ari with the use of a nickname. Then, a sharp, nettled inhale is taken through his nose, disregarding our opinions on the matter. "She put the cuff on, and while I was confused, two other creatures entered, though I could not see their features."

"What do you mean you couldn't see them?" Ari asks.

"The two figures entered, but before I was able to capture a better look at them, Delphi temporarily blinded me and hexed pain through my body." He pauses, legs trembling as he struggles to stand from his place. His hand reaches to Ari, silently asking for her help.

"No," I say firmly.

Ari turns back to me, puzzled. Her eyebrows furrow, head cocking in the direction of his cuff to remind me that there is nothing he can do to her. While I am the first to acknowledge her strength and ability to defend herself, I am still skeptical that this is a ploy.

Choosing to spare an argument, Ari sits down at my side, placing her hand in mine. It is with her that I find gentle serenity.

"How'd she blind you before you could react?" Ari continues to question. "I know we can magik temporary blindness, but she shouldn't be able to hex you while holding your loss of sight."

He coughs roughly into his hand while struggling to breathe. It's after the final cough when something comes out. Blood. Dark Fae blood that runs nearly black. He wipes his hand onto his pants, a nose wrinkling at his fluids on his clothing. "As I said last night, she studied texts which revealed magik that is untaught by your kind's schools."

"Were you able to find what restricted magik she learned?" I question, hopeful all information she has acquired are ones I am familiar with.

"I was never allowed access to the books," Adonis admits. "Delphi had given the excuse that I am not Magik, and it made little sense to have the information since I cannot perform the spells."

Though deeply dissatisfied with this answer, I hold my composure when feeling Ari's hand touching mine, reminding me of where we are and how powerless we would be against Delphi if she were to enter. It's unclear as to whether Adonis now sides with us, being that the woman he previously devoted himself to destroying Ifaeris with has placed him in a locked cell.

"Okay," I exhale. There is nothing that Ari nor I can do at this time to obtain further answers from him. Not about this subject, at the least.

"Now I do not know if I ever truly loved Delphi or if I fell in love with the life she imagined for us," Adonis says.

Side glances between Ari and I are traded, her face falling to the ground and debating how to react. Adonis is unable to lie, but that does not mean he won't do anything, such as using us for information, in order to gain back Delphi's trust.

Despite the squeeze of my hand and the look I give Ari, urging her to follow my lead of saying nothing, I feel her shake from me as she is about to speak. "I get that."

"She only ever wanted me as a means to her ends," he admits. His face casts a doleful look, betrayed by how easily he was abandoned. It is something Ari knows all too well.

However, unlike her, I don't understand why I should feel any bit of sympathy for Adonis. His past is unfortunate, yes, but not enough to earn forgiveness for the acts he committed. For the lives of others he destroyed. I still find great difficulty seeing him as anything more than the Fae who helped capture and harm the woman I love.

Ari too is struggling to offer words of comfort. Instead, she titters awkwardly. About to do something she consistently does when she's unable to console.

"Welcome to the club of people used and left by Delphi for her own ego."

Adonis looks between Ari and me, vaguely embarrassed that he now sits just as devalued as the two of us. "She kept me long enough until she could acquire a power higher than what I offered."

My mind is still reeling with different reasons that would explain his appearance here, but when Ari leans her head into my arm, nudging it twice, I wrap it around her, and the thoughts disappear.

It *should* matter. I should be concerned and dissecting every word he has said, assessing any possible suggestion of deception, but I am given no time to question him.

"I see the three of you are talking about why you hate me," Delphi intrudes, surprising us all with her unexpected presence.

The cell door opens, and a Cyclops, who is over four times my height, enters. He has a tuft of dandelion hair that braids from the top center of his head and icy blue fur coating around his whole body. In his right arm is another mattress, his left hand holding a pillow with a tawny flat sheet.

The Cyclops throws the mattress down at the corner between the wall and cell bars, having it sit perfectly diagonal from our mattress. At the drop of the sheet, the creature turns back, gazing sorrowfully at the three of us. A look of remorse crosses his face, but Delphi twists her fingers, forcing him out.

"I'll let the three of you get acquainted." She flashes a sly grin, walking away with the Cyclops, whose footsteps are heavy on the stone.

"You have no one," Ari calls out to her. "Adonis doesn't even want you anymore." While some of her lashings stem from blurted thoughts that directly pinpoint one's insecurities, this remark is spit with blatant truths and irritability.

The sound of Delphi's shoes tapping with each step can be heard from the distance. "No matter. I can dispose of him."

XII

Jump Scare

Arabella

"Wake up!" a voice shouts. The banging of two pieces of metal clash together before they're hit along the bars of the cell, the sounds distinctly different from each other. I don't register that the slightly congested voice belongs to Delphi until I open my eyes, and I see three sets of feet.

Being the closest to the cell, Adonis is the first of us to jolt up, hands over his ears.

"No," I groan upon seeing who stands next to Delphi. As if this situation can't get any worse, there stands the freckled Fae with hair as brittle as twigs.

Korine.

She's standing in an ombre gown that blends from white to green, the sleeves sheer, with an additional silver collar piece that pads out sharply past her shoulders.

On the other side of Delphi is one of the worst people to ever grace my life. A short, brown-eyed man with hair to match his height. My rapist. Grant Santos.

Amid my realization, Luka rests his arm weighted around my waist. He tucks me into him, but I can't tell if he's awake.

"Hello, witch," the nasally, mid-toned voice greets through a smile. "Or whatever Cassius calls you now."

Korine is basking in the glory of this all. Her smile is uncomfortable to look at, and I'm not entirely sure she wouldn't use her powers to topple the building from above until the whole thing crushes to rubble.

I return a gritted smile, my jaw clenched. "Hi, Korine."

Luka's arm removes from me, fingers tapping at my shoulder so that we may both sit against the wall that faces the three. I turn to him, his expression typical. Permanently angry and ready to fight another if pushed past a breaking point.

Grant is staring at me, trying to pull my attention towards the gravity that I once always fell into. His old jeans that he wore on a near-daily basis when I knew him are more faded than his graphic T-shirt. He's attempting to curl the corner of his mouth, but it comes off as nauseating.

My heart is accelerating to where I can feel nothing but that. I'm blinking so many times that everything I see feels like flashes of pictures playing in the same position. I think I've forgotten how to breathe.

"Arabella?" Adonis calls, but I can't force myself to turn to him. The most I can do is flicker my eyes.

"How rude of me," Korine says to the room. "I'm Korine."

"We've met." Luka scowls.

The Elemental's eyes go wide while her face frowns. She motions over to Grant, who is brushing a hand through his curly hair. "And this is Grant."

All of a sudden, my body feels chilled. I don't know why, considering I know he's there. I can see him clearly, but someone else acknowledging his existence makes it more surreal.

Luka's hand goes to mine, which is slack between us. Adonis turns back to the two of us, only knowing of Korine but not the other.

"Ara, can we talk?" Grant asks.

Chiming bells from worship temples ring loudly in my left ear, setting off swarms of my nerves. My calves are tingling with a numb sensation, and the next thing I realize I'm doing is walking out of the opened cell while being led down a hallway towards the torture room.

Except that's not where we're going. We pass the door and continue until we take a right. I'm taken past the showers, around two corners, and into another room. Inside, there's a square granite table that freezes my upper arms when I rest them on its surface. There's the door where we entered from and another larger-sized one on the adjacent wall, with a stained glass window behind Grant.

Three small cages, no bigger than the length of my arm, hang above fragments of stones in the far back. An unmade, child-sized bed is pressed to the corner, with the blankets thrown to the ground. It could be that this is where some of the common fae were held, which adds to the poor treatment that those under Delphi's control endured.

I study every corner in such disbelief that Delphi would bring Grant into this, knowing that he's human. He knows nothing of our world.

I wonder what the Council would say if they knew about this.

Cassius already gave her land and power. There's nothing I can offer her.

"Do whatever you need to do," Delphi says, a hand holding the gray handle on the smaller door that is carved from the larger wood.

When she leaves Grant and me alone, neither of us talk. My eyes focus on the multicolor of the window that shines behind him, while he tugs and fumbles with the sleeve of his turquoise, unzipped hoodie. Though we aren't making eye contact, he's trying to more than I am.

I never thought I'd have to see him again. When things ended between the two of us, after I found out he was cheating on me, all I got was a text giving a half-assed apology. I let him take advantage of my heart, just to find out I was viewed as an object. And when he physically left my life, every sweet nothing that he had me believe he meant had stolen any hopes I had of being loved.

My arms cross right over my chest, eyes glaring at him. I decide I want to break the silence before he can. "What do you needa say to me?"

"I uh…" His voice trails off. Thoughts are gathering in his head, but meanwhile, my heart thumps so loudly in my ears that I would take any sound to draw my attention elsewhere. "I wanted to say sorry. I feel bad for what happened and wanted to see if we could work it out."

A bitter laugh escapes me. He feels guilty, sure, but he isn't genuinely apologetic. Honestly, I can't understand why Delphi brought him here. She risks the repercussions of the Coven by informing him of our world.

"You're not sorry," I spit, wearing a sardonic smile and sending a glare that he has the honor of receiving. "If you were sorry, you wouldn't have waited *years* to apologize. You wouldn't have waited until Delphi offered you a way to ease your own conscience to confront me."

He clears his throat, fiddling again with the sleeves of his hoodie. Clearly, he wasn't expecting this from me. He still thinks I'm the same person I was when we dated.

"You could leave with me." He pauses, his gaze softening and reaching out across the table. "You were never meant for this kinda life. We could go back. Back to our summer. When you were happy to be with someone like me."

His words don't miss me. It's not about being human. "Someone like me" just means accepting the absolute worst treatment.

"You're so full of shit, Grant. Don't you have your dead-end life to get back to?"

"So you're gonna go back to being fucked with by Delphi when you have the chance to leave with me?" he bites out in a grueling tone. "Faking your happiness until the blond disappoints you too?"

My lips spread across my face, teeth grazing the edges of my bottom lip as my mouth opens. "I know you're used to women faking things around you, but other people know how to make me happy. Shocker."

"You'd choose to fuck your way through every man that life hands you as an opportunity?"

For reasons of the cuffs holding my magik prisoner and the fact that Delphi very likely used protection magik on Grant, I have to constrain myself.

"You forget it isn't just *men* I'd happily sleep with before ever going back to you." I pause, reminding him of the fact. Just like before, he refuses to acknowledge my interest beyond men. "You wouldn't understand 'cause you haven't had sex in how long? I guess you could count with all the fingers on your hand. Or," I smile, brows raised, "you could just check the hoodie for the stains."

Grant goes stunned at my comment. Mouth shut from my words alone. He carries his chair to my side, sitting beside me and putting his right hand to my thigh.

Since our breakup, I've learned how to become bold enough to defend myself and fight back. But with his body being this close in front of me, I'm regressed to such a feeling of smallness that I don't stop him. And as I sit here, I'm no stronger than who I was at eighteen. That terrifies me.

"I wanted to talk so that I could say my piece." It's an offering. Waving a white flag of surrender.

"You have no piece to say," I snap, done with his deflection and excuses. "I have *every* right to say mine, but you don't even deserve *that*. I'm not entertaining your pathetic attempt at whatever Delphi's using you for."

He removes his hand from me, sucking in his cheeks before sneering at me. "You're not shit with those," he taunts, motioning to my cuffs. "Remember that with these on, you're just as defenseless as I am. Human and all."

My eyes shoot wide at his comment, immediately pressing my lips down on each other. I exhale through my nose, narrowing my eyes at him in hilarious astonishment. "Do you really think that being without magik makes me equal to you?" I laugh, and I think that maybe I'm going insane. "We have *never* been equal. Don't flatter yourself. I'm literally a queen."

"But no one knows that," Korine interjects, appearing at the side door of the room. She walks over to Grant, giving him a pointed look before shooing him out and taking the chair for herself.

She smiles at me, the fabric of her dress irritating my skin when her knee brushes mine as she sits.

I hate that Korine is as gorgeous as she is powerful. She carries the kind of beauty that is horrifyingly intimidating–sea green eyes big and round, which don't fail to laser past my exterior and into the core of my being. The Fae knows her place well within the lower courts while not wanting to rule, unquestioning of who she is and the superiority she assumes herself to have over others. An attitude that I'm sure most of the Elementals carry.

"Figures you're working with Delphi to kidnap me."

I'm sweating from behind. With every biting or rude comment I make, it's like I'm one missed step away from choking on my words. It feels like I'm not entirely in control of my actions. A stranger in my own body. I'm witnessing everything from my perspective, and while I'm aware of the things happening, I can't contain my impulses. Not against any of them. If Delphi's doing this just to kill me, I might as well make everyone else miserable too.

Emotions are chewing on me, and I can't help myself from asking, "Do you love him?"

Korine looks at me in surprise. She crumbles from exposing anger with the ball of her fists. "What?"

"Cassius. Do you love him?"

Her high-raised brows meet in confusion, her face turning pale–nearly sick. "What does love have anything to do with this?"

Head slightly angled, I glance off to the side. Her expression and reaction give me enough information to devise an area to exploit her. Utilize her possessive feelings against her to free me.

"It's a simple yes or no question." I lift my arm from the table, using my elbow to steady my head as I rest my cheek on my knuckles. "I guess it's none of my business, but I can't really see you teaming with a witch unless you love Cassius."

Seething rage flames her eyes, and her skin flushes from a pink to a near red, making her cheekbones more prominent. "I will have you know, before you got here, Cas and I–"

Suddenly, her voice is drowned out by my thoughts. However angry I am with him, to hear her utter his name stings in ways I refuse to acknowledge.

I need to stop and create a better divide between Korine and her loyalty to Delphi. I'll likely regret the scorn that I'd receive by inciting the Fae's jealousy, but it benefits me more in the end.

"It's not my place, but if you wanted to date him again, maybe *don't* team up with the witch that killed both his family and people he rules over."

My comment earns a stone flinging in my direction, hitting me so hard that I fall, and black stars coat my vision.

When I return to my seat, she is still stiff, unapologetic, and has her nostrils flared. Her hand has lowered to her lap, breath loudly coming from her rosy, thin nose. "What I feel for him matters very little. But he does not *truly* love you. Why else would he leave you here?"

She makes a devastatingly valid point. Cassius *did* leave me here.

"I never said we weren't faking being lovers. Maybe he trusts me to take Delphi on my own," I suggest with any false composure I can. It's a lie, but if I'm going to be successful in deceiving her or planting a bit of doubt into her mind, the lie harms no one but me.

"Trust?" she laughs. She smiles in gleeful terror. "Trustful is the furthest thing he must feel towards you. You tell him what to do, what to say, and how to say it. Do you assume he hadn't revealed this to Harrison and me on a drunken night?"

Shit. I haven't thought about how they must have met while I've been here. Cassius is able to think so little while overly drunk.

Korine continues on, paying no attention to anything other than the sound of her voice. "Why should Cas have you as queen when he and I are much better suited?"

I huff, the little filter I have completely gone. "Do you actually care about me being queen? Or do you just not want to accept he stopped loving you?"

In one look, Korine's appearance turns from contemptuous to deviously patronizing. Her smile is wide and frightening. "That can change if Delphi uses the Stone of Elestial."

My blink is slow before my lids gape open. "The stone's here? In the building?"

"It can't be used for the purpose I'd intend, sadly." Delphi appears before the two of us, the door opened but never having made a sound. She's so painfully average-looking that I could mistake a random person in the street for her, which, at times, spiked my anxiety after our friendship ended. Her eyes go to Korine, waving her hand with a mouth commanding, "You can go. I need to talk to her."

The Fae rises from her seat, her nails scraping my cheek before exiting through the door Delphi came from. I have no idea where she's going.

"So..." I say lightly, my fingers tapping the table in line, "you still having fun torturing me for no other reason than your personal enjoyment?"

"You're too caught in your thoughts and feelings."

I'm not sure what she could mean by that. Delphi's done nothing besides cause me harm, but *I'm* too caught in my feelings?

Bashful remarks won't give me the information I need. I bite my tongue from proceeding, filtering everything down to nothing but, "What do you mean?"

"You forget what you wield as queen," she answers. She moves her seat farther back, hunching her torso forward and putting her weight on her arms that lie on her thighs. "Despite how little I think of you, it doesn't dispute the fact you hold the power to rule. You share equal power with Cassius since you're queen, correct?"

I nod, remaining in my silence.

Delphi hums out a low sound, followed by a blithe smile. "You can offer me more. More than Cassius has given me. You'd just have to say the word, and the king would fall to your every whim. I can easily let you go, but I need your power as queen first."

"The lower courts' rulers would never agree to that," I point out. Of all the Fae, Elementals hate Magiks the most. Many of the Fae had been wiped from the lands during the war against us, but for Elementals, Magiks practically cleared their bloodlines to nothing.

"Their opinions mean very little when you're the High Rulers. You have final say over all."

In theory, she *is* right, but my power doesn't hold when no one but those of us here and Cassius know of it. Regardless, if I did hand over power to Delphi, it would wreak chaos. The Elementals would have none of it, fighting amongst each other or dying trying to battle against Delphi's rule. And when that settles, she'll barely have anything to rule over.

I don't know why I'm riddling myself with all these hypotheticals when I want Ifaeris' king to rot. I could give Delphi power, and I'd be free to leave, but I won't allow for my friends there to suffer for my actions.

I'm selfish, but not *that* selfish.

"I'd have to speak to him about a decision that big. And even then, I don't know if he'll agree. He doesn't want me."

Delphi's proven that ten times over.

"Maybe he doesn't love you, but no one, not even Korine, can convince themselves into believing he doesn't care for you. Not when he looks at you the way I've only ever seen Luka done." Delphi takes me by my arm, ripping me up from my chair.

She leads me back to the cell where both Korine and Grant are waiting. Unlocking the cell, Delphi turns back and says, "Think about what I've said, and you'll be free to live a life without me. Unless you want to keep being tortured."

"Why now?" I ask. I'm so confused with this information being dumped onto me at once. "Why not just use the stone and be done with it?"

Her mouth quirks to the right. "The land has to be freely given. It'll reject another creature if it's not offered by its current ruler or it has chosen the ruler itself. Besides, I told you I wanted to have my fun too. And now you're broken enough to give me everything I want, as long as I keep Luka alive." She turns to the two others that stand outside my living area. "Let's go. We have some things I need to speak to you about."

I'm handed to Grant, who slides his hand to the small of my back. I can feel him lowering it as he guides me into the cell.

The beating rhythm in my ears is back. So is the knot that's grown exponentially in my stomach since I last saw him. My body shivers, legs rushing me back onto my bed and refusing to look at him.

I don't hear when the door slams shut. I only somewhat perceive it. My vision's going hazy. Focusing in and out. Only able to ground myself by touching the rough feel of the wall and comparing it to the softer touch of the blanket.

Luka is asking me questions while Grant stares at me when walking away. My boyfriend's going about different ways of asking me what happened, but nothing's processing.

Both Adonis and Luka are staring at me like a child who, if asked what's wrong, would fall into tears. I don't even realize I'm rocking or counting my fingers against the mattress until Luka's hand goes to mine, freezing my movement.

My hand whips from under his, my breath jolting from my mouth. I feel physically sick. What comes from my mouth can't be classified as breathing, I don't think. They're only short inhales that are erratic and shallow. My thumb speedily taps my other fingers at fast movements while my eyes squeeze shut.

I can't breathe. I can't breathe. I can't breathe. I can't breathe. I can't breathe.

Logically, I know I can, but that doesn't mean it feels like it.

I feel my teeth chattering, my body uncontrollable. When I'm able to open my eyes, Luka tries to put an arm around me, causing a crisp scream from my throat.

It's not that I mean to do it. Actually, I scare myself from the sound of my voice. I blink again, and I'm in the corner between the walls and on the edge of the mattress. Adonis hasn't moved from his place, and Luka looks upset with himself. He thinks he's done something wrong, but he hasn't.

My breathing finally controls itself when I find myself back in Luka's arms. Contradicting what I can't handle and the guilt that

I needlessly pushed my boyfriend away, I sit between his legs, his arms cradling around my waist. His touch I'm able to recognize. My mind has rationalized itself enough to realize that I'm with him and not Grant. This whole time, I've known that it's Luka, but the panicking side of my brain refused to register any touch without thinking it belonged to my ex-boyfriend.

"Ari?" Luka says softly.

"I'm fine. I don't know why you guys are so worried," I respond. Adonis looks at me with what I can guess is doubt, and I realize my hands are still scraping up and down my thighs. "No, really, I'm good. I just think that it's crazy that Delphi would use these people to hurt me more, as if everything from our friendship meant nothing, and she's using my absolute most traumatic things I told her in confidence and–"

"Arabella," Adonis cuts off. He keeps his distance, barely bringing himself closer to where we sit. "You're rambling."

Taking in a deep breath, I recenter myself. "Sorry. I just wasn't expecting her to use Grant against me."

"Is this the Grant that..." Luka trails off, not finishing his question.

I turn to him, nodding a few times as a response. I shouldn't feel ashamed of what Grant did. It wasn't my fault.

Or so you keep telling yourself.

"I knew Delphi did shitty things to me, but I never thought she'd sink so low to work with..." I pause, swallowing and unable to say his name, "him. Not after everything I told her he did to me."

Luka looks at me, and I clench my hand into his. He doesn't voice his thoughts, but I'm pretty sure I can guess them. "She's kept you locked away for months. Why would you question her doing something this obvious?"

"I mean, yeah, she basically emotionally treated me the same way that Grant did when she and I were friends, but physically, the most she did was choke me."

Adonis' reaction is immediate, leaning forward while both invested in our past and disgusted. "She choked you? For what reason?"

Unintentionally, I laugh. I blame my mind that immediately goes to the comical scenario. "It wasn't in a sexual way, unfortunately. Delphi knew that she was one of the few people I was comfortable with in terms of constant touch, and she used it to cross boundaries. She thought it would be funny."

The arm around mine loosens, Luka's hand peeling away. I stop him, holding tighter and reassuring him that his touch is almost always welcome.

He dips his head into my neck, moving the hair towards the other side and breathing out against me. Lightly, he presses his lips against the skin, chuckling when I squirm. "Don't do that, love."

I'm flooded with amusement, feeling the hardness that presses into my back.

A throat is cleared, reminding me that Adonis is here, sitting right in front of us. "If the two of you would control yourselves, what did Grant want with you?"

Begrudgingly, I scoot towards the edge, putting enough space between Luka and me so that we can contain ourselves but not far enough to expose him. "Delphi knew that forcing me to see him would make me crack. It would weaken me and leave an opportunity to accept her offer."

"The offer she was speaking about before you came in here?" Luka asks.

"She said that, as queen, I have the ability to give her more land to rule over. It's why she kept me for so long and why she refuses to let me go."

Adonis lifts his left brow, crossing a leg over the other. "Here I was to assume she did such a thing out of pure evil."

My lips purse, and I cock my head. "Both can be true at the same time."

"Delphi mentioned that she can dispose of me, and I suppose she's right," says the Fae.

I look at him, my mind trying to reason what he means. "Right about what?"

Refusing to meet my eyes, Adonis' hand lightly teeters on his thigh in a clenched fist. If it's not heartbreak, it's something close to it. Disillusionment. "With her deal, I'm expendable. I no longer serve use to her. You do."

Pity knocks to the front of my mind. Though he's done horrible things, assuming he would rule alongside Delphi just to realize he's her patsy is something worth feeling sorry for. I warned him, but he refused to listen.

"Ironic, isn't it?" Adonis says, changing our topic of conversation.

"What is?" Luka asks.

Adonis laughs to himself. "Well, Grant means tall, does it not? The human lacks in that area. He is height deficient."

My mouth opens, nose blowing out air multiple times in short spouts of an exhale, my head tilted to the side. Of all things, I didn't expect a short joke to come from the Fae.

"You're not wrong."

Luka might not find the joke funny when Adonis tells it, but I do. The Fae and I are cracking different jokes about the two brought to me today and their difference in appearance—when the door opens.

Delphi calls Adonis, beckoning for him to join her. The look on her face assumes her to have sinister intent. She stops me before I can walk towards him, keeping me in place the moment I stand.

And after testing her patience, she twists her fingers, the magik yanking him towards her as he looks back at us with a face full of woeful presumptions.

The former couple departs, their footsteps echoing down the hall, leaving Luka and me wondering exactly what Delphi plans to do with or to Adonis and what can be done to exploit him when he returns to us.

XIII

Kingly Duties

Cassius

Morale around Nexus has reached a low without both Luka and Arabella. The servants know nothing of what I have planned, which has only spread talk amongst themselves, with their hushed whispers coming to a screeching halt whenever I enter the room. It is only a matter of days before the success of my scheme blooms into fruition.

Come soon, I will have the two safely returned home with me.

As a young faeling, being royalty always seemed full of mischievous authority, thrilling rendezvous, and no dire need to trouble myself with the smallest of burdens. As king, there are hints of what my childhood self had imagined, but such not are they the sole of my schedule. Rarely have I found time to make merry in activities outside of the crown the way that I once had as prince. Socializing is sparse unless it is for the sake of gathering information or the crown's obligation, and many things have become dull.

On occasion, I receive letters from the rulers of the lower courts regarding their irritation with those who demand that we find their loved ones. Many common fae seek an audience with me, pleading for some minimal favor or coming with insufferable disputes and inconveniences they face, which have become my issue.

Right now, a small Pixie with sparkly, translucent wings flies before me. She is a tad taller than the size of my hand, with antennas on her head and wearing a rose-puffed dress. She has been petitioning, beseeching for a leave from the lands, though I'm not particularly listening to the details.

Two guards stand at the door of the throne room with white tunics under black leathers and boots, which rise to the midst of their calf. They carry a sword strapped by a belt around their waists, the weapon prepared to be drawn at any given notice.

My enervation from the past days has come to collect its due. Since my dinner at the House of Smoldris, I have been more lenient when granting favors in hopes to keep busy their minds, and so that word of Adonis and Arabella's disappearance does not continue to grow the worry of common fae.

The position of my body drapes diagonally across my throne, with one leg propped on the armrest. A tinge in my throat is craving to be fed, and the warmth from the sun adds as an extra obstacle when forcing myself to stay awake.

"As it were, your father would oversee the passing and goings of Fae through the lands, but I would hope more gracious of a ruler than he are you," the Pixie begs in a high tone.

Though you need the approval of the High Ruler to live outside of the lands of Ifaeris, many Fae do not go through the unneeded formalities of the process. My father was never one to keep tabs on the lives of common fae unless something strictly demanded it, and rulers of the lower courts do not truly keep tally of who is born.

Ultimately, this law created by my father is rooted in power superiority, which I ought to get rid of.

Her request piques my interest, curious over her intentions to live among the humans. The Fae before me speaks in such a way that I would assume mortals deem it odd. I lift my leg from where it dangles, facing her in a full-frontal position and crossing my legs. "Whyever would a Fae wish to live among the humans, if not to torment them?"

"I am aware that as Fae, we ought not to care for mortals, but I have fallen in love," she says with eyes as wide as a doe's.

If she is hoping to use my affection for Arabella to sway me in her favor, she may be more clever than I give her credit for.

"I do not want to risk the possibility of exile if I leave without your blessing," she continues on. Her attempt to convince me into granting my approval through a different path only raises her nervousness when I make no reaction. Fingers of salmon tap against the back palm of her other hand, the sepia of her lips being bitten down upon. If she sinks her fanged teeth any harder, blood would be drawn. "I love my family and would very much like to bring my betrothed and future children here one day."

"You would endanger not only your human lover, but your unborn, half-human children to lands which would happily trick them to their deaths?" I muse cheerily. Her face turns crimson, not having taken these actions into consideration. "Have you made your betrothed aware of your blood? Or where you come from?"

She is flustered, stammering over her words and sounds that ultimately come out as nothing. I give time, watching as she searches for an answer, ultimately bowing in shame. "No, Your Majesty. I have not told him."

"How can you claim to love him and make plans for marriage when he does not know who you are?"

The Pixie turns her head up at me, brass hair covering most of her face. Through the strands, her expression appears sullen. "I do love him."

My lips press tightly together, rendering my judgment on the matter. "You love him, but he does not know who you are truly."

Her face turns unruly, dissatisfied with the truth of my words. She, just as many others, assumes I know nothing of love with the reputation that I carry.

An assumption most incorrect.

As the Pixie parts her mouth to speak, I stand from my throne, prepared to announce my verdict and to excuse myself from duties for the day. "Without harm or punishment to come to you, you are free to live among the humans and with your betrothed... Your name?"

"Zora," she squeaks. The Pixie trembles, petrified of what I could do if I held the power of her name in its whole.

I let out one breath of exasperation, pushing past both her fear and my aggravation. "I do not wish to hold that level of power over you. Your first name will do."

Zora lets out a sigh of relief, glamouring herself to the height of a short human with round ears to match. She bows her head before me, kneeling on both knees, eager for my command.

"Zora of Ifaeris is free to live in the Human Lands, on the very condition that she keeps her form from exposing the existence of Fae to the human public, therefore protecting the identity of all creatures' existence."

"Thank you, my king," she says as she rises, bowing her head once more. "I will be sure to keep good on my word."

"You have found yourself in luck to seek me on a good day. See that you never put our kind in danger," I warn as she is escorted out.

At her exit, another guard with hair the sunset shade of calendula enters, a missive in hand. His tight curls flop around with each jogged step, carefully keeping the letter from creasing.

Yet another impatient demand from Delphi. Repetitive

paragraphs asking if I have signed over the land, passing the information to the other rulers.

Every day I have been sent another letter, each more abrasive than the last. If my plan is to work, I would need to act cautiously and with haste.

XIV

Everything Goes According to Plan

Cassius

Hooded cloaks that I requested from the tailors to be made have been given to each of the five creatures. The power of my shadows would expose our group, so the tailors made sure the fabric would conceal the wearer. Made from the blackest velvets gathered from the lands, the cloth is dark enough to absorb any light that still appears.

The time in Gigantia is half a day ahead of Ifaeris. At the time of arrival through okkaring, it will be the dead of night, with nothing but the nocturnal creatures coming to life.

We could slip in and out of the darkness without being noticed.

Sweetness from the Etherfruite releases a small ease from my worry. If I am to fail today, I, at the very least, deserve to gorge on the taste of golden honey and heated jams.

Open windows and doors allow fresh air to circulate through Nexus, bringing in light from the brightest of days. Kabir stands at the door with Gavin, who opens it for Cel, Damien, and Juliette.

The Magiks gaze around the waiting chamber, gawking at the walls and the feast of tasty treats that sit on the table.

They are who will be joining me, each a volunteer. In the case of the Magiks, their abilities aid where glamouring fails. Delphi is of their world. While the whole of their group has joined me in Ifaeris to rescue their friends, they still mistrust me.

I'm not sure if I have much faith in myself.

For the generosity of their time, I have told all servants that whatever it is any of the Magiks want, they may have it.

"Sorry," Damien says, strolling to the elongated settee that presses against the wall. "We went to the throne room first. I didn't realize you meant this room until Celeste got us."

"So, out of curiosity, there were humans wandering around the towns when we went around," Juliette comments, nearly accusatory. She grabs multiple pieces of the boring fruit that is blueberries onto a plate. "Why are they here if you don't like them?"

"If a human hadn't taken the offering of Fae food or drink, they would not be bound to our lands," Cel answers plainly.

Looks of revulsion–possibly indignation–are shared by the Magiks and directed at the Fae within the room, as if they are personally offended on behalf of the humans.

"They can't leave?" Juliette asks, voice rough with anger.

"Your issue with Fae morals is not my problem to have," I respond. The few humans who remain within the lands are here due to glamouring compulsion as a source of entertainment, most for foolish deals made. I have come across some, a few being affairs of my father, but many who exist within Ifaeris do not stay for longer than years unless a Fae has taken a particular interest in the being.

That is the way of the Fae. Our culture and mannerisms may change over the course of lifetimes, but so long as an action does not go against the laws of the lands, each choice is one made by the own by the individual Faerie.

"So we're getting there, how?" Damien asks, shifting my focus.

It has been just over a week since my eyes beheld Arabella. I cannot bring myself to think how the last she saw me, she seemed prepared to murder me in my place. In that rage was a tinge of betrayal.

I remove the ring that mixes both metals of silver and rose gold from my neck, placing it on my left's fourth finger, right above another gold band of mine. Arabella's ring remains on my body at all times, whether near my throat or near the finger that closely connects to my heart.

"The building will be on the edge, so we will okkar to the land and attempt to break inside," I respond. The structure is unguarded, just as many of the abandoned sections left for those exiled from Gigantia are. To my knowledge, this one in particular has not been occupied in decades and has since been left for the lands to consume. I doubt many would be near the area, being that Gigantia's ministers reside in the heart of the land.

There will be many areas which we will have to search through. If Delphi dressed Luka as she did Arabella, he no longer wears the pants he had on when he was taken. There is no precise way to locate his exact location.

Cel plops themself onto a chair that was previously tucked into the table. "We're blindly running around just hoping to find them? That seems dangerously ill-prepared."

Their sentiment matches closely with Esme's. They believe me not to have a plan. That without one, it will be our downfall.

I only hope their point is indeed wrong.

Scheming and planning are not things I am versed in. That responsibility is why I previously looked to Arabella. I was simply given orders by her and would follow them. Now that I am left to rule without her level-headed mind, I am completely on my own.

Worry overtakes me. Delphi has never once mentioned Arabella or Luka in her many missives. If she believes me to care nothing for them, my ploy has worked. Her hubris has blinded her to one's true intentions. I did promise her land to rule over, but that promise would only be followed through after I had met with the rulers of the lower courts. Though the signing itself would take no more than a week, I have yet to meet with the rulers to discuss such a thing. Even so, this all poses the danger that, for taking time which she views as overlong to approve her ruling, she may rescind her word on murdering the Fae.

I do my best to frame my thoughts in such a way that Arabella would, preparing for every possibility and outcome, though I can admit many of her plans fell to luck or torture. A need for circumspection is called for when rescuing them.

"It is, unfortunately, our best option," I reply. "Additionally, it will be night, so our movements must be quiet."

We could not inform Gigantia's ministers of what occurs on their lands, as there is no sureness as to who could listen into our conversations and possibly be a spy for Delphi. And in any case, they themselves may take long to permit access that pardons any damage to significant buildings or deaths done while we are there. So our movements must be careful and precise when retrieving Arabella and Luka.

Kabir takes a chair from the table and places it at my side. He is in plain clothing, yet with his size, he remains too noticeable. "We retrieve them and get out? What about Delphi and Adonis? Surely they would notice the two missing by morning."

"Can't y'all just glamour an animal or something into looking like Arabella and Luka?" questions Juliette with crossed arms.

"Adonis is Fae," Cel reminds Juliette, who still does not understand the power of glamour. "He would see through it."

"Princess Maude can glamour cows to deceive Adonis," Kabir suggests. I am sure he does not wish to entertain the idea but offers such to appease the witch. "We can carry the bodies with us and drop them in place of the Magiks."

Damien raises his right eyebrow. "Delphi isn't stupid. She'll realize it isn't them. I'd give it two days at most before she figures something's wrong."

The sorcerer makes a fair assumption. A lack of speaking between the two of them would appear abnormal. I have to produce an idea far better than what I have.

My brother is more powerful than we had assumed. He has formed an alliance with a witch, murdered our father, and put the lives of common fae in harm's way. All to result in ruling a small portion of land. I don't know whether I should be scared of the lengths he underwent or laugh at how poorly it fared.

"Their rescue is our priority. However, if, perchance, anyone spots Adonis, you will chain him with these," I say, revealing cuffs for each of us.

"Killing him would probably be less consequential in your future," Damien comments without care.

Gladly, I ought to order for Adonis' death after all that he has done, but I know that if I'm to remove Delphi entirely, it would pay better to sway him towards a less hateful demeanor towards us. It should not be too troublesome since the two hadn't agreed when I met them together. "He knows things about Delphi, which we do not. Pressing him for information will prove useful," is all I say, keeping my tedious thoughts from divulging and delaying us further.

Keeping Adonis alive matters greatly when his remaining alive and being taken back to the lands may result in a fate that eradicates the existence of the Fae.

"If you are ready, I would like to set ourselves for Gigantia before dawn rises," I announce to the room. I attempt to brush away Damien's comment, but my mind refuses to allow for it.

Many thoughts have already taken control of my nerves. Last night had been one of little sleep. I have some confidence, but many things are working against me.

Everyone comes closer, all of us joining hands with each other. I muster all the energy I can. To take all five of us to the far land requires a large feat.

"King Cassius?" Gavin, my personal knight, who is shorter than I but no bigger than Atticus, calls with a bow. "Please return safely." His head remains pointed towards the flooring as he exits, going forth to fulfill Kabir's duties while we are gone.

We okkar to the cliffside of Gigantia, the storms from rain causing Juliette to slip backwards. She nearly falls off the side and into the seas, panicking as Kabir grabs her by her arm to pull her closer inland. Meanwhile, I feel as if I may fall unconscious from energy drained.

Thunder is loud, competing against the ocean's water crashing along the land. The moon is hidden, barely peeking through the clouds, with lightning striking from afar.

The building is no more than six floors high, but such floors are suitable for the size of large creatures in stature. No wards keep us out, nor are there any markings above the mahogany door that warrant suspicion. Juliette whisks her hand, and with the action, the door creaks open slightly, wide enough for us to enter.

Kabir enters first, halting us outside until he signals otherwise. Once inside the harrowing place of stone, the doors are immediately locked.

The light is dimly shining, most of which coming through

windows from the sky. There are switches high above on the wall alongside the door to trigger a chandelier above us, though I would not play into the possibility of being caught.

On the first floor, there is nothing but tumultuous voices booming from a room. Gathered inside are Fae and creatures from Gigantia who sing drunken tunes while playing games with sharpened darts. Two are asleep with their heads on the table, others in a state of delirium due to alcohol.

I should have known better than to hold Delphi at her say-so of freeing all Fae she held.

We do our best to sneak around them, keeping ourselves out of vision. Cel keeps their hands up, focusing on any that may face the door, each of us quickly rushing through the wide, exposing opening until it is their time to move.

One by one, we fall into a line, pressing against the wall past doors in search of the stairs. At the top of the first set of steps, I listen for the voices of Arabella or Luka, but to no such luck.

We search through the sconce-lit, empty floor, ensuring not to make noise or draw any attention from the clamor below us. Unlike the first floor, the second comes with twists and turns, high-rising ceilings and doors until we are able to find a direct pathway. It's after much time exploring individually that Cel notices a route to the floor above us.

To get up to the third floor, we must climb the next staircase, which can only be accessed after passing through a wide hall without doors indenting into the wall to reveal chambers. Rather, beyond the hallway stand two Ogres at the feet of the bottom step. They are roughly the same size, with large stomachs, accentuated muscles, and a circle that runs through the septum of each creature. Their communication is uneasy to understand, both laughing between the words of their language, though those born in Gigantia have the ability to communicate with anyone of all languages.

The one dressed in a flushed gray makes a noise. "Hey, you there!" he yells.

"Shit," Damien mutters.

Juliette lifts her hands, blasting magik through her fingertips. "Celeste," she calls. "I could use your abilities right now."

"Right," they respond, lifting their hands, which causes a change in the expressions of the creatures. The creatures of pale sage drop their faces from focus into a relaxed smile, the tusks from their bottom teeth slacking with their jaw into repose.

Dashing towards the stairs, Juliette is the last of us to reach the curving steps, keeping her attention focused on those guarding the area.

"What have you done to them?" Kabir asks.

"She's casting a spell and having them believe they're in a blissful space. Celeste's abilities are making it more believable," Damien responds. He lifts his hand, laughing. "Juli, there's an easier solution to this."

The witch does not part her attention from the guards. There are beads of sweat coming down her forehead, the Magik holding her focus while she climbs the tall steps. "What is it, Damien?"

"This," he says, twisting his hand before snapping his fingers. At the motion, the Ogres drop to the ground, eyes closed.

Kabir's face holds no reaction. He turns to the side, saying to the two, "You did not kill them, I trust."

"Why the *fuck* would Damien kill them?" Juliette asks coldly.

Damien elbows the witch, shaking his head at her response. "I put them to sleep." He scans both bodies, eyes slightly widening. "Gods, what absolute fucking units."

"Let us hope that the sound of their bodies crashing to the floor didn't alarm the others," Kabir mutters as we reach the top step.

There are markings over the open archway, written onto the large stone, which juts out, though I cannot read what they symbolize. I remove my cloak, summoning my wings through the black shirt, which puffs widely down to where it wraps around my wrist. As I reach near the ceiling, I trace my fingers around the mysterious symbol, etching it onto paper that Kabir had given me in the case we needed to map the building layout.

The confusing symbol itself wraps inside a circle with a 'W'. The beginning and ending points of the letter finish with arrows on each line that crosses in the middle, with another that swirls through and curves into two separate swirls. Connected to the dash is a cross that curls at the end, dots near each corner.

I ponder what it could mean. Many things I have learned during my schooling, but little we were we taught about subjects outside of the Fae. In history lessons, we had delved into the topic of Magiks but never about what they would learn in their education.

"Have you ever seen this marking?" I ask either of the Magiks as my feet reach the floor, handing the paper over in exchange for my cloak.

Juliette points to the 'W', tracing it with her finger. "That's the sigil for warding against something, but the rest I've never seen. Damien?"

She beckons for him to view the mark himself. He studies it with his head tilting quizzically, responding by shaking his head. "In all the courses I've taken, I haven't seen these other symbols put together. The dots inside this area could be a protective ward against a threat, but for that to be effective, they would need to stand above the arrows."

"The meaning behind this may endanger us in the coming future, but we must move forward. We may not have much time," Kabir cautions.

With one missed step, Cel falls to the ground, triggering a plate of iron to fall from the ceiling. Pricks of iron and other needles shoot from both sides of the corridor. Faerie cloth of velvet protects us as we run, the lands offering a shield from its natural material.

A small blade cuts Damien at his ankle, striking him down. Cel turns back, going in to save him, but is struck by something I'm unable to catch, knocking them unconscious. The sorcerer picks my sister up, carrying them until both reach past the hallway to join us.

"What hit them?" I demand.

"I don't know," Damien says as he sets Cel down.

There is a glittery, neon green powder that clings to his cloak. "Starrdust," I inform the group.

"Starrdust?" Juliette repeats, bringing her ungloved hand to the substance.

My hand reaches to hers before it is too late. "A powder made by grinding the needles of a Starrywreath tree," I hurriedly explain, voice louder than it should. My sister is on the ground, and I cannot stop my heart rate's panic. I need to exert this energy in any way, but with every possibility that comes to mind, it would only expose us. "For a Fae to ingest it would cause their body to collapse in on itself within hours. Kabir, bring my sister home."

He nods, scooping their larger body into his arms and attempting to okkar the two of them. Focused concentration gleams from him as Cel's hair covers half of their horns, yet the two remain here.

"It isn't working," he tells me. "I cannot okkar."

Damien exchanges a look of concern between the others of us who stand. "Let me take them."

His eyes shut, but he too is unable to leave.

"The sigils," Juliette says, though this seems to be more of a comment for herself. "It's probably a trap that keeps us in, and we must've triggered some response when entering."

A loud cough booms through the floor. If I did not hear a voice follow it, I would have assumed it to be thunder.

Kabir throws Cel over his shoulders, and we all meander towards the sound.

This floor is full of cells for prisoners, each uninhabited with doors tightly shut.

"Ara," Damien calls out, jogging ahead towards the sound of the voice. "Is that you?"

The stones are rough and dingy, matching the smell of the air. A hint of the ocean and rain battles the stench of sweat and blood, though the pleasant scent seems to be losing.

Together, we stride down the hallway until we find a barred room with two figures lying on a mattress opposite the door. Here, the brightness from the moon shines the most thoroughly. It illuminates the Magiks enough to see their bodies but not enough to see their faces.

"Arabella. Luka," I call. I send out my shadows towards the switch at the end of the hall, flipping it so that light may shine through.

Something in me stills when I see them. I'm overjoyed that I can now speak to Arabella. I can hold her. The incessant pang in my chest has been disposed of.

The two refrain from answering, their eyes going to their friends. "Damien? Juli?" Luka says, leaving Arabella's side and moving towards us. "What are you two doing here?"

Damien puts his hand through the bars and lightly punches Luka's shoulder. He smiles at his friend, shaking him lightly. "Death made you dense, didn't it? We're here to save you."

As the sorcerer speaks, Juliette brushes back her cloak, cutting through the metallic bars with magik.

The bottom half of the door breaks in half, each bar falling to the floor separately.

A high-pitched siren goes off, constant vibrations and a cacophony of sounds coming from the corners of each wall. The sound blares in my ears, causing my body to bend in reaction. Then, I hear Delphi's voice.

"Our prisoners are trying to escape. Search every floor until you find them."

XV

Reluctant Faith

Luka

Delphi's voice repeats the same thing over and over. I'm not sure how much time we have until we're caught, or how soon it will be until Delphi is here.

Ari is still in the corner, wide-eyed and staring at us as if terrified. She is muttering something I cannot hear, crossing her arms around herself.

My thoughts are conflicted with anger towards the Fae king and the priority of getting Ari as far away from here as possible. Terror is coated on her face. While she can mask her emotions in the right frame of mind, being woken in the middle of the night with the surprise of those we know is not as easy for her.

Damien and Juli are standing outside the cell, studying us. There is a look in Cassius' eyes that seems to be relief. If our friends have followed him here, I will put aside my antipathy long enough to question him at a later time.

Cassius is swiftly walking towards her.

He is an idiot.

"Arabella," he says lightly, placing his hand on her arm.

Her eyes shoot at his contact. He is bent down so closely that I can easily decipher the reaction from her that he wants.

Without missing a beat, her right leg curls near her chest and kicks him. He is sent backwards, falling flatly onto his arse, and I'm chuckling. That is, until Ari launches herself at the king in a frenzied rage, screaming and swinging her arms. The metal that traps her wrists is doing more damage than her fists, taking me pulling her back several paces before she finally stops.

"If you wanted me under you, you needn't use violence as an excuse," Cassius says, smiling at Ari. As he readjusts his clothing, I take notice that he is without any jewelry or makeup. The only piece of accessory that he wears is the ring that Ari had given him. Other than that, he is completely bare.

"Bells," Juliette calls worriedly. She's cautiously moving to Ari, who has become paralyzed in place.

Ari's breathing is not calm. Her skin feels feverishly warm. She shakes her head. Rocks her body back and forth.

"Delphi, stop. I can't do this again," she begs. She scuttles to the mattress, sitting with her back against the wall, slamming her head twice before I'm able to grab a pillow and place it along the wall as a barrier.

"Ari," I shout, trying to grab her attention. It does not stop her actions. Her eyes are still screwed shut. As a solution, I drag the mattress from the stone. "Arabella," I try again, shaking her body until her eyes open. "Breathe. Delphi's not here. Open your eyes, love."

"No," she croaks, repeatedly shaking her head and whispering the word.

I'm at a loss. She cannot be easily convinced, and fighting with her if I carry her out will only make our mission more difficult. I catch her by her chin as her head slows down, holding her in my hand. "Your wrists," I say low enough for no one but her to hear. "Look down."

She blinks three times, glancing down on the third. Her face returns to a neutral state after taking deep breaths. Gulping as her eyes flit between everyone standing in the cell. For a moment, her body recoils, placing her hands around her ears.

"You shouldn't be here," she reprimands in the direction of Damien and Juli. Standing, she walks over to Kabir, who is holding Celeste in his arms. Her expression is gleaming at her friend, then turns full of concern. "Why's Celeste in your arms? Are they–"

"Poisoned," Kabir answers.

Cautiously, she looks to a bleeding Cassius, who steps closer to her. "They were hit with Starrdust."

"Then we needa get out of here," she says, her lips going tight.

It's almost another form of magik entirely to see Ari compartmentalize as rapidly as I do. Her emotions have faded, with formulating plans running through her head.

"Alas, that is not possible," Cassius says. He waits for a reaction from us but receives none. "We're trapped. We have freed you from your cell, but we cannot okkar. There are wards somewhere keeping us in."

"Did you already get Adonis?" Ari asks. Her eyes roam outside of the cell in search of him.

Those who have come for us are exchanging looks between each other. They are just as perplexed as I had been when Ari had kept me from killing the Fae.

Unwilling to explain in detail, Ari stands in her place, staring the king down directly. "He's helped me more than you'd think. We have to find him and take him with us."

"No. We have no time," Cassius states. There is a command of finality in his tone.

She crosses her arms in protest. "I haven't seen him since he was taken yesterday. He could be anywhere."

"So could Delphi," I remind her.

Juli searches around the area, possibly for any possibility of dismantling the alarm, picking up one of the metal bars that had fallen. "How'd she cast all this anyway?"

"She's become horrifyingly powerful," Ari answers, condensing what we have learned from Adonis' generous admission.

"All the more reason to leave now," Damien says.

Ignoring his comment, Ari brushes her glance past him, gazing at the others. "If we can't okkar out, it's more reason to have Adonis. He'd know what she did to this place more than us."

"Where will you go?" I ask.

For two seconds, Ari's eyes peer towards the ceiling. "Up, I guess." She kisses me vehemently. She's breathing from her nose onto my face. "Wait here, and don't die."

Instantaneously, she is taking off. I suddenly wish that I could go with her in the case a brawl plays out. Though she is capable of fending for herself, she is without power. Her brain is more than enough to keep her safely hidden, but without any magik, with months away and the things she has told me have invaded her thoughts, I worry. Moreover, my heart rushes faster when I think of Delphi's newfound magik. The horrendous things that she could do to Ari if they were alone.

Never have I been placed in a plight similar to this. But had I been, I would not have hesitated to make the necessary sacrifices to get us out. I've been brought to such a weakness that I would do anything for her, even if it means watching her risk herself for the Fae who aided in her capture.

I won't act like I comprehend why she cares so much for those who do not deserve her kindness, but I know better than to question her. I won't question her reasoning for her decision to return with the Fae.

"She is being reckless," Kabir states the moment Arbella is out of view.

"I agree with the big one, mate," Damien agrees.

"Arabella just now thought our plan to rescue her was a farce," Cassius says. "She is not thinking clearly."

"If you think she is incapable," I say, "you're an idiot and will never understand her."

Their misplaced doubt in Ari angers me, though the others may be right. Arabella *isn't* thinking clearly. But even so, I doubt any of us could have stopped her. She may not be as sharp currently, but she has never once shown an inability to fight for herself.

Juli bites her tongue, not saying anything through this argument.

Cassius lifts one eyebrow, a sleeve held to his head. "*Do you?*"

Two words. It is a question with five letters that keeps my face remaining still while sucking in my cheeks. "Not always. But I would rather burn than doubt her."

"I said nothing of doubting her," Cassius responds. He does not seem to show a lack of confidence in Ari. "I simply do not think searching through this building is worth the risk."

My friends are smiling with joy in my presence, all of us conversing as discreetly as we can to hear each other over the alarm. Damien and the rest of the Wands I have known since childhood, but after befriending Ari and Juli at Lazipeus, the two tied our group together in a much tighter sense. The two forced me to come to terms with the fact that Damien, Grayson, and Violette have always been my actual friends.

I have to keep myself contained, though it is entirely useless. Their presence is one that I have been waiting for. Kabir has handed Celeste over to Cassius while my attention was on my friends. If it had not been for that, I would have had much more than words for the king myself.

"Should we try opening the panel blocking us so that when Bells is back, we can just go?" Juli wonders after a suspicious amount of time has passed.

"No," I say. "Removing that protection leaves us vulnerable. We'll leave the gate down until we absolutely need it gone."

"So we're going to wait here for Ara like cattle for slaughter," Damien reprimands. "Are we just going to do nothing?"

"Waiting for her is *not* doing nothing," I respond harshly.

I'm sure we will escape once Ari returns. When it comes to things such as momentary plans, Arabella is incredibly resourceful. She may not consciously plot everything out in such a rush, but she has learned to act on improvisation.

Loud footsteps are approaching us from around the corner. Accompanying them are the sounds of multiple voices. We have less time now to protect ourselves.

I brush up the hair that falls to my face.

Think. I have to think of something.

"Make us unseen," I whisper to my friends. We cannot physically turn invisible, but magik can manipulate the mind into thinking the area is clear, similar to tampered security footage. "We need to stay out of their grasp if they're looking for us."

Juliette nods once. She raises her hands and projects her magik. None of us should be able to be seen, but that now raises a substitute dilemma. We all must stay silent while finding a way to move.

A Cyclops with their hair in a bun is leading four other creatures, who reach heights incomprehensible to most humans. I don't have the faintest idea what they would do if we are caught. They are under Delphi's orders. From what I can piece together, we may have to be brought to her alive.

"They are not on this floor," a grumbling voice says. It belongs to the shortest Giant with unhealed cuts. He carries an unsavory lump on his bicep, wearing hide that covers most of his body.

"Another observant comment," the Cyclops leader with raven hair chastises with sarcasm. "The iron door remains, you imbecile."

There's a pounding on the other side of the iron as the Cyclops' underlings search through each room and cell. Dents form imprints into the plate, lines cracking through the stone that locks the metal in place.

Then, I see magik act to secure the door.

"Ramina," a voice yells. She looks at the lot of us who are spread out. Visible to her. "There are more of them."

"*Juli*!" Damien scolds.

Kabir is glaring at Juli, who is blushing red, with a face apologetic.

"Fuck, sorry," she utters. "I panicked."

The Fae guard draws the shield from where it is held. He swings it, landing a few hits but ultimately causing no lasting harm to the Giant. He kicks Kabir, knocking him over and stepping on him.

When the foot lifts, Kabir is breathing. Alive with his sword next to him, he collects his last strength, willing himself to rise and puncture the Giant from the foot's most sensitive spot. The big creature groans in aggravation, plucking the sword from his foot and throwing it.

Soldiers containing the group of Ogres, Giants, and one Cyclops stomp forward, backing us into the iron panel. The leader roars with fury, pounding her fist against the stone, shaking the foundation around us. "Where is the witch?" she yells.

XVI

Run Arabella Run

Arabella

Up. Up. Up.

I'm dashing up the stairs, sparing no time to stop and catch my breath. Because I know the second that I do, I'll feel so winded that I might throw up. The rise between each step is large. Additionally more tiring since the most consistent thing I've done for exercise in a while is walk about two hundred feet from my cell to the bathroom. There are about twenty steps from the bottom of the staircase to the top, with the walls on both sides being my only support.

All of that, and the siren is screeching so loud that it sounds like metal grating against concrete. I can feel it in my teeth. I'm contracting my ears to muffle the sound. Twitching, with my head jerking to the side.

Where is he?

At the last step, I see black stars in my vision and feel fuzzy. I'm coughing from breathing so hard. I swear a lung might come out.

Weird that I have more energy with little sleep than if I were to have gotten a full night's rest. Let alone the fact I've only been eating a little more because Luka's been rationing his meals.

The large door that opens to the new floor splinters at the hinges, nearly broken, though there aren't any openings I can fit between. Its lower handle, that's closer to my height, is locked shut, with the old wood about to give. As a last resort, I collect my energy and kick it multiple times until it finally busts open from the wrong side.

This floor is just as confusing as the twisting maze that it took to get up here, lit with torches rather than electricity.

I hear the sounds of heavy footsteps approaching from the corner I can't see. The door nearest me doesn't have a handle low enough to reach, pushing me to silently hope for a miracle. By the third door, it's already slightly cracked open, giving me a temporary feeling of relief. I push the door shut as fast and quietly as I can so that those running in my direction don't detect me.

"The door's broken," a low, gruff voice from the outside nags.

"I can see that," says another growling, feminine voice, followed by the sound of wood bouncing off something and hitting the stone.

"The Magiks couldn't have gone far," the first voice utters. "Search downward firstly. We would have seen the witch if she were on the floor."

Their footsteps begin to echo far from my earshot. Air fills my lungs from a deep inhale, catching my breath from before. I peer firstly under the opening at the bottom of the door, ensuring there's no one there. Then, I take another beat, berating myself for being so weak.

Cassius was *right there*. I had the chance to kill him, and I didn't. I figured that he would be coming–I prepared myself for it–but upon seeing him, my impulses had taken over. If I had been more focused, if Luka hadn't pulled me off, maybe I could've done it. But now I have something much more important to think about.

We have to get out of here alive.

My eyes shut, and I slowly breathe one last time before leaving whatever dark room I'm in. I search around blindly for something to climb so that I can reach the handle.

Just then, something from behind me lights the room. A Giant, who looks to be just under the height of a two-story house, is staring directly at me in a state of perplexity. He's balding at the front, with sections of his head growing strands of hair sporadically spread. And though he's taller than I will ever reach without assistance, he is still under half the size of most Giants in this land.

My heartbeat speeds up, and I know I'm done for. All while I thought myself safe from those hunting me, I set up my failure. I feel so stupid for not checking the room for others.

The Giant raises his right hand, and from the way life pauses, I prepare for my death.

He doesn't hit me. I'm pushed aside, the Giant creaking open his door and twisting his head in both directions. "They're gone," he says, closing the door and looking at me.

I furrow my brows, glancing around the dimly lit room. I shouldn't trust this. "You're helping me?"

"You are looking for Adonis," he assumes.

My face is unmoving, still suspicious, but I hum in agreement anyway.

The Giant grumbles out a noise of understanding. "He's on the fifth floor. Delphi embedded a room full of iron to keep him from escaping. There are guards keeping watch beyond those who just ran down the stairs."

"*Why* are you helping me?"

"I owe him my life. If I save his, my debt is paid."

Taking time to process this confirmation, which adds to my

long list of reasons why Adonis is better than he thinks himself, I move forward to open the door.

"I will go first. If you're spotted before me, your chance of living decreases." The Giant takes the lead, his beige tarp that he wears as clothing stiff when he walks.

We make three turns before we get closer to the next set of stairs. The halls on this floor are a bit more narrow, the Giant just managing to squeeze through as he walks frontally.

At the bottom of the next staircase, there is an average-sized Ogre that has the skin of the sea and a Cyclops that looks about seven feet taller than I am.

"Ah, Zander," the Ogre greets, placing his hand on the Giant. It doesn't take much for him to lift it from his side onto Zander's shoulder. Zander barely reaches the height of the Ogre's elbow.

I hide behind him, pressing myself as close as I can to the back of his leg.

The shorter Cyclops speaks, but I can't see him anymore. "You've left your room and did not go with the others to find the escaped Magiks?"

"I've come to check on Adonis," Zander says, partially a lie.

The two creatures grunt in a humming tune. There's nothing to prove this, but I get the sneaking suspicion that they're already suspicious of Zander's motives. If he's caught, we're both doomed.

"I can assure you he has not left his holding," the Cyclops guarantees. "Why are you truly here? No lies, boy."

In the small glance I got of the Cyclops, he looks one trip to the floor away from becoming dust. I hear a blade drawn, and Zander's stance widens.

"Go!" he shouts.

Low, unsuspecting grunts of confusion come from the other two before Zander charges forward, and I'm climbing another flight of stairs to the smaller door. Sounds of blades are clanking together. I hear the breaths being knocked from each other from the fighting as I pant.

The door's locked. Because why wouldn't it be?

"It's locked," I scream, hoping Zander can hear me–or that he's still alive. When turning around, the Giant has a foot on top of the Ogre, and the Cyclops hangs on the wall in place of where a torch once was.

Zander steps to where he placed the old Cyclops, taking a ring of keys from his belt and throwing it to me. It misses my hands, landing directly at my feet, each key a size longer than my hand. "I cannot go with you. Grab Adonis and leave."

There are ten keys on here, none of which I'm sure will unlock the shorter opening of the door. I take a random guess and try the fourth one in the keyhole, but it doesn't work.

Luckily, the second key does, and I'm met with emptiness on this floor with no one guarding it. There are only three main rooms on this floor, the staircase to the next floor up being more of a direct path.

"Adonis," I shout with the blind confidence that these rooms aren't soundproof. I take slow steps, careful not to make a mistake of setting off a trap. Saying his name aloud again, I can only raise my voice with every reprise.

It's when I hear one loud sound against a door down the hall that I'm able to locate where he is. I rush over, using the first key to unlock it, and there he is. He's about two steps away from where the door was closed, and I can only assume that he backed away when he heard me unlocking the iron.

"Arabella, what happened?" he questions while I try other keys on the hoop to remove his chains from him.

At least one of us will be able to use our powers.

"They came for us. We have to get out of here. Come on," I blurt in panic. We have to leave if there's any chance of Celeste's survival. We have less than two hours before the poison takes its full effect.

We step out of the room, but instead of following me down the stairs, he glances towards the staircase leading to the last floor. The keys are snatched from my hands, and without a single word, up the stairs he goes.

I run fast. Following up to grab him, but he's much swifter than I am.

"What are you doing?" I hiss. "Celeste got hit with Starrdust. We gotta get out of here."

Adonis doesn't pay attention to what I say. He slows his steps a bit at the mention of his sister's name, but it doesn't stop him from reaching the top of the stairs. "I need to grab books. Delphi leaves this floor unlocked because none have access to it but us."

"Is that really important right now?" I scold. I'm so irritated. We're wasting time, and he focuses on books that can easily be replaced.

"They could be the ones that she used to resurrect Luka. It's how she's become so powerful," he answers. The door remains slightly ajar, and he peeks his head outside one last time. He wears the unnerving face of his father, demanding that I return to the third floor. "With what's been done, I know it's hard to trust me, but you'll need them. The key to free you and Luka is in here as well."

"Do you need me to help you? In case Delphi catches you." My voice echoes off the walls.

"Delphi doesn't reside in Gigantia. She would keep me here to watch over you. When Luka came, she would leave at night to an undisclosed location that even I do not know."

At the end of his last sentence, he dashes back into the room, and I can hear the rustling of papers and objects being thrown around the room. Though I can't see what he's doing, I can tell that what he's searching for is not in the places he thought they would be.

"Will you meet us back on the third floor?"

By now, I should've already left. I hate how I didn't make an immediate choice to help search for the books or go back down the stairs. No. I'm waiting at the bottom of the steps for Adonis, completely out of my depth in a situation I have no clue how to navigate.

"What are you still doing here?" he scolds, irritation evident in his tone. "Go down!"

I'm sprinting, and out of breath, and partially grateful for the fact that going down stairs is much easier than going up them. At the bottom of my first set of stairs, Zander is gone.

The Ogre is still on the ground, but I can see from how his body moves, he's still alive, simply unconscious. The Cyclops too is still hung on the rotting wall, showing little signs of death.

I brush any feelings of guilt for leaving them aside and reverse my steps to get to the last staircase down to my friends. While I'm descending, there is a rumble of someone's voice alongside the clang of metal hitting the wall so loudly, I flinch in place.

There's no way of telling how many creatures, both from Gigantia and other Creaturelands, that Delphi has taken under her control. I have no clue how many are down there surrounding my friends that I left. Never mind that since the iron gate on the other side of them can easily be broken, creatures from the lower floors can attack from behind.

Weaponless, I sprint halfway back up the stairs to the fourth floor to search for anything I could use. Chains, an iron bar, or even a wooden torch would be more useful than nothing.

Inside Zander's room, after ransacking through thrown items and a mountain of cloth pieces, each over two times longer than my bed sheets, I find a long, bent metal torch that I doubt is sterile. It's probably broken. It looks similar to a crowbar with sharp edges, but in this case, that might be an advantage.

I have to be careful when I wield this weapon. I've been out of training for a while, and I definitely don't have the calculated precision that Kabir tried to instill in me right now.

When I get through different turns on the third floor, I see my friends cornered and huddled with backs pressed against the door. There are five creatures, most with heads a few feet short of touching the ceiling.

For a split second, Juju's eyes flicker to me. I shake my head, moving my flat hand back and forth, close to my neck, begging her not to give away my position.

It's too late. The rest of the group looks in the direction that Juju is, and their eyes all light up. My bottom lip curls into my mouth, letting out a defeated sigh from my nose.

"Fuck," I breathe. There goes the element of surprise.

My feet are moving me faster than my sight can process. My arms are raised, lifting the tool. I slash the metal in every direction, just hoping it'll land in a critical place while dodging from their huge hands that reach for me. It's not so heavy that I can't swing it around, but the heavyweight on top makes it more difficult to be precise in my swings. I move between their legs, from under them, desperately wishing I wasn't barefoot so I could use the heels of my shoes to damage them in some way.

The first one I strike is an Ogre with hair like a mane. I can't climb him, so I run from over his foot and stab the metal into the back of his leg. The claws from it are so sharp that when I whack it into his skin, it digs deep enough to break flesh. I drag the weapon down, creating an open gash through the back of his leg.

He goes down in pain. I'm panicking. Trying to yank the weapon from his skin while two are coming together and piling on me. From what I can only guess, the other two are still crowding my friends.

By some stroke of good luck, I'm able to escape the pile of creatures that weigh heavy on me with the torch.

As I'm about to strike a head, a hand reaches to stop me. It picks me up by my arm, and I can feel my ligaments tearing from the gravity of being held by that limb. It's the same as dangling a gummy worm between your thumb and index finger.

Yelps of pleading crawl from my throat before I have the chance to think of what I'm screaming for.

"Stop," a voice commands as I fight against the hand. It's Zander in armor of metal. He places me on his shoulder, patting the fabric that sits comfortably on his skin to hold on. Then, he is moving, tackling the other creatures and knocking them out.

There's a Cyclops woman a bit taller than Zander, her hair the color of the darkest blueberries and tied into a high bun. She holds a polearm pointed at the two of us. Her face is pissed, livid with the treacherous action against her. "You would kill me, brother?"

Zander laughs. "After you left me to die by Delphi's punishment? Without hesitation."

"Then you wish to wage war."

There is a long pause, a merciful opportunity for her brother to surrender before she makes her first strike.

While the two are distracted with each other, I catch Damien's brown eyes. I'm praying he understands what I'm trying to silently communicate as he nods in agreement.

I wait patiently while the two nearest me are bickering, seeking an opening. The Ogre and Giants that once laid on me are now up again, standing in flank behind Zander's sister. Their swords are raised, preparing for her signal to attack.

"You allowed for bloodshed at the hands of the witch," Zander berates.

His sister scoffs, letting out a cackle that sounds as stereotypical as what humans expect a witch to sound like. "I seek to be the general of our quadrant's army. If I can secure an alliance with Delphi and regain the trust of our minister, I can protect our people. And I will stop at nothing."

"You do this for your call to violence, Ramina."

"Believe whatever truth fits for you," she returns, taking one step closer to the two of us.

"Fuck!" Luka shouts. He's been cut. There's blood soaking his shirt with an opening to suggest exactly where.

The Giant with apricot hair, which stops at her shoulders, chuckles. Blood stains her crescent-shaped siphon.

Luka's blood.

There's a look on Kabir's face. He ducks under a creature and grabs his sword. He's stabbing it into areas vulnerable to the creatures approaching him, but his combat skill alone is a difficult match for the size of the others.

Juliette and Damien are weaponless. Her hands point at the door, but Damien hasn't used his magik to transform anything into a defense.

Out of the corner of my eye, I see it. A shadow that crawls along the walls in a motion similar to oil on water.

It moves too slow for it to be my eyes mistaking me, but faster than a normal play of light would.

"Damien!" I shout.

He elbows Juli, and both of their hands raise, knocking down the huge creatures to the ground. The echo of their bodies falling hits the air before I view them on the floor.

Ramina and her soldiers turn around at the commotion, an opening for Zander to bring his sister down. He uses the torch that he took from my hand to whip across her head. While the torch measures up to my chest, Zander carries it like it's the size of a stick.

The Cyclops tumbles, her body falling.

The floor is a mess of bloody stone.

Zander lets me down from his shoulder, putting me next to those I know. "He's helping us too," I tell them, the clenching of their bodies instantly relaxing. My glance goes to my two Magik friends. "They're dead, right?"

Damien and Juju shake their heads.

I don't understand why they wouldn't kill the creatures, but maybe not everyone looks to death as a solution. I keep those thoughts to myself, though my facial expressions may have given it away because Adonis appears in my line of view, fully solid and snorting.

"They can't kill those from Gigantia," he informs. The room's energy turns hostile, both of my friends raising their hands in Adonis' direction and Cassius' nostrils flaring.

Kabir raises his sword, angling the tip towards Adonis, and I hear Zander from behind me, heavily huffing in disdain. He is too focused on the debt he owes Adonis rather than the bodies of his peers regaining consciousness. Is quick to take notice of my friends taking cuffs from their sides, readying an arrest.

Not enough distance is between Adonis and the blade.

"I told you," I say to everyone in the room, glaring at Kabir and tugging Adonis by the brown satchel around his shoulder, *"we need him."*

I scan everyone's reactions, but no one objects. Banging sounds from the vibration of iron being rammed into shakes the walls. Kabir lowers his blade to his side but keeps from sheathing it back to where it previously was. My friends also lower their arms while Luka stands beside them, still distrustful of the Fae.

Cassius, on the other hand, raises a brow, questioning my decision, with his sister in his arms. He's smiling as if he's happy to see me.

And then the stinging lump in my throat is back.

I want to take the siphon and stick it through his chest.

"Hands," Adonis' voice calls out. It takes him knocking the back of my palm for me to realize that he's talking to me. He has his arm extended, with his hand holding the key that will free me from the cuffs. For him, I don't move fast enough, the Fae impatiently grabbing my wrist to unlock the cuffs.

Metal crashes to the ground, and Adonis pushes himself through everyone to get to Luka.

"Why can't we kill the creatures from this land?" I ask, what Adonis said earlier just now registering.

"It would wage war against Gigantia and Ifaeris, breaking our treaty," Zander answers. I hear Luka's cuffs fall to the floor as I turn to the Giant for clarification. "Their presence here nearly breaks it."

My head twists back to Cassius, who nods his head.

"How do we get out?" Damien asks. "We tried to okkar out, but we couldn't."

"Delphi warded the building," Adonis says. He doesn't try to use his powers to escape for himself. "She created them in the case that someone would try to break you free." His eyes are on me.

"Us using magik on the cell bars must've been what alerted her," Juju adds.

There's something turning in my stomach. Too long has passed without Delphi making an appearance. If she's been alerted, why didn't she immediately come to us?

The iron panel is barely standing. It looks like it's on the verge of breaking down, indisputably due to those from below battering their way in. I'm thankful to whoever decided to keep the door shut, holding an advantage from being attacked from one side.

"The only way out now is through the front, but that is only accessible after fighting through those below us," Adonis confirms. "She's now the only one who can okkar in and out of the building."

We only have one way of escaping. I don't know how much more my feet can take against the terrain of the stone. Not to mention the other debris on it that looms.

Suddenly, the attempts at busting the door down stop, and there's distrustful silence coming from both sides. Quiet enough that I can hear heaving breaths.

"Get behind me," Zander demands. We abide, gathering ourselves in a group behind his right foot. "You will blow the door apart in their direction. Stay behind me until my fate is sealed."

"You're sacrificing yourself for us?" Luka asks.

"If Delphi is here…" Zander hesitates, swallowing hard. "If she is the one to kill me, that breaches the treaty between Gigantia and the Magiks. Should there be war, my people will stand behind any against the Magiks."

And I understand exactly what he means. Gigantia would fight alongside Ifaeris. We would be potential allies. I only hope it doesn't come to that.

With the power of four Magiks, we raise our hands, pulling them back towards our torsos before pushing the air forward and magiking the solid gate to topple from its placement. Part of the wall follows with it, startling back a handful of creatures to another panel of stone.

Zander charges forward with us right behind him, the Magiks in our group using sleep magik on the creatures he does not knock out. I see creatures that I've never seen before today as we breeze past their unconscious bodies. One is a Fae, just around Cassius' height, with a tail that points like an arrow at the end. Her skin is scaled with sunset along the sides of her cheeks. Another body we pass belongs to a Troll who is under Zander's size.

More intricate details are hard to take in as we run. Everything appears and leaves my sight too quickly as we bolt through the second floor.

They outnumber us. Despite having magik accessible and using it to hex others, the nine of us are no match. Especially not with one of us unconscious in another's arms.

"You won't escape." The voice rings as we get to the next staircase. I recognize the arrogant tone, the lift at the end of the sentence, the smile I can hear in the voice. "You can escape here, but you'll only protect Ifaeris for so long."

On the floor below, I can see Delphi standing, her magik more visible as she controls the other creatures to remain still. Rather than the usual color of silvery-white that lingers after magik, hers is that of a darker ladybug.

With the twist of her wrist, Zander falls down to the floor below at her feet. I hear multiple gasps leave the other creatures in front of us as his blood paints the stone. One escapes me as well, but I don't have the luxury to mourn.

Damien's pushing us back up the stairs, using magik on as many of the closest creatures as he can while they're still distracted. Once at the top step, Luka magiks the weapons of the unconscious to work as a barrier.

"Back stairs," Adonis yells. He leads us back to the third floor, past numerous turns until he opens a hidden passage in the wall, making me wonder why we didn't take this way in the first place.

As a precaution, Damien magiks the door unopenable once it closes to hold off all who follow us for as long as possible.

It's pitch black in this area. There aren't windows or lights to show where I'm going.

Similar to a child forgetting something right in front of them, at hearing my friends whisper to summon fire, I remember again that I'm free. I can use my powers.

I try focusing on my magik circulating, but it's been so long. I'm having difficulty using it. The most I'm able to get are flickers of flames coming from my fingertips, my hand a candelabra, lighting the smallest few feet ahead of me.

This secret staircase is a claustrophobic person's nightmare. I'm suddenly worried for Juliette, who clutches Luka's arm so tightly I wonder if it will pop like a balloon.

I hear the scurrying of animals near my feet while we descend the staircase, though I don't dare look and freak myself out. We're going as fast as we can, keeping one hand on the wall for balance.

The long trek down is frightening. Possibilities of death from every side block my mind until we reach the first floor, and Adonis cracks open a door. We're in a kitchen area, stuffing ourselves inside a cabinet, when we hear a large creature stomping near us.

"They came down the back, not okkared out, you ninny," Delphi's voice scolds. "No one touches Arabella when you find her. *That's my kill.*"

"Lady Delphi, we've searched but cannot find them. Perhaps you could track them," another feminine voice urges.

"I suggest you keep from ordering me. Do you want to have a reunion with that Giant?" Delphi cautions as a caveat. Their voices go quiet, but their footsteps were never heard. And suddenly, the thick wood that hides us rips from where it once was. We're exposed.

Damien pushes his hand once, magik knocking Delphi against the sink's cabinet. We each jump the small two feet onto the floor, out of reach from an Ogre. I don't know where we're going, but I'm trusting that Adonis is leading us towards the exit.

Grant appears just ahead in the same direction we're going. I think I'm going to vomit when pushing him aside and feeling his hand on mine during the brief period that our skin holds contact.

Delphi is casting hexes in our direction, a few other creatures behind us rampaging. It doesn't matter how fast we run. We all have to get back to Ifaeris as a whole. Together, we're easier targets.

When we get to the main entrance area, the door is locked. Juju and Luka are magiking a wall from the stones of the floor, while Cassius hands Celeste to Kabir and allows for his wings to come from his clothing after dropping his cloak. He hisses out in pain at the touch of his hand reaching the knob of the door. Either iron or some sort of poison.

On top of the main door, there's a sigil, which I can barely see, but it must be what's keeping us here, based on its location. I send magik blasting towards the symbol, my friends and Luka following suit, turning the stone above the wood into rubble and splintering the door itself.

As we rush out, I notice Luka's absence. He's not in front of me or at my side.

The others are already well past the door, nearing the edge of the land. And as I turn back, the magiked wall has been destroyed, and I see my boyfriend lodging Kabir's sword into my ex-boyfriend. Luka drags the weapon out from Grant's side, blood flowing with the blade.

I'm unable to move from shock. Grant had no powers. He couldn't hex us in any way.

"I told you what I would do to him if I ever saw him, love," Luka says as he takes my arm, running with my hand in his towards the group. It's pouring hail, and as we go, I nearly slip on a patch of mud.

When joining hands with the group, I hear Delphi yelling in the background. I shield us, but something from her magik comes through. It knocks Juju to the ground, and as she screams next to me, I realize that she's lost the cloak that may have protected her. Her shirt is torn, a hole visible from her mid-back. She's also bleeding from the front. The hex had driven straight through her.

I put pressure on both sides of her, using my magik to temporarily close the wound until we can get a healer.

Juliette is hyperventilating. I don't think she realizes tears are rushing down her face. Damien and Luka are trying to support her while also joining themselves with the Fae.

Once all our bodies are connected in some way, we okkar back to Nexus. We're in the throne room, but I don't remember aiming for a specific place.

Cassius flops onto the throne that's no longer the scarlet that it once was. In fact, the whole room has changed. All the reds that once decorated the room have changed to black. Instead of two thrones, there's one.

Gavin and three other guards I've barely spoken to are standing at the door with mouths agape.

"Celeste was hit with Starrdust and Juliette got hit with a hex. Get them to a healer," I command them. They take too long. Staring at my friends, who look death-ridden and unable to carry themselves. "Now!"

The guards rush over, carrying the two out of the room to the servants' quarters, where the healers set up their practice.

Slick droplets of rain drip from my oily hair onto the pristine marble below me. I look back to Cassius, who is still draped along the throne, his body sinking to the cushion. My eyes widen at the realization.

He okkared all of us back to Nexus on his energy alone.

Okkaring a long distance can be tiresome on its own if the group isn't able to visualize the destination, but to okkar this many back to Nexus without the shared power of everyone else could send him into a coma for over a day.

Kabir's face softens as he walks to me. He's staring at me with disbelieving eyes. If I were less delusional, I'd think he's smiling. When approaching, he wraps his arms around me and squeezes my tense body. "You're alive, Creature."

"Sorry to break it to you, Curly," I tease. His hold is tight, and uncomfortable, and weird. This might be the first time we've ever hugged.

When he unlatches from me, he puts his hand on my shoulder, patting it harshly to the point I bend my knees a bit from the impact, wincing a bit. His brows raise, blinking deeply and letting out a single chuckle.

Luka joins me, standing at my side and glancing down with a nod, stopping himself before linking his arm in mine. I'm unable to handle the romantic touch at this moment. I need time to readjust. A few minutes at least. It also doesn't help that our drenched clothing sticks to my skin in a way that makes me want to jump out of my body. Yet his nod makes something in my heart flutter. He loves me the way I need without me having to explain how.

"Arabella," Cassius' voice calls out. He sounds like he's pleading for something.

My body turns to see him sitting on his throne with a posture so straight that I nearly don't recognize it outside of how he presents himself to the other Elemental rulers. I can see the sticky blood half-dried and clotting around the gash where the metal cuffs had impacted his temple.

His face is hard for me to make out. He looks at me so intensely that I'm nauseous again. My heart is pounding, but all he's done is utter my name while beckoning me up to his side.

"Did you forget your role in this kingdom?" he asks simply.

I don't understand anything he's saying. There are a million answers to what he says, but none of them are plausible, so I keep my lips from saying something that could embarrass me.

The king takes my silence for a game. I'm stiffened with my feet planted, and I can feel Luka's presence so close to mine that I'm overwhelmed. This whole room is overwhelming me. If I don't leave soon, I fear for how I will react.

"Come," Cassius commands. He thinks I'm weak enough to do whatever he asks.

My body reacts oppositely to what he says. "I need a shower. I haven't washed in days, and I feel gross. We can gather everyone after."

Luka takes my hand, okkaring us both to the queen's bathroom, where I immediately strip from my clothes, throwing them into the metal bin and using my magik to incinerate them.

As the shower heats, I wash my hands, lacking the energy to speak as Luka throws his clothing into the bin, allowing the physical proof from Gigantia to burn.

Part 3
Coping

XVII

The Queen's Back

Arabella

It's strange. The feeling of smooth flooring is unfamiliar to my wet feet. For the first time in a long while, there's a soft touch of steady flooring against the calluses written beneath me.

My feet probably look gross right now.

The shower, though. That had consumed me in warmth that enveloped my skin. Now that I'm clean, I can finally breathe without constrictions from everything.

Luka's already changed from the towel. He's freshly shaven, wearing a black-and-white, windowpane-style blazer with slacks. Under the jacket is a plain black shirt that has a mock turtleneck. Unlike how my style shares some similarities to clothing worn by the Fae, his is completely different.

I rummage through the extra armoire, eventually settling on suede pants and a white shirt that has airy sleeves cuffing just below my elbows. Other than my necklace from Luka and the ring that coordinates with his, I don't bother with jewelry. It feels slightly better to be out of the dreary clothing I wore before and in ones I recognize as mine.

Both Luka and I leave the bedroom, descending the singular staircase to the second floor and farther down one of the curving staircases to reach the first.

Only Luka, Cassius, and I are sitting in the council room as we wait for the others. I feel uneasy, my eyes continuously alternating from the door to Cassius, who is intensely staring at me with the demeanor of someone furious.

His face has been bandaged by the healers.

I still don't think I can handle another person touching me. I'm pretty sure if anyone tried, I'd have a panic attack and fall to the floor. But when I look up and see Xavier emerging through the doors, I smile so hard that I'm running to him.

"Oh, I know," he says with a light, mocking tone. "I would have missed me too." His brows cross, scanning my body up and down. "You look terrible."

"Least I don't smell like shit," I respond. My gaze shifts to the left. "Anymore, I guess."

After I speak, I notice another presence beside him. A feminine Fae that I recognize is in a skintight dress, which finishes a hand's length below her knee. It patterns with medium-sized maple leaves, all spread along the black fabric.

The Fae has looser, corkscrew curls I doubt I could forget if I tried, and she's smiling at me sheepishly like I don't recognize her. With her hair clipped back, a few strands fall like bangs to shape the sides of her face.

What's she doing here?

My reaction is involuntary, but I can feel my face twitch into something that my friends always describe as judgy, though in my head, I'm just curious.

"Oh, I know you. Hi Iris," I greet with a smile.

"Hello, Arabella," she replies back. There's no makeup on her round eyes, but with lashes so voluminous, I would think she's wearing some. Even her lighter, olive skin tone, similar to Celeste's, radiates exquisitely from the sun.

Immediately, my attention goes back to my friend, who hasn't said anything. I'm agog, shaking my head at him, trying to unspokenly ask about her presence through eye contact.

Xavier holds her hand in his. He's smiling brightly, fixated on her and forcing me to loudly sigh and lightly stomp on his foot.

"*Ow!*" he yelps. I repeat my actions of staring at him, this time cocking my head towards Iris. "Oh, yeah. Iris and I are together now."

"Always full of surprises," I say with the lift of my brows.

"Like getting sick with a virus."

Disbelief parts my lips, my head flopping forward with an exhaled breath of amusement. I'm happy for him. Confused, but happy. "So in the time I was gone, instead of worrying about where I was, you found a way to get yourself a girlfriend?"

"Are you not happy for me, Reaps?" Xavier teases with a playful kick to the side of my leg.

With a humming sound of question, I look at my friend, my brows knitted. "Reaps?"

"Y'know, like what mortals call Grim Reaper. Since you keep almost dying."

The point of my shoe goes to his shin, causing him to bend to my height. While he does, my fingers go to his forehead, flicking it. "I hate you."

"Come on, don't be mad. You know very well that I'm right." He laughs harder, the peachy shade of his skin brightening.

I have half a mind to kick him again.

"Where's Monty and everyone?" I say instead.

"Right behind him," Monty announces, pushing past his

brother and slightly dropping his face towards me. "And spirits, was it great to witness all of that."

Iris snorts in response, saying her goodbye to Xavier. As she raises her arms to hug him, the thin straps from the side of her upper arms come up, the semi-sweetheart neckline rising too. He softly kisses her cheek before sending her off and sitting beside his brother at the table.

Then files in Dyana and most of the rest of the Disaris family. Each of them pass me, eyes astonished that I'm actually here.

After the Fae all enter, there's a group following them. People I should have expected after seeing Juju and Damien, but shocking me nonetheless.

My friends. All my closest friends from the Magikal world. All but Juju, who must still be with the healers.

From behind me, Luka wraps his arm around my waist, settling his body directly against my back. We're both pulled into a hug, and I can feel the energy of each of my friends. I can't bother to be upset with the touch. I'm in such a bewildered state of disbelief from them being in the same room as the Fae.

They also might be the only people in the world whose touch I can handle at almost any time.

"Arabella, Luka, we have matters that need discussing," Cassius interrupts, breaking our focus from each other.

My friends are pulling apart and exiting. I've seen them for less than a minute, and they're already leaving.

"What are you doing? Where are you going?" I ask.

Gray turns and stops in his place. "You have to talk to the Fae, and they have to secure the borders before they leave. We only came to make sure you were okay."

"Do you have to go?" I rush out. None of them say anything. "Am?"

Amber steps in front of our friends, standing less than two

steps from me. She keeps glancing out towards the flowers like she's waiting for her grandma to come in with a bouquet and give it to her. "Ara, we have lives and jobs. We can't stay in Ifaeris."

Maybe it's the selfishness in me, but I thought I'd have more time with them. I thought I'd get more than this.

A few accepting blinks from me later, Evie moves to Am's side. "We can't just upend our lives, Bella," Evie says. "If I could drop everything and *not* have to deal with a shitty job, debt, and someone accusing me of trying to curse her, I would. But I'm not exactly High Queen of the Fae. And besides, it's not like we won't still be here."

"Am just said–"

"We can't all leave at once," Vi interrupts. She turns at a sound, and we both notice Gray's absence. He's so ungraceful as he moves that, though he can't be seen by either of us, I can hear him bumping into things while he makes his way to the servants' quarters. "Some of us will stay and keep the protection strong."

"No," I reject. "You're not fucking putting yourselves at risk like that."

Damien is at her side. All the grime and blood that was once on him has been washed away. His arm is wrapped around Violette's shoulder, holding her close. "You can tell your boyfriends what to do all you want, but we all agreed to stay here in shifts."

"At least until Delphi's gone," Reyna says before I can deny Damien's words. All our mutual friends begin exiting the palace, but she hasn't left her place. She looks past me, glancing up at Luka. "We're glad you're back."

My whole head turns to him, and as his head tilts the smallest of degrees to the side, my breath exhales into laughter. She almost never says anything nice to him. He must be just as surprised as I am, because his face changes from a neutral state into slight amusement.

"Don't get used to it," she snaps quickly. "I've gotta go. Have a shift at the Cove. But my room's on the second floor if you need me."

Luka clasps our hands together after Reyna okkars away, and I'm thankful for its warmth.

Kabir shuts the door from the outside, leaving me and Luka with the Fae. They're not arguing with each other, which I half expected after everything Luka's told me. Instead, they're sitting quietly, staring at me like a stray they took in.

Cassius sits at the head of the table, with me to his left and Luka to mine.

"Is Celeste okay?" I ask openly. A way to steer the conversation away from me. Though these are the Fae I've spent months living with, my actions are akin to the mannerisms I have around new people I meet.

"They are constrained to bedrest until tomorrow's end, but they'll be fine," Atticus responds.

I nod furiously. My thumb is scraping through the nails of the other fingers on the opposite hand as a way to combat my thoughts.

"What are we going to do about Delphi?" Monty questions.

During my shower, I pondered that. While the water ran hot down my skin, I decided that I would stay in Ifaeris.

While I do *want* to leave, it's imperative that I stay until either Delphi's dead or she receives something that works in the same punishment. I can't let her roam free while it risks undoing whatever magik she's used to bring Luka back.

Alongside that, now that I know we've warded the lands, it offers extra protection for the time being. It'll keep the Fae safe, give me time to heal, and it offers strength in numbers if Delphi does plan on attacking.

"That decision is Arabella's to make," Cassius answers, motioning his hand towards me.

"She just returned," Esme scolds, irritability held back. Almost as if she's keeping herself from throwing him a look of challenge.

She's gotten an eyebrow piercing since I last saw her.

And when I look at everyone around me, they all keep in their silence. I can't tell if it's from being afraid or some respect they now have for him as king.

"What matters at this moment is that Arabella is safe. But her return does not negate Cassius from his duties," Helena reminds the table. The responsibilities that I helped with before I was taken.

I don't know if the family knows that I'm queen. That now, Cassius and I *both* carry the responsibility of keeping the Fae safe.

"Before any of you begin to throw questions at the two of us," Luka says while turning to Cassius, "how did you find us?"

That's something I've been thinking about too. While we were running for our lives, looking for an escape, I didn't remember to ask that question. I was too pressured by the time sensitivity we were under.

When I glance down, my legs are restless, and I'm waiting impatiently for Cassius to say something.

"On the day I was to meet with Delphi for our exchange, I slipped the earrings that directly track a location into Luka's pocket," Cassius details proudly.

My lips clamp into a thin line. The vision that Delphi had shown me was true. He sees me as nothing more than an irritation that he regrets putting in power. And although I know my anger is about Luka, trickles of bitterness still flow through my body on my own behalf.

Luka's hand is clenched on his lap. He rolls his eyes and exhales heavily enough that I put my hand over his. "And you arranged that how?"

Xavier's head pops from down the table with his index finger stuck out. "We told him that was a bad idea."

"They said it many times," Cassius laughs next to me. He moves his body to angle diagonally, with his palm cupping the glass he drinks from.

"He said he would find a way to locate Ara if he had the common fae returned first and sent Luka to her," Maude adds.

Dyana's mouth parts with a dropped jaw. Her head bends forward, finally piecing together what happened. "He didn't tell you?" she asks, directing her question specifically to Luka.

"No," Luka responds sharply.

Cassius' mouth is twisted in a smirk. He finds this entertaining. As if all of this is a minor setback that will be resolved no later than tomorrow. "This exchange is more dramatic than I had thought it would be."

"You abandoned her," Luka berates before Cassius can speak further. "The two of us saw Delphi hex Arabella for walking to us. She had to spend her birthday tortured by Delphi."

The room is stunned into nothingness. The whole of the Fae family hasn't spoken up to defend Cassius. Too floored by the reveal itself.

Cassius glances at me while I have said nothing through this. I don't exactly know what to think.

I wish I didn't have to.

"You must believe I wanted you here with me," he says.

I cannot stand him. I knew it was a trick, yet I still hate the confirmation. And I hate that no matter how angry I still am with him, no matter how much he's betrayed me and broken my trust, I still find myself attracted to him. It's so humiliating that I want to scream until my throat burns from numbness.

"Why should I? You tricked me and sent me back to Delphi. That isn't exactly telling me that you wanted me here."

"How else would I have the missing common fae returned with

you alongside them?" he counters. "You know that we Fae are ones whom you should consider cautiously when striking deals."

He actually managed to get us away from Delphi.

Cassius used psychological manipulation against her, but he didn't think well enough to account for others he'd hurt in the process. He didn't think about the power I have as queen and, therefore, the ability to give Delphi what she wanted if I broke.

"You could have left Luka out of it!" I scold. It feels like I'm arguing with a brick wall, with me raising my voice while Cassius sits in his chair. The only indication of his anger is through his downturned lips.

"It was the only way to locate you," he returns. A certain look still lingers on his face, and I wonder what he must be thinking.

Luka stands from his seat. The chair shoots back from the impact of his rising. There's a feeling of rage that I can feel both from knowing him and the tension he's causing in the room. If only Celeste were here to stabilize emotions, including mine.

Tension tightens my boyfriend's jaw, fists clenching to the color of white. "I suppose your failure to inform me was an oversight then."

"It was of the utmost importance that your reactions be just as genuine for Delphi to believe the trade was true," Cassius says. Not a lie, making it worse than what one could be. "With her magik, she could easily look into your mind and see the truth."

I see Luka staying in place. He's thinking at such a fast pace that I can't keep up. Debating between assaulting the king or not. His eyes are narrowed, his decision made.

From the corner of the shadows, Adonis appears and hands me my phone, long unheld by me. I don't put it past him to have been here the whole time. And even if I'm on decent terms with him, that doesn't mean the rest of the Fae in this room want to be. Neither, I think, would my friends.

"Are we not going to lock him up again?" Dyana voices, her tone fuming.

"It's not too late to kill him," Monty suggests.

"For the last time, *no one is killing Adonis*!" I shout over others in the room, who are yelling over each other about what to do with the Fae. I take the books from the satchel still hung around Adonis' side. "Here's what's gonna happen: I'll go through these and study them to learn the things that Delphi has. I'll note anything I can and teach things to myself in case she tries to break through the wards. And Adonis will stay in Nexus under my permission as the High Queen's guest. He's here to help us."

At the end of my rant, I turn around towards the door. In the queen's chamber, I throw the texts onto a desk. The edges are foxing. Aged and bronzed from its time spent under the sun. Conditions I'm sure weren't there prior to Delphi's care.

The practiced silence I have disciplined myself into a routine of has fallen off course. There has to be some way to block out all these thoughts. Some way to keep me from going insane.

XVIII

Lonely Rulership

Cassius

Everyone in the room is staring at me. Their faces are riddled with emotions ranging from shock at the information to anger at my own doing. All but the sorcerer, who was in the room when the queen had been crowned. Kabir himself is standing at the doorway, which still peeks open.

She knew. I did everything I could to ensure no mistake would be made, yet it still happened.

Adonis, our apparent newest addition to Nexus, does not appear bewildered. He stands awkwardly in place. As if he is waiting for a place among the High Court.

I would have all my jewelry stripped from my chamber rather than grant him this.

"Cassius," Maude utters, a pause after my name, "you didn't tell us that you made Arabella queen."

"Does that matter?" I respond.

Xavier stands from his chair. He takes determined steps towards me, kiwi eyes glaring through his movements, and I think that he may hit me with the force that Arabella had intended in Gigantia. "Of course it fucking matters."

The door from behind him shuts loudly, drawing our attention. Kabir clears his throat, reminding Xavier just who he is speaking to, though I do not think my cousin much cares. In fact, the guard may just be doing his sworn duty, as he too jerks his head to face me with widened eyes and a face seething.

For over a year, after my mother was murdered and I was given a bedchamber within the palace, my family would often regard me with fear or aggravation. A palace full of servants, my father's court, and my kin, but I was a sole heir forced into isolation whom none wished to deal with. Save an artist who painted many portraits of my family and Gavin, who, to the bafflement of myself, did not often mind guarding me, despite the horrors I had done unto his face.

Though much has changed since then, I am undoubtedly sure such regard for me is resurfacing. But I am the furthest thing from a hero in anyone's story. My choices are too full of selfishness and that of an unkind nature.

"You hadn't just endangered our friend by not informing Luka of your plan. You endangered our queen!" Xavier shouts.

"Xay, calm down," his twin cautions.

Xavier's eyes dart to the side, not that he is able to see his brother. He huffs out, looking at me once more before reluctantly returning to his seat.

During this, Luka has again taken his seat, with Adonis having taken Arabella's.

"Well, she's alive and here, so there is no point in being upset with what's been done," I say. It is something Arabella would say. Reminding others that there is no way to change what has already occurred, to which she makes excellent points.

This may be something I must tell myself in order to persevere through the remaining duration of the meeting. Their anger is merited, and in truth, I ought to receive the scathing lashings of those in the room, but their opinions needn't be said when the obviousness had been made clear upon my telling of the scheme.

"You don't get to push past the fact you made her queen without our knowledge. Discounting already that you left her with Delphi in exchange for the common fae," Dyana argues.

"I enacted a plan that Arabella would have devised herself. Had any of you known and mistakenly spread word of her queenship, the common fae and Elementals would have revolted. Many in this room once made a mockery of my ruling and said that Arabella's being here would aid in decisions made for the Fae." My eyes wander to my mother and siblings, who are the very ones that made such a comment. "How is making her my queen much different than the position you suggested?"

Helena, from the middle of the table, crosses her arms. She takes a calm inhale, the same way she would when my siblings would argue in our youth. She is not often in attendance during court meetings, but she offers great counsel as a previous ruler when she is. As if attempting to make amends for all the decisions made by my father while they were married. "With Delphi now aware you have invaded her station in Gigantia, what do you propose we do going forward, Your Majesty?"

"We could–" Adonis attempts.

He is immediately silenced by Esme. "You can't allow him to offer his opinions," she says in my direction. "Not after everything he did to Arabella. To the Fae? *Our family*?"

"There is no doubt that he is our father's son," Atticus laughs. "He speaks where his opinions are not welcome. Offering up ideas that will harm more than help."

"I don't suppose that she would have taken Luka's pants as she fled to a new hideout," Maude says, redirecting us to the importance of my court gathering. "With no way to track her, how will the Fae be protected?"

"That's why we will have Magiks alternating through shifts to keep the protection of wards intact," I reply. It is the only answer I'm able to offer without admitting my ignorance. That I am unable to find a way to keep the lands safe. Our only method is dependent on staying alert on the edges of Ifaeris. To charm rulers of other courts and areas across the Creaturelands, asking them to side with us against Delphi if it so comes to that. Mostly, to hope the rulers of Magiks will take action against what their own is doing before it is too late.

"Can we take no firmer action?" Monty asks.

"Arabella is currently in her room learning ways to combat Delphi's power," I say.

Esme's glare that she sends to me is scalding. She wishes to burn me with an ability she does not carry. "What does learning about Delphi's new powers do when she still has the Stone of Elestial? Even with multiple of the Magiks here, how do we know if their abilities fare against Delphi's?"

"Delphi no longer has the one whom the common fae believed to lead their revolution, thus taking away many of her followers," I answer.

"A Fae we still can't trust," Monty reminds.

I agree with my cousin's comment. Though the eldest Disaris is free to remain in Nexus, I have every reason to assume his disloyalty. I cannot place trust in the Fae who had been so willing to murder for the crown.

Our father deserved such a fate, and perhaps so did the other Elementals, but I cannot shake the uneasiness that comes with Adonis' presence. I cannot help the resentment I hold due to his plans wreaking so much chaos.

From the side of my eye, I see Adonis tense. His eyes are

focused on the table below. Guilt freezes his body nearly as still as frozen water during the harshest winters. "As the one who warmed Delphi's bed for the better half of a year, I know more of her plans. She has lost her advantage."

"For that exact reason, why should we trust that you wouldn't help her if she offered you a position back at her side?" Monty asks.

"You would be an idiot to flat-out disregard what Adonis has to say," Luka defends. He glances around the table at all who were not with us in Gigantia, a face hardened by any who refuse to see truth from his knowledge. "Adonis was thrown into the same cell as Arabella and me, when he did nothing more but remove the chains from weighing down our wrists. I don't like him. And I agree that he needs to be monitored at all times, but his intimate relationship with Delphi allows access to information we have only guessed at."

With clarity, I now understand more why Arabella was so determined to risk herself to retrieve Adonis. She sees him as an ally. And as for our current state, an ally who knows of Delphi's secrets is needed.

Adonis gives a small gesture of thanks to Luka. "He speaks the truth. Magiks may have the ability to tell lies, but I will give all that I know for sparing my life and taking me back from Gigantia. And I know well that you would rather me here on your side."

"You offer information only because Delphi has decided she wants nothing to do with you," Luka condescends.

That could be entirely true, though I disregard the comment. Luka should be upstairs helping Arabella, but instead, he has not left. With a head angled at my seneschal, I say, "In any case, why do you remain here?"

His jaw tightens. It's locked in place, with his hand having never left from its clenched position. "Arabella will have to be informed of what occurred while she was absent. As someone you appointed to play seneschal, I also report to the queen."

My eyes shift back to my brother. "Go on, Adonis."

"Delphi seemed to harbor a stronger opinion about our family than I did," he admits. "She would fuel my vengeance against our father by displaying pictures of her younger self with her family each time I visited her home. And then, she would emphasize that each child deserved the love of their family, so if mine could not be bothered to care for me, I was owed something in return. I was convinced that the best way to regain the throne would be by usurping those who stood in my way."

Maude scoffs. Her eyes roll while picking up the tea she had brought in. Not only her, but others at the table find trouble believing this to be his full tale when, in the past, he has twisted words in such a way.

"For a long while, she didn't believe me to be loyal. She trusted no one. I promised her a crown, but she decided it best to test me," Adonis says.

By now, the table has become intrigued with stern looks and the resistance to outright attack him due to the queen's orders.

It's silent for a prolonged collection of moments until Kabir speaks. "What did she ask that you do?"

As if for his protection, Adonis stands from his chair and moves to the other side of the table. "While I was included in the decision to resurrect Luka, his death was preordained."

My eyebrows rise, nearly laughing at the reveal. I am but a bystander in this pile of revelations. While it goes quiet, I look around to view the reactions from the table.

Luka's entire being hardens into something more steady than it ever has. He closes his eyes too quickly and takes a sharp inhale. "What do you mean by preordained?"

I too am curious by this. "Why would Delphi have you murder Luka, only to bring him back?"

"I do not think she originally intended to have you alive again.

Your death was not meant to serve purpose beyond a test." Adonis is careful with his words, moving farther down the table. Faster, when Luka stands and takes strides towards him. In no time, he stands by Kabir, who is just as much a danger to him as my seneschal. "We began to draw suspicion after hearing conversations of the prince who became encapsulated with a witch. I slid between shadows, glamoured myself, and spoke to those in taverns. And when I spoke with Delphi of my findings, we began our plan."

Luka stops in his place. "While in the cells, you were given ample time to admit what you had done to me."

"I was in an enclosed space with the two of you. Do you truly believe you were reserved enough to have held composure if I revealed this? I'm not sorry for the anger that festered from years of neglect, but I do mourn the decisions I made for the childish desire to be loved," Adonis answers grimly.

His response appeases no one, least of all myself. Much more than himself had been treated unfairly by our father. He has made that very point a topic of subject when speaking to me while he was in Phantom Tower.

"As a last resort to prove my love to her," he goes on, "I was told to kill Luka. Delphi had me believe that Luka was a man who had harmed her so deeply that his death would prove I had the ability to murder Fae when the time came."

"Luka was the first person you were told to kill? All this in the case you'd be faced with ridding a common fae who looked to you as their leader?" I laugh. It's delightful to hear of another sharing the foolish acts committed for approval.

A small part of myself—my younger self—would have reacted too similarly to Adonis if Delphi had approached me with similar tactics. Hardly any information on my upbringing would be needed to do so. I would prefer to think that I am not so easily drawn into petty resentment, but had that not been something which swayed me into returning my siblings' irritation with words much more terrible?

Adonis shoots a sharp glare at me. "I never took pleasure in murdering common fae. Hence why they were poisoned in a matter so quick, it took their life in sleep. I killed Luka to prepare myself for the death of our father. It also served as preparation for when I would inevitably be faced with killing the rest of you."

"You still think we should keep him alive?" Xavier asks, with a body leaning forward to gain my attention.

"Delphi's course of action was always to rule," Adonis says, ignoring our cousin. "I don't doubt that learning of our history enticed her, but I know for certain that it was not the primary reasoning in why she wished to be my queen."

"Your care for her is where your mistake lies," I remind him with a smile. "Delphi was quick to throw you as a sacrifice."

My brother's jaw rotates and adjusts in frustration. "Yes, and while we do have the books she has stolen from the archives of the Magiks, she will only be without them for so long before she finds something in their place."

"We are making no progress," Helena says. Despite wishing for a life of peace after my coronation and no longer being queen, her words still hold a great deal to me. To all of us when she played such a heavy hand in our upbringing. "We already know well that Delphi wishes to rule. What we must now do is act in accordance and protect the Fae without exposing that we are as unaware of Delphi's power as they are."

"Then that is that. Until the High Queen has something to say further, we shall table how to proceed. You all may leave."

At my declaration of dismissal, the room empties. The last to leave is Luka before I am left with Adonis.

"I ordered you out," I tell him.

"Your words said that we may leave," he returns, "not that we must."

I cannot find fault with him when the specificity of my words was bleak. Rather, I reply with, "If there is more you wish to discuss with me, you will have to request an audience with the king."

He reaches inside his bag and pulls out a thinly bound book with rough, walnut-colored leather and tanned pages. The purpose of such a gift, I know not. "Arabella kept a journal. You can do with it what you wish, but if you ever want to understand what she endured, I humbly advise that you read it."

Then he exits. My knight holds the door open for my leave, but I am too absorbed in what I have been given.

The journal does not have many pages written in it. Approximately half filled out, with most being scratched-out lines, sketches, or written words. From the first entry alone, I am astonished by the suffering she experienced. Wishes to end her own life.

A quick glance into Arabella's innermost thoughts. Words written from loneliness and separation from others.

I am a terrible Fae, but not one so terrible I would invade more than what I have already read.

I assumed that, with Arabella safely at Nexus, my uneasiness concerning handling royal duties would lessen. I thought, perhaps, that she would be at my side. She would be presented with the new throne that had been designed specially for her, and I would have another to discuss any challenging issues of the Fae. But when a single day of her not leaving the queen's chamber stretched longer, I knew it was a belief of fantasy. Her periods of short silence, while common when she can no longer put on a facade, are not nearly as worrying as this. She does not leave her bed, nor does she speak much to anyone as of late. The lack of speaking is due to something else entirely.

For two days, neither she nor Luka had emerged from the queen's chamber. On the fourth, Luka left only to fetch the two more refreshments.

"Your guests are here, my king," Damita, my advisor, informs.

I nod at them. Their hair, which braids into a low bun, gets stuck between the gold of their bracelet when adjusting themselves after their bow.

At the opening of the throne room doors, the representatives of the lower courts enter. All present themselves with a bow that is too shallow for my liking. Seemingly an insult. When I dart my eyes around the group, I notice there are two unaccounted for. The rulers of Enthar are missing.

"King Cassius," Fatima says, "we have received your missives that Arabella has safely returned to Ifaeris. With her return comes the assurance that we will be kept safe. Am I correct?"

My tongue clicks. "You put too much emphasis on the notion that any are truly safe. Both Adonis and Arabella have returned, yes, but that does not promise the safety of the Fae."

"He is, at the very least, locked in Phantom Tower?" Pyrros poses as a question. His muscular arms are crossed at his front, an eyebrow pointed.

"There is a guard always watching him, yes," I respond.

"That is hardly an answer," Cassandra says with a frown. She scans me, though utters nothing to avoid disrespect.

"He remains free to roam the lands, doesn't he?" Lady Jiya guesses. When I say nothing, her piercing eyes grow wide, lightning striking outside the windows behind me that are not quite parallel. "You are allowing the Fae who nearly destroyed our ruling to walk the lands?"

All of the other rulers are livid. An epiphany hits me far too late that delivering this message in a secluded room with other Elementals may have been a terribly poor idea.

I straighten my posture. Both to listen more intently, as well as to serve a reminder that I am their king.

Pyrros holds back his feeling of disdain. The look on his face holds that of a humbled man who will not risk the safety of those he rules over unless he has a higher scheme to accomplish. "Is this why you've allowed for more Magiks to remain on our lands?"

"If you wish to keep our loyalty, you owe us the truth," Rebekah, wife of Jiya, demands, the purple of the fishy scales at the side of her face seeming to deepen. "For instance, where is the witch?"

My hand runs itself through my hair, pushing it back. There are many things that I must keep hidden from them. I cannot lie, but right now, I am so nervous that I smile and titter at my failure. "She has been through a great ordeal and is currently occupied with things outside my knowledge."

Cassandra appears more agitated than the others. I would think that it was she and Tanzin who had conspired to depart from my bloodline's ruling. "While some understand that the ill-mannered girl is a personal consort of such to you, she is a danger. You already invite more Magiks to the lands. Have you learned nothing from the previous Elemental who fell prey to a witch?"

"I hate to agree with Cassandra," says Jiya, "but with the return of Arabella, Magiks roaming the lands, Adonis unchained, and the witch who captured Arabella in the wind, how are we not to assume this is a ploy to kill our kind once and for all?"

"Are we to trust you to have no bias when it is clear you are blinded by your infatuation with her?" Cassandra hisses out.

"Doing as I command does not require you to trust my word." As I say this, one of the doors behind all the rulers cracks open, and Arabella peeks her head through. I suspect she thinks she is sneaky, but what she does not know is that I can sense her whenever she is near.

"The waters of Searucks move in more consistent patterns than the way in which you make your decisions," Fatima voices, displeased. "You are still but a feckless Fae. Too young and inexperienced to handle the rulings of others."

While she has not said much otherwise, it is clear she thinks me as immature as the others do, though I doubt she would stand against the crown if the opportunity were to arise. Not when our lands have yet to object to me as a ruler. Those from Hearthis respect our traditions too much.

"Ah, how nice it must be to finally speak your true thoughts on my kingship," I return with a smile.

When traveling into the different towns of the lands, I see the effects of the lower courts' ruling. I see how many common fae have become neglected, though they survive well. None have rotted away into nothingness from a lack of supplies, but many experience sorrow from war's past.

Swirling droplets of guilt create designs in my mind when I think of all the harsh ways my father allowed such treatment. More so, when the Elementals standing directly before me express concern for their people. A facade too easy to see through, as I am sure the common fae they rule over occupy only a small section of their minds.

Certainly most hypocritical for me to think such things when I am not a Fae much for altruism, but as king, I ought to show *some* care.

"If you believe me to be unable to rule due to my age alone," I say, "I should remind you that many of you have ruled or lived in the world of politics for over thrice my lifetime, yet there is not a positive word of your leadership among those you govern."

Arabella is spectating everything. She is filled with nothing but anger and sharp-cutting glares, which target every creature in this room.

"We've not been informed much of the other witch that we have been warned about," Jiya says, pulling me from the queen's reactions. "Arabella could easily instead be using you to steal more power for that witch."

I cannot help from my impatience bursting. "She does not care for what my crown has to offer her."

She does not care about me.

"Heed my words," I proclaim. "If you take issue with my ruling as High King, you are welcome to challenge me for the crown. As I have said before, this is a responsibility none of you will handle with grace, being that you cannot care for the common fae under your singular land of ruling."

For a partial moment, I believe Arabella to soften her animosity, but it is quickly diminished when my thoughts remind me that her hatred is stronger than the sliver of care she once felt towards me. The only possibility is that she is perhaps intrigued that I have become the authoritative king she has berated me into becoming.

Nonetheless, I am smiling to myself that she cannot take her eyes off of me. I am staring back with such delusion that it would dance to the melody of a mortal lying. A comforting lie that I can convince myself to sleep through.

"Perhaps, if you wished to earn popularity among the common fae, you would do more to ensure the Zips they pay are distributed in ways that benefit them, rather than your comforting lifestyles," I chide. Their faces and clothing made with the utmost of fine fabrics only remind me of my duty to discontinue the common fae's poor treatment.

"What is expected of us until the safety of the Fae is guaranteed?" Fatima asks. It diverts the conversation but not enough to ease the tension lingering.

Cassandra is pointing her finger and waggling it furiously. "Exactly, Lady Fatima. Are we to live in fear until the life of the witch expires?"

Arabella was one to give her full confidence in me as king. It's high time I carry that same sureness.

"If you would have simply bestowed me with your ears upon entering, I could have explained the singular reasoning for summoning you here without the gossiping mouths of those who give you counsel." Mouths in the room shut with such obedience that I assume even the rulers themselves are astonished by their involuntary action. "The Magiks are here to protect the lands with wards. Therefore, you are not to interfere with what they do. You are not to make demands for their leave, and you are not to worry the common fae of their purpose. Let them continue with their theories until we can put an end to this."

"My king, there must be more that you can trust us with," Pyrros says, undaring to attempt discourtesy, unwilling to look into my eyes as he speaks while holding a bow.

Those in the room's eyes point towards me. I am thoughtless. I was not raised to be heir to the throne. Groomed by my birth mother for that reason, surely, but not raised by my father to do so.

Is anyone truly ready to rise to power? Is it more than just myself who acts as if they know precisely what ought to be done, or is this the result of years due to unpaid attention?

"Many things must be conferred with Arabella, and until we are to be rejoined in each other's company once more, I command your patience."

Before the Fae catch sight of her, Arabella lightly closes the door and makes an escape, so as not to be perceived by those who think so little of her. She departs with an angry scowl, briefly meeting my gaze on her going.

My eyes shut, and my head tilts back as others in the room leave towards their carriages, or in Cassandra's case, okkars to her land.

Arabella loathes me once more, and it is entirely from my doing. But she is here.

XIX

Avoidance and Distractions

Arabella

A dim light greets me as my eyes open. My breathing is shallow, no air coming in, and my throat's closed up. The inner corner of my left eye, all the way to the side of my right, is wet, the silk of my pillow, damp. My right arm has gone numb from the weight of my head, and I can't see much, but I can feel myself screaming. My body thrashing.

Awake.

I'm fully awake in a cold sweat while Luka has to once again hold my body to keep me from falling off the bed. My neck snaps around the room, and suddenly, I can actually feel myself breathing. Heaving, but it's there. My hand grasps around my boyfriend's arm, gripping at any skin I can hold onto.

I can remember all of it so clearly. Memories of my bones cracking one by one with no one to help me. A reminder that I was utterly helpless and alone.

The curtains are shut, so the light I saw when I woke must have come from the desk lantern made from citrine, which lights from magik.

I haven't used a nightlight since I was a child.

If I'm not dreaming of exacting revenge on Cassius, I'm having terrors about my time with Delphi. Every night, when I wake from these, I have to slow my breathing to ground myself.

The aftershock of my kidnapping has long kicked in. I repeat affirmations reminding me that I'm okay and safe, but it barely does any good when Delphi is still out there.

Thoughts trying to rationalize, just like my poor attempts at calming myself, do nothing. I'm always in constant distress that I'm going to wake up in the torture room or next to Luka's corpse. My friends and I have used our magik to cast a protection spell on him. I make sure he keeps holly leaves in his pockets wherever he goes. But my anxious mind remains.

Whenever I wake up, I can barely find a reason for staying alive. I haven't told anyone that.

I *can't* tell anyone that.

Without realizing how long I've been sitting in silence, I hear a knock at the door.

"My queen?" a servant asks. The tapping is soft. I'm called with hesitation. It sounds like Lizette.

All of them have been overly fixated on attending to me left and right. I know they're doing their duties, but it feels smothering.

My body untangles from Luka's before throwing on a robe that grazes the touch of the floor. Upon opening the door, Lizette is standing a few feet from the frame, stiff, with her tall height and hair roughly the length of her whole self.

"Hi, Lizzie," I say.

Lizette pushes a cart full of food for both Luka and me to eat for breakfast, the Fae respectful towards the two of us, while I am grateful and smiling for what she brings. On her leave, she bows to me, shutting the door after greeting my boyfriend.

Luka stands, stabilizing himself with one of the bedposts, and brings the cart towards one of the tables in the room. There are so many that have different uses, and I really don't understand what I'm supposed to do with this much space in a bedroom. One table–by the green, stylish loveseat–is for invited company to place their items on. Another is where I do my makeup, which is next to a full-body mirror. There's one at the desk that sits towards the windows, and a few more that I've let Luka decide the placement of. My workspace has turned from an elegant pedestal desk–decorated with art that I can only relate to the enchantment of glamour–to a disorganized mess of restricted magik books and notes of my understandings. I've rearranged the furniture in the room and added so much more since returning, but everything still feels empty.

After collecting a few books that I left on the small dining table together, Luka neatly places them back on the bookshelf while I lay out our food. A meal I don't quite have an appetite for.

I try, but my fork only pushes around the meat and eggs that had been carefully prepared for me. All I'm able to digest is the water that bubbles and tastes faintly of apple and lime, which isn't considered digesting much at all.

"I know you're upset, love, but don't forget that I still hold enough strength over you and will force-feed you if I have to," Luka states. His voice is so one-noted, I know he'll hold me down if I don't eat something.

One bite in, and I already feel full enough to take on anything. Honestly, the only thing that's felt safe to eat for the past weeks is bread. Everything else is so unappetizing that my stomach twists at the thought of chewing it. But really, everything's been hard for me to eat whenever I look in the mirror.

That is, until I broke two of them in the room.

"This isn't healthy, Blossom," Luka murmurs in a somber tone, brushing my hair to my back. He gingerly kisses my forehead before slipping his hand into mine. "I talk to you, and you talk to me, remember? We fight everything together and not each other."

He's stopped eating. His free hand is at his side, out of view.

A high velocity is driving defensiveness straight into a crash site.

"Fuck would *you* know about being emotionally healthy?" I ask. The nicest things he constantly reassures me with, but I won't allow myself to accept it. Because I would rather deal with everything in my head than admit it out loud. Maybe that exact way of thinking is also the reason I overindulge in isolation, incorrectly believing that in order to heal, I must solely rely on myself. But simultaneously, another part of my brain cannot survive without wanting love so much that I hate myself for it.

It's hard believing Luka. Words work like object permanence, but instead of a thing, it's forgetting a person's words exist the second they leave. Finding time to address the things I'm feeling is difficult when there's so much pressure to end what's started. There are so many things that I haven't confronted because I'm too overcome by stress to do anything except escape in reading while also trying to comprehend the things that Delphi has taught herself, which only induces lethargy.

I've been disconnected from everyone. Nothing's exactly wrong, but nothing is *great*. Luka and I have become stagnant, and that's all from me kicking everyone out. If, after everything, he wants to leave, I wouldn't blame him.

All my efforts and energy have been channeled into finding Delphi. I can't allow myself to fall victim to my thoughts. They're the same ones constantly reminding me that everything may be one big false reality. I want to believe I'm at Nexus, but with my brain being rebooted so many times, I can't help but question everything in my day-to-day life. My mind won't keep still. I'm suffocating in thoughts of my worthlessness. My inability to cope might kill me as well.

"Fuck," I let out with a sigh. "I shouldn't have said that. I'm sorry."

Shame creeps into my conscious mind as I look at Luka's face. I leave my seat and go into the closet, changing into something more fitting for training. I never *intend* to hurt others when my emotions overwhelm me, but it always happens outside of my control.

I wonder if I will forever punish those who only want to stand alongside me.

"I'm gonna go spar with Kabir."

"You're deflecting again," he lectures as I dash out the door. He's too used to me reacting so abruptly in a splitting anger.

He really shouldn't be.

I'm immediately on my ass again, with Kabir holding a sword that's over half my size to my chest. His foot is on my lower stomach, making it seem impossible for me to lift myself.

My body is now just an eternal ground of bruises. I'm in a permanent state of soreness. Working out this consistently again has gotten to a point where I don't start blacking out or seeing stars, but there are still a good amount of times when I've vomited from overworking myself.

A free hand reaches for mine as he pulls me up to stand against him. The fact I see him every day aside, his height will always stagger me. He's so tall that I don't know if I'd reach his chin even in my highest heels.

"I don't think I'll ever be as skilled at combat as you are," I admit.

He wraps cloth around his hands before slipping on padded

gloves and holding them up for me to work on my punches. A grin lights his face before he slips into soft laughter. "I've had a hundred and sixty-eight years of life to train. Do not expect yourself to hold just as well."

Multiple punches later, I already feel exhausted. I'm disappointed in my stamina and its ineffectiveness to work during training but hold through in a dire situation.

That's because you're weak.

"You are resilient at improvising where you fall short and have been trained well enough in your magik to keep safe in battle," he says in an effort to comfort me with a pointed look, telling me to stand in the correct stance before I throw another set of punches.

Air feels like nothing as I try swallowing deeper breaths. Bits of hair from my overgrown bangs slip from the clip, the strands oily and covered in sweat.

After the twentieth punch, I'm given a break. Both jugs of water are at the corner of the training room. This is the biggest one in Nexus, filled with mock weapons, which is why I'm only in here when I spar with Kabir.

On one of the wooden mannequins for sword practice, I rest my body. The exertion from my work with the Fae has finally caught up, and I feel like my legs could give out from under me. "I guess it helps I always wanted to protect myself growing up and learned fighting skills when I was younger."

"And that's why you're so quick to pick up on things. You've trained more than you think."

Sweat glistens down from the pores of his forehead all the way to his aquiline nose. He pauses to guzzle down at least a third of his water. Drips from the ceramic bottle fall onto the curved lines of his tattoos that spread all around the upper half of his front torso, the diamond dotting looking similar to period marks between symbols. There are certain drawn-out lines that are shorter than others, which connect to the longer ones, showing the same as half of an arrow.

"Have you made new headway with the books?" he asks. His thick, groomed beard has also captured his drink. "Or are you still using them as an excuse to do nothing but train with me and avoid speaking on other matters with the king?"

I'm always on edge. Worried that Luka and my friends will change their minds and become so exhausted by me that they realize I'm too much to handle. So, to divert my insecurities and thoughts of the kingdom, I train with my Head Guard. It's where I can absolutely lose myself in my exhaustion to take my anger out in fighting. Before, when we would train, he would briefly introduce swordsmanship to me, but ultimately, we focused more on hand-to-hand combat.

"That doesn't involve anyone but us." I give him a look, telling him not to get involved, chugging more water and wiping my forehead with a towel that rests over a wooden bar.

"You have sat around with three books for what is now nearing a month and a half while only occasionally leaving your room to eat, attend court meetings–*where you hardly speak*–and train with me. When the two of you rule a kingdom, it *does* affect more than just yourselves," he tries to convey with a scowl. Quickly, his face lightens at my eyes, jumping in surprise, and bows his head down. "My queen."

Really, I should be angry at him for bringing this up when, by now, he knows I exercise to clear my head. But when he is nervous from speaking up against me, I can't find it in me to be mad. It's pretty funny to see him find so much repentance in his disrespect.

I take wooden swords that are hanging with the others, handing one to Kabir and changing our focus to sparring. I don't understand how Kabir is able to strategically strike when all I can think of is to aim at open areas while protecting myself with magik as a shield.

Whenever he swings, I'm able to dodge or jump back, but when I do it, his sword blocks me.

"While you have good instincts and can fight decently enough against untrained Fae, you would find yourself in trouble when battling against armies without your magik." He swings again, but this time, I'm able to block the sword with mine.

The blade nearly hits my face and would have wounded me deeply, if I hadn't gripped the weapon with both my hands and held it so close to my skin. I move to the side, where I'm able to twist my wrists in a half circle, forcing his sword closer to the lower half of his body. He's going easier on me than he would with the trained guards, pulling his strength when he knows he could easily outpower me. My reaction time clearly isn't as fast as his.

We're going in slower movements to improve my technique, but my inclination is to constantly rely on my magik to defend myself.

Lately, though, that's been nearly uncontrollable.

The reminding thought nearly throws me off guard from the sparring, forcing me to dodge back from Kabir's sword swinging my way. I'm going from lower strikes, to middle, to high, each narrowly hitting him with the tip of the practice sword.

"Pivot your foot before pulling back and lunging," he reminds sternly, adjusting my stance with the wood and allowing me to plunge forward.

He bests me two more times, and during the third, he manages to take the weapon from me. My head throws back in defeat before he hands me the sword so that I can return to position.

"So you're trained like someone from our armies, but you're a guard for Nexus?" I comment. "Why not fight with the armies?"

This time, I make the first move, squatting low for balance and striking towards his knee. He's quick enough for my weapon to miss and aim his sword directly down towards my head. I drop to the ground, securing the sword in my hands and rolling away.

"It is a great honor to be chosen as a guard," he answers while I am down.

My hand pushes me up from the ground, where I feel my knee—tender and already forming a bruise.

"That's bullshit." I use my magik to freeze his body still and use my strength to bring him to the ground. It's a successful offense, but I doubt I'll have enough concentration to do something this precise in an actual fight.

This time, I'm triumphant, putting my foot on his chest and pointing the weapon towards his throat at an angle. I kick his sword aside with my free foot, leaving him with nothing. "Maybe it's part of the reason, but I know that isn't *the* reason."

He sits up, using his hands to support himself. "I was trained under General Callian. He's my father."

"But you look nothing like him," I state. My brows furrow together in confusion. General Callian, the man just passing the height of the Aeon twins, is still much shorter than Kabir. The general has skin the shade of lapis lazuli and hair as pale as frost flowers in the ocean. But then I remember a feature they both share. "Other than maybe the fact you both have long hair."

"He married my mother after my father died." Pulling himself to his feet, his walnut eyes glance down to me while taking in a sharp inhale. "The general raised me as his own since I was eleven, but being under his command was humiliating. When training me, he pushed me harder than the others. Once the other Fae realized my back tattoo matched Callian's and my brother's, they assumed my high rank to be attributed to being his other son."

Kabir grabs the sword from the ground, standing five paces away and in position to charge. Immediately, he speeds towards me.

I duck from left to right until I'm standing behind him, knocking my weapon to his back from the base of the handle.

His head snaps behind him, and he reaches out a hand to grab my arm that isn't properly stiff, demonstrating a lack of control over the weapon's swing.

Hard enough to hurt but not enough to break anything, he forcefully smashes his forearm onto mine until I drop the weapon. He follows by sweeping low, grabbing my waist to lift me, and slowly trapping me between his arm and the ground. I'm pretty sure if I were one of the guards training under him, he would have used his strength to slam me down.

"And you asked Elliot to place you as a guard?" I ask. Perspiration beats down my body from my chest into my sports bra as Kabir helps me up.

"All current guards were trained under General Callian. Only a select few from the army are graced with the honor of guarding Nexus Palace. And only six are chosen as the knights of the crown."

Kabir raises my arms in a fighting stance for punches again, only now, he is without the gloves that protect his hands. He's swinging back, forcing me to work on my defenses while I punch. There's a look on his face that's urging me to end training for the day, and I don't think he's going to let this go as easily as others in the palace do.

My hands turn to fists at my side. I'm glaring, but not at him. More like if I were looking at myself in a mirror. "I can keep going."

He pauses, shifts my left arm closer to my face to protect it, and squeezes my right hand more. "Tighten your fist."

His right arm swings from around me, this time with me able to block him. Right after, I use my right hand to grab his wrist and draw him closer until the mock dagger I summon to me is against his throat with my left hand.

"Better," he says.

Block after block, I'm able to keep myself from being hit. But with one incorrect assumption, his swing knocks into my head in the same area that Delphi struck the night I was taken.

Unintentionally, fire shoots from my fingertips towards the floor. As I groan, Kabir rushes to the nearest towel, frantically putting out the flame. Everything is a mess. I'm taking every little interaction too personally, and harnessing my fire is as difficult as ever.

"Control yourself," Kabir tells me. He says it so harshly, it sounds more like he's scolding me.

"I can't."

"Then your magik will remain chaotic. This is the second time today that you have done this." He points to the sword across the room that's broken off the hilt from my fire splitting it.

In a squat stance, I throw a punch to his hand. *Hard.*

He keeps pushing. "I may not be one that you would seek advice from, but I'm an excellent listener."

Punch. This one weaker.

"You can trust me." He sounds convincing, but try as I might, I can't make myself believe him.

I work all my strength into my fist, but my wrist bends on impact, and I start feeling the tears well in my eyes. My forehead drops to the open area of my fist between my thumb and index finger, keeping hidden anything that may come out.

"I don't know who to trust," I confess. The emotions are consuming. A weakness that I can never come back from if wounded from exposure. "And I just want to spar."

We sit silently for a good amount of time before he picks up the wooden sword and hands it to me.

Finally, a nod of understanding.

"So you trained hard and worked your way up to be a guard?" I ask to break the awkwardness.

We both walk towards our water. He sits on the bench near the mock weapons, while I rest with my back against the wall before ultimately lying on the floor.

About five giant gulps of water later, he answers. "I was given the option of being my father's second in command or join the guards."

Now I'm more confused. "But you basically brought yourself to the bottom of all the ranks here."

Standing, he prepares himself again in stance, and I realize the break isn't as long as I would have thought it would be.

I briskly start towards him. Always striking lower, painfully aware that I don't have a height advantage over him.

"Yes, but now you are here, and I am Head Guard, which you can say is above the rank of the general since I would hypothetically give him command." He says this all like he didn't put in any of the work to get where he is now. The only thing I've done for him is tell Cassius to make him Head Guard when he wanted to strip Ezra of his position.

Somehow, I've gained enough stealth to swipe upwards and make what would have been a crucial hit on his shoulder. I grin to myself, but keep in mind the knowledge that I must always be alert in a fight.

"I train the guards with drills that my father had done with them. With Prince Ezra, he did not know of the harsh training we endured and therefore never instructed us under the same conditions," Kabir continues on.

The wind is knocked from my chest as Kabir holds the weapon close to his, bending down and pushing until I am nearly off balance. I try to grab the wooden dagger I placed at my side, but he too swiftly restricts my arms and flips me slowly until I am on the ground.

His knees are keeping me in place on my thighs until I tap his leg and surrender. "Now," he says, smiling, "are we going to keep speaking about my life to avert from the important topic at hand, or will we continue avoiding it?"

I'm back in a fighting stance, now without a weapon at all. I refuse to ever be in a situation where I cannot hold my own again. I need the practice, but I do this more because I'd rather not admit to him that he's right. I'm so tired of everything. Of the memories, and the trauma, and the voice playing on loop that keeps pounding, repeating to me my worst fears. That maybe Delphi's right about me, and I deserve every shitty thing that's ever happened.

Kabir looks towards the door, presenting an opening while throwing a punch that I dodge when using my forearm to knock his. I go behind him, punching the small of his back, causing him to drop his sword.

I kick him from behind his knees before toppling him down with another kick to his back. Upon hitting the ground, I keep my weight on my knee, which digs into him. A dagger flies into my hand, and I lift him by his hair, pressing the weapon against him.

"We talk about anything other than him, or you leave," I warn.

Right when I think we're getting back into position, Kabir grabs his towel and water. He walks towards the door with a grim look on his face. "You may carry a strong face, but I am disappointed you'd let your petty anger keep you from doing more for the kingdom."

At his leave, I'm left with unresolved anger resonating within me. For time I can't keep track of, I'm trying to fight against this wooden dummy–which I imagine having Cassius' face–but I've yet to do anything of significant damage.

Eventually, I'm full of so much fury that I take a real sword and swing it until I break a piece of the figure.

As I'm walking towards the stairs, from the hall, I hear the sound of a melodic harp. The music is so beautiful but heartbreaking.

Without words, you can sense the emotion that is behind the piece itself.

I follow to where the music takes me and see someone I don't expect to be listening.

It's Cassius. He's using pencil-like graphite on paper, peering up at me standing in the doorway when the harpist finishes the last of the song. I myself don't know why I didn't leave when realizing it was him. The music was so hypnotic.

As the musician takes his exit, he bows to the two of us, though I hardly notice it. Cassius and I have locked eyes, neither of us breaking apart.

"I thought it was Luka in here," I blurt as an excuse. But Luka doesn't even play the harp. "I'm gonna go."

Before I'm able to leave, Cassius says, "Have you found anything recent worth noting when going through the books from Delphi's archives?"

"Yeah," I reply, taking one extended blink before turning to face him. I venture deeper into the room, leaning myself on the piano, whereas he stands on the other side. Papers compiled together lie on the lid full of Cassius' discarded sketches. All with different concepts just as aching as the music that had been playing, art as beautiful as ones Juju creates.

"Do you care to explain then?" he says.

"Delphi's learned something that has to do with blood magik. Basically, it amplifies spells more intensely, depending on the Magik's intent."

A hand goes around Cassius' chin, his finger tapping his lip a few times. "This relates to Ifaeris?"

"Yeah, but the two books I told you about before are less so about spells and hexes and more about their research," I admit. Unfortunately, there isn't much information in the books that I can understand. Worse, the first two books regarding the experimentation of magik are the ones I read prior to the book that's fed me the most information. "A lot of things are either in an ancient language that Luka and Gray can't understand, or they're the findings after experimenting with blood magik, so right now I'm trying to figure out what limits blood has."

Everyone knows that restricted magik exists. Some are more known than others, but just like the Fae, certain magik is taught to be myths. Killing another with magik, though not taught in schooling, is probably the most common form known to the masses, but Luka has taught me of others.

"Over a month, and all we have learned from these books tells us nothing?" he says.

"Not as much as I was hoping, no. But at least we have Adonis on our side and the wards across the lands."

"The lower courts' rulers may want to know. They have been questioning me as it is." His annoyance with them is evident. "Is there anything more regarding blood magik that you have learned?"

With the way he looks at me, when there's no one here to stand witness, I feel like my heart will vomit up from my mouth.

"Uh, yeah. For us to gain more power or to control someone unwillingly, blood has to be drawn."

"That's all to say that if Delphi breaks past the warded borders, she could control a Fae if she had used her blood to cast a spell on them," Cassius says, more of a statement than anything.

That's not something I've given much thought to. The hit of the realization fully sinks in. She may not have done anything yet, but it doesn't mean that our protective magik can last forever, especially with time going on and my friends needing to live their lives beyond this.

"Yeah. I'll make sure to check on the wards tomorrow and strengthen them if needed."

But that response didn't seem to satisfy him enough. There's more that he wants, and I can't quite pinpoint it.

"Must I tell you that checking the wards falls under the duties of others?" he comments, almost as if concerned. "What do *you* plan on doing, apart from collecting information?"

I can't stop focusing on the visible marking on the back of his palm. How so many of his scars can be seen. And, instead of answering him, all that can come out of my mouth is, "How did you get your scars?"

The exact moment the last word leaves my mouth, I regret asking my question. I've convinced myself I have no interest in Cassius' life and am prepared to leave as soon as I can, yet I keep finding myself wanting to know more about him.

"My parents." He brushes his thumb over the faint mark on his left hand, smiling and acting like the question is nothing of importance. "It was their way of showing me affection. Those on my back are from the affection of my mother, the front from my father's."

My arms drop to my sides. I know that his mother was horrible, hardly acknowledging her only son unless it advanced her status among Elliot's consorts, but this knowledge causes guilt to circulate inside me like water filtering through a statue fountain. A knot in my throat pings harshly, and I can feel it becoming more sore with the swallow I take. My mouth is trying to form the words, but a breathy sound comes out as I start to speak. "I- I'm sorry."

"You still have yet to tell me what you plan on doing with your time here." He leans his body forward, putting his weight carelessly on the piano and watching me intently.

"I'm only staying to see things through with Delphi. Either to make sure she's dead or taken by the Council."

He moves, striding towards me with my every word. I hope he

understands and remembers that I'm free to depart with the crown whenever I so choose.

"Do you stay for anything else?"

"No."

Then, Cassius' eyes drop. He breathes once, and I feel like time is stopping. We do nothing but stare into each other's eyes, drawing me in closer. He doesn't touch me, though I can sense the faint of his fingers tracing my skin. How the barely there heat of his hands is radiating from his body that is so close to mine.

With a quick, accidental touch, his fingers graze my skin. They're warm but not soft. *Why aren't his hands soft?* He's always had soft fingers–or at least softer than mine. His bones are more prominent through his skin's outlines. Veins more visible than usual. He hasn't blinked, but I've done so enough for the both of us. I can't hold the charcoal of his eyes for longer than two seconds without feeling the speed of my heart making my breaths shorter.

I've spent too long analyzing this. Way too long. I'd kill to be high right now so my mind doesn't have to remain where my body is grounded. My head shakes, breaking me from our locked gazes and allowing me to back away from him.

"Something else you wanted?" My foot is already turning towards the door.

"Yes, actually." Cassius takes one step towards me. He looks directly into my eyes again and softly whispers, "I want you to kiss me. Dally your time and suffocate me with your lips."

On occasion, maybe I *do* act with intentions of reminding him of the sting of what he had done unto me, smiling wide without acknowledging his existence, refusing to communicate with him and thus enraging him further. But this is something I still can't do, even if it is to toy with him.

Using the momentum from not too long ago, I revolve my

body and don't stop my steps until I'm in the queen's chamber, accidentally bumping into Maude outside of the music room.

Inside, there is another box from the tailors waiting for me on my bed. It has an emerald green color, with the box itself being made from glass-like material. When I open it, my breath is caught by its beauty. A pair of silver, four-pointed star earrings that are coated in diamonds with pearls on a ring around the star is placed inside. It's not subtle in any way.

I go to put it with my collection of jewelry, but before I'm able to prepare for a shower, there's a knock at my door.

"Ara, let me in. I know you're in there," Celeste's voice says from the hallway as I'm approaching.

"It's unlocked."

The door opens, the princess sauntering in upon their entrance and sitting on a chair. Their hair is tied into a bun, a ballet blue dress cinched at their waist by a brown belt, highlighting the bigger curves of their body.

"How'd you know I was here?" I ask. I don't bother welcoming them with a greeting. Everyone here is too acquainted with each other for that. I follow behind, sitting adjacent to them on the sofa.

"I could hear you moaning up the stairs in pain."

My reaction spreads my face wide faster than I can stop myself from doing it. I didn't realize I was being that loud.

"I heard you spoke with Cassius," they blurt.

"Gods, Maude's faster than a hummingbird." I cock my head, crossing one leg over the other to rest my foot on my knee.

There's an awkward unspokenness between the two of us, with an even more tense topic of conversation. "I think he is trying to impress you without smothering," they admit.

"He doesn't care about anything besides making sure his kingdom is safe."

I'm not sure why this makes me discontent. Isn't it what I wanted after all? For him to care about his people?

They send a glare of irritation at me. A weary sigh of disappointment. "He has been discomposed since you were taken. He was drunk and moping. But above everything, he was scared."

How do I process this information? Reading Cassius' emotions is hard on its own for me—more so when I've lost base with reality. "Cassius isn't afraid of anything."

"You say this while forgetting that I have felt his every emotion when it comes to you."

I'm more tense than before. I open my mouth to deny it, but I can't.

"He knew nothing of what happened to you, Ara," they continue on. "Do you know what that did to my family? Esme couldn't find you when she traveled through the unconscious. You were missing, and none of us could sense if your energy was dead or alive."

My heart begins pounding faster. I've been so focused on myself that I haven't put much thought into what others' panic must have been while I was with Delphi. I never once thought that my being missing affected much.

Celeste is studying me. They're trying to gauge my reaction to this information, but it seems unnecessary.

"I can feel every emotion my brother feels. When you were gone, there was something shattered inside of him. Something I am unsure will ever return. He feels something with you." They move to sit closer to me, taking the seat that was previously tucked into my desk.

I clear my throat and feel my toes anxiously curling from inside my socks. My foot is scraping against the floor and bouncing to remind me that I have to say something. It feels ridiculous to be feeling such high levels of anxiety when I'm the one keeping my distance. "What does he feel?"

"It's the feeling you get when you're truly seen for the first time."

On instinct, I don't know whether to push away the comment or reprimand myself for letting their words make me feel something I can't explain. I swallow once and avert my eyes to the stack of books and paper on my desk.

To change the subject, Celeste offers information of their own. "My partner, Damita, has told me the ways in which you still held influence over Cassius."

I make a sound from shock. "Your what?"

They smile at my pure surprise. "Your advisor is my lover. Mother managed to convince Cassius to assemble more of a court while you were gone."

"No, not that part. I know about the court," I playfully dismiss. "I was just in- So you're dating the same Damita who played the flute at Cassius' coronation?"

"The very one," they brag with a smile. "I saw them exhausted one day, and we got to talking, and... They're *also* who informs me of the notable change in Cassius' attitude towards leadership."

"Oh yeah?" I goad. "*Do tell.*"

Celeste lifts one of their brows as if asking if I'm serious. "For one, Cassius has already put into motion giving reparations to those hurt by our father's selfishness towards Aquatius. He's begun funding more Zips into the lower courts to help tend to those raising livestock and providing food. But I think one of the bigger things he has done is freeing those that father had imprisoned in Phantom Tower over minor squabbles."

I can't help my jaw from slightly dropping, or my mouth from parting open. My small smile grows with each accomplishment that they list. The first two things I partially know, but the last one hadn't been told to me.

"How much does your *partner* know?" I tease.

They roll their eyes with an exhale of a laugh. "They are sometimes the one who writes the letters sent to other rulers, so I would say a fair amount." For a short-lived beat, they pause, snorting to themselves before continuing and saying, "Well, that as well as spying in on the audiences that prisoners would have with Cassius."

"I have a lot of work to take care of," I say, the two of us in good spirits as I walk us towards the door, allowing for their exit. "So, I'll talk to you later."

Once they leave, my back presses against the door, and I take a breath of relief. Kabir is right. I've been shut down completely. Angrily simmering in silence during our court meetings. I need to put my hatred for Cassius aside so that we can expedite finding Delphi. There are so many necessary things I need to do rather than going over the same few texts, attending court gatherings for an hour each week, and meeting with my Head Guard to spar.

More than ever, right now, I desperately need to bathe my body before icing it.

XX

Exposing Power

Arabella

Magik doesn't work in this room, I've learned too quickly upon entering.

Lazipeus holds no information. I've sifted through multiple sections in the library, the databases, and anything that could be hidden, but the most significant piece of information I could find is about the theory of blood magik and what it may contain, though with no actual proof of its existence.

Files I've stolen from the staff offices earlier also have nothing that could help me in my search for Delphi. Her records have all been blacked out, and her place of residence has changed its status. I guess I shouldn't have expected to find much, since her graduation last year meant that administration no longer kept track of her whereabouts.

At least I know where her friends live. Plausible places for her to stay and jump locations for.

However, one good thing has come from skulking around the offices. While printing records I was able to access, I overheard a professor expressing a need to retrieve one of the texts meant for the other educators from the library. Obviously, I wouldn't be allowed into the backrooms, so as that professor was leaving, I snuck in.

Sigils are marked high on the wall to keep magik from being used. Two magik locks are used on the door. One locking upon entry, and one locking upon exiting.

Not only are both of those security precautions in place, but there are also enchantments that keep thieves from okkaring out. My last resort is now reliant on sneaking past someone who would open the door.

Either the school keeps secrets, just as the Coven does, or they really have no idea of the capabilities our powers could extend to.

Keys twisting from the outside kicks me into high alert. The door opens, and I quickly rush to hide, thanking whatever luck I've been blessed with that a worker's come to reshelve a few books.

Step by step, I go in the opposite direction of the worker, slinking while crouching as low as possible. The door is propped open with enough Magiks passing that I can get lost in the raucous crowd.

Once I escape the room, I allow myself to take in deeper breaths, my mind relieved that I'm able to walk close to others leaving for dinner. Coming to Lazipeus to collect information during the busiest time of students bustling through the buildings may have been my smartest decision ever.

I keep my head down, blending in with the Magiks around me, until I make it to a bathroom and okkar back to Nexus.

Luka's not in the room when I peek out from the closet. But upon further searching, I spot Adonis sitting on my bed with one leg crossed over the other and a book in hand.

I really hope those aren't his outside clothes.

I'm not positive if I'm caught or how much he knows, so I must act as if his presence is of no shock. I casually lead with my back on the frame of the closet door, watching to see if he's noticed me. "What are you doing in my room, Adi?"

His mouth cracks into a fox-like grin. "I think the bigger question is, where were you, my little vixen?"

My eyes widen at his question before rapidly narrowing back down. Adonis has yet to put the book down, so my surprise is still disguised well enough. "I was checking the wards."

"This morning," he chimes smugly. The book is set on the bed, and his body fully turns to face me. "I thought your newfound motivation to leave Nexus the past weeks suspicious, and it seems that my theory may have been correct."

With his freedom as my guest, the arrogance he originally carried is higher than ever, growing the longer he remains within the palace. It makes me regret not forcing him inside Phantom Tower at all.

"Okay, and? I'm doing my job and making the lands safer by searching for Delphi," I fire back. He offers up his hand in defense. "How'd you know I wasn't actually in Ifaeris?"

This, he perks up to. As if he was waiting for me to ask. "I figured you weren't spending all your time alone in your room or wandering the grounds without a knight to know your comings and goings. Not when you were so antsy alone in your cell."

Now, he's standing next to my bed but not coming any closer to me. My eyes are searching for any indication that he's looking for a way to double-cross us.

"You gonna tell Cassius?"

Adonis waves me off with a face to be dismissive. "He already does not want me here. Why tell him something that will upset him more?"

"Then why'd you come to see me? Were you just waiting to prove your hypothesis correct?"

"It was my main reasoning, yes," he returns in a mocking way, and I let out a groan. "I also came to ask for your opinion."

Both my brows go up, eyes slightly raised. "On?"

Nothing is said between the two of us for a while. His hesitation has passed musing thoughts and is now prolonging an answer. "My family, I suppose."

His answer isn't something I expect. I thought maybe it would be about Delphi and what she was like, but not this. Since coming to Nexus, he's avoided talking about her, and I haven't thought it was my right to bait him into telling me.

"They're not exactly cool with you being here," I tell him.

Four blinks pass his face before he says anything more. "I never wished for this." He sighs, with eyes unable to look in my direction. "I suppose you would not believe me, but I only truly wanted my family. I wanted a home. After my aunt and uncle died from an accident caused by humans, I thought perhaps she could give it to me."

Delphi's name doesn't come from his mouth, but we both know she's who he means. And it's something similar that I had thought she would do for me. Rather than saying this, I tilt my head down in acknowledgment.

"I thought that ruling Ifaeris alongside her and taking my father's place would remedy for what he did, but instead, she wanted the power for herself." His voice is shaky, tangled with tempestuous self-anger. "I hate her." He pauses. "But I can't let her go either. Is that pathetic?"

Consoling people, especially in the department of emotions, is something I find very awkward without making a joke to lighten their mood. "No. I think it's human-" I cut myself off to correct myself. "Well, in our case, living nature, to wanna belong to something. We can hate people all we want but still crave a sense of community. She offered it to you but ended up using you to her advantage."

What I'm saying doesn't seem to be helping him, as far as I can tell, but I think he needs to hear this. "She's never really cared about using people if it benefitted her in some way, even if it hurt the relationships that she said she cared about. I guess her need for power outweighed her feelings for you."

"Do you think they'll ever reconcile with me?"

I'm not sure if he's asking me this since I'm one of the only ones who will hold a conversation with him or if he asks this because I can lie to him. "Honestly? I don't know. Their relationship with each other is already messy and broken because of your dad. And as much as they were all annoyed by him, you killed Ezra. The only one who didn't mourn him in any way was Cassius, but even then, I don't know if that's something that can be easily forgiven."

Adonis thins his lips to nearly a straight line. "You know a lot about Cassius' feelings towards both me and our brother. The two of you are what I thought my love with Delphi to be."

"I hate him," I correct much too quickly, but deeper, I know my abhorrence is directed at the fact he left me and Luka with Delphi. My anger is misguided, but I can't help holding firm in it.

"Don't play coy," he scolds in a dry tone. "You do not hate my brother any more than you hate Luka. You are in love. And that is a poison far more dangerous than hatred."

Why does everyone insist there's love between me and Cassius? I know better than to consider myself in love with the very Fae who can do no more than make me question my trust in him. But Adonis is wise in his words. Love holds much more dangerously than hatred.

Saving me from thinking more into this, Luka opens the door and cues Adonis' exit from the room.

He doesn't say a word, and I'm instantly filled with dread. I can't stop from repeating to myself that I'm driving everyone away with all my constant problems. I question what it must be like to be absolutely certain that you're not a burden. No second-guessing or a need for reassurance.

Quickly, the thoughts lessen when he wraps his arms around me, keeping me locked in until we are in the bathroom and both of us shower.

"Any difficulty with duties today?" I tease in a jovial tune.

Luka's smiling at me, a toothbrush in his mouth and wearing nothing but a towel wrapped around his waist. His shoulders are broad, and with hair still wet, the wavy texture is at its most natural state. I can't stop staring at the fern fronds between his lower waist and hips.

He hands me a shirt that reaches the middle of my thighs before rinsing his mouth and throwing on his underwear. His whole body is toned. So muscular yet lean and I just want to–

"Staring at me like that does little for you, Blossom."

I hesitate, stumbling over my words to find an excuse, but he cuts me off. "The job was as monotonous as usual. I speak with the creatures that already hate our kind while also having to remain prepared to execute them if they show indication they're unrecovered from their trances."

While I apply moisturizer to my face, Luka goes from the foot of the bed to putting a dry towel on my pillows. He crawls back to the edge, rising to sit straight.

"Today was more socializing than paperwork then, I assume?" I take his left arm and wrap it around me, joining him on the bed.

He gives a light-hearted smile. "It's hard to disagree with the common fae's resentment after hearing the effects of Elliot's ruling."

"Well, if they try to do anything to you, let me know so I can rip their hearts from their chests and return the favor you did for me."

"I'm glad you didn't say that killing would make us no better than them." He presses his lips to the top of my forehead, lingering. We go to our respective sides of our sleeping position. It's earlier than we usually sleep, but the day has exhausted me.

I snort, kissing him lightly before flipping sides and scooting my body back into his arms. "We aren't better than them."

We're probably worse.

He's playing with my hair, which should be drying on the towel placed over my pillow. "How was checking the wards? Any trouble?"

I flirt with the idea of telling him that I visited Lazipeus, quickly deciding against it. Lying to him is something I hate doing more than anything. I'm used to being harsh and honest to the point where it hurt Luka in the past, but he's far too stressed with his other duties for me to add needless worry over my well-being. Not that it matters much when I hadn't been gone long and wasn't in any particular danger.

"Good. I found a not-so-interesting read after I finished." Just then, I recall how late it had been when Luka entered the bedroom. "Why were you staying out so late tonight?"

"I can't sleep without knowing you're safe first. I was asking the knights if they knew where you were." His arm moves down from my chest to my stomach. At some point, while he talks about the correspondence he had with the rulers of Hearthis and an interaction he had the other day with a common fae, I feel myself falling asleep.

The throne room feels empty without the presence of anyone

else. However, this reason is due to me for organizing this meeting. I put off training with Kabir and ensured that Cassius would be occupied with something else. In Luka's case, he was already out and about in the town center of Mindae by the time I woke up.

The ornamental trimming on the throne's frame is exquisite, with spirals and thorned design. It rises above where my head would fall back without jutting out to the possibility of injury. From what I've been told, there is another one, but it's currently being kept in one of the storage rooms on the upper floors.

"The Elementals and Lady Theodosia's mother have arrived, my queen," Damita informs, hair falling to their brown skin.

I'm pulled from my admiration and give them a nod of approval. "Let them in."

Ladies Jiya, Fatima, and Cassandra enter, but Lord Tanzin is nowhere to be seen. Suspicious, considering his daughter is one of the few who knew where I was being held. Better for my running mouth though, since Tanzin's face resembles too much of a praying mantis, and I don't know how well I'd be able to keep from making a comment if he's rude.

I've met the rulers of the lower courts on very few occasions. Since Cassius was decided king, I've met Fatima three times, the others only twice—once being during the reception of Cassius' coronation. I first saw them, of course, on the night of the ball, but I was not properly introduced.

"Ah, Arabella. My advisor says great things of you," Jiya says. Her son, Harrison, looks so much like her. Their eyes are both the same color of teal, both with faces of hearts—though her skin runs two shades deeper and more golden than his. Alongside that, their hair colors are different. "Will the king be joining us soon?"

"He busied himself with kingly duties," I respond. "I've gathered you to inform you of what I've learned about Delphi."

Cassandra is glowering at me. Then a scoff. "Such a need would not be necessary, had it not been for the problems that your kind caused."

A low-hitting comment, but an accurate one. My tongue is swiping across the front of my top teeth but is still covered by my closed mouth sucking in. "I know you blame me for what Delphi did, and sure, now there's a need for higher precautions, but whether you like it or not, *my kind* are the ones safely securing *your* people."

My reminder is something they all know in logic, but it is still something they do not like to hear.

"So what must we be informed of that couldn't have been said in a letter from King Cassius?" Fatima asks. Her shorter nose is flared, while her downturned eyes narrow, expecting an answer.

There's too much information I've come across that serves as important. I think of the most vital pieces–more importantly, the ones I can trust to divulge on–and condense them. "Delphi's become more powerful because of something called blood magik. For some creatures, names serve as importance, but for us, blood is said to be the ultimate form. It's quite literally a way of putting our whole selves into our magik. I wasn't aware of this until recently, and it's not taught in schools."

"Do you believe that the witch hasn't put some spell on Adonis?" Jiya asks, doubt in her voice, hands held together in front of her blush dress with a fitted bodice that drapes out under the bustline. Her questioning is something of a guide when inspecting possibilities.

My eyes shift downwards to the right, then back to her. "I can't say I believe that with absolute certainty, but after the things I witnessed, like her casting him out, I do think he's on our side more than hers."

I don't expect them to believe me. After all, they've only been fed bits and pieces of my return. None of them know that

I was being held in Gigantia. They know nothing of my personal connection to Delphi. Not even the possibility that there's a higher chance of her still holding control over some common fae more so than Adonis.

When it comes to my kidnapping, the details that the lower courts' rulers know are sparse. That only prompts me to be mindful of the subjects I touch on. I need to be meticulous about my wording while allowing them to fill in the gaps with their imagination.

The real issue lies within balancing between not shutting down and saying nothing and overexplaining. My communication with the Fae is a complex match of a game where I learn the rules as I go. I have to move among them the same way that Luka has taught me to speak to the Magik elite. A missed step and I am doomed, a purposeful sacrifice, my damnation.

These Fae assume that I can be easily tricked due to my disconnect for so long. Probably thinking I am innocently unaware that they are more conniving in their tactics to extract information from me. But I'm scheming for my own angle. I want to earn their trust so that they will explain why the wards keep weakening at points in the most vulnerable areas.

Fatima makes a hummed sound. "I must confess, I do find it interesting to have a witch aiding in our protection this century around."

"Have we suddenly forgotten what Magiks are to us?" Cassandra screeches. Her head falls back with a bitter laugh, her hooves of a deer dragging along the rug. "Since Arabella's return to Ifaeris, there have been no attacks. No imminent warning or danger to suggest Delphi thinks highly enough of herself to hold a chance against us." Then she turns to Jiya. "Lady Jiya, you said yourself that this could be an elaborate ploy. Perhaps the king just thinks the lie to be true."

"I do not believe that Arabella would orchestrate this whole ordeal when King Cassius told us that she cares not for the crown's advantage," Fatima argues in an attempt to sway the other rulers in my favor.

Jiya turns to the other Fae women, tilting her head at an angle where I cannot see her facial expressions. "I believe Cassius' intentions to be pure, and he would not place his faith in Arabella if she were not willing to help. Perhaps not for our benefit, but her intention to aid is of very little matter when we have the same end goal."

Cassandra's petulant and misdirected animosity is becoming less and less tolerable. But I hold my composure. I remind myself of the importance of their loyalty so that they won't challenge Cassius for the crown.

One. One, two, one. One, two, three, two, one... I tap the sides of my thigh while keeping my eyes focused on the women in front of me. Counting in my head up to eight and down while the Fae argue.

"Are you so narrow-minded that you actually accepted Delphi would stop attacking?" I berate. "Just because I've returned and Adonis no longer serves her, doesn't mean she's stopped caring."

The room goes still. Silent and responsive.

"She wants power. She wants to rule," I keep to my point. With bitterness, I prepare to admit the stinging candor of his treachery. "If you think Cassius was doing this without the thought of his people, I can tell you that when he was offered the opportunity to have me, he traded my life for the common fae stolen from their families."

Responses to this revelation, while all containing similar reactions, are various. Widened eyes, a taken aback straightening of their posture, a parted mouth.

Jiya's lips purse into a half-smile, her pupils turning to a more open state. An unmistakable showing of pride that would have never caught my eye if my gaze wasn't constantly jumping between the three. "What was he willing to offer in exchange for their return?"

"A piece of land." Before any of them attempt to speak out in rashness or objection to the act already committed, I add, "A small piece. Only the corner of Enthar where the old Oris manor remains."

Fatima's expression of neutrality turns to a face of furrowed brows and downward lips. "We were never told of this bargain."

"Because he, a few other Fae, and my friends found me before Cassius drew up the final word of their negotiation. Something that might be relevant to all, had Lord Tanzin decided to come today."

The last sentence causes passing glances between the room. From that, I remember the lord wasn't here when I spied in on Cassius speaking to the rulers. By now, I think it isn't just me who has taken notice of his constant absence.

I'm certain that Cassius has no idea about Korine being aware of where I was held. She didn't torture me during my time there, and I don't know how long she knew I was in Gigantia, so I choose to say nothing. It's a big accusation. And when Korine is an Elemental, I have to be sure I can present this information with proof.

Looking directly at Fatima, I say, "For Delphi, one piece of land might've turned into something more in the process."

"You said that she asked for a mere piece of land in exchange for our people," Jiya says, her voice tailing up at the end of her statement.

"She asked that of Cassius," I respond, though my attention is on no one specifically. "If she ended up ruling a section of land, small or not, what was stopping her from taking all of Ifaeris and leaving you with nothing?" For a few seconds, I debate if I should offer up more. "On top of that, Delphi asked me for more land."

"Only someone without any sense at all would think Cassius to keep from giving up land if you asked," Cassandra insults. "But I doubt that, as incompetent as he is, the boy would give up a kingdom." She brushes a hand down the crimson of her chemise dress. The trumpet sleeves have silvery embroidery along the sleeves. The color differs from that of the element she is representing, regardless if it's her daughter who is of the Wateriever bloodline.

"Moreover, it cannot be your word to offer her land," Fatima says. "Ifaeris' land rulings are given by bloodline decree unless the land chooses the ruler."

That much I'm aware of from being imprisoned by Delphi.

Fatima is the kindest to me out of the three. She is headstrong and fights fiercely, also becoming the peacemaker between Cassius and the other rulers. Those things aside, she still isn't my friend. I can't trust her with all that I know.

"The point is," I cut myself off from exposing my exasperation, "Delphi is much stronger than you give her credit for. I've lived through what it was like with her newly acquired magik. To cast her out of our worries is a mistake."

"A noble tale," Cassandra says, "but one of a lie."

This time, I glare at her. She so desperately wants to believe me as malicious as Delphi that she refuses to see reason. "Why would I lie about this?"

"You lied to assemble us here," Jiya expresses. A reminder that their trust in me is as empty as mine in them.

The Fae already don't like my kind. They especially didn't like *me* when I worked under Elliot. And even though I work alongside Cassius, their opinion hasn't changed.

I'll never be given the same respect as the Elementals, but I *can* be stronger.

I scan the three of them and take a deep breath. A stabilizing inhale. "That was because you wouldn't have come otherwise. Be honest, without my lie, would you have come if I sent word to meet with me and me alone?"

Nothing.

An irritated smile of validation widens from my mouth. "You see? Since hearing of me, you've had no reason to think I posed a threat. I found where and what happened to the missing common Fae. But even with the knowledge I give to you, I'm accused of being a liar."

It occurs to me then how arduous it is to be a ruler. There are many decisions to be made, and more times when I have to keep myself from trading information or terrorizing it out of them. I think about the times that Cassius has dealt with this without my presence. The other Elementals must have been conspiring together against his ruling since he was decided to be king.

Despite recently appointing Atticus as Lord of Mindae and that responsibility being lifted from the piles of decisions to be made, there are many more things that must be followed through on. The rulers have implemented the changes that Cassius has demanded, but they remain hostile with the decrees. If they become unruly, we may need to assign new ones entirely.

It's time to test how far I can go with my command. "I need you to keep from bombarding Cassius with your concerns. Part of your obligations is to send aid when we need it in tracking Delphi and sending guards to patrol the wards. If you hear anything of them being tampered with, you report your findings immediately."

"You have no power to demand things from us," Cassandra barks.

"Actually," I say with a belittling smile, "I was Cassius' High Reeve before the night of his coronation. I've held power over you regardless. But now, I'm the queen. Therefore, your loyalty to the lands equates to loyalty to me."

Fatima is the only one not outrageously appalled by the news.

Her body is tense, but she doesn't go against my declaration. "That means that if you had given Delphi–"

"Yes," I stop her. "If I gave Delphi what she wanted in exchange for my freedom, the land would've been freely offered by the High Queen. She would have become a ruler."

Rather than being met with a bow or respect, the Fae women stand rigid with their expressions agape.

"Other than informing Lady Theodosia, I expect you to hold yourselves accountable and not say a word of what I told you to Cassius or Harrison before I have," I order. "Understood?" I make eye contact with the women, each of whom nodding when I glance at them.

Relatively, at the same time, all three utter, "Yes."

"I will send word for a meeting soon. Please see your way out."

They each leave, and once they're gone, I notice a head inching through the small opening between the doors. I whisk my hand, and the two large doors open fully, unveiling my advisor playing with the buns that tie up half of their hair.

"You might as well have come in if you were gonna be eavesdropping," I tell them.

"Forgive me. I was only curious as to–"

Their nervousness is laughable. I don't think the servants nor my advisor understand when I'm not being serious. I step down from the throne and walk until I'm at their side. "Calm down, I was just joking. But you can't tell Cassius what you heard either. Not until I do later."

Damita nods their head multiple times in promise. They scurry off to do something of their own accord, while I begin to list and organize how to tell Cassius of the things I know.

XXI

Quality Time

Cassius

Days have begun to blur together as one. I cannot recall what happened at which point in time as I sit within the garden, just past the stroke of a new day.

Helena tends to the gardens quite often since her abdication as queen. I may have ruined one of her hedges by crashing into it in my sweet state of drunkenness.

Effects of slumber are slowly overtaking me. My eyes are slightly open, and the moon is in its phase of waxing. Then, I am overwhelmed by the gelid sensation of water being thrown to my face.

Though the outside is no place for a king to retire, punishment ought to be served to whoever thinks it funny enough to disturb me. My irritation only increases once I sit up and find Harrison cackling. In a fit of heaving breaths, he's fallen into a squatted position, laughing so hard that he knocks himself over and falls back into the hedge that I have wrecked, creating a larger indent.

The mess of a Fae, bushes, and other flowery objects overlay in a heap, none composed.

Eventually, he collects himself before sitting on the crafted bench, leaving me to remain on the ground, where I have yet to get up. One look at our height difference, and he bursts into laughter once more. I throw the precious metal chalice I hold at him, though it misses horribly.

"I did not invite you here for your entertainment," I sneer, glaring at him until we switch positions.

Pleasure in his attitude brings about a smirk. "You did not invite me at all."

"Am I expected to feel sorry for that?" I ask with crossed arms.

"I suppose not."

Nocturnal creatures roaming around the Darkened Forest are so loud that the pounding in my head cannot drown out their sounds.

"You appear miserable, friend. I've never seen you so bothered. Trouble with your unruly witch?" He flips a coin, one created of silver and serves as a Zip higher than most, save a Gold Zip.

Thoughts of her ought not to pass through my mind tonight. That is what the delight of consuming lasialic and sugary sweets is for. But alas, the slightest mention of her reminds me why I am out here alone in the cold of night in the first place.

She remains at Nexus, unnoticing of my presence projected beside her but feeling its haunting all the same. Lingering in the shadows of every corner of the prison that she desperately tries to escape.

There are still so many things I wish to ask her. I want to *share* everything with her, though I know it is not me whom she desires. Not anymore.

"You were not at Theodosia's revel tonight," Harrison says rather than forcing the information from me. "I am aware of the duties you have as king, but I'm surprised you take them with any seriousness at all."

The tone of my friend cannot be described as mockery, if that is what he intends. Instead, it emphasizes how greatly he disregards the rulership of our lands.

Over the course of being left to rule alone, I could perfectly hear Ezra taunting me daily. Calling me useless. A disgrace. That I have no business being king, and less so a glimpse of success without Arabella to speak sense into me.

So each time I was burdened by decisions, I would begrudgingly choose the opposing option of whatever it was I had thought of firstly. I would think of clever plans or means of trickery far more intelligent than what I would have thought to come up with in years past.

I have responsibilities I never wanted, and it is entirely her fault.

All of this I hate, not solely for the obligations, but due to the reason that the lives and deaths of the Fae are under my leadership. I can laugh at the minor misfortunes of common fae, but the life of another is not something I ever wanted power over. I don't know what to do, and that very thing churns my stomach. Strategy was never something I paid much mind to when my father ruled, but now I have to think of other possibilities outside of myself.

Ezra and my father may be dead, but their insults follow me in their afterlife.

Sometimes, I hear their voices so clearly, I think I could materialize their spirits.

To admit this to Harrison would result in ridicule. Rather than doing so, I say, "You can ask your mother where I had been tonight." I crack a smile at him. "Both of them."

He sends a smirk at my words. "Finally, I missed this side of you." Taking a snort of iceheart dust, Harrison giggles giddily. Three years over me, and he still acts the youngest of our trio of friends. "I miss the days when we would take any that we wanted. We used to be fun, the three of us. We were horrible and unapologetic. What happened to that side of you?"

"Perhaps I have outgrown your childish games."

"Oh yes, this from the same Fae that once watched as Korine charmed the human lover of a common fae." His laughter erupts with coated sarcasm. "Do you not recall when she glamoured the human so well, he used his pen and stabbed himself in the neck to pledge his undying service to you?" His head faces down, hunched over as he laughs harder at the memory. "You have become dull."

And you thrive off sadism.

"In any case," he moves on, "have you heard much from Korine? I feel as though I have not seen her in weeks. And you know, for my dramatics, that seems like a lifetime to me."

I think over his question. Korine *hasn't* been around much. Though I have been occupied since the night of my coronation, I find it odd that Harrison has not seen her either. She does not attempt charming others the way the two of us do, and Theodosia was too young to have joined in our debauchery during the time of our raising. Though there are other Fae our group has joined together with in revels, none are so close who I would think know of her whereabouts.

Exchanged looks between us while saying nothing was once worrisome for others. When Harrison, Korine, and I were silent, it meant that we were thinking the same thing before something egregious would occur.

I think that reasoning is why the common fae continue to harbor fear of me and find trouble trusting many of my decrees. The resentment that the common fae hold towards myself has little effect on me, but how they view the crown does. Perhaps my rulership will be doomed no matter how hard I attempt to present myself in a better light.

"I have not heard from her, no." After ongoing silence, I ask, "Are you attending the meeting at the behest of Arabella's request?"

The meeting is to take place in one week's time, with the other Elementals in attendance. Not only are the rulers of the lower courts expected to attend, but all future Elemental rulers are invited as well.

"I would rather not intrude," Harrison responds. In truth, he would rather not be bothered by the politics of his mothers. I'm sure that he will wait to sire an heir and pass off the responsibilities of being a ruler to them.

"It is not an intrusion when your attendance is demanded," I tell him. I doubt my friend would willingly go without an order.

Harrison shoots his eyebrows up in surprise. Our dynamic, where I allowed him to do whatever it was he liked until I said otherwise, now functions as it did before. "You are being unkind. May I not send a representative in my place as your father did in meetings such as these?"

Immediately, I am seething with enough aggravation to evoke alertness in the presence of my friend. Though he does not know the extent to which I hold disdain for my father, he knows well not to bring him into the topic of conversation.

I glance at him, saying, "You will do more than attend. Convince your mothers that to cast Arabella away will do nothing more than bring harm to their court."

"Why must I tell my mothers to offer refuge to a witch?" he remarks playfully.

Persuasion does not work well on someone who finds glee in creating dramatic torment for others, though I ought to try regardless.

"She's your queen," I say. "Her survival is just as important as mine. If not as my friend, then do this with the knowledge that her queenship upsets the other rulers."

"You should have led with her being queen. I thought that was perhaps a jest." Attention to the smallest changes in attitude is something Harrison lacks, yet his eyes scan me. "Had you informed the other rulers of this when you spoke of her importance during the search for her?"

"It was too tedious to detail," I reply. "I cannot be faulted for missing a few things."

While humming, he taps a pointed finger to his curved mouth. The sharp spikes–similar to horns–that poke from his shoulder are covered to hide the true mood that exists within him. "I shall do as you command, but they will likely have reservations of a queen that can lie. My mothers think Arabella capable of betrayal and working with the witch they know little of."

My head tips back in frustration, hoping to disguise my nervousness before I return to my friend. "Their apprehensiveness is understandable, but they ought to be grateful rather than distrust the same witch who saved them from the common fae demanding their heads."

Once more, Harrison's eyebrows go up in surprise, the corner of his mouth lifted in a smirk. "I do not think your lady lover likes me very much. And I may like that all the more. I think it would be intriguing to get under her skin. See what makes the anger truly tick."

Had Arabella been here, she would scowl at him with warning intent. After, of course, her reaction of being taken aback and rolling her eyes. She would have said something so scathing that Harrison may as well have signed over his death. That, I know with absolute certainty.

That, I laugh at.

"I have heard that she's shown nothing of interest in you any longer. If you no longer wish to romance her," he insinuates with a smirk, pushing the golden of his hair back, "perhaps you would not mind granting me the kind honor of a night well spent in her chamber."

Though I know he jests, uncaring for Arabella in any such way, I hate his words all the same. Harrison is a friend, but he remains a particularly inconsiderate Fae.

A heat of rage pushes to my fist. I feel a pound nagging at the front of my mind. A voice urging me not to explode at the Elemental. I remind myself that this is something Arabella would not do over a minor provocation.

"Your face is not one I think she should have to bear."

"I would think my face is a fine one to bear." He stretches both arms, resting his hands behind his head.

I do not allow for curiosity to get the better of me. My energy is far depleted, and if I do not force myself inside Nexus within the next passing minutes, I will spend my slumber on the dew of the grass.

XXII

A Special Evil

Luka

Irritation, sleep deprivation, agitation. All three are what best describe how I feel.

Unsurprisingly, those within Ifaeris have their guesses regarding the constant visits of my friends. We do our best not to draw attention when checking the wards, but only so many rounds can be done without adding suspicion to the common fae. If anything were to slightly confirm their assumptions as to why there is a need for protection, the result would be catastrophic.

I skip a rock between my feet as my friends approach. Juli's wheelchair is being pushed by Grayson, with our other two friends walking alongside them.

"Luka!" Violette greets. She hands Damien a bag that is filled to the brim with food and runs to embrace me. Initially, my body is stiff. I've spoken to them numerous times since my return, interacting as if nothing has changed, but they have all kept their distance from any physical form of affection with me. Instead, they will stare as if they cannot believe I am real. Today, it seems, they believe it. Or at least, Violette does.

"Gods mate, I've seen frogs change their appearance more than you," Damien mocks as he draws near. "You *do* remember Vi and I design clothes, don't you?"

"As much as I support your fashion capabilities, you have never designed something which matches my particular taste in clothing for day-to-day wear."

He rolls his eyes at me. "Whatever you say."

"You look like you haven't slept in days," Grayson rudely comments as he joins us with Juliette.

I haven't.

All I feel is tired. Exhausted in every sense of the word. Smaller tasks of my duty have little effect on me, but I need Delphi to be brought to the Council soon, so that, if we stay in Ifaeris, at the very least, she is one less burden on my mind.

"As seneschal, I spend late nights bettering myself at my job while also doing research," I explain, not bothering to mention that I have also taken on Arabella's previous role as High Reeve. Their heads all move around, echoing familiarity from a period when Grayson, Vi, Damien, and I discussed topics that they only knew half the truth of. "Most nights, I lie awake thinking of different ways I can murder those who watched Ari imprisoned and did nothing."

Their facial responses are all more or less the same. Variations of shock or thoughts of concern.

"You have so many issues," Grayson comments.

"I'm aware. You've listed them quite extensively while intoxicated."

Fae stare at us as we stroll through, detestation on their sneering faces, while curses aimed directly at us are muttered. I cannot be sure if this is due simply to their loathing of Magiks or if it extends to our bodily appearances and the way in which our clothing differs from theirs.

"How *is* Ara?" Damien inquires. "I know you said she's still not dealing with the withdrawals well."

My heart slows its beating. For our first weeks back, Arabella could not go one day without the high of valskull or some other substance. She would claim that she wasn't reliant on it and only used it as an escape, but then, she'd retreat to her mind, keeping others at arm's length while laughing in giddy. I did the best I could to help, but it typically ended with her forcing me to sleep away from her. I've had to remain cautious in my words, the same way I had in the past when her mind was in a similar place.

It's turned to something much darker since the nightmares began, increasing after a month and causing her to break down.

We cross over a rickety bridge made of tree branches, with plants climbing through the open spaces and vines that weave through the rails. Moss seems to coat everything, from the trunks of trees, to broken-off pieces of wood, to the boulders that line an edge of Mindae. The wards seem to be intact, aside from the erosion that occurred from the storm two nights ago. For safe measure, Damien, much better at the topic of warding than I am, takes a carved knife to etch the sigils into where the magik previously painted. He then flips it back down so that the ward cannot be detected by anyone who is possibly a spy for Delphi.

The method is much simpler than drawing on the symbols constantly. This way, it guarantees a lower chance of the magik being tampered with. It may be time to revisit the areas I had previously examined.

"She's progressing," I answer Damien, but I'm speaking to the group as a whole. "Her decisions have turned from impulsive to constant distractions and throwing herself into her responsibilities as queen. She spends most of her time searching for answers on ways to understand blood magik and the rest of her time training with Kabir. I wouldn't call that better, but it isn't worse."

Juli must sense that this is something that I do not want to discuss, so she reaches into Violette's bag, made from canvas, and tosses plates of paper for us to use on the ground. "She should invite us on one of the days she checks the wards. Least then she'd have company."

"What else has she been doing for research anyway?" Vi asks. "She told us about some of it—obviously, we've all helped a little—but she hasn't told us anything new for a while."

"She rarely tells me where she goes off to when she leaves Nexus. There are hints of her doing duties, but never specific."

It worries me endlessly that I never know where she goes off to. I always fear something is going to happen to her again. Without her, I am terrified. She's holding herself together by nothing but a determination to see through what she's started.

"That's ominous," Damien says. "Is she planning something?"

I shrug my shoulders. "I don't particularly think she would tell me if she were."

Grayson opens his mouth to say something, shuts it, then opens it again to speak. "That's even more unsettling. You know, her anger issues and all. Hell, the last time we were going over translations, she almost threw a book across the room."

We gather in a circle and sit. Juli struggles to stand from her wheelchair, Grayson and I becoming her crutches. Then, slowly, she lowers herself to the ground, her curls pulled back by her clip. She has regained the ability to walk small distances, though the healers said the likelihood of her needing assistance from the wheelchair may extend to her whole life. This may have been prevented if I had not taken extra time to kill someone so worthless out of rage.

The pizza that Damien pulls out is plain, with cheese and pepperoni. Garlic butter coats the crust, much to my dismay.

Grayson looks at me with a raised eyebrow, laughing at my reaction before handing out napkins and utensils, which only I use. I cut the food into pieces and use the fork to bring it to my mouth, freeing my hands and clothing of the greases, oils, and mess.

Before university, I was never allowed American pizza. I never knew I would enjoy it.

Our food comes from our favorite late-night restaurant. The same that we frequented on nights we stayed awake for study sessions at Lazipeus. Those would be the same times the others laughed much more than they learned. Stuffing their stomachs so full that they would look in pain if they were to take another bite, which only resulted in more laughter.

No one says anything as we enjoy the food, satisfying our hunger. I eat at a steady but fast rate, my schedule for the day packed with obligations that do not grant the luxury of leisure conversation. However, against what my father would have allowed, I have made a slot for precisely one hour to finish examining the wards in Mindae and intermingle with my friends.

The next on my schedule, however, will be more serious. I must okkar to Aquatius and ensure that those whom Lady Theodosia is sending to follow through on Cassius' decree are continuing to do so up to the crown's standard.

No matter how many times I assume to prefer isolating myself in paperwork, there is a certain satisfaction that comes with commanding others and taking lead of things on my own. I enjoy it. Without having any sense of excitement in productivity, I feel as if I am useless.

From the peaceful quiet, Grayson says, "It sucks that Delphi took you, but it couldn't have been all bad if you got to beat the shit out of one of the two people keeping you."

Juli lightly knocks him with the back of her hand, her blue-green eyes narrowed. "Why would you say that?"

He shrugs while saying, "It was funny."

Face glowered, I stare directly at my friend. "Your empathy is greatly appreciated, Grayson. I'll be sure to remember this in the case you're taken hostage."

Damien stretches his legs and crosses them as Violette lays her head on his lap. "Would you ask your father for any help?"

"Yeah." Juli leans back with one arm extended to support her. "Aren't y'all rich? Why not just have him open an investigation with the Council or something?"

I sit acutely upright. "My family has persuasion in the decisions and laws made, yes, but ultimately, we do not have the capability to open an investigation so easily, just as Vi's and Damien's can't. That power lies with our leaders and executives."

She gives me a quizzical look with a hummed sound in question, unsure of the difference between the Council of the Coven leaders and Coven executives. Neither she nor Ari were raised the way the rest of our group had been, leaving them with only a morsel of an idea of how our leaders operate. To her credit, there is not much of a distinction between the two leaders' role types, outside of certain things outlawed and how they will be dealt with versus overarching decrees made.

Violette waves me off. Clicks her tongue and rolls her eyes. "Oh please, even Gray's father knows the Council only *really* acts whenever they think something poses a threat to their power." She laughs once. "Or if something could expose magik to humans. And that only results in the erasure of their knowledge of our world or death of the Magik who exposed us."

"Yeah, and without memories of the craft and their families, they're left to live a life of confusion among society," Damien adds, shamefully aware of the system that all of our families participate in.

There are different severities in punishment when exposing

magik, depending on the executive's law, but if the person who has been exposed becomes a liability, all parties involved would first have their memories erased. Considerably merciful to leave the Magik alive, but much more damaging to be set into the Human Lands without a support system or ability to recall who they are. A prolonged death sentence of sorts if their magik spirals.

Despite knowing this fully, Grayson grimaces. Rubs his hands along his arms, which are losing their tan, returning to a lighter color. "From what I know, knowledge on restricted magik *should* only be known to leaders and executives sworn into the Coven. Probably more kinds if we're talking about the magik exclusive to the Council. *But as we've seen*, it depends on who you are in relation to them."

"Gods, I knew I was right to never trust them," Juli complains, her arms lazily thrown into the air before flopping onto her lap. "So you're telling me, not only do twelve corrupt fucking Magiks get to control everything 'cause another hundred and seventeen executives elected them, but when it involves a serious matter, they'll hoard information and do nothing?"

"A fairly accurate assessment, yes," I admit.

"What else are we doing then?" Damien asks. "If you're not going to ask your parents, what's the next move?"

"Jefferson," I respond. Cassius and I had reached the conclusion that the Stone of Elestial was stolen from him by Delphi. He has insights into the most powerful objects and their location. Collects antiques and ancient relics, which he has stolen, distributing them throughout Magiks for their benefitted use.

"What are you going to do? Form an alliance?" Violette teases, nudging me with her foot. "Just in case?"

Joking aside, Jefferson would be a potential threat if he were to use his collected items as an advantage over other creatures. Deeper insight into the Stone of Elestial and its powers is needed.

There could be more than just the ability to attract another into the control of the stone. How it can be destroyed. A visit to the collector is long overdue.

"He should if we're going against Delphi," Juli responds, a light sense of curiosity crossing her round face. "You think she's gonna ease off since Bells is back and her boyfriend left her? My ma wouldn't even let her boyfriend forget he cheated when he was on his deathbed."

Damien chokes on his drink. "Doubt it. If she followed Luka to another continent out of pettiness, I don't think she'd give up on this."

"Did you ever expect Delphi to become something this destructive?" Violette asks me. She flicks her hair with a snap of her head. Takes a sip of the pop. "We knew she was capable of *normal people evil*, but she had you killed and brought back to life for fun."

"Maybe she did that to Adonis at one point too, just to test it out. She *does* bring 'crazy girlfriend' to another level." Grayson chuckles, slapping his thigh and says this all with a mouth still full of half-chewed pizza.

I look at him with a deadpan expression that matches my innermost thoughts. Only he would say something so immature with a face stuffed with food.

"You are an abomination to my sanity. Do you ever listen to what comes out of your mouth?"

The sorcerer laughs harder at his perfectly indecorous statement.

"I'm serious," I continue. "Do you ever think about what you have to say before you say it and stop yourself from speaking? You sound insufferable and look even more like a child while you speak with food still in your mouth."

Everyone in the group begins staring at me and wheezing alongside Grayson, as if enabling him. It calls into question whether they were taught how to socially interact at all. I wonder in further detail what it says about me if these are the ones I consider myself closest to. My most reliable friends, who stop at nothing to remind me how much I have been missed.

283

XXIII

A Deathly Agreement

Luka

When I enter our shared room, I hear the sound of the water shutting off. Ari, I'm sure, has finished her morning shower after her time with Kabir and is setting off for a day, which I have persuaded her to take for herself.

She has been overworking herself much too hard. So, after a night of sprinkling promises into our conversations, she let me convince her into spending today relaxing. Her idea of a day well spent is to go through a pile of her unread books and read whichever she feels most drawn to.

I knock on the bathroom door, calling out her name to say goodbye before leaving with Cassius to Infinite. As it turns out, he and I are not the only ones to assume Jefferson's relationship with Delphi. Ari told me that, while being alone in a cell, it gave her time to recall the words said by Jefferson. She mused over how the thief spoke of the stone being stolen from him but never how it was stolen. Only admitted to knowing nothing of the missing Fae, which, when searching through his mind, is true, considering he couldn't have known Delphi's plan.

"I'll be out in a minute," Ari says from the other side. I hear four objects fall and one muttered curse from her side of the door before the sound of her voice speaks to me again. "Putting on clothes."

My hand reaches for the door, turning the knob to open it. She's facing away from me, bent to the floor as she picks up her clothing to throw into the barrel of unwashed garments. Two of her towels are thrown over a hook, and she hasn't noticed me yet. I lean on the frame that previously held a door between us while the steam from her shower exits through the open space and into our sleeping area.

There's a smile that forms on my face as I take in the gorgeous indents on her skin. The ones which show similar to the rippling waves in the middle of the sea. Her body was formed by the most sightly things in nature. "You're beautiful, love."

Ari turns around, jolts back in motion, and yanks a towel from where it hangs, loosening the hook from its secured place. She cannot hold in her blithe sounds that come out as nothing more than a sighed laugh.

When I see her laugh, I know I would gladly take on a battalion of armies if it means listening to it on loop until my last breath.

"You have places to be," she warns me as I stare. "We don't have time."

"Come here, Arabella."

Nothing is as inviting or tender as her name when I say it.

She drops the towel that covers her soft body, and as she remains standing, I find my eyes sliding down to scan all of her. My hand goes still, gaze watching her move until I bend to press my lips on hers while she roams her hands around me, undoing the buttons of my slacks and part of my shirt. Her touch is premeditated, her icy fingertips wandering, loosening my tie. As she moves my hands to her waist, all I know is her and nothing more. I'm stumbling back, my feet nearly tripping on the rug as the two of us fall onto the bed.

Hands are exploring each other, mine becoming slick from the wetness from her cunt. Our bodies are moving, and while sitting up, her knees lock around me with enough space for my fingers to work around her clit. She goes to undo the closure of my pants. Until my underwear is exposed, and she is so close to losing herself with me.

I cannot speak.

Can't move.

At the loss of movement, she shifts around, her right hand palming me beneath my underwear. My cock is stiff, hardened for her.

"Mahal, *please*," she moans. Her previous anxiety to me seeing her body has fallen. She's rocking her hips, her body bucking against my hand. And when I pump in my fingers, curling them, I plunge at such a pace that I feel her cunt releasing enough wetness to drip onto my underwear. Fabric that hides the one part of my body that screams to be inside her.

"Not yet," I tell her. My mind is out of sorts. I vainly need to hear her. Need to feel her around me. "Not until I'm inside you."

Ari's mouth closes over mine. The harder I press around her clit, the more erratic her breaths become. Her back arches, lips parting from me as high-pitched sounds leave her mouth.

I groan against her touch. At her pulling down my pants just far enough. As she lifts her body to adjust and prepare herself, I'm in absolute ecstasy. So close to entering her.

Until there is a knock at our door.

This can't be over. *I don't want this to ever stop.*

Despite her smile, Ari is frustrated. Her breathing also sounds angry. She shuts her eyes, once with a head turned to the door to be sure she heard correctly, twice in disbelief, with a longer blink. Her hand combs through her hair, which is still wet from her shower, and on her sweet face is an expression of disappointment. A second after, she presses her body against mine, kissing my cheek. "You have to go."

To my chagrin, Ari's right. She lifts herself off while I tuck myself back into my pants and straighten out my attire. My shirt has become wrinkled, my whole appearance disoriented.

While I walk to the door after washing my hands, Ari remains in the bathroom, closing the door to keep our intrusion from seeing her.

Cassius stands there, and all I feel is irritation that he appears just exactly when he is not wanted. An impeccable talent, really.

"Is everything settled?" he asks.

"Yes."

No.

He wraps his hand around my wrist, and I okkar us to the top stairs of Club Infinite. The building is silent, and the only ones in the club are the workers who are cleaning from the previous night. I have been here on many occasions–when Damien, Vi, and Grayson dragged me along on a night out. This, of course, was during our first year living in Los Angeles.

Hickory wood creates the door with a nameless, platinum plate displayed. Each door on this floor has a name etched into the metal, but this is blank.

"What have you to say?" Cassius asks. He doesn't care that he interrupted a very intimate moment between Ari and me. "You cannot be upset with me. It was you who suggested we come together."

I keep from answering. Instead, I point to the unclaimed door, Cassius giving a sharp nod. First, I press my ear to the door. There is nothing audible but the aggressive writing of a pen against paper. They are quick movements, sounding like a signature.

Then, when I open the door, Jefferson is sitting at his desk. He grunts out something of annoyance and perks his head up to see who came to disturb him this early into the morning.

"Back to beg for information about the Stone of Elestial?" Jefferson taunts in Cassius' direction.

"Only to ask about how it was stolen," Cassius returns.

Jefferson's smile of amusement turns into a raised face of intrigue. His hair looks to be unwashed for days, though it may just be due to the thin limpness and an oily scalp. He turns in my direction, returning quickly to Cassius. "I see you've brought the son of the unofficial Coven executive."

I want to know why he is not surprised at my being alive. It suggests he's more aware of Delphi and the stone.

"You're fighting a superfluous endeavor if you think I will help you in any way," Jefferson laughs.

The mercenary is in grave peril. Had anyone in the Council reached him first, sharing the same knowledge that we have of him, he would not still be alive.

Jefferson's greed for monopolizing his business and handing it to those he views would bring him the most attention is not unknown to those in power. More importantly, word of his folly of falling in love with women that he seeks to share in such a mindset is his biggest tell in revealing his work with Delphi.

"What if we inform the Council about certain dealings that occur with you present?" Cassius challenge.

He only laughs more. His hand shoos Cassius off, attention brought back to me. "Two Magiks and a Fae conspiring together. In my most wild dreams. There have been many instances of the Coven officers using certain criminals for themselves."

It's not at all surprising to learn that Jefferson is on good terms with the government workers of our world. His bluff may deter others from questioning him further, however, I happen to be smart enough to call him on it. He is not unexpendable to the Coven. Other thieves exist within our world.

I've seen many things as the son of a wealthy family, but there are things that even the executives believe to be reduced to legends. I suppose that is why I was uninformed of certain restricted magik and why, until recently, I believed the Fae to be extinct. I am constantly met with new information that surprises me, which makes me question what my father is aware of and what has kept from him.

I cannot solely blame my parents for this. Though I was raised in the politics of our world, within the past few years–due to schooling at Lazipeus–I have not often been in association with the political elite, and the result has disconnected me from my understanding of the now. So much may have changed. Even so, the game of strategy remains to be moving through intimidation or manipulation.

"I have trouble believing that your rulers place faith in you without precaution," Cassius says while stalking closer to Jefferson.

"You're funny, Your Majesty." Jefferson stands a bit straighter to hold himself in the same position as Cassius, to which he fails. His left leg is bouncing slightly, fingers twitching. "At your side is a sorcerer who can lie, and your witch is someone known to be the liar of your court. How different am I?"

Cassius sends a scowl to the sorcerer. Unfortunately for him, Jefferson is right. Both Ari and I, as Magik, use our ability to lie constantly in order to gather information. In some cases, such as when meeting with the common fae, it bodes well, but more often than not, it makes it difficult to get the common fae to believe a word we have to say.

To prevent from revealing his thoughts further, Cassius returns to an appearance more entertained. He throws on a smile, folds his arms while leaning his shoulder on the wall. "You assume that I ought to distrust them, but they are the ones who have kept me from a foolish king's death. Whereas *you* had not revealed it was Delphi who stole the Stone of Elestial. I recall you consider yourself a high-value collector, so consider our meeting collecting a debt of sorts."

Suspicious, Jefferson darts glances around the room. Searches for anything stolen from his collection. "Are you going to send a mythical creature into my club? Exploit your power and therefore exposing who we are to humans around?"

Being confined to Ifaeris often muddles me into forgetting that there is more out there. Until this very topic is brought into conversation, I will forget that others would view something of this sort as unimaginable. What we do, what we're capable of doing, I remember then why we keep our identities a secret from humans.

"And I suppose that Arabella has dropped all her feelings for the poor king at your return?" Jefferson continues to taunt. He sends a suggestive look at Cassius, who is all too uncomfortable by the words. Next, he turns to me. "Do you still spend your free time allowing yourself to take any little attention she gives you?"

His mockery draws me back to a time when I was nothing to Arabella. She heard stories about me, calling me a cold, heartless man who treated everyone as if they were nothing. Such gossip is what drove her from me for so long. Then she saw me as more, but not enough to keep herself from proceeding warily around me. She shielded herself–her heart–away to ensure that she would never be hurt.

Jefferson is vibrating with an energy of self-importance. He prides himself on his collection but is unskilled at magik for the most part. A coward of the highest degree, evident when he throws a bag of different jewels and pieces that seem valuable. If the sorcerer assumes this to be a good enough bribe for us to leave him and continue about his day, my questions about how Delphi infiltrated his organization without strain no longer need to be asked.

I cannot let my insecure emotions rule my decisions. Emotional outbursts lead to sloppy mistakes. Again and again, when Ari was missing, did I make poor choices out of anger. Information went amiss because I did not think to ask common fae the correct questions. When it comes to her, I lose all connection to logic. My ability to think reasonably leaves my thought process, and I am inclined towards anxieties until I'm sure she's safe. If that means leaving a line of bodies behind me because of it, so be it.

"What you know, or we expose to the Council your involvement with the Fae and the Battle of Hearthis," I express in a matter-of-fact tone. To ruin not just him but the empire he has accumulated for himself in popularity among all mortals alike.

Jefferson's leer drifts from me to Cassius, then around the room. He breathes loudly, leaning back on his reclining chair while he racks the options in his head. His fingers clench into a fist, with each finger moving and the thumb scraping along his knuckles. Finally, he glances up at the two of us. "I've heard nothing circulating about the Coven's involvement or the Fae. According to rumors spreading through the club's floor, the Council specifically heard of a mishap at Gigantia, but it was said that it was quickly resolved."

"As someone who was there, it most certainly was not," I respond with a glare. "We barely escaped with our lives."

"One of our own had her insides ruined," Cassius informs. From the wrath in how he says this, I would think that he may care about what happened to Juliette. Shadows leave from the palms of his hands, summoning the silhouette that fights his battles for him. "My sister was nearly killed."

As the silhouette creeps towards Jefferson, Cassius' posture grows abrupt and stiff, causing the sorcerer to take a gulp of fear. He lowers his hand at the side of his desk, pulling out a paper with numbers scribbled on it.

"I steal from Magiks too," he manages. There is a mischievous smile that forms on his face. One that appears when someone assumes that they have the upper hand. He stands from his desk and walks behind us, hitting a ficus on his way. Then, he lifts the rug from its edge, revealing a safety deposit box after removing the disguising floorboards from their place.

That is his fatal mistake. To give me sufficient time to steady myself and sharpen my senses enough to concoct the ways I will kill him for his betrayal.

The inside of the safe is filled with items that I know to be stolen from the Coven, many dating further back than my childhood. There is the wand of Kaiman, the sorcerer who created the Council of the Coven. A diadem that belonged to Saoirse, Empress of the Forgotten, is also kept inside. A plethora of other things I thought were recovered and returned reside in this safe that is the width of a small clothing hamper. Items I do not doubt were stolen from other creatures as well.

Cassius and I glance at each other from the corner of our eyes. A mutual agreement. Jefferson digs deeper into the safe, eventually finding a toffee-colored book. He stretches himself up to where he now can face the two of us, though he does not reach our height.

"My loyalty is to me and myself alone. Though I *did* learn of the powers the Stone of Elestial contains, if that interests the two of you," Jefferson says. He dumps the book on the desk in front of him and gestures to the seats across from his, waiting for the three of us to have distance.

Cassius, whose chair is angled in a way that I can see both his and Jefferson's expressions, points his focus to Jefferson in suspicion. "Do not bait us with words as you would with others."

"Its power was created by a sorcerer in hopes he would raise an army large enough to have Magiks bow to him," Jefferson says. He taps his fingers on the book for three rounds, then slowly slides it to our side. "The book that goes more into the history is yours if, and only if, I am granted a favor of my choosing when the time comes."

I feel no sense of remorse when I harshly snap out, "How much more could this book be of use when the stone is still with Delphi?"

"Wouldn't you rather know its power and how to destroy it?" he questions in reply. Jefferson clearly, and incorrectly, assumes that we need him more than he needs us.

"Let me clarify," Cassius says. "Why would a boon granted from me equate to a simple book? The only promise I will agree to is if you also vow your loyalty to the Fae. And from what I have heard, you make good on your promises."

The sorcerer takes time to formulate a response. He sucks his lips into his mouth and eventually lets out a popping sound. "I'll promise my loyalty. And as an addition, I will not say anything if the Council or any executives come to question me. But you cannot betray me and reveal it was me who told you all of this."

"I, Cassius Disaris, vow to keep your name from spilling from my lips if there comes a time when you are called into question by any of your rulers," Cassius says carefully. "Luka?"

My head turns to him as he extends both hands across the table. Jefferson does the same, reminding the Fae that the agreement is one that cannot be broken. I use my magik to bind the two. The color of silvery magik enters the air, coming from both Jefferson's and my hands. His magik spirals around his and Cassius' individual bodies, meeting together where their hands hold the other's arm. Similarly, mine circles around both of them, a long stretch of magik passing through their torsos. As non-Fae, promises are flimsy, but when magik is involved, a broken vow causes slicing pains through your body at the beginning of the betrayal until death.

Before the spell finishes, Cassius calls my name again. "I want to add the stipulation that instead of death, if Jefferson breaks our deal, all promises are void, and I may give him up to the Council of the Coven."

Jefferson's eyes widen, but his hands are unable to pull from the connection. I nod, slightly chuckling and adding to the magik that binds them tighter for nine more seconds.

Out of spite or a sudden spout of good conscience, which I highly doubt, Jefferson turns to me with a feigned, apologetic face. "Did you know that I have spies everywhere?" I don't say anything, prompting him to continue. "My informants have told me that they heard from Delphi's friend saying she came to see Cassius earlier, where he offered Arabella up for his people. He called her rotten and said she brings nothing but grief."

Cassius stands in his place. Silent and denying nothing.

The former half I am aware of. I have already understood why I was necessary in finding Arabella and retrieving the missing Fae, but Cassius' words are something I did not know.

"If you care about Arabella, you would know better than to trust the High King."

"You have been misled into the notion that what you say affects me." I have to keep myself from revealing my true feelings on the matter. My hands twist, and Jefferson falls to his knees. He clenches his heart before pounding the floor for mercy. "I don't care if you live or die. I suggest that you remember that."

I relax my hand, releasing the magik that holds the sorcerer, who is gasping for air. Jefferson's head makes a soft *thud* against the wood of his flooring before Cassius and I separately okkar to the foyer of Nexus, where it is filled with fewer bodies, as many of the guards are in the open field training.

There are things I consider unforgivable. My morality is skewed and inconsistent, but one thing I've known since the day Ari walked into my life is that if someone hurts her, I will find a way to make them regret it in whatever way I best know how.

I'm shaking. I feel the furthest thing from composed as my hands turn into fists and knock Cassius at his jaw. Thoughts of shock and curiosity cross onto his face as his hand goes to rub it, but it's not fast enough.

My magik slams him into the front doors. He tries to fight back, summoning a sharp javelin from his shadows and launching it at me. It slices deep through the side of my lower waist. A sting so strong, I drop my magik and him to the floor.

Cassius rushes to me. His rings brush against the side of my cheekbones, his left fist narrowly missing. "You can go back to whatever realm they raised you from."

Sweat drips from my face.

No. It's not sweat.

Blood.

My fingers touch my cheeks to feel the red fluid falling from the sides of the pierced skin. And I'm smiling. I do not generally engage in immature fighting, but this is something beyond a small rift.

"Are you going to be the one to send me there?" I laugh. Regain enough strength to use my magik to drag him from the high-hanging ceiling to the marble floor. Cassius isn't trained in combat, whereas I was taught how to kill a man over fifteen ways by the time I was eleven, thanks to my father and the many Magiks who want him dead.

I rush until my foot stands on his wrist, my magik rapidly lifting and twisting the rest of his body until I hear a popping sound. His bones dislocate from each other, from his scapula to his humerus. Along with it, a scream of immense agony.

Ari may feel vengeful and angry towards Cassius, but, as I already know, killing him would only upset her more. She does not hate him. Not in the way that she thinks. I'm confident that *I* do not hate him. For that alone, I can't kill him. It doesn't, however, mean I must stop myself from inflicting blows. Nor does it mean that the king should not hear these words and face the ramifications of his actions.

I can't be bothered to listen to what the guards have to say as they pull the two of us apart. My thoughts are directed, filled with only emotions of rage and the need to exact it. Kabir finally knocks me back, forcing me into my body and recognizing where I am.

Multiple guards are pointing their swords at me. The next thing I know, Kabir, Cassius, myself, and other guards whom I should know but cannot currently bother to remember the names of are sitting in the waiting chamber by the throne room. The sound of a high-pitched ring has been playing in my ear, but when a tray of food is presented in front of me, I realize it is lunch.

Kabir is asking what led up to the altercation, to which I refuse to say. So Cassius explains.

Blood has seeped into my clothing. Comparable to a splatter design clothing piece put together by Violette and Damien.

Cassius is given ice wrapped in a wet cloth tied together by a piece of twine. He is shirtless, his arm in a sling while his slender body relaxes. And as we eat our lunch, Cassius presses the pack to his shoulder, where a contusion is already beginning to form. I twist my fingers when he isn't paying attention, relocating his bones back into place. Immediately after a yelp, the king looks at me, giving a half smile in gratitude.

He takes a sip of the Arctic blue wine he is so fond of. Says nothing while he takes several bites of his food. Then, he moves his head from side to side, cracking the tensed areas. "Jefferson was telling the truth."

A poor thing to tell me.

"Why would you admit this?"

"I cannot lie," he reminds me. "But it does not have the intention to which you believe. Everything I said was to trick Delphi, and for that, I was able to bring the Fae back and gather information of what they knew. By doing so, whatever Delphi is planning, it ensures that those Fae will keep from attacking us. It will keep us from being surrounded on all fronts."

Previously brainwashed or not, there are many Fae who would still side with Delphi. Most have suffered the Elemental rulership and unfair treatment for time dating back to the war against Gigantia. To break onto their land and take Ari back only incites the possibility of violence. It means bringing about war against the same creatures who killed many of the Fae's loved ones. Many of which, still in mourning.

His eyes glance to his food. "I truly did not think Delphi would harm the two of you much more, given your history with her. For that, I am forever regretful. I never sought to bring harm to Arabella, but I had to act as if I didn't care when speaking with Delphi."

The words sound earnest, and I know them to be genuine. He cares for Arabella just as much as I.

"Is she well?" he asks.

I take in a deep breath without answering. I can't reveal to Cassius what goes through Ari's head when the only answer to that is everything. Information that is and isn't to be shared must be balanced. I still require time before I can fully forgive him. "She's been trying hard, incredibly hard, to make sure everyone is okay. I think she assumes if she can make everyone happy, she'll be distracted enough to not focus on her emotions. She overanalyzes every emotion she has and pushes them away, trying to rationalize her feelings as insignificant or wrong."

"I only wish that she would speak to me. Hate me loudly or say something that lies outside the realms of our co-rulership."

Cassius is hurting in a way that I understand.

Gratitude, in a twist, sets in. If I had never been brought back by Delphi, I'm glad that there is someone who is willing to fight for Ari as hard as I am.

"Empty promises are not something I partake in. Ari has a strong heart and passions that push past extremities, so I won't force her to forgive you, but I can explain to her what her stubbornness won't allow her to see past."

We both finish our meals and head to our respective rooms. Ari has her body leaned forward on the bed with one leg hanging over the edge, the other bent, with her body fully resting on her calf. She holds a black pen and smiles with eyes wide in anticipation.

"How was Jeffers-" She breaks off as she takes in my state, dropping her pen and whipping herself to her feet. "What the fuck happened?" Each word is jumbled on top of each other.

"Cassius and I had it out," I say. Her face hardens, anger jumping onto her face. "I'm okay."

She leads me to the bathtub and takes a fresh cloth, dampening it with water and pressing it to my skin. The blood dissipates with each angry pat, the look on her face tight. "He keeps putting you in danger, and I'm getting fucking sick of it."

Though her worry is sensible, my thoughts do not heavily lean into it. Yes, there are points when I question whether a physical pain stems from something external or if Delphi has found a way to breach past the wards and undo my lifespan. But these debates quickly wash away once I recognize that the area in which I am sore is where I had increased my exercises the day before.

"This was my doing. Besides, the cuts won't take long to fully heal," I assure her. I gingerly place my lips on the skin of her forehead before starting the shower. Other duties I have today do not warrant leaving the palace, and I can smell the acidic sins of Infinite and the copper of my blood radiating off my body. "I think speaking with Cassius about what you're feeling may not be the worst thing in the world. He isn't as bad as you think he is."

Her eyebrows furrow together as she listens, shooting up when I finish. "Okay." She rolls her eyes and laughs. Shuts the door while dismissing my comment entirely.

At my shower's end, Ari kneels between my legs while I sit in my underwear at the edge of the bed. She's in her sleeping sports bra and underwear, smiling at me. After bandaging my head, she softly presses a kiss on the area.

"Is it wrong I think you look *more* attractive when you're bloody?"

I place my hand on her cheek, guiding her up and joining our lips together. She crawls until she reaches the pillows, placing her book on the foot of our bed, when my foot unintentionally kicks it off.

Every second is excruciating when she pulls away from me with a grimacing look, as if I had violated her most prized possession.

"I'm sorry," I murmur against her cheek.

"I'm sorry," I say again against her neck. My lips drag down all the way to her collarbone. I press my mouth to her chest, sucking roughly enough to mark her. "Forgive me."

Her thumb brushes my lips, directing my attention to her. An index finger curves, and I'm drawn upwards, resting my head on her chest as she plays with my hair.

Guilt weighs heavily on me when I think to the night Ari had been taken by Delphi. I was negligent.

So I hold on to her tighter.

XXIV

Unfriendly Reminder

Cassius

Three nights consecutively, I have dreamt of her. Incessant reminders of where she is not. The dreams are more or less consistent. She lingers in my room. *On my bed.*

A knock at my door forces me awake, but before I am able to tell the nuisance to leave, the door pushes open. At the frame stands Arabella, the light behind her illuminating her full figure. She's in nothing but a white, high-rising nightgown. The lacing extends only to the form-fitting chest area, the skirt starting right under her breasts. It's silk, cutting unevenly at the bottom of the dress, and ends just at the top of her dragon tattoo.

"Hi, Cas."

"Hello."

She crawls onto my bed, and I am too powerless to stop her. My hands go around her waist, pressing into her skin. My restraint is nothing but fickle and imaginary in her presence.

"Tell me this is happening," I beg, pulling myself up, kissing her with my arms wrapping around her. "Tell me you are here with me."

"I didn't want to hurt you," she breathes, kissing me deeper, shifting her body while clutching me closer. "I lov–"

But before she is able to complete what I long to hear, a door whips open, and my lids jump from their resting position.

A dream within a dream.

Both containing the same content.

Both wounding me.

If it took never sleeping to rid myself of these torturous illusions, I would sooner take the opportunity.

Arabella and Luka stand in the open area. She is with arms crossed, wearing loose lounging pants and a shirt that ends at the middle of her thigh. Luka, though, is in clothing that appears slightly different from his usual attire, wearing a modest shirt of garnet red under a tailored suit of naval blue, which has light touches of brass coloring all over the set.

"Cassius, get up," she groans, exhausted. She magiks over a regal set of clothing that has been tailored specially for me onto my bed. "You're gonna be late."

"This is your first time meeting the rulers of the lower courts as queen," I say. "Will you be dressing more according to your position?"

Her jaw shifts at my question, slowly closing her eyes and letting out a prolonged exhale. "I'll throw on some pants and a corset. How about I even strap on a sword at my side? Will that help?"

This. This is what I know to be the sobering reality I face. Such a sick twist to that which I have been interrupted from. Yet, despite that, my heart still elevates to high degrees and sinks to the depths of the earth whenever I lay my eyes upon her.

"Ari," Luka says, her eyes flitting to him at her name, with her sucking in her cheeks and taking a deep breath before her gaze returns to me.

I prop myself from my bed, peering down at what I am to wear. "It will surely demonstrate your capabilities to them."

"Good," she says with a smile that I wonder is genuine. "See you later, I guess."

I've had Arabella's throne brought from its storage place below the palace. It is identical to mine in every way, aside from the metal framing created with silver instead of gold. We sit together as a united front, with her to my left and Luka standing behind the two of us. He lurks near the corner below the window, beside the tray full of glass and lasialic.

Rather than the ensemble that Arabella had worn previously, now she wears a crow-colored garment, designed with sleeves that puff out all the way down past a quarter of her forearm and cuffs that cling from there to her wrist. I cannot help but notice the fabric that wraps tightly around the middle of her neck and the teardrop opening, exposing skin from her cleavage into her collarbones. Then, my eyes drift to the overlay skirt, which parts in the middle of the front, revealing the breeches that cling to her legs.

True to her word, at her side is weaponry shining as bright as her valor. Other jewelry she wears is that of her usual accessories: the necklace from Luka, her moon ring that coordinates with his, a surmount of other rings, and one thing more I see when she tucks her hair behind her ear.

She has on the star earrings.

I feel foolish. The high-rising breeches I wear, with golden buttons along the front of my thighs, contrast with my layered shirt of elegance, made with the orange of monarch butterflies. Yet my cape is the dark shade of our blood. We could not appear less similar.

At the very least, our crowns twine the same.

The first of our guests to arrive are the Elementals of the Airlius bloodline. Then comes the Rokus bloodline, Flameling, and finally, Wateriever. Korine is not with her parents, and those of the Spiritus bloodline are the only ones excused from this meeting.

"Hello, Your Majesty," Theodosia greets. Her ears are decorated with jewels of the water, with her skin of warm sienna complementing well with the sunlight, appearing exactly as her father had. A diadem of pearls crafted in line under a wreath of golden leaves rests over her curls of thickness. Her hooves are visible, however, her tail is not.

The Fae bow to me, yet none bother to show Arabella the same respect.

"Thank you for joining us," Arabella says. Her lips are painted with the dead of night, dark and confident. "You're probably curious as to why I have called you here."

"More so wondering why we are attending at the command of some lowly witch," Theodosia belittles. She crosses her arms over her feathered dress that brightens with the colors of a parrot.

Arabella rolls her eyes at the comment. Sucks in a breath and says to them, "You're here so that we can inform you of things regarding Delphi. While I haven't been able to collect enough information about *where* she is, I've learned there's a possibility she still has control over the common fae we've taken back from her."

During Arabella's explanation, I pay attention to the reactions of the other rulers. I notice faces that appear dismayed over being forced into this meeting. I also peer at the panic on some others' expressions, who do carry worry regarding Delphi.

The information is distressing, putting in danger not only the wards that protect our borders but the safety of the Fae in the lands.

"And that is of strong relevance?" Tanzin asks. He pulls Vaela closer to him and speaks directly to me. "Can we not have those Fae murdered?" There is merriness in his tune and a joyful gleam in his eye when saying so. It's as if the matters of those under him serve no importance. He cares not, so long as he is rid of those against him.

"The common fae still demand to know where their loved ones are. They'll stop at nothing if they find out we imprisoned *and* killed their family," Arabella states with eyes narrowing at him in suspicion. Deservedly so for a man who assumes his responsibility can be tossed to the crown.

Fatima had seldom interjected in meetings such as these when we have met prior. Though, given the matters regarding the newly presented information, she says, "You have said that you've collected this information from her books. Is Delphi still able to control the Fae now?"

"No. That's why the wards are so important," Arabella chimes on. "They keep her from using any magik she's possibly cast upon the imprisoned Fae. She can't control them while being far, less so when there are shield barriers preventing her from penetrating the grounds of Ifaeris."

"You have given us no reason to trust your word," Rebekah argues, creases of anger sharpening in her glare. "And it isn't as if we can glamour the truth from you."

With what I imagine to be great resistance, Arabella does not appear bothered, though I know she is undoubtedly holding herself from releasing the discomposure that brews within her. "I've ventured through the archives of my school. I've gathered information on restricted magik that Delphi's studied." She flattens her hands on the fabric of her breeches, turning it from a tensed claw to nails gripping into the clothing. Nothing strikes the other rulers. Weapons are sheathed, with only her words slashing the air. "Do you think I would put myself at risk of leaving the protected lands for nothing? She took *me*."

Her words stun my mind, all other thoughts coming to an abrupt halt. Arabella has informed me that she searched for evidence independently, but she did not mention leaving Ifaeris without any protection.

Curiosity beckons me to ask what it is she has done, but to appear as if I know nothing of what she does would only present the two of us in a disadvantageous position. I do not think she has shared this information with even Luka.

"And can we not lure her here by removing the symbols?" Cassandra asks.

"Removing the sigils puts all Fae at a vulnerability," Arabella answers. "It would allow the possibility of Delphi's magik to control the common fae. No winner would emerge but her."

My silence is being noticed by the other Fae. Jiya, Pyrros, and Theodosia are staring at me. From the three, Jiya is the one to speak. "What say you, my king? The Fae are your responsibility."

"Is it now?" I say. "I would have thought you to handle it on your own since you do not enjoy being ruled by a boy such as myself."

"Your Majesty," Cassandra says in irritation, "I beg you not to make light of this."

I turn in her direction, inclining my head at an angle. Words of their uncertainty in my leadership have arisen such a response. I want to laugh. Remind them of their previous desire to rule over their individual land. It hadn't been too long ago that these Fae wanted such a responsibility.

Now that they are faced with a crisis which they cannot manage, they look to us for support.

My leg falls to the floor, the right staying propped by the wide arm of the throne. "I am not. Are you denying saying that I was too young and ill-suited to rule?"

She does not respond.

She cannot respond the way she wishes.

"The witch's very presence jeopardizes our existence. Stealing her back from Delphi only incites further danger." Theodosia is angry, though justified in such. There is a look of burning enmity in her eyes. "Arabella cannot possibly be of that much use to us."

"To throw me to her whim is dooming yourselves to a war against her." Arabella glances at me, blinks, then returns to the rulers and kin. "You think if I'm given to Delphi that my friends will keep the wards up to protect you? Or that it'll keep Delphi from killing each of you until there's no Elemental to claim the throne?"

Theodosia's face holds firm, reflecting bravado and blindness. "You do not know that. If we were to believe you, it would make us unthinking fools. You're a mortal *and a witch*. Most of all, you are a liar."

"I would hope you'd remember who you are speaking to," I warn, glaring at the Fae.

She meets my glare, grins with teeth sharp enough to puncture flesh. "I am well aware of what I've said."

Arabella sighs a sharp sound of displeasure, throwing her head back. "Allow me to clear this up. I understand the severity that comes with my rescue. Of all people, I know what's threatened against everyone."

"Your speech is full of words that speak as if you are one of us," Tanzin mocks with sarcasm. "Are you truly aware of what you jeopardize by breathing alone? It seems that you have brought back the one Fae set on murdering what small population of us there is left while the king heedlessly does whatever you ask."

"What do you suggest then?" Arabella challenges. "Since all of you think you know better than Cassius after years of neglecting the Fae you rule over?"

Silence hangs in the air like fog lingering over the ocean.

During such time, I cannot help but shift my eyes to the side at Arabella and smile. I have very little thoughts on matters such as these. Least of all during meetings. Often, I allow others to speak, taking note of things said so that I may discuss them with my court to form decisions that are not made in haste.

It is best that I focus on the subject at hand. My mind should remain on course on crucial things, such as the danger of Delphi's location remaining unaccounted for. Or, I should think of the second half of Arabella's words. We must ensure that there does not happen another uprising due to rulership.

Reacting too largely would only prove that I do, in fact, have a bias. So I must speak as sensibly as I can. "Well then?" I demand, my eyes back on the rulers of the lower courts. "This question is free for any to answer."

Theodosia strides in front of her elders and all those in command. There is a look of smugness on her, which I cannot say I am able to predict the intentions of. "Marry a Fae instead. You've had countless lovers in the past. *Make one of them your co-ruler*, and rid our lands of the witch and her plaything. Are the lives of the Fae, *your people*, not as pertinent as a silly affair?"

To my side, Arabella is rigid. Her knuckles have turned a shade of white, with hands balled into fists. However, I am unsure if such reaction is due to her being slighted or Luka.

I am livid for both.

Luka's steps click against the marble behind the thrones. In this silence, it is the only thing audible. He makes his way to Arabella's side and has a hand up, prepared to punish Theodosia for speaking out of turn. And I might as well allow him.

Arabella stands from where she sits, not moving forward but clenches her jaw tight enough to be visible. "Lady Theodosia, I've already disarmed one Elemental. I will gladly maim another."

She speaks this with a smile I only recognize from her threatening encounters with those whom she rightfully puts in their position.

It lights the room the same way that her flames do, forcing

some to recognize that she no longer is a prisoner. Delight spreads through me, excitement hopping.

The Lady of Aquatius should not have spoken so carelessly. As high as she carries herself, she is not the queen. Her insults will not so easily be forgiven.

Harrison's eyes brighten with amusement. His eyebrows lift, lips curving into an enthusiastic grin. "Where was she during every meeting I was invited to prior to this? I would have attended had I known she carried such fire in her."

"She was being held captive by the same witch you demand her to be sent to," Luka snaps dryly. His stillness makes every definition in his face all the more sharp. I find myself surprised it has taken this far for him to say anything at all.

"Well, perhaps if it had sooner been made aware that it was our queen who was missing, we would have been more attentive," Harrison says playfully with specific emphasis towards my direction.

This meeting is performing as well as I had thought it would. It has completely strayed away from its purpose, the loathing aimed at the incorrect Magiks.

A huff coming from Tanzin disregards what Luka says. "As it still stands, I refuse to bow to a witch as my queen."

"Bow, don't bow, I don't care. But *do not* come crying and begging when your family is the first to be condemned for treason," Arabella says in a horrifyingly monotone tempo.

"Treason?" asks Vaela, her owl eyes growing wider than they already are.

"Have you not questioned where your daughter runs off to?" Luka asks in return. Arabella is gripping his arm, as if to hold him back from casting a deadly hex. "Korine has been conspiring with Delphi and knew of Arabella's torture. By that action, she has gone against the crown, breaking her oath of sworn loyalty. It makes her a traitor."

I am at a loss. Too many pieces of information have been kept from me.

Not only has the first I had ever loved hurt me so grievously with my brother, but now she stands at the side of the witch who wishes to take everything from us. Yet all I care for is how Arabella did not bother to inform me of this. Or how she cannot look at me for longer than seconds before her eyes shift into resentment or hollowness.

Unconvinced, Tanzin continues his dismissal of Arabella's queenship. He seems unsure of the accusation against his daughter. "If what you say is true, you need not say more. My daughter is ours to punish how we see fit. You ought to recall that this is Enthar's law when a lesser crime has been committed, Your Majesty." The lord may be in disbelief, and that causes him to listen to nothing more when hardening his face at the queen, whom he sees as inferior. "She is *not* my queen."

"I was crowned on the full moon the night of Cassius' coronation. Per your tradition, I'm the queen. And in no way am I teaming up with Delphi as a ploy," Arabella fires angrily.

"We cannot be sure her words are truthful," Cassandra chimes in.

"You and your brain are useless if you assume that both Arabella and I would collude with Delphi," Luka retorts coldly. His eyes have locked with the woman while he holds the face of neutrality. "Or your age has declined your wits."

Smiling, I drop my other leg, announcing my full attention. "I'd hate for any of you to bring about a king's displeasure. But I must say, it would be a delight to partake in my old activities if you do."

"Cassius. You're drunk. *Shut up*," Arabella mutters in

seriousness. She would rather take on the ungracious mannerisms of the others in this room than allow me to come to her defense.

I drink the nectared juice in my glass, which I am sure the queen is unaware of, swallowing the chalice that is half full. "I speak nonsense most times, and I will not refrain from doing so now, my goddess."

The other Fae in the room are staring at me and awaiting my response. I have yet to acknowledge Arabella as queen. For me to say so would be to confirm everything as truth. But to attempt lying would cause a twist so horrid in our throat we cannot utter the words.

"Trees work much too hard to create oxygen that is wasted on the likes of some of you," I say, eyes flitting between Tanzin, Cassandra, and Theodosia. Then, I turn my head, not peering at anyone in particular. "Those who have accepted Arabella, you have my most sincere gratitude and nothing else. Consider making better attempts at fulfilling your duties so that we will not have to continue compensating for your failings."

"You make a mistake if you do not relinquish your crown," Theodosia grits out in the direction of Arabella. "You were never meant to have one in the first place."

Head turning to the Magiks, I say, "Arabella, Luka? Might you leave the room for a moment?"

Arabella looks at me with eyebrows thrown upwards. "I can handle myself."

My head tilts closer to her. I know that whatever I do, whatever I say, it will not return the trust that took so long to earn before. The way the light of night touches her skin, how the beaming of the sun reflects off the dark brown of her eyes, any true smile she wears will forever be one I am not the cause of. "Yes, but I have a few things of my own to say, which do not require your presence. I will meet you in the council room after, if you could."

Luka links his arm with Arabella's and starts towards the stairs. "You've barely touched adulthood and propose something as stupid as marriage," Arabella derides. "Keep making unthought-of plans, and you'll end up right next to your father." Her eyes narrow, scanning all the other Elementals before descending the steps.

Though Theodosia is much taller than Arabella, when they stand facing each other, the Fae seems to shrink to the size of an insect.

"The next time you address me, let alone in a formal manner, you will *all* show respect."

At that, the two leave the room, and I am able to speak freely to the other Fae. Once the doors close, the room erupts into chaos, with the rulers speaking loudly over one another to make their point.

"She has been had once by Adonis already. You believe her incapable of being deceived many times over as queen?" Harrison interrogates. As he is the only to know of Adonis' omission in relation to the letter sent by Delphi prior to the taking of Arabella, his words earn the attention of the others, the rulers shutting their mouths after he speaks.

"My faith in her may be perilous, but you believe a marriage of alliance will bring peace to the lands rather than to accept the faults of our ruling's past." I turn towards the rulers of the lower courts. "You were ready to secede from the Spiritus rule not too long ago. When had the decision changed?"

"We–" Jiya attempts.

"No," I halt her from continuing, slightly moving my head towards Theodosia. I refuse to dignify the other Elementals with the pleasure of what they want and allow disrespect to my queen with their imperious demands. Nor will I allow a single ruler to send for her death. "I am assuming your proposal was suggested by the other rulers. If you are their puppet to deliver their message of cowardice, know that if you ever suggest something as outrageous as a marriage to another Fae, I will have you thrown into Phantom Tower at the highest cell."

I stand from my throne, lingering closer to the edge of the steps. "If any of you threaten harm to your queen again or are foolish enough to question her sovereignty, she will not be the only whom you should fear."

My shadow silhouette slips from my palms, stands before Tanzin and his wife, and shatters the bones of the woman's left fingers.

"You need not remain in place," I tell the others over Lady Vaela's shrill screams, which bounce against the creamy walls. "You may go."

The honey from this drink tastes sweeter than usual. Delectable.

They all stagger out of the room, pushing each other so that they may leave my presence. Lady Vaela's bones may be able to heal in under two weeks, but the reminder will last much longer.

The queen is in the council room as I enter. She is on her phone, scrolling through something of interest and letting out huffs of laughter every few thumb flicks. She has yet to notice me.

"Where has Luka–"

"He left to work out. Told him I'd get him if I needed to," she answers without looking up. "Are you gonna marry one of them? Y'know, one of the Fae."

I shake my head. I cannot fathom why she would think I'd take any as a spouse but her. A marriage of convenience may provide advantages, but the ambition of Arabella has already shown superior to a Fae who knows nothing of leadership. None fight the same way as she.

There is also another matter of annoyance to discuss. I stroll to the area across from her. "Why was our meeting with the Elementals the first I was informed of your unguarded leaving of the lands? How could you be so neglectful?"

Immediately, she places her device onto the table, screen down. She glances up at me, face hardened and scowling. "You don't get to lecture me when you put *my* life at risk with your plan."

The reminder of my carelessness troubles me constantly. I cannot forget the day I saw her when exchanging land for the freedom of the common fae if I tried. Nor have I been able to disremember the look of anguish and loathing Arabella had on before being taken back to Gigantia. Too many signs had there been of Arabella's suffering, yet my mind convinced itself that she would be able to endure days more under Delphi and Adonis.

"Of course I get to lecture you," I retort. She treats me as if I have no right to be upset with her. "For every wretched day, I worried for you. And now that you've returned, I have to worry that you will go about this on your own, since you now view Delphi's involvement as entirely your responsibility. You do not get to take on the burdens of the world as if you have control over it all."

She plays with the pendant around her neck. Her eyes blink faster than her normal rate, fixating towards the floor. Still, she says nothing.

"Dragon," I murmur, "let me–"

"Arabella."

My eyes drop, a sigh exhaling at the confirmation of my worst assumption. Just as I open my mouth to speak, the queen tucks her hair behind her ears, and laughter rumbles through me. "All the jewelry I send, but not once have you responded to me. You reject me, but not what I offer?"

"Wait, wha- *Huh*? I didn't know the jewelry was from you. I thought the tailors sent it with the clothes," she says with eyebrows crossed, hands moving as she speaks with more disarray than rage. "And what do you mean I haven't responded to you? We talk every day. And the only thing I got was some note saying how everyone in the palace knows the truth and that I'm 'unbecoming'."

"Never mind what I said," I retract. If she knows nothing of what else was sent, then it serves no purpose now.

The High Queen frowns with pursed lips and irritation. "No, I'm here now. We're not kids. So if you have something personal you wanna talk about, say it."

A liar, but not one who would lie about such a thing. Perhaps what I had said has disappeared and cannot be found. The fault would only be mine for not ensuring my words were received by her personally.

I should feel relieved. It would make me be seen as a pathetic fool all the more had she read the contents.

"You are already discontent when we speak. So I had asked you to forgive me for my wrongdoings." There is a pause in my words when I notice she remains unaffected. I exist purely as a villain to her. A minor one, perhaps, in comparison to Delphi, but one nonetheless. "I would have done anything. Dragged my body as my flesh scraped into the grounds. Whatever it took to bring you home."

My honesty may have shocked her, or she, in earnest, does not care. She has become still, with arms limp at her side. Her eyes, in contrast, are empty and wandering. They are detached from all that is occurring in this room.

Hands clasped behind me, it is the last chance I have to uphold my pride. "Perhaps you will spend the rest of your days gloating or yelling at me until blood rushes from my ears. I care not, so long as you say something."

She is taking a ridiculous time to respond for someone who has plenty to share with others in the palace. "You saw me and the way I looked under Delphi's care. How am I supposed to believe you give a shit when you gave both me *and* Luka to her?"

"Please," I say. "Since your return, you have hardly spoken to me beyond our crowned duties."

"What do you want me to say?" She again refuses to meet my eyes. There is an emptiness in her, similar to when she was no more than a vessel for Delphi's mistreatment. Misery summoned from months due to torture rises to the surface, and every bit of wrath, hurt, and betrayal she feels blasts through me the way strong winds of a storm will splinter glass.

"That you still see something in me," I say selfishly. "That you do not care about how broken I am and will stay beside me as you always have."

"I'm not saying that."

"That you desire me, or that you will stay with me?"

"I–"

"Then, at the very least, pretend with me."

I carry myself until I stand above Arabella. She looks at me with an unmoved face but leans back slightly when I near her.

Carefully, I take in every detail. How her hair now falls over her shoulders. How the straight strands still carry a thick volume. How she stands too straight for my liking. As if I am a stranger to her, and all she can be is stiff in my presence.

Arabella should be yelling. There should be a sense of resentment in retort. Unbridled fury that she must feel after all this time. But ultimately, this is worse.

She feels nothing.

"Would you like me to recount everything I have written? I can recall many of my words." Unable to leave her, my hand goes to her, bringing her eyes to me. It lowers to her neck, thumb stroking her jaw, but that is still not enough. "I'd rather endure your hatred than believe you truly think I would hurt you."

Nothing is turning out how I would like. We rule together, but we are not partners in anything but that. My hands depart from her, moving back to my body. I take a step and put distance between us. "What must I do to earn back your trust?"

Without taking longer than a short stare to consider my questions, she says, "You can't. You already know I have one thing left to do here, and that's to kill Delphi. So don't even bother with me."

"What is it you're saying?" I ask.

"Do whatever you want with whoever you want. I don't care. After we deal with Delphi, I'll leave you alone for the rest of your infinite life, and I expect you to do the same until I'm dead. I'll go back to my life and renounce ruling. You can continue being king or hand the crown off to someone else. It won't be my problem anymore."

I have always known my tricks could hurt others, but never did I think it would cause such repercussions that harm me so gravely. I never imagined the pain could be so severe. When I look at her, intense emotions burrow into my chest, boiling my blood so hot that it could forge my bones into weapons. I have admitted things to her that I have never told anyone. Not Harrison. Not Korine.

My expression remains the same, but my eyebrows lift. "Is this what you want?"

After harrowing moments of silence, she finally meets my eyes. "Yes."

My mouth is pulled upwards, my gaze lowering to her lips, fixated for an indecent amount of time before returning to her eyes. "Then I wish us luck if that is your desired end."

Nothing. She does not stop me as I move away from her and begin towards the exit.

As I am ready to close the door, I turn back to her. "So you may hear it from me, I thought Delphi would believe peace and was likely to be less cautious when divulging details to Luka."

The door behind me shuts, and with it, my heart.

Watching her struggle to form a sentence has torn something from me. I am hers, but she is not mine, and I am miserable for it.

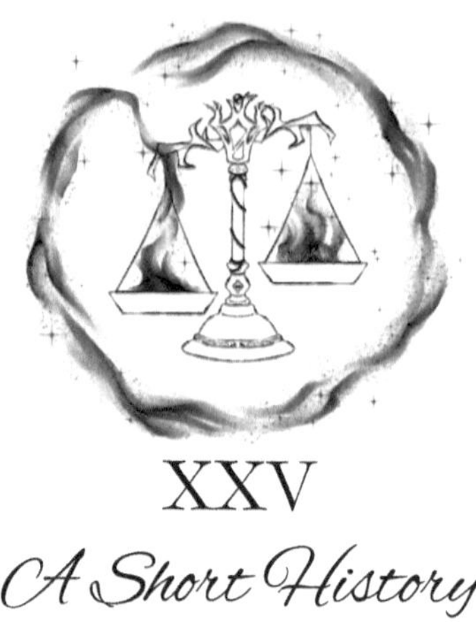

XXV

A Short History

Arabella

The fetid smell that emits from Phantom Tower is not something I missed. Until enough time passes, the lower cells are to be filled with those who were under Delphi's control, leaving the higher cells free for those who committed more severe crimes.

I promised to have Kabir with me today as I go to speak with a common Fae named Orella. I don't know much about her except that she was once a courtier of Cassius' grandpa.

At the foot of her cell, I enter with a bubbly drink of sweetness. It's not a soda I've ever drunk, but a juice that tastes similar to strawberry lemonade. The Fae turns when I offer the drink, snatching it from the floor and downing it until she belches from the carbonation.

"Queen of the Fae and Magik, a privilege," she greets in a grumbling tone. Her rags are worn down and torn, veins bulging from her skin, her sullen eyes that of a meerkat. She appears like she's made no effort to nourish herself. She scans me with a questioning yet arrogant expression, and I wonder if it's because she expects the same manners in return.

"You've spent over ninety years down here with no attempt to appeal your sentence. Why are you requesting an audience now?" I inquire. There's a voice in my head speaking over the other disorderly fragments, telling me not to be tricked again by another Fae.

She opens her mouth, flashing a sharp, toothy smile. Each fang is still as black as soot produced from a candle, accentuating her once-wealthy status, contrasting with what she wears now. There are some fangs missing and some that have holes. Others have grime on them that looks the color of moss. At most, she looks sixty, but I have no clue how old she really is. "Let me tell you a tale, witchling queen."

I glance at Kabir, who still waits at the door, one arm at his side and the other glued to his sword. Turning back to the woman who seems taller than the Head Guard, I sit on the ground in front of her but stay far enough not to be in line with her breath that smells of rotten cottage cheese.

"When the king was in his most malevolent age, he was known to send his shadow and chase others off the lands," she begins. "He'd haunt them until they feared for their safety in Ifaeris, which eventually caused them to flee to the Human Lands. And without King Elliot's approval to live among mortals, those Fae were no longer welcome back. If word of their leave or return reached the king, they would be killed. This left the Fae to a life of hiding."

"But couldn't your glamour hide—"

The Fae snarls at me for interrupting. Tangled hair that knots into a hive stiffly whips up with her head, her tail slamming against the ground, emphasizing her frustration. "Our glamour does not hold as strongly outside Ifaeris. Surely you've been told this by your lover. The *lands* fuel our glamour, and cut off from it for extended periods of time, Fae powers become uncontrollable. If our glamour failed, or a human with sight were to see us in our true form and cause trouble, it would become the High Rulers' responsibility to ensure those involved are dead."

Cassius told me he never killed anyone prior to Adrik's death. But I don't think this is that much different.

"He found it amusing," she continues, followed by a snort, possibly sensing my discomfort. As if this were the true reasoning behind why she had requested the presence of the crown. "Not once did King Cassius physically touch those common fae, but instead, he found joy in that intimidation."

I thought I'd heard the worst of what he'd done at the ball.

This is so much worse.

Get a fucking grip. Don't let someone talk over you. Command respect.

"I didn't ask for a history of the king's past. So unless you have information to offer about those under Delphi's control, this audience is over." I stand from my place, dusting off the remnants of rubble on my pants.

"Word carries in the tower, my queen. Do not think I would ask you here if not for passing along information." The Fae cracks another uncongenial smile. My head and body back in response. She's horrifically unnerving. "I have heard that her spells come from many books she kept in Gigantia. She was seen to carry different titles, though not one knows where they would come from."

Not allowing myself to give away my reaction, I don't move, my posture communicating for her to elaborate. What books the prisoners saw are too important for me to slip up with an incorrect question asked or show any sign of overinterest.

"There are other Magiks they had seen, but from what I have heard through the bars, none were recognizable enough to describe key features." Her information means nothing without a name. A face even. "One once overheard her speaking with another regarding sneaking into the archives within Magik Cove and stealing her mother's key."

A throat is cleared from a neighboring cell. "The books I heard her reference the most often were *Sanguis et Maledictiones* and *Theories of Magik*, but they were missing from the archives whenever she searched," a gruff voice inserts. It must be the Fae who told Orella this information.

Orella's brows raise with an inclined, quirked lip that seems to have been raised by the other Fae themself. She makes no attempt to request her freedom. She must figure this would be the case, as it is the other prisoner who feeds me information. "Find those, and the two of you may just be the saviors of the Fae."

Trepidation is crisp inside my body as I approach the throne room, mostly for the reason of the last time Cassius and I spoke. He is hurt and furious with me. I drove him away.

I would much rather play the fool than grovel at the feet of someone who cannot return the love I hold for them.

He said that once, yet to Delphi, he said I bring him grief. So by leaving when this is settled, I'll prevent from causing him further harm.

Maybe I'm protecting myself.

At the push of the door, the High King is lounging on the throne with an expression that even I can tell is boredom. Like he doesn't want to be here. I'm sure that I've seen him return from the most wearisome of times with more liveliness than this. Instances of when he's spoken with the common fae and when he had attended tournaments but come back to Nexus with his Zips lost come to mind.

A stunning Fae, who has branches that spout from her neck through her hair of silky green and a protruding stomach that hangs low, is kneeling in front of Cassius. One of her hands is playing under his shirt, the other inside his unbuttoned pants.

Every semblance of me stops working. My heart drops to the ground with my eyes, and I think my stomach is about to go with it. I blink a few times. Swallow down the lump in my throat.

Nothing is different from the last time I was in here, but for some weird reason, the black accents in the room seem bleaker, and the gold flecks around the room don't light the way they used to. Trimmings and mountings surrounding the wall appear bland. The room is too bare for the size, pillars and decorative marble accent pieces too uninspiring.

The Fae positions herself differently. I'm afraid she may do something with her mouth. But Cassius' fingers tilt her head from its place. Guides her up towards his lips. A discomforting sensation twists my stomach, and I have to clench my body fully to keep from a noticeable reaction.

My hand closes to knock on the wood, snapping myself into a different frame of mind. If not to, at the very least, draw my attention from the Faerie whose lips move around Cassius. "Sorry to interrupt, but I need to speak to the king about pressing matters."

Actions from the woman don't stop. She's sucking so harshly on his neck that I think she may overpower the shadow mark he was born with.

"Leave," he commands with a slight gleam in his eyes as he sends off the earthy Fae. On her way out, she hits me with her shoulder, and I wonder if she's aware I am his queen. "This matter is so urgent it could not have waited?"

This feels too familiar. Like I'm reliving something Delphi showed me. Shrugging, I reply with, "Too late now."

He rolls his eyes. Fastens his pants. "You spoke with Orella today."

"Yeah. She told me what she knew, and another common fae told me about these two books that Delphi wanted constantly. I think she and one of her friends searched through one of the archives. I just don't know which friend it was."

"Would that matter?" he asks with brows furrowing and the tiniest movement of his head.

"I mean, I wouldn't tell you if it didn't," I respond, an annoyance badgering at the front of my mind. "Magik Cove's two main offices are where the Council leaders work from and where executives meet for summits. And then you have the different buildings where they have trials and keep some other texts, so there's a few different places to look if I don't know which friend."

The king's eyelashes, much curlier and longer than mine, follow his blink. Slowly. Seemingly unable to comprehend what I have to say. "Our archive has much of the same information that their books contain. Why search through the spread of Magik Cove?" It takes a beat for me to think of an answer, but before I can speak, he continues. "The Fae have not had consistent correspondence with your leaders in centuries, so we cannot just ask them for the books."

"Well, maybe if you spent your time communicating with the Council, rather than inside other Fae, then we'd have better headway," I bite out too aggressively, my mouth once again moving before I can think.

That's not why you came.

His makeup is more detailed than mine. Under his eyes' outer corners are complicated linework with mixed black and gold, while his lids are shadowed with a metallic cobalt. I think I've been staring. His gaze narrows while strutting down to me. "You're angry over a few exchanged kisses? Truly?"

A scoff of disbelief at his unending arrogance comes out. It wasn't just exchanged kisses, and he knows it.

"No."

An amused hum and grin twitches on his expression at my lie. "I ask then, what ought I to do about your leaders?"

"Figure it out. Not like you aren't capable of deception." A beat passes, my brows raising. "You *are* king, after all."

He looks at me with such intensity that it burns sickly into my bloodstream.

"And you're the queen."

Delusion is a debilitating thing. Just like when I thought Delphi and I were something more than what we were, I look for signs in everything that Cassius does.

I grow attached to people too quickly. But I'll push them out so I'll never be hurt again.

"I have sent letters to your Council detailing the activities occurring within Ifaeris, as well as Delphi's involvement," he tells me. His tone makes me think he meant to explain this at a later time. "And though I mentioned how her actions border on breaking our treaty, I have yet to receive word from them."

While I'm reminded consistently by his actions, it never fails to surprise me how Cassius takes on responsibility without being forced. He has grown into being king in the same way that someone would take up a hobby and be instantly good at the craft. I just have to be patient for the days he decides to take interest.

"I made you queen to deal with matters such as these," he throws out in a delightful tone. "Now that you're back, by all means, resume doing what you had before." He strides out the door, and I can hear him stumbling, chuckling before he makes an incoherent comment, then chuckling again.

How dare he ask all this of me and leave me without intentions of helping? I have half a mind to kill him before I get to Delphi.

XXVI

Explanations

Arabella

Mango Sago is one of the best foods ever created. The condensed milk, chewy tapioca, and mango make such a perfect combination that I imagine this is what food in paradise must be. What's even better is its taste with the crispiness of the waffles prepared by the chefs. Usually, this amount of sugar as a first meal is too much for me, but as of right now, it's perfect.

Luka already left for Hearthis. Some of the Elementals have agreed to meet with him on the condition that the crown doesn't withhold protection out of pettiness or anger the same way that Elliot had. A fair enough trade, especially if this means their cooperation. If he can convince Fatima to join our cause, we can work our way towards uniting the other rulers.

Sounds of laughter and the faint smell of caramel popcorn enter the palace. From the dining area, I follow to where the noise grows. All of the Wands, except Luka, are standing with Cassius. They're cracking jokes, becoming louder with each thing they say.

Cassius has glamoured himself to have rounded ears like us,

but the jewelry that he normally accessorizes himself in gives away his riches. He's in tattersall pants with thin lines as a pattern, and the low-buttoned long sleeve he wears looks designed by Damien. If I didn't know him, I'd assume the king to be a human-passing creature.

I have no sound reasoning to be upset, but the sight of Vi with a cut on her leg sends a spike to my head. It's like Cassius is taunting me with those I hold close so he can put them at risk.

The sting in my throat scales its way up until I can no longer hold in my frustration. "Why the *fuck* are you hanging out with him? He's nothing to us."

My friends are all staring at me in bafflement. I feel myself crumbling into an episode. Screams are clawing at me, and any progress I've made, no matter how little it seems to others, diminishes to nothing as the toxic habits find their way back into my thoughts. I'm warping back into my scornful teenage self who lashes out over the slightest thing. If I could condense my body into imploding, I would.

"What are you on about, Ara? Are you okay?" Violette asks, walking over to me. Her chestnut eyes are full of concern, but my heart is beating too fast, and every little sound is causing me to be angrier.

I don't even think the cut is from today.

I'm relapsing into a spiral. No amount of grounding or breathing is going to stop it. Aware of what's going on, I can't stay. If I do, I know I'll say something I'll regret.

Nothing since I've returned to Ifaeris has been pretty. It's not some kind of passing of events in chopped segments with a beautiful music score in the back. It's ugly, and ruining, and the dread you feel when presented with the consequences of your actions. It's the night demon you're told is a myth, only to find out just how real it is. When you have the epiphany that the collection of ugly, monstrous emotions has glued together and created the thing that is you.

Most of this is my issue, I know. I just can't help but consider that there's a truth to them.

"Here she goes," Grayson says. Candy is tossed into his mouth, a playfully annoyed expression winding him tightly. "The last time we were all together, you were asleep in his lap. Now we can't like him?"

If it weren't for the reminding voice telling me that he's one of my best friends, I would freeze dry his lungs.

"You're right," I breathe. The rage refuses to simmer inside of me, but I can try to refrain from any hateful words.

Cassius' lips thin into a line. I can see his jaw shift. "Allow me a moment with the queen," he pardons, beckoning me to walk with him to the waiting room.

He shuts the door, excusing the two of us in privacy. Glamoured or not, his unnatural beauty remains the same.

"I–"

"You needn't explain yourself."

I can feel my gaze shift into leering when my brows knit downwards and my cheeks upwards. "That wasn't what I was going to say."

Do *I* even know what I was going to say?

"Then what incursion could I have possibly made to bring about such untrusted hostility on this day?"

Urges to scream at Cassius vibrate through my nervous system. They beg me to tell him that we only fucked because Luka was gone, and now that he's back, I don't need whatever relationship the king wants. But even *that* is something I recognize as my extreme, transient emotions. It's not what I really think. Definitely not what I feel.

"On this day?" I argue with a jerked shake of my head. Just

when I think my anger has been put out, the flames reignite, rising to prompt this argument again. "How am I supposed to trust you when you put Luka's life at risk?"

"He forgave me for that." Aggravation pauses him. His chest falls with every breath he exhales. "Why can you not?"

"Because fucking I lost him! Not the other way around." Explosions of cracks come out through some of my words. "I was given another chance, and just throwing him to Delphi was thoughtless."

My body is too expressive. Movements sharp and animated. After months of manipulation, hallucinations, stabbings, beatings, and being near death, I can still be angry at his plan. Even if it was a necessary one.

I know he's remorseful and wants things to be okay between us, but whenever we talk, my brain reminds me of his false betrayal. Images of his grin before being taken back to Gigantia by Delphi play out in my vision, despite only looking at his face.

"Not to mention the fact you left me too."

"Will you not grant me a pardon for my scheming ineptitude?" He comes closer, his arm wrapping around my waist. Unsure of himself. A test. The other skims me with his nails, a prickling sensation alarming as it moves up my arm. "Will you not let me *atone*?"

His mouth is close–*so close*–to my face.

My breath is treasonous. Whatever I don't say, my breathing pattern does. Or lack thereof.

"Cassius," I whisper. In hesitation. Warning. Pleading? None of which I make sense of.

It's easier to remain in denial when he is not in the room. When he's far enough away that I can't feel his eyes watching me with my every step.

I hate him. Or I hate what he did. But I don't think my hatred and attraction to him are mutually exclusive. They're more similar to battling opposites—neither truly satisfied with whatever I do.

His lips find themselves on my neck. It feels like I'm falling from the sky with nothing to save me. And I'm so terrified that if I allow myself to fall again, it will turn out worse than before. But I'm still letting him move around my skin. I'm tilting my head, not fighting him from creating marks on me.

"You still want this from me," he taunts. "How unfortunate for us both." He's snickering in sadistic joy. About to press his lips to mine.

And everything crashes down.

It takes all the willpower I have to extend my arm and step back. I can't let him kiss me. If he does, I don't think I'd want him to stop.

Cassius thinks I hate him, but I hate myself more. And while he can be trusted on some things, I don't trust him with myself.

I know I want him. But it *hurts* to want him. I want him so badly it stings in my chest in a way that hurts more than the torture did. I've never been so drawn to someone the way I feel intrinsically tied to Luka and him.

The problem with wanting is I can never just do it in minimal amounts. With wanting *someone*, it drives me to the point where I destroy everyone around me, including myself, if it means becoming who they want me to be. I become a specific kind of internally obsessive. The person won't ever leave my mind, no matter how often I try ejecting the thoughts away.

Then I realize, just as I have before, we are two beings who have learned to build a tower so high that no one may ever come in. After Luka died, I never would have thought myself dismantling it for someone else, but Cassius walked through it as if I left a key in his pocket. I just don't know if that will ever be enough. I don't know if our walls will ever come down, even if we scrape each layer one by one.

Cassius is studying me with wide eyes, quickly lowering them after blinking. "Go," he says. He moves away, placing his hands into his pockets. "You've arranged a day with my family."

Sorrow is swallowing him whole. And I keep watching, not doing a single thing to help him.

The two of us exit the room, parting ways at the back door's entrance. For a brief, passing thought, I think to look back. Maybe to apologize and tell him that he's not the one doing anything wrong.

But I don't.

The day has become addled. Everything blends together, and I think that I dissociated at some point. When I do return to my body, it's nearing sunset, and I'm in a carriage taking us back to Nexus. We journey past a deteriorating bridge built over a bog, traversing along the border by the cliffsides, hills, and smaller mountains of Mindae. When I peer out of the other window, at the bottom of the cliffs are five warships that are being refurbished by workers. Repairs are being made where they are needed, with bodies moving on and off the vessel.

About forty percent of our army comes from Mindae. Though war has long ended for them, the common fae of this land still work as though they must prepare for one.

The crashing of waves is tumultuous. In spontaneous, unrhythmic timing, different animals and creatures peek from above the water. I've seen pictures of some in my schooling, others from human sketches in their mythical creature writings.

Esme and Dyana have departed for the Human Lands, leaving the five of us. Monty's arm is wrapped around a Fae woman with eyes of amber, skin slightly lighter than Helena's, and beautiful hair that has been picked out into an Afro. Xavier has his hand closed over Iris', arms linked together, and her head on his.

Iris and Daraja's looks are otherworldly. Daraja has cheeks round as the moon and features as mesmerizing as the celestial's hypnotic beauty. Iris has the elevated fullness of brows I could only ever achieve when I fill mine with makeup.

My being here feels unneeded as the only one here without a partner. Something that is made exceptionally clear as we all hike down, entering the grotto-like cave that contains the overflow of water. Outside the entrance we've climbed down from, the carriage and horses wait with Kabir, who has told us that he would keep watch of them.

The pool of water in front of us splashes from the waterfall above. It shifts from the white, rushed bubbles into a lavender shade the pool colors with at the time of calming. Cascades of foliage that dangle from the sides trickle the remaining water into the body. The greenery and animals of nature swim around, radiating light, quieting down with the end of the day.

"Wait, what did you say that family was angry about again?" I ask Daraja, my attention drawn from peering around the area.

"Oh." She turns, with her torso moving back slightly, an expression furrowing with the quickest movement. I don't think she expected me to have been paying much attention to her story. Her eyes roll from side to side, disappearing when rolled too far back behind her lid. "Well, the father told me he believes something ought to be done about Prince Adonis' crimes."

That is something Cassius and I have taken into consideration. It's why Adonis wears a prosthetic arm made from iron—though not pure enough that it would kill a Fae—created by Gray and our smiths. Although it is a gift, I've reminded Adonis that the iron will keep him from using his Elemental abilities, and alongside that,

Damien also enchanted the arm to seize the Fae if, at any time, he betrays us and okkars outside the lands.

Curiously though, I am too interested in how much the lovers of my friends agree with sentiments regarding my decision. "Yeah, but you two *do* trust I wouldn't let him do anything bad to the Fae, right?"

"Some assume we ought to be more cautious of you, but as far as my family has said so, they do not care, so long as the crown's rulership does not return to the way it had been under Elliot's," Iris responds.

Both her and Daraja's attention is focused on our conversation, whereas Xavier and Monty are having their own while laying the blankets on the ground. It takes another few seconds before any of us realize that we left the food in the carriage.

Patiently, the twins and I sit, waiting as their lovers retrieve our food, the women insisting they don't need any help. My friends' backs are aligned with the entrance, mine facing the water.

"So you were friends with the witch who stole you?" Monty asks carefully, biting into the Etherfruite from his pocket. The juices leak down the fruite from the imprint, but the crunch is that of an apple.

Shame admits my answer as my cheeks lift upwards. My top lip curls inward, my bottom overlapping it. "Yeah. Delphi and I were best friends, but shit kinda hit the fan when she started hanging out with the people we used to hate. I guess once she got bored of me, we lost each other." I blink, head turning at a large, dull sound hitting the water. "I think the day that group offered their friendship to both of us was the beginning of the end."

"But one of their mothers works within Magik Cove, if I'm not mistaken," Monty stresses.

"And?"

"Would that not suggest which collection to look through?" he asks, turning his head at the sounds of the women far behind him. I don't know how he hears their steps above the waters showering near us. "I'm guessing there can't be *that* many who have befriended Delphi *and* have mothers working for the Coven."

A sarcastic breath of laughter comes out of me. "You're forgetting that the group of friends she kept are all connected to the elite in some way. They all kinda flock together."

Glancing up, Xavier's expression is one more playful, mockery sure to follow. "You said that you and Delphi were romantic. Care to elaborate?"

Yes and no. I don't know how exactly someone would describe what we were without it taking hours.

"I don't wanna talk about my feelings for her."

"Feelings for who?" Iris teases in a singing tune, her question a sneaking surprise, before handing Xavier a tray full of food and sitting on the blanket.

The Fae women pass the glasses and pitcher of water around the circle, filling up each cup.

"King Cassius, gods willing," Daraja says in a joking but hopeful tone, both her fingers crossed. Her guard father tells her too much of what occurs in Nexus.

"It's nothing," I answer Iris, ignoring what both women say.

I think Cassius would smile at what Daraja has said.

I blink, my eyes rolling while closed. Luka would find it funny that this is where my mind has immediately gone to.

Our meal is eaten with pleasant conversation and many things spoken. Hypotheticals and unrealistic questions are posed, most making little to no connection to the last question. When they talk, I wonder how different their answers would be if Fae could lie.

"So," I look at Iris, my tongue making a sound when it sucks the back of my teeth, "how *did* you two become a couple?"

Iris becomes effervescent, full of excitement to tell the story.

Her smile goes wide, with eyes popping from eagerness. "My brother was one of the Fae taken by Adonis. When he was brought home and set free, he told me of the fire-haired Fae who saved his life during battle. I had to thank him, and–"

"And when she saw me, a simple 'thank you' and honeyed pastries wouldn't do," Xavier interjects.

"So you dated him as a thank you instead? A bit overboard for gratitude," I joke, kicking him with the side of my foot in play.

Xavier shoves my arm, moving me from a seated position on a damp rock onto the ground. "Don't be mad you and I won't happen anymore."

Monty chokes at the comment. Drips of water leak from his mouth and catch onto his hand, which he throws at his brother. Daraja's reaction is similar, snorting and choking on the water.

I take a pea off my plate and flick it at my friend. "I'd rather have more needles shoved into me."

Iris doesn't show outward worry, but her eyes carry a deep edge and tenseness. Uneasiness I recognize from myself.

At the look on his lover's face, Xavier nervously apologizes, fumbling over his words as he tries to reassure her that he is only joking.

"Xavier," Iris says, finally getting him to stop talking, "You have nothing to worry for. I understand well what you meant."

"Well, I have had too many misunderstand my jests," Xavier says, continuing to justify himself. "I enjoy the dramatics, but only when it bodes well for my entertainment of fun watched, and it is not my life."

She glances between Xavier and me, raising her eyebrow as if to prompt more amusement for herself. "Did the two of you ever..."

Both of us start cackling. I'm wheezing so hard I feel my insides cramping. I try to get the words out, but each time Xavier and I make eye contact, I fail, hunching over and gasping for air while coughing.

"*Hell no*," I'm able to finally get out.

"She's had her fair tumble through my family, but never us non-royals." Xavier turns to me, half-heartedly feigning heartache and offense to my reaction. "And I'll have you know I could be the most handsome Fae in the lands."

"You and your brother are identical twins, Xavier," Daraja says in her lover's defense.

"And I'm clearly the more attractive one," Xavier boasts in response with a smirk so deep, I can see his and Cassius' relation. Regardless if they have no blood shared.

Iris raises a challenging brow. "Isn't that what you said before Monty gave you that scar on your nose?"

I bring a closed fist to my mouth, biting down on my index finger. In one rhetorical question, she's managed to shut down Xavier's false, overzealous confidence.

The sun's fully disappeared, and the stars have come out in its place. From the lake glows a color of abstract, bright purple, curiously calling into question how the lands created something so aesthetically pleasing. I want to jump into it. Swim until its essence flows around my body.

"It's late," Daraja says. "I hardly slept, and I am afraid that slumber is beckoning me." She stacks the spread of plates, dumping what remnants of food are left before going towards the entrance.

Monty follows behind her, spinning her in a circle with her free arm. He picks her up from her waist and kisses her gently. A delicate exchange from the more reserved twin.

From her seat, Iris stands, dusting her earthy frock from the debris of dirt. Xavier rises with her, pulling her into a hug, holding her so tightly that I'd assume he never wants to let her go. His larger hands rub around her back, resting his head on the top of her. "I'm afraid I must go as well. My parents will begin to worry. They have been extremely protective since my brother went missing, despite having him returned."

Even when she doesn't pay attention, Xavier gazes at Iris with the look of someone completely in awe. A lovestruck man wearing a goofy grin while her face turns away from him.

"I will escort you," he offers at the end of her explanation, leading the two up.

"Wait!" I call, halting them both in their place. "I actually needa talk to Xavier for... royal reasons. Please feel free to take the carriage instead of okkaring though!"

She smiles, kissing Xavier on his cheek before climbing up the cave.

The long-haired Fae plops down next to me. He pats the empty space beside him, using his extended arm to keep himself up. "What's up, Reaps?"

I think that nickname annoys me more than Dragon ever has. My eyes roll, joining him while he stares at the glowing lake in front of us. "I need you to do me a favor."

"Anything." He turns to me, angles his head and crosses his brows. "Okay, not *anything*."

"I need you to glamour yourself into looking like me," I say.

"Reaps, when I said you're the mirrored version of myself, I didn't mean–"

"I'm gonna visit one of the Cove offices. I know what I said to Monty, and I still don't know which friends met with Delphi or whose mom it was, but I've gotten info on which office Delphi wants a book from."

His focus becomes interested. The Fae sits straight, fully perpendicular to me. "May I ask how you came across that information?"

I shake my head. "Not important for you to know."

"Then why am I changing myself to appear as you?"

"No one can know what I'm doing, especially if Delphi has spies in the lands. You're the only one I trust who can act the same way I do."

He brings his knees closer to his stomach before he stands and walks to the water with hands held behind his back. "I'm flattered you place so much faith in my ability to imitate a witch three-quarters my height, but the other Fae would see me as glamoured."

Jumping to my feet, I pace in steps until I am at his side. "I convinced Maude to glamour you into me. I'll only be gone a few hours. Swear to keep it a secret to the crown." He's becoming suspicious. I need to find a way that would convince him better. "*Oh come on*, last week I walked around Nexus painted blue 'cause you dared me to."

"Shorten me up," he says cheerfully, though doubt is still clouded on his face. "Or down, I suppose."

And I shove him into the water.

XXVII
Caught

Arabella

This room of books smells strongly of parchment and the outdated methods of their documentation. Pens, inks, and quills from ripped feathers scatter across the desks by the door. In the age where other mediums to note information exist, I wonder why so many creatures live in archaic times.

The aroma of old mothballs and spicy cologne, favorable a century ago, permeates my nostrils. It's a horrible combination that forces a nauseated expression from me.

I walk around the room, peering into each section and tapping my fingers across the spines of books I pass. A poorly bound book comes into my hands. It's the size of a textbook but looks no different than a grimoire, with its golden edges and personal insights written along the findings. I take it, along with another book I need, before placing the two books from my bag in the stolen books' place.

Creak.

My heart beats faster.

"Shit," I whisper to myself. I didn't think someone would be

coming back to the archives so soon. I still have another book I need to find. This area is a dead end. If I'm to be discovered, there's nowhere I can hide.

Footsteps come closer to my aisle, and all I'm able to do is press myself against the shelves, hoping I can manipulate the mind of whoever's there for more time. Clack by clack, their shoes hit against the wood of the floor.

I wonder if Luka's been in a situation like this. Just as I think I'm safe, my weight shifts to one side and sounds the wooden slab below me.

Scuttling feet are making their way to me. I hear the sound of multiple books knocking down as he sends magik through each aisle trying to find me. And after multiple failed attempts, he reaches the aisle I'm hidden in. It's a sorcerer in a long navy coat, black slacks, and combat boots–the security uniform of Magik Cove. Protection of metal acts as a belt while tying around the closed coat, which is covered in buttons made from the same material that lines his shoulders.

He cowers behind a protective shield, assumedly shooting spells in my direction with the twists of his wrist. His magik misses, hitting things behind me. I have no choice but to fight back. A countercurse blasts from my hand, hitting him in the knee. The dagger I've brought comes in handy as I remove it from my bag. I march closer to him, prepared to plunge the weapon, but am struck at my side by a hex.

Three other security officers swarm around me, pinning me to the ground and dragging me out of the room and into the hallway.

"The Council has requested to see you," a witch spits.

After going up a story in an elevator, I'm hauled into a room farthest down the hall. The floor inside the room is blank in color, other than the crescent moon that lies under a skull. The art is encapsulated inside a circle, which I'm standing over. I'm forced onto the ceramic flooring, being presented in a way that feels like I'm on trial for a crime.

Elevated on a semicircle table are the twelve Council leaders. Each differs in their styled clothing, but all attire is worn under a regalia robe of light silver, designed with sharp lines of black.

"Miss Huǒ," the sorcerer with tired eyes and crow's feet greets. His accent hints at a southern raising from the United States. He's in a burgundy suit, a white undershirt showing through. "We've been expecting you."

Expecting me?

I say nothing in response. I can't afford to reveal more than what they know.

"You break into the archives of Magik Cove and do not expect to be punished? You've spent too much time with the Fae," a witch with a Spaniard accent accuses. Her fuchsia-colored clothing is blinding.

Her words prove how much the Council hides from the rest of the Magiks. So many things I've learned from my schooling are made from half-truths. Our history that was taught could just as well be lies.

I suck in a sharp breath. Standing and swallowing a gulp. Each time I try to take in more air so that I can speak, a pain squeezes in my chest.

My eyes dart around the leaders. With the way one leers at me, his fingers curling from pinky to index multiple times, I imagine him patiently waiting for a reason to hurl a curse at me. His mustache is long, hairs curling into his lip.

Wonder what it would feel like to have that burn.

"We've heard of the uh… What is the word?" He pauses, speaking in a heavy French accent. "Ah, 'issue' a witch has supposedly caused the Fae. Do they not remember the last time they thought themselves powerful enough to battle us?"

"You are one insignificant witch. We know magik beyond your knowledge. I can kill you now," another sorcerer next to him threatens.

To evade a possible curse, I jump behind a security member and onto his back. He flails his body around, swinging to get me off of him, but I'm changing my position as quickly as I can. I move my body down until I'm able to hook my leg between his, relocating his center of gravity.

He topples to the floor, where I'm able to flip us. My dagger is in his hand, and he thrashes it, trying to stab me. In retaliation, I paralyze his body to keep him from moving, take my dagger back, and slit his throat.

When I glance up, the French leader with the mustache twists his fingers while wearing an insidious smile on his face, and I'm brought to my back, screaming in misery. Thoughts of those I love and unbearable pain take turns at the forefront of my mind. My limbs feel like they're slowly being ripped apart. That might be what's starting to happen.

Doors from my right are flung open. I hear Luka's voice before I'm able to see him.

"Don't any of you dare touch her with magik. You hex her any further and I'll kill you myself." He says nothing while the magik is undone, my breath recuperating, senses once again available to my body. The security member, who had been standing next to the one I killed, is on the floor being hexed by Luka the same way that I had been while also being forced silent. Then Luka steps over the sorcerer and enters the room with Cassius, whose black wings are spread, making the Fae appear all the more threatening. "And so you remember, I have the knowledge from books you've allowed my father to slip into our home."

Luka glares scathingly up until the moment his face turns to mine, immediately softening. He reaches his hand out, helping me up. The immediate feel of his touch is tender, his magik healing me enough to bear through this. His all-black attire is closed together by a singular button at the blazer, shoes made from leather in the same color. He has all the intimidation his father raised him to become with all of the gentleness he shows towards me.

I should be thankful. While I have a small understanding of the readings from the restricted archives, it still wouldn't be enough to combat twelve Magiks who are much more acquainted with such knowledge. But instead of gratitude, all I feel is irritation and fear towards the two men close to me. Despite this, I bite my tongue and everything back.

Cassius, who is in a Hollingsworth green top that appears similar to a blazer, looks entirely out of place. There are lines of fabric in multiple 'X' formations, which stitch the two sections of cloths from around his biceps and forearm together, beading and fabric designs protruding off the piece itself.

Leave it to him to dress as dramatically as possible when he comes to save me from being hexed.

"Apologies for our lateness," the king chimes from the doorway. "I incorrectly assumed Arabella would have enough patience before meeting with her leaders."

Designs from his overly wide, black lapels catch my attention. The left side has a blossom ornament sewn near his shoulder, while the other is embroidered with a wingless dragon along the whole lapel. Both are the same color as the rest of his open-cut top that exposes his bare, lithe body, which is as radiant as his face. Even his lips are colored in a heather purple near the corners, blending into a nearly black, deep eggplant color in the middle.

With the clothing he wears and a smile so charming, it's dazzlingly manipulative.

XXVIII
A High King's Performance

Cassius

Arabella's eyes flare with fury. They are widened with a clenched jaw as I venture into the room, pushing away the dead sorcerer with my foot. Her ferocity will never fail to amuse me.

"How long did you assume my sister's glamour on Xavier to fool us?" I say into her ear.

"Longer than this, I suppose," she responds bitterly.

I abhor the other Magiks in this room. I should have all their hands cut off for taking part in bringing harm to Arabella, even if by watching, but I far more worry for her current state.

Luka, who stands at my side, pulls Arabella in. "The second he walked into the room, we knew something was wrong," he murmurs, though loudly enough for us both to hear.

Grunting in a low huff, Arabella narrows her eyes. She tilts herself to the side, scanning those behind us. Her position is ireful, gradually more menacing when she refrains from commenting further. "We'll talk about this later."

"Your Majesty," a witch with hair tied into a bun greets,

"sending our own to spy on us?" There is a block in front of her with the name 'Odette Thatcher' carved into the silver.

"It is unseemly to accuse royalty, even for your kind," I insult, standing in front of Arabella and Luka.

The sorcerer who was cursing Arabella writes something on paper. His name holder has the name 'Ambrose Blanchet'. When finished writing, he passes the note to a witch, and she hands it to a sorcerer with graying hair. The elder sorcerer nods, summoning a flame from the fireplace across the room and disintegrating it in laughter.

A blonde witch, the same who gave the note to the older sorcerer, pricks herself with a sharp object. The doors are shut within the same moment, and the room weakens me with iron particles gathering in the air, surrounding only my being. This magik works so fast that I do not see its remnants floating in the air until everything has been done.

Why is her magik remaining silver?

Sigils are set across all the Human Lands to hold Magiks' power strong, differing from creatures whose abilities wither when venturing outside the lands of their kind. Due to this and iron being Fae's greatest weakness, the power of my shadows may have a slim chance of manifesting.

The witch shows a smile that rings insincere, glancing around at the others around her. "Our safety is most crucial. Say what it is you must. We won't kill you, but make no mistake, if you think to use your Elemental abilities against us, I will not hesitate to send iron straight through your heart."

"Your lack of trust insults me." Pausing, I pace around the floor and acknowledge the eyes that watch me. "Have each of my missives not been sent with kind gifts promised?"

From the mouth of the curly-haired witch, she responds with, "I thought the Coven came to an agreement with those who ruled before you. The Fae keep to their business, and we Magiks would never interfere."

"Yes, well, the time has come for such agreement to be reviewed," I say. "For your kind has stirred up quite troublesome events within Ifaeris."

Measures must be taken a step further. They have received my letters, I am sure of it. Outright denying so by evading my question is futile. I have already informed them of the way in which Delphi has destroyed the lives of the Fae, yet nothing has been done.

No justice has been settled by the Council for the balance of both what Delphi has done and for being remiss when knowledgeable of such information.

"What grounds do you claim this on?" Odette asks in a dismissive tone. In the Magik leaders' prideful beliefs, they are the ones most powerful and cannot be bothered to inspect matters which paint them capable of such atrocities.

I roll my eyes.

"On account of Luka standing before you, raised from the dead?" Arabella says, her voice raised, as if those sitting are without skills of critical thinking.

Their faces appear grim, without a hint of surprise nor motivation to make amends for what Delphi has done. Unless it directly affects their reputation, they see no problem with the deaths of the Fae.

It reminds me of my father's rule.

Of course, he had times of spreading great rewards and offering the best of sweets to the common fae, but instances such as those were only done so to keep the Fae tolerable and to turn their anger towards the lower courts' rulers.

I have to take a deep breath to keep from saying something. It causes a stinging heat to prickle in my throat the same way that the iron around me does. If the Council of the Coven is to be uncaring, they should do so while taking ownership of their stance. To act as though they have no knowledge is a cowardly move.

In my experience, while reading from our history, I would suspect the Council of the Coven to reject any evidence given of Delphi's crimes, perhaps remedying her magik by undoing Luka's life.

Something I would not allow.

A sorcerer in closed robes under the uniform gown, which matches the others, pounds his hand on the porcelain table. "Why should we believe it was Delphi who used magik to revive Mister Caedos?"

"Your inability to comprehend this matter is staggering. I could not come alive by sheer will," Luka states plainly.

"His funeral had many people there. If not by any of you personally, I'm sure you heard about it because of his father," Arabella argues on.

"What he means is," the bearded man next to Ambrose Blanchet, named Lingyun Zhao, whose hair has begun thinning and disappearing, clarifies, "why is Delphi the only suspect? There are many others who have motives. A loved one with access to our archives for one."

Luka remains stiff and alert. "You are all well-acquainted with my father. He would never use restricted magik to bring me back. I am not important enough to him for that."

I would think him more discomposed when saying the last of his claims. We hold similar relationships with our fathers, the difference lying in him being raised to become identical to his, whereas mine kept close watch over me to ensure I did not bring an end to our bloodline's ruling.

"Why are you acting like Delphi and Adonis' relationship is completely separate from Luka being brought back with restricted magik?" Arabella berates. "He was dropped in Ifaeris when he regained enough consciousness." She attempts to reason but to no avail. Her posture is deflated, and I can see her viewing an allyship as a lost cause.

Expressions on their face show substantially that they think themselves clever enough to absolve their involvement. And they may be able to elude responsibility, so long as there is reason to suggest Delphi's involvement falls more onto Adonis' vengeance.

Hatred exists in many forms. There are varying levels of it, but the word carries enough strength to imply solid reasonings behind an action done. I'm quite practiced in the art of tolerating something worth hating–it has been the motivation for charming those into my favor–but those once loathing thoughts against common fae within Ifaeris have become ants when thinking of my anger towards impudent rulers.

While this area is decorated with the formal dullness in which these Magiks present themselves, I think that perhaps I am not best fit for leading our victory in this battle. The leaders are accustomed to viewing those whom they meet with suspicion at their untruths. I may not have the ability to charm them with words adorned by others, but there are tactics much better respected that can be taken.

"Should Delphi not be punished for stealing from your archives alone?" I question.

"Miss Huǒ is the one we've caught trespassing through our archives," the sorcerer, named Remus Hilton, informs in recollection. The color of his face nearly matches that of his burgundy attire. He has the mortal neck equivalent to a giraffe's– long and surely one that slows down his digestion. "That's why it's she and not Delphi whom we are holding here. We have received your letters, King Cassius, but I'm afraid there is nothing to be done for what you ask. Unless you would reconsider what your ancestors before you have rejected and allow an ambassador to remain within your lands. Ensuring that the Fae never attempt to strike against Magiks."

"I will not forfeit to these terms," I assert. "I am not so weak that I can be manipulated to your whim."

"You're naive to think that our terms are unfair. You are young, uninformed, incompetent–"

"I'd let you go on, but then, you would perhaps need one of your mortal thesauruses." I flash him a grin, causing another witch to grind her teeth, shifting her tightened jaw.

Luka runs a hand through his hair as he puts on a tight smile. His frustration can be detected by any, though his communication says something otherwise entirely. "May I remind you that to discipline Arabella for lurking within the archives would also mean investigating how she was able to access it in the first place? I would withhold from requesting space within Fae politics in such an uncouth manner. You act as if your leadership is superior when *you* were unaware of who was stealing from your archives for months. You also deem it improbable for Delphi to steal and partake in restricted magik, yet I have heard from others the panic that has ensued within these very walls."

To Remus' left is a witch–Noel Volkov, who appears no more mature in age than ourselves. A bit older, possibly, but in mortal aging, that cannot be by much. Her body is youthful, but her face sags. Eyes wide and thin lips curved, a single sound of a giggle is directed. "Correct me if I misunderstood, but you think that with all the work we encounter, letters without substantial proof would warrant priority over other proceedings? We regard allegations against one of our own to a high degree, but we are pragmatics. There are *proven* Magiks that roam free, using their abilities and sigils unauthorized by the law, so you'll pardon us for prioritizing those with more urgency."

"There are curses that you teach in your schooling yet are

not permitted to be used. How is that sensible?" I berate. I do not burden myself by mentioning that curses, though some not restricted, still cause harm.

Noel opens her mouth to speak but pauses in thought. What the Council views as immoral may still be taught, but insights into their knowledge—with books that expose the immense power they hold over untaught skills—are not ones they would risk making known to other Magiks. "Many are shown horrendous atrocities in their fictional media. That doesn't mean everyone is a murderer."

"Yes, but if given the means and necessities, some very well could," Luka emphasizes. Warning shoots through his eyes. A reminder that he is one of them and can play politics as well as any of the others. "How many underage Magiks are you sending out to do your bidding?"

There is a lingering pause of tension, though no denial is attempted. I think it frightens the Council enough not to argue, though it takes a great deal to keep myself from expressing my amusement.

"From recorded texts and keeping secret our feud with the Fae, you grasp enough to know they cannot lie," Luka goes on. "The High King has told you that it was Delphi who not only took Arabella but manipulated his brother. All of the elected bribery will not erase this if your negligence continues."

My hand holds up, stopping Luka and allowing me to speak. "I have had the misfortune of meeting Delphi. And in that, she made a bargain with me, offering Arabella's freedom in exchange for land."

"Your ignorance is noted, Your Majesty," the witch in pink says.

I do not believe she cares whether I grant them the favor they request. Since our arrival—since I sent word—the Council of the Coven has shown no empathy towards what another Magik has caused. Perhaps their apathy stems from a rivalry that dates further than any of them have lived. The leaders uphold a system that wishes to thrive under a clouded mindset, firmly convincing themselves that they are the most powerful among creatures.

"Regardless," Remus ignores, "nothing can be proven from what you had to say about Delphi's connection. If she aligned herself with Adonis, the murders would not constitute a breaking of our treaty with the Fae."

Arabella's face becomes impatient. Her leaders purposefully give me no chance to elaborate. I dread the inevitable consequence that is to come from her.

"I'm witness to these things *and* the torture Delphi enacted upon me!" Arabella returns.

"You are one of our own. If she had harmed you, that matter is to be dealt with under different circumstances," a witch with hair of wood tones argues. "This is exactly why we need a Magik representative in the Fae lands. At any given moment, the Fae may retaliate against us for Delphi *possibly* taking someone of importance to their king."

Ambrose nods and turns to his fellow Magik. "Un menteur qui prétend de telles illusions est ridicule."

"Ne sous-estimez pas l'ambition d'une sorcière avide de pouvoir, quand vous pouvez regarder dans l'esprit d'Arabella et prouver le contraire," Luka replies. He does not miss a beat in his words, crossing his arms in displeasure at their exchange.

This language is that of which I have never heard spoken. I do not recognize a single word, save the sound of Arabella's name. "Did he speak another language?" I ask.

Without glancing in my direction, Arabella keeps her attention in front of her. "Yeah."

"And what was said?"

"Leader Blanchet said something about me being a liar,

delusions, and being ridiculous. And Luka said something about my mind proving otherwise," she explains.

As she speaks, my chest constricts tightly. The Magik leaders are too callous when discussing Arabella's experiences. My eyes jump constantly, focused mainly on the queen, though darting to those at the table and scanning for a hint of magik aimed at her.

"I'm pretty sure," she goes on, turning to me at last. Her face is unchanged, irritated, and aggravated, though I do not think it to be caused by my asking. "It's been years since I took French classes."

The man, who appears similar to the looks of Arabella's features, mutters something to himself in another language I cannot detect. He glances past Luka, towards Arabella and myself, as if he is better than us.

"Ngóh léih gáai néih. Chēut sēng lāai. Yùh gwó néih m̀h chēut sēng, m̀h hóu góng lāai!" Luka says curtly. His remark stuns the leader. Others around the table react with gaped mouths or pursed lips.

I would appreciate such assailing comments that I do not understand, if only for the look of mortification on their faces. Arabella appears as puzzled as I. Nevertheless, I am hopeful she understands the exchange. Asking her, "Did you understand any of that as well?"

"Uh," she drawls with a look of confusion and twisting expressions, "I know it was Chinese, but I don't speak any of the languages."

Without diluting his stare against the sorcerer directly center-right of the group, Luka says, "It does not translate, but I have essentially said that Leader Zhao must speak up with what it is he has to say, or he should say nothing at all."

His clarification incites additional outrage. In a multitude of other languages, their words topple over each other, becoming incoherent. They have become starving piranhas–floundering and fighting amongst each other.

"How many languages does he speak?" I ask.

Luka moves his head around to face us. "I am fluent in multiple languages, including English, Italian, French, Mandarin, and Spanish, though I can carry a conversation and understand eight." He turns himself back to the Council leader. "*Which*, Leader Zhao, is why I can also understand your Cantonese."

"Told you he was smart," Arabella whispers, leaning into my side. It is the closest that she has come to initiating contact with me, to which I savor every generous bit I am given.

The bald sorcerer with darker skin frowns. His sleeves open widely as his arms cross over each other, revealing his nameplate, engraved with the name Ryan Morrison. "After the necessary tools we provided for your growth, you choose to align yourself with him?" he insults, tilting his head at me.

"You provided me with an education that, despite learning with the highest teachers, I was kidnapped by Delphi," Arabella rebukes.

In a fluid movement, similar to a snake coiling around something, she comes behind me, her foot kicking the back of my knee. My legs fall forward, while my body backwards. I am on my knees, paraded in front of all, when I hear Arabella flip the blade from her knife out. She presses the iron to my throat while holding me in place with her other hand.

I make no effort to fight her. The burn of the metal is excruciating, but she is touching me.

"Do something about Delphi, or I kill the High King and we go to war against the Fae," she threatens. Admittedly, I find it intriguing she has not revealed her power as the queen.

A clever move to keep hidden.

Threats from Arabella are not to be taken lightly. Her hatred for Delphi and demand for her justice may very well overpower any other emotion she feels. The Council doubts that she would truly have me killed. An ignorant mindset when she would not mind drawing blood from me. I don't know, in honest, if she would do so now or if this is another trick, which makes my emotions on the matter all the more confusing.

The contact is a familiarity I recall with fondness. Even in her most threatening state, while she holds my life in her hands, I crave this.

Easily, I could break free. One flap from my wings, and she would be sent rearward and flat.

Instead, as a ruse, I put my right hand to her arm that holds a weapon against me. To appear as if I am attempting to escape her grip. Even as I try that, the blade of the knife begins to press into me deeper, causing me to flinch back.

"Your feeble attempts, while valiant," Remus chuckles, "are fruitless. No one knows of your existence here beyond these walls. We could expunge this problem at once. A tragic accident may have happened to Miss Huǒ. Mister Caedos is already confirmed dead. And as for the king? Are the Fae equipped to handle another war so soon?"

Fists clench directly under my view. Arabella releases her knife against me, tucking it into her shirt while I stand.

A sorcerer in green smiles at Remus' insinuation. "Your quarrel has nothing to do with us. We take no blame for what Delphi does on your land." By the way in which he enunciates his words, they come out nearly the same as how Luka speaks, though this sorcerer's accent is much thicker.

"Indeed, you have made that very clear. If only you cared to tend to matters of your own kind rather than stare at my face. Though I cannot blame you for taking to my comeliness," I return glibly, grinning at the pathetic man.

Arabella elbows me at my side, her patience less tolerant of me than before.

"Furthermore," I continue, stepping aside from the two Magiks at my side, "the harm you have cast onto Arabella is to threaten a ruler of Ifaeris itself. You throw your coins where they ought not to be spent if you expect me level-headed for such a violation of our treaty."

"Cassius!" Arabella hisses loudly. She holds her tongue, but I wager on the fact she is upset with me for revealing her power as queen.

Let her be wroth with me. I would prefer that to feeling terrified for her well-being. She seems to find a rush when it comes to throwing herself into murderous plans, and I just wish she would halt from doing so.

To harm the queen is enough of a reason for me to unleash my silhouette shadow. Yet, I am strongly aware that Arabella expects more of me. I am to hold my composure no matter how little I wish to do so.

Faces of the Council attempt to hold straight, but their synchronized reaction gives away their true feelings on the matter. Hexing Arabella means an attack on Ifaeris, though I am not so senseless to declare war in this very room. We hold no advantage while entrapped by their magik. I must think as Arabella would and say nothing.

"Shrewd Council leaders," I begin, "I do not wish violent offenses committed unto us when there is an option for peace. I would hope you do not carry the same bloodthirst as those preceding you."

After exchanged glances, a consensus must have been reached. Leader Morrison rises while wearing a wide smile, clearing his throat. "Okay, Your Majesty. Since neither of us want to hurt the other, this will be your single and final warning. If there is an unjust cause of death upon a Magik, or you do anything more to disrupt our system, we will not hesitate to rethink our agreement of peace." For seconds, he pauses, allowing for the information to settle. "We'll consider the death of our security guard equal for the hexing of Miss Huŏ. As for Mister Caedos, count your blessings that you have another chance at life."

Odette stands, looking at us with flaring eyes, flickering them between the three of us. "You are free to leave."

The guard whom Luka had hexed stands at the door, handing Arabella her dagger back, which is coated in blood from the dead sorcerer's body. She snatches it, huffing in anger but contesting nothing.

"Oh, and King Cassius?" Leader Hilton says. "Please change your ears and wings for us before you leave."

"The books you have taken, Miss Huŏ," Leader Zhao says.

Reluctantly, she opens her bag, pulling out two leather-bound books with metal-sprayed edges, and shoves them into the guard's chest. I glamour my ears round, drawing in my wings, and in defeat, we wait for the witch to drop the veil, which imprisons us in and exit the room.

XXVIX

Brilliant

Luka

As we leave the room, a Magik with a build similar to Gavin's escorts us out. He orders us forward, the three of us walking in front of the large man, passing investigation offices, conference rooms, and other doors that Cassius and I had disregarded on our way to find Ari. Each area in the hallway is lightly embellished, with floors and walls made of immaculate ceramic tile. The doors too are made from heavy metal and painted a faded charcoal.

Hardly anything has changed around here.

It still has decor meticulously chosen, which presents the Coven as artificially perfect as possible. On a wall are pictures of Coven workers, dictating the line of achievements some have accomplished. The exquisite flooring appears similar to a historical glazed carpeting with designs on the outer framing.

We roam until we reach a lift, where the security allows us to depart freely. Our group stands in stalling silence filled with tension. I could have easily led our group out without issue, but there seems to be copious amounts of distrust.

After ascending four floors, Cassius glares at Ari. "You did not think before this."

"I did, actually," Arabella replies. Her face is stone and forward without a hint of regret while she crosses her arms. She has done something beyond what she says, and I am not sure what it is.

"You were nearly ripped apart by your leaders," Cassius says. The golden, winged eyeliner on both corners of his eyes remains still while the rest of his face narrows, the outline portraying himself to look more similar to a crow. The belt that wraps around his waist and meets in the middle at an ornamental buckle, adding to such a comparison.

Ari's body tenses. Her head crooks to the side while her lips press into each other until they turn to nothing altogether, offering no rebuttal.

"Luka nearly killed the guards on duty for neglecting their responsibilities to keep you safe," the king laughs. "And when Cel lowered his levels of anger, I sent every guard and knight across the lands in search of you."

I make no apology for my worry. Whenever Arabella is gone and none know where she is, the fear that she's been taken by Delphi again skyrockets.

From the corner of my eye, I see Ari's face pucker while blushing. She rocks to the tips of her toes, then back down to her heels.

On the next floor, the doors open. A sorcerer in too-bright and mismatched colors for my liking enters. He whistles through the silence for another two floors before ours is reached. The man strolls out first, and upon his exit, Ari glances to the corner, making a sound of laughter. I can practically hear the thoughts in her head.

Her reaction is one I am in total agreement with.

Cassius' boots make nearly no sound when we walk. His steps are light and differ from the trainers that Ari wears, which squeak against the freshly polished floor when her footsteps stop.

"How'd you figure out it was Xavier?" Ari asks with a sigh. Her hands drop to her side, arms swinging and brushing her thighs.

"When he spoke, it only took seconds before we knew something was amiss," I respond. "And in less than two minutes, he admitted where you were."

Ari stops again. Places her hands on her waist.

It's clear she is frustrated that her unilateral plan had been foiled, but I find it adorable to see her stumped. She thinks that her looks alone would render me unable to spot a difference, not thinking of the quirks she does subconsciously. I would know her, even if my senses were stripped and the Council removed my memories.

I will always gravitate to her.

She throws her head back, turning in both directions to see who is around. Under her breath, she mutters, "He promised me. I thought Fae couldn't break their word."

"They can when the promise was held together by swearing to the crown," Cassius says smugly. "Which I am as well. Lest you forget, my queen."

Ari glares at Cassius while exhaling in understanding. Holds a thin smile and continues towards the revolving door. The two of us hurry our steps to meet her without difficulty, despite her walking ahead.

Xavier had told us that she went to Magik Cove, but due to him having no knowledge of the many offices, Cassius and I had okkared to six separate areas. That is until I, like a man inadvertently obtuse, realized that Ari would go looking through the main archives. We first arrived there, and when we saw the books flung from the shelves, I rushed us towards the Council's chamber.

"We would have been here sooner if we had chosen the right office building from the start," I tell her as we catch up to her side.

The grip around her sleeves tightens. "Well, it would've gone better if y'all didn't show up." She attempts to restrain herself, but it fails upon her steadfast line towards the revolving doors.

"Arabella," a voice hisses. Arabella stops before either Cassius or I do. At the turn of my head, I realize it comes from the front desk. "Luka. Arabella. Come here."

Our names beckon us to her. As we get closer, I see the witch's hair in twists, with the color of magenta towards the bottom. She has matured since I last saw her, but my memory recalls her well. Imani, daughter of Leader Morrison. She is two years my senior, but she has barely aged from when she was fifteen.

"There's something you should know. If you can provide undeniable evidence that Delphi has used restricted magik against the Fae, they'll have to move forward with your case." Her voice is hushed. It can barely be heard over the sounds of workers bustling through the lobby.

"We've tried showing proof. But they won't listen," Ari says with a shrug.

Imani looks from side to side, scoping for any onlookers. "My father's colleagues are lying. I've heard him speak endlessly to my mother about the Fae and Delphi specifically. Right now, the executives suspect, but only the Council is aware of their existence."

"Okay, so if they're going to lie, what do you think can be done to prove otherwise?" Arabella presses.

"If more Magiks knew of the Fae's existence and other secrets the Coven hides, Delphi's case might be taken more seriously. Spread word. Raise suspicion." Imani turns the monitor towards us and reveals a list of missing texts from the archives. On the list are names, many of whom are the more notorious workers of the Coven. Next to some of the texts are em dashes, exposing if what was taken was returned by a member or if it is believed to be stolen. "Since the first letter from King Cassius, the Council's been working on damage control, and it's eaten the entire Coven from the inside out. Leaders have been questioning the executives and investigating what has and hasn't been taken from the archives and vaults."

If the Stone of Elestial isn't the only thing that has gone missing, there is reason to wonder just how far any of our leaders are willing to go to hold power.

"The Council said, as recently as minutes ago, that they do not regard hearsay of Delphi's involvement as high priority," Cassius explains.

From a bag, Imani pulls out a book that is too large for the storage holder. She digs through, the leather of the orange stretching outwards as her fist hits the borders of the inside. After rummaging for a short period longer, she pulls out a letter of correspondence between her father and Leader Volkov, mocking Cassius' letters, which plead for them to intervene. "You can't keep that, but you can see that the Council's more convinced that Delphi is involved than they say."

"Why do you have this?" Cassius asks.

"I keep a couple of my dad's letters with me at all times," Imani responds. She takes the letter and places it into her bag, trying to force the book back in after dropping it twice. "Sorry, it's hard to get this in here."

"If they suspect that Delphi *is* guilty, why haven't they done anything to stop her?" Ari asks, staring at the witch as she continues struggling against the accessory. "And if that's too big to fit, why do you keep shoving it in? Why not just carry it?"

Off from the side, Cassius looks at Ari, his mouth quirked and brow raised. When she turns to him with a face of puzzlement, her chest and shoulders jerk forward, chuckling once when realizing the secondary meaning of what she has said. She holds in a louder laugh while my eyelids shut, eyes rolling with a sigh.

"Anyway," Imani ignores. "It isn't that they don't find it

important. They just think there may be more positives to her endeavor than negatives."

"In what way?" I interrupt. Wondering questions ponder whether the Council assumes themselves to benefit from Delphi ruling over the Fae. Perhaps they think themselves right to rule over Fae. After all, that *was* something Leader Hilton hinted towards.

Imani simply shrugs. "No clue. Maybe they think they can use Delphi for their gain somehow?" She peers at me. Puts on an arrogant smile. "Unlike *you*, my father never forced me into a life of politics. I only know the things I've overheard from my parents' conversations."

"*Hmm*," Cassius hums. His rings clash down, clanking to the desk. "What more of relevance can you tell us?"

Fingers type on the keyboard in front of us. Imani shakes her head no, just as another employee strolls by. "Not much I can say besides Delphi's no longer friends with some of the daughters of the Coven. From what one of them told me, they never made their fallout public, but if she confided in anyone prior, they would be the ones you should speak to." Just as she is about to go on, a group of Magiks stop, peering in our direction. "Si testifican, ni siquiera el Consejo podría negarlo."

She just admitted that if any of the Coven's children testify in our defense, the Council could no longer deny the accusations. Theoretically, this helps in our favor, but I'm unsure if it will result positively if played out.

"Why do you help us?" Cassius asks with skepticism. The questioning is understandable, given what he has witnessed our leaders doing to Ari. The fact also remains that we can easily lie.

"I know the long-ass grudge the Fae must have against Magiks. If I can prevent your people from taking out their revenge and having us pay for what our ancestors did and what Delphi's currently doing, I'll happily help stop it."

With one last click of her mouse, the printer starts. She grabs a piece of paper from the machine beside her. On it, lists the addresses of several confidants who Delphi has recently cut contact with. A few are Magiks I had interacted with as a child at the request of my father when my parents socialized with theirs. Others, however, are those that continuously harassed Arabella at Lazipeus. If they are no longer acquainted with Delphi, they likely would be the few to reveal her secrets. Though, even then, that is very implausible.

Ari takes the paper, thanks Imani, and folds it into her bag. "I think we should go. I don't feel like taking my chances for loitering longer than we already have." She takes the hands of Cassius and myself, okkaring into the foyer of Nexus.

"What did you expect to come out of meeting with the Council?" Cassius demands from her immediately upon our arrival.

"I don't know, okay? I was hoping they'd at least listen to me about their archives being stolen from. They wouldn't communicate with us otherwise." Arabella's eyes glance towards the floor on her left, her breath marginally heavier than normal. She refuses to make eye contact with either of us. "Didn't think it would go that way."

Cassius' eyebrow perks up. He smiles, the corner of his mouth pointing with his eyebrow. "Did you not think you would be caught?" He never reveals to her his worry. Instead, he says this as if he finds it amusing.

Ari grins to match his stature, but differing from the king's, hers stems from a place of provocation. It is my own doing that she put herself in imminent danger. I'm the one who pushed her so hard to remind her of her strength. I hadn't thought. I did not take into account her insistence on fighting against the world as if it is her burden to bear alone.

"You're acting like that wasn't my plan," she brushes off.

Suspicion makes its way onto my face. I turn to her. Scan her up and down. Her vice is being quick to anger, which makes her reaction to Cassius questionable. "It was?"

"Please," she dismisses with a scoff, grabbing two books from the table that were not there before we left for Magik Cove. One I cannot see, but the other is a grimoire. Old, but in fair condition for its age. "I okkared back here and left these a little before I was taken to the Council. There are benefits to having Reyna and her boyfriend working in high-level security at the Cove."

Ari's face is full of pride, but with how she scratches her thumb's nail with her index finger, I think she's more nervous than letting on. "I knew they'd wanna see me for breaking in, but I didn't think they'd try hexing me."

My theory proves correct when she drops the books onto the table, wincing and holding her shoulders.

Cassius takes a step closer to her. "You would have come home perfectly intact, had you been more careful."

"And no one would've risked a kingdom if you didn't come along and fuck everything up!" she retorts. "*The two of you could've died.* They threatened to kill you like it was nothing."

"So you expect us to be okay with you being tortured?" I berate. Discounting my love for her, she was impulsive. She risked her life without so much a thought as to their apathy and willingness to kill her.

Ari looks at me with a face of confusion. Her eyebrows are crossed, and she blinks a few times, a blank expression apparent. "You're mad at me." Not a question, but a statement.

"Yes," I admit. "But more importantly, you shouldn't have done what you did so early."

Her face falls into more spouts of angered confusion. She assumes that I find her strategy stupid, when, in fact, I think she jumped to a last resort too soon. Imani made such a revelation clear when speaking about the others who were raised within similar, elite backgrounds. If my appearance were known, some would wonder how I have come alive. It is one of my greater ignorances to have never taken that into consideration.

So deeply do I respect Ari's need to save others, but not if it is at the cost of her life. While she is a powerful witch, she also forces herself to endure perilous actions that endanger none but her.

"You didn't factor in that the other children of high stature would question their parents," I explain. "Many of us resent the ways we were raised. If we had gone to them, we would have allies willing to side with us."

In a quick movement, Ari's eyes widen. She whispers an "oh my gods" to herself while turning away. Rather than admitting her error, she pulls out a piece of paper from Jefferson.

To the leaders of Ifaeris,

Inside my package is an artifact that was stolen from the Fae so long ago. Along with it is a payment and reminder of what my loyalty means.

Recently, I overheard a son of one of the Council leaders disparaging his mother. He claimed to be the only one with knowledge of the missing books that were recently returned. After an exchange between the two of us and an offering of exclusive festivities that will occur in Infinite, the boy easily parted with the information. Below are the book titles.

— Sanguis et Maledictiones
— Ceanglaionn Magikal
— Magik with the Afterlife
— Histoire du Traité des Fae

You may want to hurry and collect these before any of the Council leaders find out they've been returned to the archives.

If I can be of more assistance, contact me.

— Jefferson

"I managed to find another book that some prisoner told me about when I saw Orella," Ari says. "I didn't tell either of you 'cause I *knew* all of us going would be dangerous. It would've allowed easier access for Delphi to rule. I was careless. And yes, I almost died, but I couldn't let the books sit there waiting for her to take them."

"And what of the other books we've stolen from Delphi?" Cassius asks. "Have you committed them to memory?"

Ari scowls at him. Rolls her eyes as they shut. "I took notes of all the important details. Anything else, I had duplicated into empty journals. The ones I put in the archives were our books that I knew they'd have as well."

It takes little to no time before I calculate my error. It had been an oversight to think Arabella didn't have a deliberate reason for what she did, but her disappearance struck a fear in me that makes me incredibly angry with her. She may not want to endanger others with her plans, but this is not something so minor as closing herself off from the world.

"I'd rather not dishearten myself with ideas of harm befriending you without another present, so if you are to go about your mission, see to it that Luka, at the very least, joins you," Cassius requests. He shares equal power with Ari, but she is hard-headed, making his demand of little effect.

"Fine," Ari calmly agrees, though reluctantly. She removes her shoes, exchanging them for slippers from one of the servants. "Luka and I will go back to LA and find some of Delphi's ex-friends."

Cassius nods. "I will attempt not to interfere with your plans moving forward, but I implore you, as co-ruler, you divulge your ideas of leaving ahead of time so I do not hinder them in the process."

"Okay." She walks towards the servant's quarters, supporting her left arm with her right hand.

Part 4
Gathering Information

XXX

Pop Goes the Fae

Cassius

I would have thought that appointing the role of Master of Amusements to Xavier would have been ideal, considering his expertise to incite joy in whoever is around, but it appears I am incorrect. The bard he had sent to me today only held my attention for minutes before his tale became uninteresting. I do let him continue now, but only for the reason that there is nothing else of pleasure to do in this palace today.

Stories of fiction captivate me far more than those of truth. A retelling of events done by one individual does nothing for fascination. I had learned enough of that during schooling in my youth.

I am sure I have smudged the kohl while mistakenly running a hand through my eyes due to boredom. A yawn and a careless action are all it takes to ruin my appearance.

Night cannot come soon enough. I would much rather activities among others be occurring. In such hours, I will fly into the sky. The breeze from gliding through the air centers me, and in my past, with the right company watching from revels or other festivities, it is the greatest source of attention. However, it can also be a relaxing, brief reprieve of solitude when others during those nights grow too expectant of myself.

Perhaps the bard would be a bit more fun with more alcohol and the two Magiks.

"My king, if you're this disinterested in the bard, may I suggest another form to entertain yourself?" Gavin suggests at my inattentive attitude. He stands at my side with the face of contribution while also keeping sure to exchange glances across the room with the guards at the door.

Before me, the bard, dressed in a bright fashion for his tales, attempts to continue, though he grows worried of his dismissal. His hat is tilted at the side of his head, with his curly, rose gold hair barely poking out. Then, he becomes silent, with even the lute ending its strung tune, directing himself towards the ground so as not to face me.

"Might I offer another story if you are displeased with the one I am currently telling, my king?" the bard asks. His throat moves as he gulps while his anxieties ripple through the air. He bows deeply in my presence, lilac hat clenched to his chest, with eyes that tremble similar to a child awaiting approval.

"That may result in the rejection of any future opportunities to entertain the crown." My leg drops from Arabella's throne, where it had been propped and resting comfortably. "You are dismissed, but see to it that the next time you're brought to entertain me, you find better ways to keep me engaged."

With another bow, the bard exits the throne room. I wonder if I should have gotten his name to inform Xavier of my discontent.

"Perhaps you can attempt meeting with the chefs and try your luck with cooking again," Gavin jests. He chuckles at his comment, instantly forcing a cough to cover it up.

I cannot be insulted by his words, considering the previous time I had worked with our chefs, it had gone horribly wrong. One moment, the food tasted slightly off, the next, flames were covering the entire dish, everything was overly salted, and I destroyed the pan on which the food was placed.

A catastrophe for something mortals consider a dessert.

"I think that is a horrendous idea," I respond with a darting look thrown at my knight. "For both myself and anyone involved."

The throne room doors burst open, with Damita rushing in. They are out of breath, shakily dashing up the stairs and heaving in an effort to get the words out.

From my throne, I stand, requesting Gavin to fetch my advisor a drink.

"What is it, Damita?" I ask while they finish the glass of water.

Their hair has fallen from its pinned-up place. The twisting way that their hair braids together is in their face, with the tie caught in a section. Sweat coats them entirely. "There was an attempted attack at Windwyrd. The court's guards could not find Luka, so they informed me." They pause, catching their breath while moving the excess of their mauve breeches to cool their legs. "I ran here as soon as it was explained."

"Find Arabella and inform her there is an urgent matter that demands the queen," I command the guards at the door.

Less than ten minutes pass before Arabella is brought to the room by Gavin leading her. Tiredness is planted on her face, with her hair tied up and strands clinging to her rosy cheeks from the sweat.

She wipes her forehead using the back of her palm, drying it on the cloth of the brassiere she wears. "What's up? Gavin barged in the training room and said something about an important matter."

I step down, descending towards her. "Damita has informed

me of an attack at Windwyrd. I called for you since the lands are just as much yours as they are mine."

Rolling her eyes while smiling, she turns to our advisor, who has not left their spot.

"As the king has said," Damita says, "there was an attack at Windwyrd. Lady Rebekah sent guards to inform Luka of a common fae who attempted to remove a ward from their land, but they found me first." While attempting to recall the information they are to relay, they scratch the side of their head. Its value must be significant, since what they have said thus far does not seem nearly pertinent to have rushed in the way in which they did. Their head pops up, eyes widening with eyebrows lifting as well. "The border's offender had only been caught due to an attempt on Lady Jiya's life. Somehow, the Fae had snuck into the House of Zephys during the night and attempted to murder her. Guards found a stone with one of your sigils in his pocket, and now the rulers demand justice."

Arabella is still catching her breath from her activities. She finishes the water from her metal jug and exhales heavily. Her hands go behind her head after a guard takes it, her arms raised at an angle. "Is Lady Jiya okay? Does she need more healers sent?"

"Yes, my queen, Lady Jiya is alive. I do not know the state of her, as I was not told much before rushing here to inform you. I am only aware that the rulers request to see you tomorrow when Lady Jiya regains energy."

"Cassius," Arabella calls. It pulls my entire focus to her. My body turns, saying nothing as she undoes her hair from its tied place. "Can you handle this on your own, or do you want me there with you?"

"My dearest queen, I always want you with me," I return. She snorts at my comment as if it is a jest, but it is nowhere near the sort.

Turning to our advisor, rather than to face me, Arabella smiles.

"Thanks, Damita. And get more water. You look more out of breath than I do."

Our advisor leaves the room, shutting the doors. The queen turns to our guards and my personal knight next. "Can y'all leave the room too? I needa speak with Cassius alone about this."

All three nod, bowing to the two of us and exiting.

"It seems someone has made it easier for Delphi to break through the wards," I comment before Arabella speaks.

The queen is already starting in the direction of our thrones. Faster, her feet take her before she flops onto the steps. "Sorry," she laughs. "I needed to sit, or I might black out."

As I hand her my chalice, she takes it, taking large gulps before making a face. "This tastes wrong."

My eyebrows knit at once. What incorrect thing could I have done with *my* drink?

"You usually like your little drink more appley when you make it." She has returned to a consistent breathing pattern when handing back the chalice, yet she is still flushed. I have not seen her this spent in a long while.

My gaze drops to her revealed skin where my marking has long disappeared. Instead, her arms are covered in bruises, fingers cracking her knuckles.

Despite exhaustion, she holds pulchritude that no other creature has. No matter how it is she looks at me right now, I feel a rush from the core of my being.

The distance between us makes it difficult to communicate thoroughly. *That* is what moves me to sit beside her.

"I could always use my supposed guile to get that common fae to admit what it is that drove him to this," I say light-heartedly. It distracts me from everything I cannot take my eyes off of.

"Your charisma won't get you everything." Though she says this in a condescending tone, she doesn't appear upset with me.

Our bodies are pressed too closely. We both recognize it. The back of my fingers unintentionally skim up her thigh as I move my hand to my lap, my body heating. I can hear her inhale.

Silence is loud in my mind.

"You're free to leave if you wish," I tell her.

Arabella's lips are parted, full and beautiful. Her presence is both a treacherous thing and the single most sustaining necessity of my existence.

"I know."

But she doesn't leave the steps. Only moves off to the side and away from me, her fingers skimming up and down the opposite forearm.

"Whoever the common fae is," she says, "the attack couldn't have been random. It was during the Beaver Moon."

While my eyes remain on her, Arabella's focus is hard at work.

"But then, how would the Fae have known that full moons are when magik is at its weakest? Delphi had to have been using the Fae to do her dirty work. And *that* would mean she controlled him somehow," she continues to herself. Her knees come closer to her chest while twisting her head to me, nearly falling into a cross-legged position, if not for her arms wrapped around her bent legs, hands clasped together. "And I'm sure they had plans to do a lot more than what was done."

"Are you planning on murdering the common fae?" I ask, delighted. "I think the rulers of Windwyrd would find your murderous tendencies of use for once."

To this, she grins proudly. "I don't know if I should kill some common fae that's still under Delphi's control, but if it were anyone here that they'd done this to, you wouldn't have to ask me that. They'd already be dead."

"So what is our course of action as the king and queen?" I question with a wondering smirk. Perhaps due to coordinating together or that she suggested she would murder for me. I choose not to comment on this though. It would only result in nothing.

She crosses one leg over another, tapping her fingers in line on her arm. "I think we should do what the rulers ask. Allow them to think on the common fae's punishment, as long as it's fitting with the reminder that Delphi might've controlled him. You think they'll ask for his immediate death at our arrival before we can question him?"

"I *assume* that they would obey their king and queen, no matter what they decide."

Arabella's eyes briefly widen, her face relaxing into a small smile. "I think I'm gonna go check on the wards. Just in case, y'know?"

She has no reason to protect the same Fae that hate her kind, no less the rulers who are hoping for her demise, yet it does nothing to stop her from risking her life for our very existence. And as she saunters out the door and calls for a horse to bring her to the edges where the wards can be found, I think that her motivation has bled onto me.

Perhaps it is inane to have traveled to the Zephys' household by carriage, but wasting an opportunity to make use of our steeds would be a great shame. The ride itself does not feel tremendously long, though that may be due to conversation taking place.

Both Luka and I sit side by side with Arabella across us two, the queen wearing something contradictory to the outside's weather— just above the temperature of snow.

The dress on Arabella, which is as green as the Darkened Forest, cuts deeply into her chest. It's fitted to her waist, where it then flows down right past the head of the dragon marked on her thigh. Though the straps are the width of my two fingers, they are hidden under a corset-armor of sorts that hugs her ribs and the sides of her breasts. While not a chest plate, the weaponsmiths have guaranteed that it works as full-body protection when activated by Arabella's magik.

With the new season approaching, Luka's never-changing attire fits well. There is a return of one of his many black shirts that loosely stretches above the base of his neck. His breeches, which he has informed me are known as slacks, are the same as always, posing the question of whether he wears this to signify a uniform. There bears nothing special with what he dresses in.

Upon our arrival, Gavin departs from our driver and opens the carriage door. The cream and gold of our transportation complement well with the outside white.

Luka is the first to move, swinging a leg towards the door when I feel a tug from under me. "Cassius?" he calls, motioning to the tail of his single-breasted overcoat, which I had been sitting on.

I lift myself, swaying my body for Luka to exit and myself following shortly after. There is an odd mixture where my clothing overlaps Luka's and Arabella's. Like the seneschal, my garments are almost entirely black, save the gold accents, and similar to the queen, my tunic cuts low into my torso, with the intricate epaulets extending beyond my shoulders.

Arabella keeps one hand on the golden handle of the carriage's body when climbing out, and as she moves, the armor glides with her. The metal, which protrudes slightly past her shoulders, extends out at the bottom, serving as partial sleeves and resembling wings, whereas the rest of the shielding consists of a design with silver trimmings, shaped in feather outlines.

Sounds of her boots crash with the travertine pathway below us. She checks thrice over for the weapons she keeps on her body—some she has concealed—and puts on a coat that falls to the middle of her calf. Her face is written with the thoughts traveling through her mind while her eyes stare at the hall in the distance.

She is enchanting.

The four of us walk towards the entrance of the House of Zephys and approach Harrison, who stands outside, prepared to escort us to his mothers.

We stroll under arched architecture along an area that overlooks their flowery garden, the porcelain balustrades bordering this walkway reaching a height above my thighs. I can see the far-off town, which is filled with common fae working to create new inventions.

"Do you recall the games we played in this yard?" Harrison asks at my side.

"Games?" Arabella asks with an intrigued voice.

Harrison turns back, wearing a grin so wide I expect him to reveal the worst of what we did in our teenage years spent together. When my father would send me to the lower courts with Ezra in hopes that–while my brother learned how to communicate as royalty–I would pull something so horrible against other Elementals that it would warrant a need for my death. A strategy my father kept in place until his last breath.

"Cassius, Korine, and I used to play all sorts of things. We would prance about these gardens, hiding behind trees or anything we could before one of us would search for the other two." Harrison turns around, continuing into the house and smirking to his side. "As I recall, the High King would cheat."

My eyes roll to the side, settling on my friend. Grateful relief eases every clenched area of my body. "I would use my Elemental powers, same as you. Mine simply allowed me to stay hidden in areas harder to spot. You once sent a spike of chilled ice towards Korine for seeking you out and hitting you first before me."

A mischievous attitude with narrowed eyes is thrown in my

direction, silently but glibly insinuating that if we were to play in a game much more interesting, it would cost me nothing but embarrassment.

"What about you two?" Harrison asks as we hike up the stairs. We veer left at the top of the steps, taking a turn at the hallway's corner, where numerous windows are pristine and shining light perfectly into the corridor. Displayed vases and decor line against the walls, robust and unbreaking–such as most things in Windwyrd–despite how often Harrison would attempt to destroy them. "Either of you dabble in such an activity?"

"I was never allowed to participate in childish affairs, as my father raised me with nothing but punishment since that age. I was only allowed to speak when asked something directly and allowed around others my age, only if they were children of my father's colleagues," Luka answers.

"Such sad conversation. Is that why you hold the humor of a dry tree stump?" Harrison mocks. "Remind me of his importance here again, besides being a companion to the queen."

"He's our seneschal," Arabella's barking tone remarks before I answer. "He handles many things and oversees affairs between us and the lower courts' rulers, which includes your mothers."

"Pity, I thought he would be more fun," Harrison complains. A hand goes into the pocket of his auburn trousers, the other knocking on the door.

At the answer, Lady Rebekah opens the door in a gown of beige and sleeves of lantern, her grape hair done simply. "I did not expect both Magiks to come."

"Yes, well, at the risk of sounding repetitive, Arabella is the queen, and Luka is just as important for what is to be discussed today." At the end of my statement, the Fae bows, reminded of what we are to the Fae.

We all enter the room, Harrison departing soon after with

Gavin, who takes Arabella's coat and remains on the other side of the door to stand watch. Lady Jiya sits on an armchair across the room, resting against cushions the color of Arabella's painted lips, with the silver, wooden framing of the seat crafted in elaborated, rounded designs. Her body is turned, facing towards the window and staring out at the gardens in full view.

Upon turning, she stands from our chair, greeting us with a bow and a sullen look. "Thank you for meeting with us. Many things must be said, but I would first like to get the Imp's punishment settled."

"May I ask what happened? How did the Fae get into your room without making enough sound to alert a guard?" Arabella questions. On impulse, she stands closer to me so that we may appear as a team. Her knuckles brush along my side, but I do not assume she takes notice of the contact.

I have missed this–the way that whenever she questions others, all answers seem to hold equal value.

Jiya appears distressed, anxiously shaking her hand against her thigh. Quickly, Arabella glances down, briskly walking to the Elemental and inviting Windwyrd's ruler to sit.

Two stuttering breaths leave Jiya before she is able to speak. "I have been a ruler for many centuries, and never have I experienced a threat to my life so close to this. It was the middle hours of night before morning while Rebekah and I were asleep. I am a light sleeper, so when I felt something cold against my neck, my eyes shot open. And from pure reaction, I shot lightning through my fingers, though my hands were still under the blanket."

"Then the Imp panicked and shallowly pierced Jiya," Rebekah interrupts when Jiya hesitates to say, anger fired at both Arabella and Luka.

"You cannot blame the two of us for what another common

fae committed," Luka says with an uncaring tone. His hands are behind him, the only movement being the cock of his head.

"But I can blame your kind if Delphi is the cause," Rebekah retorts.

A singular exhale, loud enough to break the room's tension, leaves Arabella. "Okay, what happened after that?"

"Guards burst into the room when they heard the commotion. They tackled the common fae to the ground, and when searching his pocket, they found a stone with one of your carved symbols," Jiya goes on. Her hand reaches the front of her throat, running her fingers across the webs from spiders wrapped around the wound. "Everything appeared fine, but after minutes passed, nausea and dizziness hit me. I was unable to walk straight, and I felt myself stumbling. As it turns out, the blade was coated with poison."

"Have you had the healers detoxify the poison completely?" I ask Jiya and Rebekah.

Jiya rises, crossing the room towards the table, where there is a glass filled with liquid, dirt, and a squashed mushroom that colors the same as a carnelian. She moves slowly, hardly able to keep herself up. It's then that Arabella takes Jiya's arm in hers, steadying the Fae until she is able to sit near us with the mixture in hand. "I have been made a tonic that will abate the poison, but that only slows the effects for a certain amount of time."

"What of the Imp?" I question further. "Has he been taken to a secure location so we might question him before you decide on his fate?" This may have been something that Arabella and I should have clarified with our guards yesterday, but with what little information we were given and the fact that we were to meet with the rulers today, neither of us had thought to.

"No," Rebekah answers for the two of them. "We have kept him chained in a chamber on the opposite side of our main common areas."

She assumes that keeping a Fae whom she deems her prisoner is a wise move, whereas I can see the imminent danger that the decision may pose. It's as if the rulers paid no attention to how easy it was for two other Elementals to be killed. While it may have been due to my brother, those Fae were first given to him by the common fae. The same fate may have just as easily befallen Jiya.

Fatigued, my tongue lightly clicks against my front teeth. "Lady Rebekah, I surely would have thought you wiser than to keep the Fae who attempted murder on the same grounds which you reside in. She could have easily been attacked a second time."

"Of course, Your Majesty," she says, a look rife with woe shown when glancing at her wife. Possibilities of their oversight only bring about horrified fear to her face as she turns back to me. "The foolish ones are us to have kept him here."

Luka's stone-like posture remains unmoved. "It is imperative we speak with him. He may hold information that benefits us regarding Delphi. It will also do you good for us to discover the poison in which the blade was coated, so that you may find a proper antidote."

Merriness most often lacks in his tune and instead is stated with directness. Around most people, he is monotone and inconsiderate towards those he cares nothing for, but outside our politics, he allows himself to loosen himself to a more animated demeanor. That is where we differ.

Rebekah moves her head slightly towards me. Her eyes are wide, and there is irritation inside them. She is riled, but it may be due to me allowing a sorcerer to speak to her in such an insolent manner.

I think, with the three of us, most of the Fae know not what to make of it. We complement each other, stringing together in harmony, yet from the perspective of one unfamiliar with us, we present ourselves in a way that different creatures never understand what to expect.

"We would like time to decide what to do with the common fae," Rebekah says.

"If you would like to shorten the time of your wife's survival, that is completely up to you," Luka says. "She'll die much sooner, and the ruling will be passed to your son."

"Yes, yes," Rebekah finally agrees. She gifts a false smile of respect to Arabella and myself. "Then you must act with haste if there is a quicker chance to heal my wife." She scowls at Luka for his blunt candor and extends an arm for Jiya to join her, interjecting her words with such speed and disregard that she acts as if she came up with the idea herself.

When we exit, following to where the Imp is being held, I wonder if the court rulers have truly comprehended what Magiks have become to the crown. They are aware of Arabella as queen, but Luka shares just as much in the duties, only without the title.

As we are brought to the prisoner below us, I ponder the ways I can demand the same level of respect for both at my side.

"I've already told the guards. I was not in control," the Imp says, coughing while on his knees. He is small in his size, less than the length of my arm, with bony, gray skin and circles bruising below his eyes. From what we were told, he has been coughing blood for the better half of his time since being chained, unable to speak much without dangling his head back to the window and taking deep breaths to continue.

As we impatiently wait for him to return to us, I glance around the room. Next to a sofa that hosts one stands a singular, glass case bookshelf, with another wider chair against the window. A fireplace in the middle of the room sits with a family portrait hung on the wall, painted long ago, based on Harrison's young appearance.

Three rugs, all the same purple, cover the white and tan stone-marble floor. And on the rug by the fire, a low-rising wooden table is planted.

"Then it *was* Delphi," Arabella mutters with folded arms, pausing from her pacing around the sitting room.

The quickest way to achieve this would not be by rushing in and murdering this Fae. Before we approve a proper punishment, a description of whether the Imp's attempted murder is related to Delphi must first be told. For it to have been her is likely, given how we have been made aware that she can invade another's mind, but I'm still unsure how the witch had gained access into *his* mind. All of the common fae taken back from Gigantia are imprisoned in Phantom Tower. All but one. A spell of obedience must have been cast on the Fae much earlier.

Arabella had been right. This is much more than what we had assumed. It is not only those who we keep in Phantom Tower that Delphi still holds control over, but many of Adonis' other followers. Those who had fought in the Battle of Hearthis and been uncaught when fleeing after my brother's fall.

"I-" the Imp tries but is unsuccessful, succumbing to hyperventilating. His body covers itself in sweat, with his tunic's strings untied. The hair on his head chops closely to his skin, emphasizing the perspiration. "There was a voice in my head. I heard a buzzing, then someone telling me what I must do, and then my actions were not my own."

While lowering to him, I realize that each word he manages to say drains more of his energy. His skin is beginning to shrink into his bones, and it is disgustingly visible when they poke out.

"What did the voice say?" Arabella asks.

"Please, my king," he begs. "I shall not forsake you a moment longer if you're able to save me."

Arabella too bends so that her weight rests on her calves, while her feet are planted on the floor. Sympathy floods her expression as she is next to me, facing the Fae.

Another cough. The Fae scowls once at the queen, spitting his blood on the side of her in disrespect, narrowly missing her shoes. At my head's angle, I can see her eyes and balled fists. She does nothing to react, though I see her cheeks sucked into her mouth in disgust. Whatever remains unsaid, it is shown as clearly on her face as the fields on a summer's day.

Her arm shoots out, but I do not see the effects of magik. Instead, the arm holds Luka from moving forward and physically handling the already incapacitated Fae.

Immediately, I clutch the fabric of the Imp's tiny shirt, lifting him onto his feet. The action should be enough to strike fear into the Fae, who squirms at every attempt to escape my hold. "If the queen asks you a question, I think you ought to answer it."

"What is your name?" Luka questions.

"Mydior Rae Eleania," he whimpers in a state of delirium, mindlessly offering something that should not be given lightly. At that, I put the Fae on the floor.

"Mydior Rae Eleania," I say, rising next to Arabella, who is already standing. "I command you to tell us what it is you know."

Luka moves beside the queen. From the sides of my eyes, there is a murderous smile, though faintly visible, presumably recalling the many Fae the two of us extracted answers from. When Arabella was gone and we found each other at our most agreeable. Before things had taken a turn for the worse.

"A voice of medium pitch commanded that I venture through Windwyrd's border and search until I found a stone with significant marking on it," Mydior falteringly explains, perhaps frightened that I know his name in full. He takes in a sharp inhale, moments passing before he goes on. "I put the rock in my pocket, and from there was told to kill Lady Jiya or I would die a grievous death by loneliness.

I have no one who loves me, you see, so when the threat did not work, my body forced me to march until I reached the House of Zephys while my mind held in a trance. I waited all night until a shift in guards had come, and when I snuck into the bedroom of Lady Jiya–" His ribs pierce out from his sides, an edge stabbing through what he wears.

"What poison did you use?" Luka interrupts with the blade in hand, gloved and careful. "The blade that pierced her has no trace of powders." He is meticulous when inspecting the weapon, going so far as holding it at different angles, with the light reflecting off of it.

"Oleander," Mydior chokes out while coughing more blood onto the floor. He falls to all fours as a support, keeping himself up by his forearms. Slowly, his body is changing from its natural color to a deeper purple, darkening and beginning to swell. "I swiped the petals along the blade with gloves."

The Fae shrieks in pain. He returns up to his knees, hands lifting the shirt from the bottom. His body is collapsing in on itself. It is so noticeable that more than just his bones show through his skin. I can see his stomach. Other insides, I would rather not. The horns that stretch his arm's length behind him snap in half with his gaunt, sharp fingers appearing no different from twigs.

I can be a capricious Fae, but as this scene of macabre plays out before my eyes, I cannot hide my sickened state. During battles and fighting, where I would expect something such as this would be simple. Torturing, even, I know this to happen. But none have touched him with magik or Elemental abilities. He is falling to something much slower than a merciful death. Cursed to suffer with any information he passes.

Mydior's open sides have torn wide enough that blood is gushing out. Though his skin shrinks inward, everything inside him remains the same size.

"Magik isn't working," Arabella shouts, hardly able to focus without turning away in disgust, but then, her eyes return to the sight, as if curious about the small creature. Her hands are raised with glittering silver circulating in the air.

Luka joins her, but his magik is just as ineffective.

The common fae is screaming, agony pitched in each sound as blood streams from his eyes. He's barely able to hold himself up as his cursed body betrays him.

"Please," Mydior pleads, frothing at the mouth. "I think I am to suffer this if I speak more."

He looks as if he is about to vomit. The three of us exchange glances with each other, stepping aside so that the Fae may get neither acid nor blood on us. That is not what comes. Instead, he uncontrollably arches to a position that breaks his back. Screaming.

There is a burst of sound, bits of his intestines exploding out. Blood is splattered, sullying the pristine of the room.

Arabella's mouth drops from the shock, the door flying open within the same second.

"Your Majesties, are you harmed?" Gavin asks frantically before the sight of Mydior is viewable. As the Fae takes in the scene, his eyes go to the queen on instinct, to which she shakes her head many times.

From behind our knight, Rebekah holds Jiya's arm in hers. "We had decided to ask for his death, but it would seem you rightly handled it for us," Lady Rebekah mutters.

"Delphi cursed the Fae. He could not tell us what he knew without suffering great consequences," I explain, glancing at the spot where his body lies. "As I'm sure you can very well see."

Both of the rulers stare at me with a blank expression. One which tells me that neither care of the Imp's demise, only that it is done.

We ought to have figured the curse sooner so that we could have received answers better than those he gave.

Luka steps to my side and Arabella to his. "Mydior swiped the petals of oleander on the knife. I recommend charcoal as a cure within the incoming hours to save your life." He is impervious while handing Gavin the blade, which is wrapped in the cloth from the dead Fae behind us.

XXXI

Rumor Has It

Luka

One message alters my schedule for the night completely. I thought today would be ending with rest and recuperation, but instead, I am sorely mistaken. It's gone from an organized schedule of translating the books Ari had stolen, exercising with weight training, and finally finishing it with well-deserved relaxation, to setting off for more work in Los Angeles. This is not unforeseen, especially since Arabella and I had previous intentions of finding Delphi's old acquaintances, but neither of us expected a lead so early on. My eyes are dry from the texts, mind fatigued from interpreting and transcribing. Schoolwork from university would be more satisfying than the research I currently do. I do not have the energy to maintain pleasantries with others, which is something required considering who we are going to speak with.

I look similar to something styled by an eleven-year-old. While I am fully aware that I cannot be recognized by other Magiks, outside of those we are speaking with, I harbor distaste for what I wear nonetheless. Ari, less than an hour ago, handed me one of her oversized punk T-shirts that she had purchased during her first time seeing the band perform. With utmost speed, the tailors had glamoured two ghastly pieces of clothing–salmon shorts for me to wear as bottoms and a red-and-white, vichy button-down shirt that I commonly see worn by adolescent boys who try to accentuate their wealth.

I'm forced to wear that heinous article as a shirt instead of Ari's, though neither are particularly shirts I would ever choose for myself.

On a contrasting note, Ari dresses comfortably in cabernet red with black ripped jeans and platform trainers. She pops her head into the bedroom from the hallway. Unsuccessfully tries to stifle her laughter. "Ready to go?"

"Yes, love."

Before we can leave for Ari and Juli's shared house–which has now primarily become occupied by Juli and Grayson–we must tell Cassius where we are off to.

On the first floor, Cassius is already waiting for us, a pastry made with honey and Etherfruite in hand. The Fae is friendly and full of extravagant greetings, though I cannot say if it is from the overt happiness that the baked good gives or something else entirely.

"What are you wearing?" he asks with a raised eyebrow.

"A disguise. So you better not make fun of him," Ari replies, though I don't think she can obey her own command. She tosses a cap with a flat brim to me, complementing the attire well in the most unappealing way possible.

I only imagine it looks unflattering.

When seeing the piece on my head, Ari makes a face, shaking her head and twirling her finger around. "Other way."

As I flip the bill to the back of my head, Ari falls into a fit of laughter, choking when taking in my whole appearance. I'm overwhelmingly glad that I have no mirror to view myself. Others in the palace stare, a few taken aback.

"You trust your source with finding Delphi's acquaintances?" Cassius asks, redirecting us to the subject which we are meant to focus on.

"*Yeah, of course.* It's Evie." Ari links her arm in mine, and I have to hold myself from wrapping my arms around her. I'm also unsure how she can find me appealing in any way when wearing what I do. "She told me they passed through her store, so we should go. I don't know how much longer they'll be there. Take care of everything while we're away?"

"I'm doubtful any of the Elementals would request an audience so soon after the Imp incident, but should I need to, I will create a way to deter the rulers from your absence," Cassius informs with a sly smile.

"Don't wreck the kingdom while we're gone," Ari jokes.

Cassius chuckles at her comment. "I would not dare attempt purposefully wrecking something without you near." He looks at Ari, smiling. "At least, not today."

"You're the worst," Ari replies, shaking her head while exhaling laughter. "And your jokes are still terrible."

"Yet you like me for both of those things."

With lips curling into her mouth, Ari angles her head up towards me. Asking, "My room?"

I nod, and we are pulled to her bedroom in Los Angeles. It's messier than the last time I was here. Ari would usually keep this room neat unless she was busy with work or in a state that prevented her from doing anything of productivity. The plush toys are not stacked together in the corner, a pile of clothing looks rummaged through, and the books are all stolen from the shelf—which I expected, since nearly all are displayed in our room at Nexus. My single drawer of clothing I keep here is still intact, folded and unwrinkled. I run my hand over the smooth fabric created by the most renowned designers, both from the Magikal world and humans.

It is not something to take pride in, but for a few seconds, I allow myself to think of a scenario in which I live a privileged life, similar to the men who flaunt their wealth, wearing fashions identical to what I have on now.

Financially, I may be privileged, but emotionally, my upbringing is far from it.

Shutting the drawer, I turn. "Where are your keys?"

A face of puzzlement crosses her. When glancing down, the lanyard holding keys is held tightly in her hand. "With me. *'Cause I'm driving.*"

"Allow me, love." I reach out, laying my hand flat for her to give me the keys.

"No, it's fine. It's not that far."

"Ari, please let me drive us. You already do so much."

Her stance is tighter than ever. As if she is suspicious of my reasoning. "Why don't you want me to drive? You know I don't like being passenger."

"Because whenever you do, you get too angry at those around us," I remind her, but my main motive is that I need something to alleviate the violent thoughts racing through my head. Her mouth parts, crosses her arms across her chest. "That, and I haven't driven since my death. Give me this."

Unraveling her arms, Ari drops them to her side. With a taunting smile, she says, "Are you sure you *can* drive, ghost boy?"

I lean in. Kiss her forehead. "If I've already convinced *you* this easily, a car should be nothing."

Her face softens. I have no clue what she is about to say.

But she doesn't add anything. She tosses me her keys and leaves the room.

I trail behind, meeting her in the beaten-down car, which I

believe unsuitable for her to drive. The car starts, beginning our journey towards our destination, fifteen miles away from the shared house.

Throughout the drive, Ari controls the music. At one point, the driver in front of us abruptly brakes, my arm reacting by whipping in front of Ari. The shock causes her to yell, but once the music changes to that made with rhythmic snares and bass, she dances with her arms, bouncing and moving them to the rhythm, the same way she does in the privacy of a room with the two of us alone. When she has earphones blasting and she is on our bed, procrastinating her work, while I sit across the room doing my work.

When we park in the structure, Ari jumps out the door. She's taking deep breaths when I rush to her, with eyes focused on the white line that creates a parking boundary for the car.

"Are you okay?"

"I'm nauseous," she responds before picking up her phone from the seat.

"I told you not to look at your phone. You know you get motion sickness."

She rolls her eyes, following with a glare aimed at me. No matter how many times this happens, she never learns her lesson.

While walking through the indoor shopping area, we pass a woman on a bench who is interviewing with a hiring manager of a common shoe store.

I recognize this woman. Her features make her unforgettable, with her hazel eyes and orange-dyed hair on the underside of her brunette hair. The clothing she wears is dirty and wrinkled, stained from the cruelty of life. Punishment caused by her desperate choices after flaunting her magik to her ex-boyfriend's new partner. She had parents who loved her. A child who is now an orphan. Now she remembers nothing of her past. All that's left for her is a future of mundane activities with knowledge barely adequate for a year thirteen.

Every corner that my gaze roams to is bombarded by different stores, standalone food options, or groups of people.

In another world, I would be strolling through here with Ari as if this were another ordinary weekday. We would be sharing her favorite food from here–a pretzel–followed by picking up ice cream before our leave. Her arms would be full of shopping bags with an iced matcha drink in her hand, while mine carried two bags at most. My face would light with a smile, watching as she became exuberant with each little thing she found to her liking. We may even pass the bookstore, where she would read the blurbs of novels. And whatever books she excitedly explained to me, I would quickly put into my arms to purchase, no matter how much she protested.

But that is not this life. It isn't why we are here. Ari scarcely offers herself a moment to breathe. She has a monomaniacal determination to complete this task so that she may carry on–moving so fast that she will never have a second to think about what is going through her brain.

She is so much the same as I, my opposite on a spectrum measuring the same content, and I don't know if that is charming or worrisome for the both of us.

As we make our way into the department store where Evie works, Ari, for a split glance, peers at the jewelry in the front. It's barely noticeable, but the slight turn of her head makes it obvious to me.

I let her drag me around like I have forgotten where Evie works. We weave through aisles of shoes, makeup, and men's clothing until we finally see the short witch with a back turned to us.

"Evie!" Arabella calls.

In a quick reaction, Evie turns to face the two of us. Her clothing contrasts heavily with many of her older co-workers. Half of her hair is tied into a bun, the rest of the black falling to her waist. As clothing, she wears a white turtleneck and bronze skirt, which complement her golden-brown skin.

"Hi, guys!" Evie greets.

Stunned in place, she surveys me, holding back her true opinion on my attire, though her grin tells her away.

"Hello, Evie," I respond. The lights of the store are off-putting, but compared to the electricity that runs on lightning and other natural forces in Ifaeris, it may just be my body reacquainting itself with the outside world. "Do you have a precise location for us?"

Her eyes flit in Ari's direction, with both eyebrows remaining up. She blinks and returns to me with a genuine smile. "Once I saw them, I had security tell other stores to keep an eye out. Said they stole from us once, and I wanted to make sure they watched their security cameras and update me until they left. Right now, they're eating at Ricetta di Famiglia."

"How'd you know it was them?" Ari asks. Her hand is at her waist, weight resting on one side.

Evie points to a rack of clothing. I skim through. Pull out a few items that unhook from the bar. It is overcrowded, full of superfluous different pattern designs and a myriad of blinding colors. "Two of them went through the whole store and didn't put anything back in the right place. When I was called to help reorganize the clothes, I caught their faces on their way out. So *please*, feel free to get their ass. I'll support it! Erase the security footage even."

"Thanks, E!" Ari says. "I'll make this up to you somehow!" She begins taking off to exit the center and return to the outlets. I am right behind her, stopping when I hear Evie call my name.

"Hold on," she adds, jogging to me. I lean down towards her, allowing her to whisper. "They said something about Delphi taking something from them. Some object that amplifies? I don't really know what she'd use it for, but I don't think it's good. Also, tell

Bella I got the ingredients she asked for, so she can pick them up whenever."

I give her a singular nod, darting off and chasing my girlfriend, who couldn't have gone far.

Unsurprisingly, Ari hasn't moved more than thirty feet. She's sitting on one of the cushioned seats by the food area. Her legs are in a cross-legged sitting position, one over the other, eyes on her phone.

"What Evie say?" she asks, rising to her feet.

"She overheard of a possible object that explains how Delphi was able to communicate with and curse Mydior."

"Care to elaborate?" she inquires as we reach the exit where Ari holds the door for an elderly woman.

We are nearly at the fine dining establishment, with prices triple the cost of most restaurants in this area. There poses a danger if there are any listening ears.

The table that the two Magiks are eating at is on the outside patio area. Luckily, we do not have to order to speak with them.

"Later," I express with a quick point of my hand to the two we need to speak to.

I've only associated with these Magiks on three occasions outside of our lessons. The witch with a flat, upturned nose, though long and skinny at the bridge, is Camila. Daughter of Executive Antonio Campos, I best recognize her by her highlighted, wavy hair of blonde and brunette that is just darker than her skin. The other Magik across the table from her is Kaileigh, whose father is the brother of Leader Hilton. Unlike Camila, Kaileigh's hair is short and brittle, damaged from the bleach she uses to dye it.

The two are so caught in their conversation that they don't notice us approaching them.

"Heard you dumped Delphi the same way you left me," Ari mocks. She's not laughing, but in her voice is a glint of humor.

Her direct words startle those eating. Their faces drop at our sight, Kaileigh choking on the burger that they eat.

"Wait, you're alive? How?" Kaileigh asks while continuously coughing from their food.

"That's not any concern of yours," I say.

Camila scoffs. She leans her head on her hand. The same hand that has an arm upright and an elbow resting on the table. "I think a dead sorcerer speaking to us is understandably questionable."

Before Camila can go on, Ari cuts her off. "Listen, whatever questions you have can all probably be traced back to Delphi. I just wanted to ask you about her since, from what I was told, you're not friends anymore."

"What y'all wanna know?" Kaileigh holds her hands together. Shifts their jaw and glances at Camila.

I can't be sure if they'll give us clear answers. I'm not sure they'll answer us at all. And it is progressively difficult when we, as Magiks, can lie.

"Why'd you stop being friends?" Ari asks. She shifts her weight to one side. "What happened?"

"Well," Camila begins, "for starters, we knew about how you disappeared to some land we didn't know existed. Delphi never fully told us what she planned, but we'd get restricted books for her from the archives. She never gave us time to read them, but we knew what some contained. Then, around the end of spring, she started withdrawing from us. Threatened to share the illegal things we did together when we kept asking her questions. And in the middle of summer, she completely disappeared after we had our falling out."

In that time frame, Ari had already been taken by Delphi. Through all of this, the group that once befriended her had unknowingly been helping torture others. Holding victims against their will and increasing Delphi's power.

They have completely turned against the witch. Dropped her

from their group of vultures, though not making it public when they had done so. The Magiks sitting on the other side of the metal barrier are smirking with malicious intent. Delphi's exposure is something they have waited to exploit. In their group, when one is forced to leave, the whole wastes no time making it known why that person is deserving of backlash. In some cases, they decide to become friendly with the very person they once hated if they are also against the supposed 'friend'.

"Was there any place she met you secretly? Or one that you met at regularly?" Ari questions.

"Nah," Kaileigh yawns. She overlaps the opening on the body of their white cardigan over her cherry, thinly strapped shirt when crossing her arms. "She did have some guy with her that she said would become king, but who knows with how many lies she tells?" Their small figure and height, shorter than anyone our age, provided a sense of innocence to her when rumors spread of Arabella and myself. Their assuredness, face, and deceit were enough to turn some people against my group of friends and others who associated with us.

Because who would believe our word over the group that was also so well-known and liked around the school and elite circles? Their reputation created followers who would excuse their every action in hopes of gaining their friendship. They had all been very immature, despite being far too old for such juvenile behavior.

"Closer to your graduation, Delphi talked a lot about you for some reason," Camila continues on. She takes a sip from the pressed green juice at the table's corner. "Something about how she knew the easiest way to break you."

"Am I to assume by that, she meant raising me from the dead would break Arabella?" I turn to stare at the witch, who pays no care to me.

"You being brought back isn't any different to the heartless asshole you were when you were alive the first time," Camila responds flippantly. "Remember when you'd hex others 'cause your father said to?"

Ari's eyes light with fire at the insult. I have to take her hand to keep her from using her magik in this public area. To insult any that she loves drives fury worse than if she were the one being spoken poorly about. At the touch, she becomes grounded, the small flames gradually snuffing from her fingertips.

Her magik has become... unpredictable, to say the least.

I don't care to defend myself to them. With their past attempts to tarnish my name, I find this one pathetic.

"So the witch who'll jinx anyone if they don't solely praise everything she does wants to talk about morality?" Ari pauses, collecting her raging thoughts in a placating breath. The attack on my character is an accurate one, but it angers her nonetheless. "I may not be able to use my magik to kill you here, but if you say one more bad thing about Luka, I'm *not* above finding you later to do it."

"Aw, bless your heart," Kaileigh mocks. "This is why none of us really liked you. You just like to feed your ego and make everything about you."

One step back, and Arabella's expression changes completely. Her hand goes limp from mine. It never occurred to me that confronting these Magiks, whom she once held so close to her, would trigger something. I did not think that being in their presence would call back memories of what Delphi reiterated to her during her torture.

I take a slow, deep breath.

There's a high chance I will snap the necks of the two in front of me.

With fast recovery and a smile, Ari chortles in sarcastic laughter, pursing her lips. "Big talk for someone whose dad isn't even likable enough to be bribed into an executive position. I became the queen of the Fae. What have y'all done besides acting like best friends while hating each other behind the other's back?"

"Queen of the Fae?" Kaileigh snorts in retort, nearly dumbfounded. "Last we heard, you were held against your will by the same one they call a king. All y'all *do* is stab each other in the back. You'll never trust each other. Delphi told us that his stupidity would just end up with his people killing him themselves."

Overconfidence brings about sureness and a brash smirk in her absolutely misconstrued telling of the events.

Ari's eyes drift to the side, rolling her eyes and blinking. "I don't think you wanna insult Cassius either. He's clever enough to depend on. Can you say the same about each other?"

Camila takes two steps forward so that she is less than an arm's length from Ari. Her halter-neck, long-sleeved shirt with orchid floral and white patterning becomes more outwardly unflattering when she crosses her arms over her chest. "One call, and our parents can send someone for both of your deaths."

"Unless you want me to kill you without magik, I suggest backing up," I warn. My stare on her is firm.

"You can't threaten us," Kaileigh says with glee, joining Camila. "If you're alive, the Council may want to know."

That— That causes me to laugh. Depraved acts I would commit unto them cross my mind. "They're already aware of my being alive."

Both their faces pale. Without any of our leaders as an advantage in this situation, they have nothing. The four of us have neither yelled nor spoken loudly enough to warrant worry from the establishment's workers. No one sits outside when they can opt for the inside restaurant's warmth. But as exchanges are becoming increasingly violent, I prepare to leave if a commotion arises from the workers.

"Although they may be the ones who allow Delphi to continue her overtaking of the Fae, you're as complicit as they have been. You were aware of her plans and did nothing to stop her." I pause. Their faces possess diametrically opposing emotions–Kaleigh assuming that if Delphi were to be blamed for this all, they would suffer no consequences and Camila holding fear that their self-serving relationships are their ignorance. To the latter, after all they harassed Ari with, I cannot help but smile. "So I'm sure the Fae would be just as satisfied to have their blood paid with yours. Back up, or you'll both be dead."

The two Magiks step farther back, creating enough distance where I can't reach them. Ari's eyes shift from me to her once friends, exhaling lightly from her nose. "What else do you know?" she asks.

"There's a few of her friends that sided with her during the falling out. Chrissy's the main one she still talks to," Kaleigh admits.

If it saved themself, she would offer up any of her friends.

"We only talked to Chrissy 'cause Delphi invited her into our group," Camila sneers as a remark. "Much like what we did with you, Ara."

Kaleigh scans me up and down. Their thin lips quirk into a grin. "Delphi's a fucking idiot for treating you so badly. You're welcome to join me any day you want, darlin'."

I can see as Ari's eyes grow into instinctual rage while her lips curve upward. Her body is tense, the slightest movement from her swallowing a gulp highlighting.

"I am not one of the dogs that you keep around to lick the scraps you give," I say, outright rejecting Kaleigh.

Baffled that someone wouldn't want her, she slowly blinks with their mouth dropped.

Ari's lips relax into a genuine smile. Tongue lightly clicks the roof of her mouth. "How about we make a deal? You don't tell your parents about what happened today, and we won't ever tell Delphi you talked to us."

"Why would her knowing be a big deal?" Camila asks.

"If I told her you gave me any information, she'll kill you first. And I don't think daddy would be able to save you." Ari turns to her right, walking with our fingers intertwined.

The distance to our car is not far, but there are still streets we must walk across.

My past is helpful in instances of duties and it having taught me how to carry myself around others, but it is hindersome in how it has resulted in my present. Delphi has become an enemy larger than the nuisance of being an ex-girlfriend, and the Council, I'm sure, is keeping careful watch over any activities we could be doing.

The Coven in itself works in such a predictable way that I am concerned why they have done nothing. Anxieties follow me while anticipating their strike. Their word of peace means nothing. None of them are trustworthy.

To the side, Ari is snickering. She marches towards the parking structure, averting her eyes from mine. Her body hunches as she moves, falling into high-pitched, breathy laughter.

"What's so funny, Blossom?" I ask, squeezing her hand tighter when she stops.

"I've just never seen someone look like *that* and be so threatening," she replies while gesturing to the clothing I am in.

It feels incredible to see her laugh, even if it is due to me wearing something so horrendous. I love how when the sounds of delight leave her mouth, her nose comes up. Her eyes are shut, and I think that for a minute, she is my blessed afterlife.

I release our fingers that are twined, slipping my arm around her waist. "What someone wears means nothing when people fear your threats enough."

Verbally, she doesn't respond. She cocks her head to her right, lips pursed and eyebrows raised in agreement. We continue walking together, moving to the sides when others pass by.

"Fuck," she hisses.

I notice in a flash that she is stumbling over her foot, narrowly tripping into the trafficked street.

I'm able to catch her with my arm around her, bending down with her.

"Sure, backward crossovers I could still probably do. But gods forbid I go on a straight sidewalk," she mutters to herself. It is completely endearing how frustrated she becomes over something so minimal. The way she refuses to look in my eyes while my arm stays locked around her back.

My only reaction is a chuckle, lifting her straight and using my free hand to move the neckline of her cropped, hooded jumper. Her head jerks to mine, wonder planted on her face as to why neither of us have gone back to walking. What other logic is there than to bring my lips to hers?

Her reflex is something intense. Hands cup my face, then immediately wrap around my neck as Ari stands on her toes to reach closer to my height. Then she pulls me in to deepen the kiss, and I can feel her body warming in comparison to the outside weather.

I'm reeling. Smiling along her skin.

"Mahal," she murmurs. I slide my hand from her back up to one side of her neck while my mouth sucks harshly on the other, combating my soft biting. "People behind you."

Three words could not have been more unpleasant.

I whip myself up, holding her in my arms while my stare stalls on her lips. In a swift motion, I swivel our positions so that she stands away from the road and, therefore, away from the moving vehicles.

"We should get to the car before parking goes up," she giggles, pulling the ticket out of her wallet. She takes my hand in hers, and

I do the honor of alternating our fingers together. As we walk, her two front teeth are visible from the opening of her mouth, similar to a bunny.

Driving, I'm tormented with my thoughts. Ari has no idea how badly I want her. All I want is to drive faster than traffic would allow so that I can throw the love of my life onto her bed. Until I don't know what to do with myself from the pleasure.

XXXII

Accidental Poisonings

Arabella

Wrong.

Everything I do is wrong. I fail at every turn when I do something on my own.

I had already tried different spells to track Delphi, but her magik is too strong. She must have set up precautions in the event that anyone would want to find her, whether it be me or anyone working for the Coven.

The magik I want to use is too complex to rely on intent alone, and the steps of this potioned spell prove harder than I thought they would be, with the needed components making no sense. I think I might be reaching my breaking point. There's a very specific order that lists the ingredients, and I thought that I would be able to figure it out by myself, but I guess that was wrong too.

I have notes of translations, but something still isn't right. Maybe I recited the incantation inaccurately? Or maybe I didn't have the right intention to match it in my mind?

My heart is beating so rapidly, I feel like I'm about to piss myself from the effects of a spell done incorrectly. If there were anything in my stomach, I'd probably vomit. Taking deep inhales to at least steady myself only makes it worse, and a headache is pounding in my head. I'm sweating, but my body feels like it's freezing. This is worse than any blackout or comedown could ever be. I'd take being stabbed again to whatever the fuck this is.

Crawling to the desk outside of the salt protection circle around me, I reach for the grimoire. My fingers accidentally close it, my eyes staring for what feels like too long on the cover. The leather-bound, mulberry book, decorated with golden branches on the cover, is mesmerizing. Even more so with the crystal in the middle that lights with a bright blue.

I realize how long I must be looking at it again and gather my thoughts before flipping through the pages to the spell I used, but I can't read anything without my notes. The words are floating off the page. They're jumbled into nonsense, which worsens when I remember that everything is in a language considered dead. I try to decipher the writings, only being able to tell what spell correlates to what writing from the sketchings drawn.

More and more, the spell is draining my energy. Dehydration is overtaking my body, and as I reach up for my glass of water, I knock it over. I can hear the water spilling across my desk, dripping onto the floor, exasperation adding to the overwhelming damage this spell is causing.

A taste of metal spreads in my mouth, but I never bit down on my tongue. Something drips from my nose, and when my hand goes to wipe it, wooziness overfloods me. I'm lightheaded, with a nose bleeding. I try to stop the spell, but I can't undo whatever it is I've already done. My eyes have lowered. They're half-lidded, and I start wondering if I may have overgorged on the potion aspect of the spell. It's not like the restricted magik that Delphi would cast, where a burst of energy would feel like it was blasting through me, followed by the same panting you get from cardio's tiredness.

Toes twitch. My legs are involuntarily convulsing. I think my body is seizing.

Everything stationary around me is moving, and my sight is hazy. Symptoms of my mistake only worsen my panic when I realize I can't call out to anyone. My tongue feels shriveled inside me, though I think it's just so dry, like my throat, that there's nothing to help me get the words out.

No reversal spell is on the page I used for this. And there isn't one on the page after. Right as I'm able to pull myself to the door and reach for the rooted handle to get help, my body slams hard against the floor. It doesn't hurt. A numb tingling courses through my arms as I lie still.

I'm completely paralyzed. I can't walk or move, and considering I'm just in my office, I doubt there's a guard around to have heard my fall. My right cheek is flat against the marble floor, and I can't decide whether I'm uncomfortable by the fact I can barely breathe, or I'm disgusted that my face is against the same space where people's dirty shoes step. Hair also obstructs my view, furthering my irritation. It's honestly grown too long for my liking.

After what feels like a lifetime of playing movies in my head, I hear the door handle turning. I hear Luka's voice calling for me, but I can't answer. The door is lightly pushed, and when Luka's strength opens it enough to see me, I hear the thing being ripped from its hinges and thrown backwards. A light gust of wind sucks the air as it flies. I'm picked up from where I lie, carried by Luka to the couch, where he puts me upright. His worry is severe, asking me if I'm okay.

He blows out the candles inside the circle while also skimming through the page I kept open in the book. When the last flame is out, he rushes away, telling me nothing of what he's doing.

But he's back in no time with a hoard of ingredients. He throws them onto the table before yanking open a cabinet where I keep numerous potion mixture bases. A medium-sized mortar is taken out, vodka and kariflare also being extracted from its place. The ingredients are thrown in, crushed by the granite pestle before being added into the glass.

Guards have come to check on what's going on, but Luka yells at all of them to leave. More is said, but my hearing is so poor that it comes through muffled. Like if I were listening to the short exchange from another room with my ear pressed against the wall.

"Drink this, love," he distressingly commands. He opens my mouth, pouring in the tonic, saying nothing as he gently strokes my cheek with his thumb.

It hits me at once. There are still remnants of spinning in my vision, but that's slowly going away.

Nausea attacks me. My hand whacks to my mouth while I'm whipping my head towards anything I can use as a garbage can. Nothing would work without it being a pain to clean up for the servants, so I rush to the windows, using my magik to fling them open and stick my head out.

Vomit leaves me, and with it, I see the colors of orange and glittered liquid from both the tonic and potion. I'm heaving after the first of it comes up, throwing up again in less than four seconds. Then, as it repeats for a third time, Luka rubs my back, holding my hair through each emesis.

It takes another minute to pass before nothing feels as horrendous. And when everything somewhat lessens, I turn around to Luka, who, since I last threw up, has a glass of water prepared for me.

"You'll be dehydrated for the rest of the day, but if you continue drinking water and the cure, it will keep you alive." Luka watches as I finish the water.

On the table sit ginger, valerian, ginseng, and bases, along with my empty glass. There's a guard at the door with more glasses of water in hand, which Luka instructs to be set on the table, mixing and diluting them with more of the cure he makes.

I can barely grip the cup, but I do what I can with the strength I have. The guard is sent away, Luka never leaving my side, his arm around my waist.

My breath reaches a composed pattern that doesn't feel like it's in survival mode. I still feel cold, but at the touch, my body's feverish. "How'd you know that would work?" I ask Luka.

"These roots work as a counter to detoxify and banish most toxic potions," he responds. His hold, which I can now recognize with feeling regaining in my body, is tight.

I didn't think of that fast enough. There are remedies or counter potions and spells for nearly everything magik, but one of the basic cures involves ginger. It's something we learned early in school, but I didn't have enough time or energy to grab it.

Luka's cleaning the mess, taking the fulgurite, herbs, and other ingredients from the floor and placing them on the table while I finish the second glass on the sofa. I'm still a little nauseous, but it's not bad enough to induce vomiting again. A drink with electrolytes might help, but I don't know how well that would react to the mixture Luka has concocted. The thought of stomaching anything, just for it to immediately come back up, makes me feel more sick.

He sniffs the empty, spherical glass that had contained the potion I brewed, which nearly killed me. "Love, this smells rancid. What did you do?"

"I tried to do a spell that would enhance our protection on the borders. It was supposed to prevent the possibility of another incident like Windwyrd, but I must've read something wrong."

Flipping through the pages of *Sanguis et Maledictiones,*

Luka searches for something. "What page is the spell you were performing?"

I move from where I sit, placing myself next to him, though it's probably as graceful as a drunk person walking in a straight line. As I approach the desk, Luka quickly slips his hand around my waist to support and keep me from falling. While my upper body shivers from freezing, my legs feel on fire.

I want to rip my pants off.

"Ari?" he voices, pulling me from my thoughts that have gone off track.

"Sorry. Uh-" I take the book from his hand, rapidly turning the pages until I find the image I remember from the spell, tapping on the drawn symbol. "It was this one."

His brows knit together. A soft, questioning hum vibrates from his lips. "Love, this is a spell to make someone permanently under your control."

I must've mixed my translations. Accidentally matched the wrong translations from my notes to the book.

No wonder it didn't call for black tourmaline.

Luka combines the same ingredients for the cure. He goes through a drawer from behind me, pulls something out, and throws it into the mortar. Never have I been so grateful to Evie for donating spare materials for potions and antidotes.

I'm internally screaming at myself for my error. I grab a pen from my desk, crossing out the translation in my notebook and rewriting what the spell actually is, but before I can finish, Luka places another glass next to my hand to drink.

The mixture tastes different this time. It's somehow colder and crunchier.

Violent coughs pummel through me, like I'm choking on something. My spit, maybe, but something sticks in my throat. After three more coughs, something is on my sleeve. It looks like the leg of some insect. It's not a natural color. There's a holographic aspect to it that reminds me of oil on pavement after the rain has hit it. "The fuck is this?"

"The cure to the mishap of your spell. The full cure requires a crushed Sungman Scarub and seeds from acorns with pineapple juice."

I think I'm going to burn my tongue off. The texture of bugs isn't something I can do.

He goes through the book again, looking more puzzled as he studies the page. "This spell requires the sacrifice of a human life."

"I thought a substitute would be fine if I gave something of mine up. A few years of my life? I don't know. It was confusing though, because I couldn't figure out why enhancing my power would take so much out of me. But I kept pushing through 'cause I thought it was a natural response to the spell."

This all comes off too defensively. I keep making excuses to justify my poor decisions. Language as a subject is where I fall short, which *should* have prompted me to confer with others who are more proficient in it.

"You thought paralyzation was just a small, passing reaction to the spell?" He gives me a look. There isn't pity or a judging look there. At least, I don't think.

When he says this to me, my cheeks burn with embarrassment. I'm probably more full of humiliation that I did this with translations only he or Grayson would've understood better.

"Also," he adds, "I hate to be the one to remind you, but with restricted magik, there are no substitutes. Calling for death means theirs and nothing else. Magik always has a price, whether it be your energy or someone else's. This could have cost you your life if you added the burnt wick of a candle."

"I missed an ingredient?"

"Yes, and I'm beyond grateful that you did. But I still don't understand why you had a reaction so extreme when, at most, your skin should have just been inflamed with rashes."

I ponder this, and after rereading the translations, I realize the counter cure for it only renders void in the case that a human life wasn't sacrificed. My impatience and skim reading accidentally saved my life. As my eyes drop to the bowl of ingredients, I stop at one. "Everything was fine until I added the red verbena. The second I touched it, my skin started itching, and when I drank the potion before reciting the incantation, my throat started closing up."

"Drank it? The spell says to waft it after spraying, not ingest it." Luka's eyes widen slightly, his face full of worry. Though I feel fine, he takes me by the hand, dragging me to the other side of Nexus and forcing me up the stairs to the healer's room until he places me onto one of the single beds.

Inside, no one's there except Isa, and I'm not sure why.

"Hey, what's u–"

In a panic, Luka frantically cuts her off to explain what happened. As he goes on, tersely stating everything, Isa notes it down onto paper. She doesn't look overtly concerned, which only aggravates and raises Luka's voice more. He hasn't let go of my hand. The splinters of this table are starting to edge into my sweatpants.

"Isa," I shout over Luka's voice. "I'm okay. Luka found the counter cure and already said I should be fine."

She doesn't take my word for it. Instead, she narrows her eyes at me, scanning me up and down. "You sure? Your eyes don't seem focused."

"Then can you get Evie? She'll probably know better about the potions," I say, my head twisting around. There are no balms, healing tonics, or potions on the shelves. Those reside in the next room up. All I can see are bandages, wraps, and things similar in nature at each bedside table. As if in stations. "What are you doing here anyway? You an apprentice or something?"

Isa laughs, uncrosses her legs and stands to face me. "I've been working with the healers in Nexus. I'm good with creating healing tonics and aid with any guards' injuries." Again, she reviews the notes that she's taken while Luka glares at her for a response. "You shouldn't have ingested it, but if Luka already made a tonic to work against what was done, you should be fine. Can you recall every ingredient?"

I could go through everything I had already told Luka, or I could just explain the worst one of them all. "Red verbena's what I think fucked me over."

"Red verbena?" she asks for confirmation. I nod, and she is already dashing up the staircase. "Let me check on something with another healer."

When she leaves, there is a resigned, stoic look on Luka's face. I rub my thumb against the back of his palm, finally drawing his eyes to mine. "Are you mad I almost died again?"

Though I try to play it off as a joke, a way for the both of us to move past it, he remains unamused.

"I'm upset that you weren't more careful. Because you couldn't wait for me to check if the translations were correct, you performed a spell that nearly killed you," he answers. His voice isn't as harsh or angry as it was when talking to Isa, but there's still a hint of it there. "Everyone has been worrying that you're going to do something that will get you killed, and I have run out of ways to defend you."

"You were busy," I retort. *I'm not other people's responsibility.* "It was supposed to be a simple spell. I genuinely didn't think it was dangerous enough to need another person."

He turns away from me, removing his hand from mine. "Love, even if you *did* cast the correct spell, you still would have been performing restricted magik that we don't know much about." With a deep breath, he runs his hand through his hair, resting it at the top of his head for a moment. "You should have had another person in the room. Magik feeds off intent, and a lot of yours seems to be dictated by your emotions. But since you refuse to accept that something is wrong, you can't control your fire magik again as a direct result."

"I handle it just fine when I'm around you, or Cassius, or our friends."

"Yes," he replies plainly. "You have some control when you're with those you are comfortable with, or when you are so overwhelmed by one emotion, it ignites the intent, but you have to learn to grapple your magik without the crutch of these things. It doesn't have to only be me and our friends who you trust. What would have happened if I didn't come to see you before our meeting with Fatima and Pyrros? What if I wasn't there in time?"

The exhaustion on his face is evident, his breath weary.

"I know it's hard for you," he exhales. "But the way you've been acting affects us too."

And for something inexplicable, my raw emotions border me to the verge of tears.

My own failures keep reoccurring because he's telling the truth. I've grown to trust some people to a certain extent, but I still cage everything too close to me. I'm so stubborn and paranoid that I have no idea what it means to accept someone's pure intentions without fear of an underlying motive.

I do everything I can to be better. I try, and try, and try. But trying doesn't mean anything when you're not perfectly successful, does it?

I really am my parents' child.

"Ari," he whispers, "what's wrong?"

"I keep fucking up everything I do, and what- wha-" I sigh to keep my voice from cracking. "What if I am this horrible person? I push people out, and I hurt them, and I'm never sure what I wanna act on. And I'm either extremely impulsive or I overthink everything." I'm speaking steadily. Rambling on and on until I feel my torso rocking. With a slow, deep inhale, I breathe out, "I don't know who I am anymore."

Luka carefully steps closer to me. "I know who you are, and you are anything but a horrible person. Your actions of atrocity committed to survive speak nothing when standing beside the things you have done for love."

"I don't know how I'm ever feeling. I guess I just don't know how to word it," I admit. How does someone admit feeling every negative emotion at once? What can I do except block the thoughts from my mind instead of succumbing to the impending black hole?

"Then throw out words, and I'll help put them together until they make sense." His hand goes to my face, stroking away a falling tear with his thumb. "You can't keep going about this alone."

"I know," I admit in surrender, my head dropped down. "I'm sorry. I'm trying, I really am. It's just taking longer than I'd like, and I feel... like I'm a failure."

Before I can continue, he stops me, cupping my cheeks in his hands and forces me to look at him. "You're not a failure. You're doing everything that you can."

He presses his lips to mine, the breath from his nose kissing lightly onto my skin. When he stops, he lingers there, his nose brushing my cheeks. And I finally surrender to everything I have kept inside.

A good ten seconds go by while we remain in this position. I've devolved from choking back the liquid rage into flowing streams of water from my tear duct as a source. He presses his body to mine as he pulls me up into a hug, my arms warm from the inside of his coat and his body heat.

"Can we talk about this later? I don't feel like going into this right here," I tell him. The outside of my hand goes to rub my eyes.

Then, I turn them to the inside and follow my thumbs with my palms.

Comforting silence surrounds the room as Luka and I sway side to side.

"So Evie's not here, but I talked to the other healers, and I think that-" Isa's voice says, barging in. "Oh shit, sorry. I didn't realize I was interrupting something."

I unwrap my arms from Luka's body to turn to Isa. Out of the corner of my eye, I catch an expression on Luka's face that seems crestfallen from me unhooking myself, but there is also an opposing look of relief, possibly pleased that Isa didn't come in with bad news.

"You're fine. What were you saying?" I say to assuage the awkwardness.

She looks at both of us, mostly Luka, since he's the more agitated of us. "The other healers said because of how fast you came to the queen's aid and added the needed ingredients for a cure, Ara should be fine."

"Should be?" he voices with irritation.

"Yes. Complications *do* exist," she reminds him. "Clay and charcoal typically combat poisons to red verbena for Fae, so I imagine taking it and adding it to the mixture will work the same for other creatures. We don't know much about Magik healing."

Isa takes two jars full of powder and hands them to Luka, who snatches them from her.

"Thank you," he says. He rarely ever says that.

"The queen ought to rest today. She must stay within the grounds and have us constantly checking on her to ensure that the cure is working at its quickest. I know you're to meet with rulers today, but you must meet with them alone, Luka." Isa hands me another item–a bronze bowl with more of the roots that Luka had mixed into the earlier drink inside. She says her goodbye and leaves the two of us alone, quiet as she goes down the stairs.

I take both jars from Luka, dumping them in the overly large bowl Isa gave me. "Okay, you'll meet with Fatima and Pyrros. Tell them I'm fine but got sick. That's why you're alone in my place."

He remains with a neutral face, agreeing with a nod. "I also meant to mention that I want to remove Adonis' prosthetic so that he can okkar us to the meeting places of him and Delphi. Guards will be with us, but they need both your and Cassius' permission to depart since you're the crown."

"Yeah, of course. The spell to remove it is in the room. Just put it back on him when you're done."

The two of us go down the stairs. When I use the walls to support me, Luka steals the bowl from me altogether.

In the foyer, two servants pass through, heading in the direction of my office, which has an unhinged door. It's almost always busy on the first floor but silent and lonely on the others.

The twin Fae with shorter hair, when compared to his twin brother, is standing at the table in the middle, carrying metal I'm positive isn't pure iron. Though it rests on his shoulders, he still wears gloves.

"Monty?" I call. "What are you doing?"

At the call of his name, Monty turns around with glee on his face. A smile instantly wiped off, turning into a concerned expression when taking in my state. "Are you okay?"

"Yeah, I just made a mistake. Things happen," I say.

"More of this will be prepared for you by the time you get to our room," Luka tells me. "We can watch that singing program when I return."

Confusion travels from my thoughts to my face. "You hate that show."

"Yes, your choice in entertainment is horrible," he replies

playfully. "But you enjoy it." He kisses my forehead, hugging me tight before marching towards my office to pick up the rest of the ingredients.

He's so handsome that my thoughts will often scramble when looking at him for too long.

Monty's eyes follow Luka as he leaves. He probably picks up on Luka's speed because when he turns back to me, he lowers the metal to his hip. "Things happen, huh?"

"I didn't die." I shrug, reaching down to help carry the weight of the metal.

"Come along," he says, leading us outside Nexus.

We keep walking, nearing the Darkened Forest. Immediately past the stables, there's another structure I've never been in. It's where the weapon and armorsmiths work. The smiths and soldiers alike come and go from the building. They're carrying different things, ranging from wood, metals, leathers, nuts for smaller Fae, or fully completed sets of armor. Most of our more notable weapons are under Nexus, but with my friends available, whenever they're in Ifaeris, they help by adding magik to new weapons.

The workers here bow to me, which only conflicts me by being both uncomfortable and proud to have this power. I don't know how many times I have to tell them that they don't always have to be so formal with me. They've known me since I was Elliot's prisoner.

I follow Monty inside, where the temperature is much warmer than outside. There are about four fires set up in stations, a bench with the smiths pounding on the cooling metal, mannequins displaying armor, and a set table where others are taking a break. He leads me up the stairs, the next story filled with things about the same as the first. Everyone on this floor is sweating, most of them with shirts tied or without shirts at all.

As we reach a workbench at the opposite side of the stairs,

Monty places the metal on one side, saying nothing as he organizes them by length.

"So you're helping with the smiths, and Isa's helping with the healers," I say, tying my hair back, my voice lifting. "Who else in the family helps around that I don't know about?"

"Helping?" he asks. Like he thinks I'm making light of what he does.

"Isn't that what you're doing? Or is that not what's going on?" I laugh, grabbing a helmet created from hide that wraps around something more inflexible.

"I'm the Master of Weapons, Ara," he informs me. My face drops, and he begins fully laughing at me. "Did you think that my siblings and I do nothing besides serve as counsel to you? We're still common fae."

How did I not know this?

I'm not able to get anything out. A horde of workers approaches Monty, asking him to inspect the weapons for flaws and if they're acceptable enough for battle. I watch as all of them respect his command, heeding each thing he says as he explains the qualities and different versatilities of each weapon. My eyes shift to each Fae, who ask me for my thoughts as well, but I have none to offer.

Another Fae, with straight, yellow warbler hair, hands me a sword that's a lot heavier than the ones I've used or worked with before. I don't know what kind of strength someone has to have to continuously wield this with ease, but whoever it is, I envy them.

Monty pats the Fae's side, chuckling at something she's said, which I didn't hear. "Will you please excuse me and the queen?"

"Most certainly," she obliges, taking the weapon from me. She, along with everyone in the room, bows to me on their exit.

With the two of us alone and others downstairs, I remain in shock. I walk to the weapons lined on a table. All blades vary, but each is shaped differently. Some are tiny and straight, others have curves on one side for certain precision.

"These weapons are beautiful, aren't they?" he asks. "They're much different than ones we have had from years past, but these are also a bit more fragile than others. Your friends have been of great help in using magik to make them a bit more durable."

He continues to speak with passion over the intricacies of how things are built, excitedly comparing newer weapons to older ones, equivalent to how one would compare models of technology.

I struggle with how to word exactly what I want to say. I'm still queasy. I ask the question in my head, but I'm just confusing myself. "I- Uh- You're Master Weapons?"

Cackling and wheezing erupt from Monty. He's slapping his hand on the table. I've never seen him laugh this hard at something I've said before. "*Master of Weapons*," he corrects. "The only one allowed in the armory at all times, besides you and Cassius, is me. I lead the forging of weapons, and taking into account my knowledge of improvising something into a fun trick against my brother in our earlier years, Cassius appointed me in this position. What did you think we did all day?"

"You're still related to Cassius. Why would you have to work? And even then, how do you afford the hall you have?"

"Our home was gifted by Helena to our mother. We're not royalty by blood, and my father refuses to take aid from Cassius like he had with our uncle, so if we wish to keep up our lifestyle and have access to tonics and medicines for our mother, we work. Since there are multiple of us working for the crown, we receive enough payment for the upkeep."

I hadn't thought about any of this. Honestly, it's extreme inexperience on my part to not question who and how the weapons are made. I've been given armor created by the armorsmiths in association with Damien, Vi, and the tailors. New weapons have been created and upgraded after the battle in Hearthis, but not once have I thought to question who is in charge of that.

Of course, I should have come to the conclusion that the others work. Xavier and Monty have taken on the role of parenting their sisters since they were children, with their father too consumed by distress over the illness of their mother to properly care for them. Who else was going to care for Dyana and Isa, if not for their brothers?

From my side, Monty hands me a necklace that I haven't seen in a while. It's the same one Cassius gave me as an apology, but it doesn't look changed. "Gray enchanted the jewelry so that when you aim it at your target, it hits with high accuracy," he explains, handing me the weapon.

"Oh, thanks," I say. Monty and I aren't as close as me and his brother, but he knows me well enough to have sensed something's wrong. "You brought me all the way over here for this and to help you move metal?"

"You're arguably more violent than our army." He shrugs, eyes the same green as his brother looking at me, hovering his hands over a few pieces of armor until he picks up a dagger. "I wanted your input."

XXXIII

Vicious Alignments

Luka

While sitting in this house, I realize why modesty is necessary when speaking to the common fae. No frivolity or flaunting of the authority my role ensues would earn their trust, so Gideon okkared us into his home.

The home is a moderately sized cottage, though large enough to house a family. I sit in a basement that has been turned into a workshop, which contains a fireplace for casting metal. Most of the items scattered in the room are scraps of materials or tools that otherwise belong with engineers. A wall of thinly recycled fabric hangs as a divider between this and the kitchen above the small staircase of tree branches.

Twenty minutes I have waited here. I've sat with nothing but thoughts playing in my mind on how to make things right between the common fae and the rulers. The Fae of Mindae have come to appreciate Atticus as their ruler more so than those in the other lands. Fatima continues to struggle with overseeing the mistakes resulting from her father while also carrying the worst end of all the

Elementals, as her land still recovers from the battle not so long ago. While Cassius has worked to amend for what he can, the common fae are still apprehensive about him taking Ari as a queen, with some, just as Tanzin, not regarding her as queen at all. Most are still unaware of the wards that protect them. To avoid conflict, we have tried to keep secret the extent of Delphi's power, and it works well due to those who were under her control in Gigantia being locked away in Phantom Tower, but it hasn't been foolproof.

Unfortunately, our wards only protect against Delphi and other Magiks from okkaring into the lands. Other than myself, Ari, and our friends, no other Magik should have the ability to enter past the borders we have created. Magiks' powers should be rendered useless when trying to break past the wards, but we have seen that with unrestricted magik, there are ways around this.

Gideon has brought me here to speak to the few allies who still trust him. Common fae whom he thinks would be open to advocating in defense of Ari and Cassius. Either to a disadvantage or to our benefit, one of them is the same Fae who helped persuade other common fae in Adonis' favor.

It has been a nonstop argument since he brought up the subject, which is why I now wait for a signal to join. Most common fae are infuriated that Adonis remains free from Phantom Tower. If I were in their place, I too would be upset, although I think that I wouldn't be so presumptuous to base opinions without examining the larger reasoning.

"Just listen to what he has to say," Gideon's voice says. The curtain of fabric is pulled to the side, and he peers through, beckoning his hand towards me to join him.

Up the stairs I go, hands behind my back and posture straight.

It is utterly offensive in this household. The decor is arranged incongruously. No furniture fits the same theme. Colors are clashing with one another, and the wallings are of different types.

Statement pieces add a touch of boldness, but when nothing collects as a common theme, the interior becomes heinous.

This cottage is one that I would consider unappealing at its nicest.

Three Fae are gathered on the opposite side of the unstable kitchen table. One is a thinner Fae, with white hair braided across the head and skin the color of indigo. The masculine Fae between the other two has the sides of their head shaved, with long, coral hair in the middle tied high. That Fae has wings of a phoenix, which are pulled down. The last of the three is another feminine Fae with tall hair. It is full near the head but thins to a singular point at the top.

"This is Amara," Gideon says, gesturing to the Fae with indigo skin and a long, fitted pink dress. "He's the most ferocious of our group, but he won't bite."

"Unless you want me to." Amara exposes a smile, teeth sharp as a shark. "And don't look at Gideon like he offended me, boy. I just don't like being called she."

"I'm Navya, Amara's sister," the other feminine Fae introduces with a hand extended. Neither of the two share any similarities in appearance, but one could argue that is possible with many siblings.

"Louder, girlie. Ants and Pixies might be the only living creatures to hear you." The masculine Fae knocks a soft punch onto Navya. Laughs while having this take entirely too long to proceed. As the Fae returns his attention to me, I take notice that his eyes are completely black. No whites, nor is there a distinction from an iris.

"Fuck off, Max. Y'know she's shy," Amara defends. "Apologies 'bout him. I'm the loud one, and she's the shy one, but Maximus here's the bully Gideon decided to take into our group."

Maximus crosses his arms over his unwashed, food-stained tunic. Kicks his boots onto the table and leans the chair back. "The queen's lover wanted to pay a trip to us common fae, huh? We supposed to bow?"

"Max," Gideon warns. He pulls a chair and sits next to me. "You can either be polite, or you can get the fuck out."

"If he wants our help, he should be treated as one of us. Why should I respect anyone the Elementals trust?"

Because I'm the reason you were not killed.

I take a deep breath to calm myself and hurry this along. A nefarious voice, which hisses in my head, wants to remind the man of his unintelligence. He seems to disregard that my friends and I have shown to work in the Fae's favor. I stop myself as the honesty nearly leaves my mouth, taking into consideration that the Fae's long-standing hatred of Magiks may sanction a reaction much worse. Instead, I take a small jar of honey from my pocket, placing it on the table and sliding it to the three as a peace offering.

"Gideon said you want information? Fine." Amara says, being the first of the trio to speak. "First thing you should know is that many of the Fae still don't know much about Delphi, so their stances are divided. Some know *of* her, but you locked up all the Fae who know how dangerous she really is. Then there are some who think it would be refreshing to have a ruler not of Elemental bloodlines, while elders, who have lived long enough to bear witness to the ramifications of the first war against Magiks, oppose Queen Arabella greatly."

"Most of the Fae now rather hate Delphi after hearing that she's behind the deaths and control of their loved ones. But they find King Cassius all the more suspicious for taking a witch as a queen and you as a seneschal," his sister adds.

"Not to mention the constant Magiks on the lands roaming around," mutters Maximus with a disgusted face.

"Our friends," I correct.

He shrugs and takes a drink of his beverage. "It makes no difference to me."

Gideon glares at his friend. "As of this point in time, most of the Fae are in a state of mourning from deaths or fear that at any given moment, they will meet the same demise as Mydior."

"I ask then that the three of you help in convincing them otherwise so that all parties no longer have to live in fear of Delphi," I say.

This piques Amara's interest, the top of his ears twitching. "Why should we believe you want anything good for us?"

"To reiterate what I have told Gideon, the three of you are important to the Fae's survival. You hold a leadership role among the common fae rebels. The High King and Queen did you a favor by sparing you during the battle, despite your treason. They've allowed you to live outside of Phantom Tower while knowing your exact location. You owe it to them to fight against the witch who held others, such as your peers, against their will."

Maximus scoffs. Drinks the ale from the glass and belches. The action is not only rude but potent. "I don't owe them shit."

"Cassius works to mend where his father failed," I challenge. My jaw clenches at their refusal to see reason. "He makes many mistakes, but he is undoing years of negligence against the other common fae. There's no denial of that."

"May I ask, why do you care so much about the fate of our people?" Navya asks timidly. She barely meets my eyes.

"I don't. Arabella has her own motives. But for some reason, despite what I have said, she wants to help you, regardless of your hatred."

"You love her enough to sit in a room with Fae, who would kill both you and her without thought if given the opportunity?" Navya asks.

Obviously. I nod.

Amara huffs out a scoffed laugh. Sarcasm is evident. "The witch queen holds power in every which way. Neither I nor the rest of us have spoken about me being taken by Delphi, as is the sworn condition of letting me roam free. I can't imagine she needs many more on her side when she can control us as well as the other witch."

"She wouldn't do that," I say, both to him and all at the table. They know nothing of her, and I cannot help myself from lashing angrily at the accusation. It is her heart which cares deeply for others that I love. Her passions have always extended beyond anger, yet no one chooses to see that.

Gideon is the only one to believe me, which is due to the fact he fought on the battlefield with us at Hearthis, as well as listening to Maude's every word when Ari had been kidnapped. I appreciate it nevertheless.

My lack of elaboration is taken as disrespect by Maximus. He snarls, glaring with eyes on the prowl to kill. "Says her lover. Your kind's persuasion over our rulers is exactly why those I care about were taken in the first place. Do you know what we do to Magiks? When we travel through the Human Lands and see an unsuspecting Magik walking by, we take them. We lure them with a sense of kindness or need for help before we sink our teeth into their flesh. The crown should have done the same with the two of you. If the queen cares about Ifaeris, she should offer herself to Delphi and be done with this."

Maximus is beginning to work my last nerve. He plays games with me, but a fatal mistake is given away in his subconscious state. When Navya spoke about a Fae's loved one being controlled by Delphi, Maximus' eyes shifted slightly to Amara. He revealed too easily where his protection lies.

Consequently, his words further cause a furor of anger to stir within me. His comment is a stab without knowing Delphi's intentions to rule the Fae as a whole.

While looking at the black-eyed Fae directly, I feel no sense of fear. "I will bury everything you love and force you to watch all of it." My head tilts slightly towards Amara, ensuring Maximus knows well that I have discovered his tell. "And while you beg for mercy, pleading for me to end you, I will set you free to a life of misery. You will live knowing you could have prevented this if you had just told us what you know."

This response elicits a guttural laugh, deep from Amara's throat. He swings an arm around Maximus, razor teeth biting over his bottom lip and sleeve flounce dangling over his shoulder. "Oh, I think we should hear him out now if he's willing to go so far to kill me for your words against Queen Arabella."

"Gideon?" Navya says. "You've met her. What do you think?"

He isn't quick to scorn her the same as his friends. His hand scratches the back of his neck, pausing to take a deep breath. "I think she's a force to be reckoned with. She could have easily given away Maude at the gathering when Adonis revealed himself, but she held silent. The queen fights alongside the crown but made clear to me and others that she understands why we common fae stood against King Elliot's rulership. She's the reason I know the king now works to ensure that neither he nor the other Elementals treat us the same way they had under the previous king's rule."

"Then why should we defend King Cassius?" Maximus asks, humoring the table. "Everything you explain only tells us why she should be ruler, not he."

How much more ignorant can you be?

"If you want to punish the king for the crimes of his dead father, I can't stop you from trying. But this power was thrown onto him. He is an abject product of his upbringing." I pause, mulling over what I have just said. I don't know if I am speaking solely about Cassius.

"His father was the reason the common fae went missing or

died, but instead of sending another to do his bidding after being crowned king, Cassius and the queen personally work to bring Delphi to justice," Gideon says to remind others in the room.

Navya bites the nail of her index finger. She eyes me with suspicion and reservations. "And if our siding with them causes a war among the rulers of Magiks?"

"Then we will recruit other Magiks against them. Our system is not so much better than yours has been. There is corruption and underhanded grabs for power dependent on bribery. Arabella and I will fight so that history does not repeat itself." It's a promise. An oath. I may have the ability to lie, but I know that with whatever comes, I will not stop until it is up to the correct standards.

All three of the Fae glance at each other, Maximus and Amara smirking, Navya grinning with a dimple showing.

XXXIV

Excursions with the Elite

Arabella

Exposing the Council of the Coven is not as swiftly successful as I thought it would be. There's talk amongst elite Magiks, and obviously, with technology, word travels fast. According to my friends who still interact with the Magikal world, a few articles have run regarding restricted magik and the books being stolen, which has only increased suspicion against those who lead us.

But when those in high power have the money to buy out media coverage, it's difficult to get information circulating outside of a niche set of people. While it's beneficial to have friends who are the children of those high in power, most of them don't have the benefit of their parents listening to them. If anything, they left the support of their parents for that exact reason. There's also the fact that most of the influential Magiks' children are exact replicas of their parents.

This isn't enough to make a change. Not with the little amount there is in comparison to those who refuse to believe in the corruption in power.

One of the biggest things to give us an advantage, though, are the rumors circulating that Luka's alive again. It's spread like wildfire around certain groups, and I've been receiving messages from others I haven't spoken to in years asking me about it.

For the reason of speculation behind Mydior's death, Cassius has decided to take a page from his father's book and throw a revel in place as a distraction. He insisted last night that I be there to assure the common fae there's nothing to fear about a witch as their queen, but since this party is the only night that Luka and I can rally more Magiks against the Council, I had to decline. Besides that, I don't think the common fae would want me there, which would only ruin Cassius' point of the revel itself.

Instead, I'm joined by my friends at a party with a guest list of influential Magiks–from music artists and actors to those who simply live among the riches of the elite. Magiks around my age, whose parents are involved in politics, are also in attendance. Many of those same children are the ones who have heard of Luka's death, so if they physically see him, there's no denying the restricted magik that the Council is hiding.

I feel unsure of my earlier confidence to attend as I walk through the door. I thought arriving at this time would be a decent amount of late for a party, but the mansion is already crowded and full of people.

Magiks are spread everywhere. Strobe lights that flow inside from the backyard trigger my heart to race, and the loud voices make me want to plug my ears to drown them out. I'd much rather be in my room with a book, but the needs of tonight unfortunately outweigh my wants.

I'm becoming increasingly irritable. Anxious. And I can feel a bundle of hostility towards others shutting down my body.

On the counter near the kitchen is a table full of cups, jugs full of mixed drinks, and shots for our convenience if we don't want to wait for a server. If telepathy were something I had the ability to do, I'd be silently thanking Troy while I dash there, taking three shots, tasting alcohol for the first time in a long while.

After the third, Evie's at my side, shouting over the music, "Godsdamn, take a breath between them."

"Fuck's sake, Evie!" I jump, holding my hands in fists.

"Sorry," she laughs. Each time a light hits the tiny jewels of her bedazzled white dress, I'm blinded. She could probably be a disco ball if we levitated her up.

The rest of our friends join us seconds later. Luka's arm wraps over my shoulder, putting me in a position where I find myself becoming too warm from my black puffer jacket. He's holding an indifferent face, taking a cup from Gray full of whatever alcohol he filled it with. I'm pretty sure the only reason Luka didn't flat-out reject coming is because tonight serves a purpose.

"So what's the plan?" Evie asks, the question open to any of us.

My tongue clicks from the roof of my mouth. I take another shot of vodka but stop myself from drinking more so I'm not drunk to the point of incapacitation. "The main thing is to make sure people see Luka. We can't say how he was brought back, but if we imply the Council has enough knowledge of this, it'll put pressure on them."

"Many of those here are too craven to ask me directly. Which is where you will all come in," Luka adds.

I chortle, smiling wider when Luka looks at me.

"You going back to being pretentious, mahal?" I ask jokingly.

He lets out a singular, amused huff, taking a sip of his drink and handing me a cup of water as he turns his head to others who look our way. Immediately, they avert their eyes. It's from that exact exchange that everyone else realizes he's right, inciting traded expressions we all find funny.

It's near impossible when he's wrong about things like this.

"But yeah," I begin, finishing Luka's explanation. "Luka's too known by some of these people for them to not take notice. Am and Reyna are around here somewhere, so y'all can go around. Treat this like any other party, but don't get so drunk that you can't understand any gossip being passed around."

Everyone in our circle agrees in various ways, taking a drink or finger food from the table before dispersing.

Others stare as Luka leads me around. A couple of Magiks here are ones I've met at cocktail parties hosted by his family, but some I've only ever heard of. The overwhelming atmosphere of the party has spectacle elements that make it feel more event-like, though there's a bit of a frat party flair with the number in attendance. Cups are everywhere, people are outside smoking and dancing, and there are others doing lines of star powder on the glass table.

The songs blasting are also ones regularly played at friend-hosted parties I've gone to. I don't know why I expected the energy to be more formal, but it's almost hilarious to see how normal the elite are. I'm not tall enough to find my friends as Luka and I navigate around the outside, and my heeled boots really only add about three inches. If they're in the crowd of people dancing by the DJ setup, I'm not seeing them.

Laughter and supportive screams boom through the air, bodies spread around the grass, deck, fire pit, and a few in the pool.

Luka and I follow to where the crowd's attention gathers, weaving through bodies around us. It's beginning to take a toll on my comfort levels. And when we finally do get to the front, Gray's tall body is mid-crouch while performing a skateboarding trick from the high-raised platform of the jacuzzi down onto the travertine deck, skating around the many curves.

None of his siblings are here. There's no one to compete with. He isn't solely known as the youngest Mariani brother anymore.

Yet he continues to act as if he *must* perform a trick to prove a needless point.

A sigh slowly sinks Luka's shoulders before moving off to the side, joining the onlookers, with eyes carefully watching Grayson to make sure he doesn't do something he'd regret. But I think that even if regret isn't the result, it may be something that lands Gray in the hospital again.

"Do you wanna go inside?" I ask Juju.

"Can we? It's cold as fuck out here," she answers at the sounds of her boyfriend cursing and laughing, joined by the speeding sound of his skateboard escaping from under him. "I swear, the only time he's sure of himself is when he's on that damn board or in the kitchen."

She ties her hair up with a berry scrunchie to match her jumpsuit as I push her inside, making our way over to the table of alcohol. I wonder if she knows what she's just implied.

As we roam around, I observe others chatting in different groups and taking pictures, all dressed in luxurious clothing that I would have never imagined myself being in the same vicinity of. After I park Juju next to a couch chair so that we can sit. The two of us scroll through our phones or listen in on conversations that are absolutely none of our business and, without a doubt, unethical, sending each other looks when something bizarre is said.

"Oh no," I mock in a deep voice, pretending to be one of the men who just left. "I cheated on my girlfriend and got publicly exposed for fraud, and now I have to deal with the consequences."

"But you don't understand! He's just misunderstood!" Juju fires back, acting as if she's a big fan of the man, the two of us giggling. "What if he goes to jail?"

"Oh, speaking of," I say normally, "I know you went to see your dad today. How is he?"

"Well, he's still in jail, so... not great."

My inattentiveness to my words hits me too late. My lips curl into my mouth, eyes widening, internal thoughts cursing. "Shit, sorry. My bad. I shouldn't have asked it like that."

"You're good," she laughs. "Just miss painting with him, is all."

"I'm sorry. But hey, soon you'll both be able to make art together, and you'll be living in one of these houses."

Excitedly, Juju pulls out her phone and tells me of her latest piece, which won the Oxanna Art Award. With each picture she slides to, nothing except praise leaves my mouth. Her easily embarrassed nature pokes through with each compliment, the pale of her skin reddening her cheeks. Lips pursed, dimples punctuated. Like she's holding herself back from insisting how much she doesn't deserve this, despite the fact that she's been using award money to help fund her schooling since we were seventeen.

Five more songs pass before Grayson and Luka return to us. Grayson's designer shirt has become wrinkled, his beanie sticking out of his pants pocket while his face is flushed and brown hair mussy, with sweat sticking strands to his face.

"Thank the gods I finally found you," Reyna says, yawning as she joins us. "You have no idea how hard it was to find a tall blond here."

"Did you come for sarcasm, or did you have something to tell us?" Luka asks, his demeanor dry.

In her glare lives such a large expression of annoyance that I'm surprised she only crosses her arms and rolls her eyes. "Sometimes, you're a pain in the ass."

"I remember you saying you missed us," he taunts, replaying her words from our return, which only makes her frown more.

"That was mainly to Ara. Anyway, I came to say that others were taking pictures of pretty boy's face."

"*Aw*, so you think I'm pretty."

His shin is kicked, Reyna beaming with satisfaction when he

bends to rub it. "Others were asking about Luka, and a few were wondering if the Council had anything to do with it."

"Yes, some have been bold enough to ask me the same questions."

"Also needed to tell you, for purposes of keeping our jobs, Dylan and I probably shouldn't be seen talking to you after tonight."

Luka and I nod, Evie joining us not long after, whisking me and Reyna back outside to the sea of dancers.

"What are you doing?" I yell over the loud music.

I've lost Reyna to her boyfriend, who takes the two towards the bar area.

Evie giggles, holding my hand and having me spin her. My friend dances, every move creating a perfect still. As if she were a crystal ball with images predicting the future. "I wanted you to come relax."

The next few songs are faster. There's a group of others supporting and holding each other as they shake their bodies, asses moving and bouncing while screaming the words to the song. I'm smiling. Out of breath, like my being here is for pure socialization and not something bigger.

It's hot. Luka excuses us while Evie and Amber continue dancing, and after squeezing between a ninth person to get inside, I think the alcohol's finally reached its peak inside me. I'm wavering side to side. Bumping into things, despite Luka guiding me from behind. With the cross-tied, twisted sports bra I wear as a shirt, nothing stops the corset of my jacket from clinging to my skin.

Finally, we reach an eggshell door. It's a coat room, and I've never been more eager to strip off an item of clothing.

"So, what did you say when people asked how you were brought back?" I ask as Luka hangs our outerwear. Without thinking, my forearms brush my legs, and I shudder at the feel–having forgotten the fishnets I wear under my black skirt. It's not irritating entirely, simply a sensation I didn't prepare myself for.

Back turned from me, he says, "I told them that when I sought answers from our leaders, many were not particularly helpful. Though, I did imply that I doubted the Council wouldn't know." Then, when he faces me, his hands wrap around my back. He tugs me, pulling me into his body. Whispering in a low tone into my ear, he says, "Remember when I said I would stay with you tonight?"

Snickering, I push him away. "It wasn't that long ago, so yes."

"Well, now I don't want to leave your side for another reason." Nothing about his tone indicates worry. It's something completely different. Desire. His hand goes to the side of my face as he leans down, pressing his lips to mine.

Swallowing my impulses, I turn for the two of us to leave. As I reach for the handle, the door opens. A woman who is slightly larger than me with medium-length, platinum blonde hair stands on the other side. She says nothing other than apologizing, but when she glances up from her phone, I realize who it is from her facial features. It's Vi's younger sister, Gee. I haven't seen her since Luka's funeral, and since then, she's changed drastically. Her hair's been bleached, and she dresses differently.

"Hi, Ara!" she greets, pulling me into a hug.

"Hey, Gee!" I hug back. With most cultures showing affection in a physical manner, I've learned to accept it. "How are you?"

"I'm good," she answers, with something between her fingers. Valskull.

"How do you know Troy?" I ask, my brain sobering. My fingers are chipping away at my nail polish. Anxiously peeling my nails' tips as my insides do flipturns. I have to take a deep breath and focus on something else to get my attention off the joint. I've gotten better at controlling myself, but not so much that I can have it again without it causing a spiral.

"Oh, his sister is one of my-" She cuts herself off, brows twisting when taking notice of something else. From their raised position, her shoulders drop quickly, her body tilting forward. "*Luka?*"

"Hello, Giselle. You look nice."

"Giselle Nicole Dimaanó!" a voice scolds quietly over Luka. From the right pops Violette, marching her way over here with Damien tailing close behind, both in dark purple velvet. "You're supposed to be asleep! Actually, you're not even supposed to be on this continent. You have classes."

The hall has become overcrowded by us standing right by the closet, blocking its entrance. Behind Vi and Damien are four Magiks who are making their way closer.

I walk, the rest following me into a more open area. Through the short walk, Vi doesn't stop questioning her sister. Others watch as we move, most of them staring at Luka, who doesn't so much as wave or acknowledge their presence.

"Ate, how in the bloody hell is Luka alive? We literally went to his funeral," Gee questions, eyes on her sister.

"I'll explain that later. First, tell me how you got into this fucking party," Vi demands. When Gee doesn't answer, Vi becomes more irritated.

Damien showers Violette with kisses and a hug, uttering hushed compliments into her ear, though that may be to sedate her. "Sweetlove, take it easy on Gee. Remember how rebellious we were in our early years?"

Scowling with a head angled to Damien, she breaks away from his embrace. "The difference is, *I wasn't caught*." Her glare is terrifying when directed at her sister. "What do you think would happen if mom and dad found out you were here?"

"Probably nothing." Gee shrugs. "Except ignoring it altogether if nothing happens. Or, if I do something that shames our family, they'll just yell and express how much we disappoint them."

Sighing, Vi's energy loosens. "We need to have a talk."

Away goes the three, Violette dragging her sister away by her suede bomber jacket, probably to hound her further.

By the door are Reyna and her boyfriend, the sight of them popping a reminder into my head. "Luka," I say, "nothing's wrong, but I'm about to do something, and you have to act normal."

Quickly, I storm to them, shoving Reyna the moment I'm at a close enough distance.

On her face is an expression of shock. Even Dylan looks perplexed, standing there and saying nothing other than a singular word, which overlaps with Reyna's voice.

"Bro, what the fuck is your problem?" she demands with annoyance at my lack of apology.

"You should fucking know," I yell back, getting in her face, which is still confused. Immediately after, I mutter through my teeth, quietly enough for only her to hear. "Just play along. Trust me." Then, my voice resumes to its previous volume. "I can't believe you told people that shit about Luka when you said you believed me."

"Then maybe you shouldn't have stopped talking to us after he died. Maybe then I'd have reason to believe your side."

We angrily say things back and forth, spewing a fake argument with truth sprinkled in our words. It draws in a small group of people to come near, all trying to gather what's going on. Another possible minute goes by as our fighting escalates, nearing a physical level. The display isn't grand enough for others to call for security, even as Dylan pulls Reyna back, yelling at me before Luka steps in and the two leave.

Upon their departure, a few gawkers ask if I'm okay–some, I'd guess, wondering if it's appropriate to ask what happened. But when none of them get the answers they want, they go back to their own business.

We mingle with others, passing through conversations where I can overhear some not-so-whispered words, though I'm sure they're trying to have them be. Those who became famous for entertaining are the ones who I feel more comfortable speaking with. It takes a little for the feeling of nerves to pass, unbelieving that I'm speaking with the same Magiks that Juju and I would keep up with in our teenage years. I still have to control myself from getting too excited when I'm talking to Am's boyfriend.

Contrastingly, there are some elite who we speak with, conversing over interests that are vastly different. In these conversations, some will unintentionally brag about their riches, speaking as if owning observatories in their backyards or something just as exuberant is normal.

I'm not sure how well I am comprehending most of these conversations.

"Are you enjoying the party?" Troy asks, taking me away from some boring discussion that Luka's having with another elite from the political sphere.

"It's... different, to say the least," I answer. The sip from the alcohol I have tastes like pears, but even that smell is less potent than whatever Troy is drinking. "Not bad, though. I'm just getting used to the fact that this is a bit classier than other parties."

"Lucky for you, this isn't an event." He laughs, dirty blond hair catching in the light with the slightest movement of his head. "No one's here to schmooze you into collaborating with them."

I think that if this were even as little as five years ago, that exact thing would have been my ultimate goal. Not with a particular talent in mind to reach elite fame, but to befriend those I idolized.

"Where's Am?"

"Dancing. Doing star powder." He laughs once, tilting his head to one side and back straight. "You know her."

"Makes sense."

Liquid inside Troy's cup is whirled around a few times, the sorcerer's eyes glancing around the room to others recording the party. "How's your little plan going?"

"Good. I think?" I cock my head to him. "I'm guessing that's why you came here?"

"Yeah." He's one of the most well-known elites in the entertainment industry. For all the money that he has, I would think he would've dressed more upscale than just suede pants and a taupe ribbed shirt. "I'm sure someone here is bound to leak to the media who I'm associating with. Might as well be you and Luka."

The younger voice in my head is urging me to ask what the musician is working on and tell him how cool I think it is to call him a friend.

She needs to be shut up somehow.

"Thanks for inviting us, by the way," I say. Desperately, I'm searching for a commonality that wouldn't portray me weirdly, but all I'm stuck with is small talk that makes my insides contort in detestation. "I know it was mostly a favor to Am, but it *does* help."

"This isn't my party, and we both know it," he laughs, clanking our two cups together. I can't deny that everything about this entire night has Amber's touch to it. "Besides, you think I don't want to see the Coven be exposed as frauds too? Obviously, I have no proof of my own to say anything, but having Luka here speaks for itself."

He's charming. He knows how to move among others while also being careful with whom to trust. At least, that's my assumption from the things I've seen about him online and the times I've interacted with him.

We all figured that Troy knows how to use his fame, but I didn't expect him to share our goals.

"Hey, mahal," I say as Luka joins us. I can see the exact second that his face changes from drained energy to curiosity with Troy. A small message is also silently being sent to him from my eyes, hoping that my boyfriend won't tell Troy the embarrassingly large extent of how much I've loved him for years.

The slightest smirk pulls up one side of his lips, his brows raised but saying nothing.

"Hi, Luka," Troy greets with a grin, extending a hand out, but it is not returned with the same eagerness beyond two shakes.

"Troy, right?"

"Yeah," he replies in response. "Nice to finally meet the man in the flesh. I was just saying that the few friends I've invited should help you lot. Fun people, horrible etiquette when it comes to guest secrets."

Glancing at Troy, Luka asks, "Aren't you worried about the repercussions you might face by having us here?"

"Not really. It wouldn't be too hard to guess why something happened to me after this party," he says with a slight raise of his shoulders, laughing as if Luka said something funny. "But being that I don't have to occupy Ara while you speak with others, I'm going to find my girlfriend."

As he departs, Troy nudges me and laughs from hints of tipsiness. "Get a drink or something. You might as well enjoy your night after that whole kerfuffle with Reyna."

Then, the sorcerer disappears. When he was speaking to us, a few women were taking pictures, and I'm sure that by now, they've reached his fans and caused curiosity. It doesn't matter if no one knows who Luka is. People are too nosy when it comes to who associates with Troy.

Mine and Luka's fingers intertwine together before strolling towards the music's origin. The dancing area has cleared partially, though as the four music artists on the stage begin their set, my boyfriend and I get caught in the horde of excited people crowding closer.

"Wanna dance?" I ask.

Behind me, as the slow-paced song is being performed, Luka plays with the sections of hair I've braided up from two half-pigtails. Then he goes to the parts that I've curled, never stopping from keeping his hands off me.

Coolness from his sleeve brushes against my skin as he places his hands around my hips and presses himself closer to me. The silk from his long-sleeved button-down *just barely* differs from his daily clothing. This one, at least, has designs woven into the fabric. Even though he expanded his clothing on the night of Cassius' coronation, wearing that would be too eccentric for the Magiks around us.

We move along to the music, the lyrics completely enabling the way everyone around us dances, with their bodies pressing too close together. I can hear Luka chuckling as I sway my hips onto his body through two more songs. His hands reposition, arms shifting from around my shoulders to my stomach to keep me locked in place.

"Have you ever taken me while others watched?" he croons into my ear.

"No."

"Well, if you don't stop grinding yourself against me, you will."

From my mouth leaves the quickest exhale of gaiety. Then, my eyes widen at the realization. Goosebumps form, and a shiver runs through my body.

"*Oh*. You mean–"

Luka leans down, kissing my neck. "Yes."

Something in my brain flips like a switch, and I'm filled with the carnal desire to fuck him with everyone watching us. I continue dancing, grinding harder against him.

His hand glides from my stomach. Up my body and past my chest until it pulls my face up to the side for a moment. His hold around my chin is firm as his eyes stare down at me, wild and craving.

He skims his fingers across my skin, unbuttoning the side of my skirt. Sliding it past the bands of my bottoms and sliding his hand into my underwear. My breath is uneven by the time he reaches my clit, fear striking me that my skirt may fall.

People are still around us, but I'm not sure anyone's sober enough to comprehend what's happening. Or if they're even paying attention. *I'm* barely able to see the other faces with the dim lighting.

All the better. I'm sure in actuality, Luka would rather strangle someone than have them see me like this.

"You're so wet, love," he purrs.

His fingers move around me with more magik than our powers contain. We try to be subtle, me keeping my legs from spreading suspiciously wide and him not bending down too far. It creates such a steady pace that, with the environment and danger of others around us, it makes it all the more sensual.

"Do you remember Almos and Keona?" he says into my ear.

They're the couple grinding a few bodies away. The last two people I fucked before I realized I didn't want anyone but Luka. Apparently, since I last saw them, they've become more acquainted with each other. Or at least, are partners for the night.

"What about them?"

"They were watching you tonight. When you were dancing in the middle. When I came to you." His fingers work faster and with more pressure, my legs buckling as he holds me tighter. "They'll never get to touch you like this."

I don't know how, but his voice is louder to me than the music. He might also be unaware that it was probably him they were staring at. His touch is electrifying, setting a heating sensation to everything in me.

His free hand is on my throat, squeezing, and with the alcohol in me, I'm completely gone. I'm clenching down on my teeth as hard as I can. Fighting back from moaning so loud that others can hear me.

"I love you," he says, continuing his motions, knowing damn well that I've orgasmed.

My body's unsteady, my hand grabbing his arm. A stern reminder that if he keeps going, everyone will know what he's doing. The reality of everything comes careening down.

Barely audible chuckling leaves his mouth as he retracts his hand. He spins me, holding me tight.

Then I see them.

I see his dimples that rarely make an appearance outside the privacy of just us alone. The two craters that carve into his cheeks.

"You're my favorite person," I say against his lips, loudly enough for him to hear, me giggling.

"Say it again, love."

"You're-" I breathe shakily. He's sucking on my neck while running his hand around my back. "You're my favorite person."

"Good."

Luka's hand wraps into mine after I zip and button my skirt, the two of us seeking any of our other friends both inside the mansion and out. I'm sure he wants to get out of here more than he did upon our entrance.

After almost fifteen minutes of searching and getting trapped in conversations–which I'm sure makes Luka wish he could fade into obscurity–we're able to find those we came with, explaining our desire to go home. Annoyingly, our group is torn over whether we should leave.

"We've been here for hours," Juju complains. Her head falls back, though her hair is still perfectly intact. "I'm tired, and I have opening shift tomorrow."

"It's still early," Grayson counters, appearing a lot more

disheveled than any of us, barely able to hold himself up straight without laughing or nearly tipping over. "I haven't even seen anyone run to the bathroom to vomit yet."

"I don't think it's that kind of party," Damien says. "But I still agree with Juli. It's nearly midnight." While he enjoys staying up late, his energy doesn't last long with a large number of people. The handful of times that we hosted parties, Damien tried to ensure the attendees were down to only our friends by one in the morning.

"Will the four of you just make a decision so that we may go?" Luka asks, expressly annoyed both in his tone and body.

"If Vi wants to stay, I'll stay with her," Damien concedes.

"Why don't me, Gray, and Damien stay, and you can take the car?" Vi suggests, not even slightly close to done with her night of frivolity. "We can ask Amber to have someone bring us home."

"Oh, I'm not staying if Juli isn't staying," Gray says, his words slurring.

"Y'all, can we just go then?" Juli asks. Her tired voice still manages to be louder than the noise around us, though it is raspier.

A voice yells behind us after we say our goodbyes and make our way towards the door, sounding closer with every step we take.

"Guys!" the voice yells. I can't hear her much, but Luka, with my arm in his grip, is rushing us faster. "Luka! Teka muna!"

That stops him in his tracks, halting and turning around with me to realize the voice belongs to Gee.

A lot of times, I forget that Luka has learned Tagalog. It was a shock when he spoke it for the first time in front of me. He learned it originally to communicate with my family, but what he didn't know from his secret lessons was, by not telling me, he found out too late that I barely understand the language myself. Outside of context clues and the few words I can understand, I'm pretty much only guessing at things whenever I hear it spoken.

"Giselle," he remarks snippily, "unless this is something dire you must tell me, please pass your message to your sister, and I will respond promptly."

"Mate," Gray says in passing, "we're going to get the jackets. Don't leave without us."

"Okay," I respond, nodding.

Gee crosses her arms over each other, wearing a snarling face that looks identical to her sister's. "I just wanted to tell you that some of the others in my year have heard about the suspicions raised against the Coven."

She extends her phone out to me. There are messages in a group chat with her and a few others discussing their suspicions, most texts brutally honest and insulting our leaders in ways that serve no relevance to the topic itself. One message is just a picture of Leader Blanchet's face with an accurate, mocking description.

As much as I want Luka right now, I have to control myself. No matter how much I'm imagining his hands on every inch of my body.

"What do they think about the Fae?" I ask, handing Gee her phone after finding nothing about them in the messages.

"I don't know if everyone believes rumors of the Fae's existence quite yet, but it would've helped if you brought one tonight."

I understand the need for irrefutable proof before believing something, but if any of the Fae made themselves known to the public, I'm sure that the Council would have them killed to keep the secret of our history against the creatures.

Luka sighs. Too worked up to explain the dangers of bringing a Fae. "If they are so curious about the Fae, I recommend you and your friends ask our Coven executives about the truth of our long-standing feud with them. Ask why we were led to believe they are extinct. You'd be idiots to go about asking for a Fae to be present among Magiks when you know nothing about them."

Before Gee can say another word, Luka is tightening his hold on my hand and exiting the party, with our friends close behind who are asking the valet to bring our car to us.

Cold, stale air breezes past me as we wait, my jacket not doing much to provide warmth. Luka's body heat adds *something*, but my teeth still chatter.

"Mahal," I call sheepishly, thoughts of the conversations occurring inside the mansion occupying my thoughts. I undo the braids of my hair and take out the scrunchies, retying everything into one ponytail. "Are you ready for your family to know you're alive?"

There is silence as Luka thinks over my question. He doesn't answer while the song that's playing is finishing. Then, finally, he kisses the corner of my cheekbone. "I know the ways my family receives intel. I would be more surprised if they didn't know already."

XXXV

Mortal Bullets

Cassius

"Do you really think this a good idea?" I ask Arabella as we venture down a corridor.

The building, tall and full of living quarters, is said to be an apartment complex. They are structured similar to tenements Atticus constructs for common fae or inns for visiting Fae from other lands. Not only do Magiks live here, but humans as well. All areas beyond the doors are the living spaces of mortals, and according to my queen, the apartment may contain multiple living within.

Arabella spent our whole trudge up the stairs explaining that though these may appear small to me, the building is considered more luxurious than many, though I find that difficult to believe.

"It was *your* idea to follow Chrissy around. She hasn't met with Delphi, so her apartment might be our last option." Arabella moves faster, us staying a distance away from the woman.

"*In jest,*" I remind her. I would have never suggested such a thing if I knew my words would be taken in earnest. The thought had been something said in passing with partial seriousness but nothing more.

Chrissy, the witch carrying bags full of food, shimmies a key into a lock, dropping it after her first attempt at pushing it in. "Oh, for fuck's sake." She turns around, glancing in all directions. "Good gods, it feels like someone's been following me all day. Hello?"

I'm pushed into a small crevice by Arabella, where the walls cave inward, caging the door. Her body is pressed against mine, both her forearms surrounding me, my glamour that changes our appearances having dropped.

She pays no attention, but my mouth twitches as she brings her body closer, leaving no space. Not even a book could pass between us.

As we hear the sound of a door shutting, Arabella peeks around the wall, ensuring Chrissy is gone. She returns her attention to me, glances down at our bodies against each other, then back up to my eyes. Her arms rigidly lower to her sides, backing away as she lightly clears her throat. "Can you sense another Magik on this floor besides Chrissy?"

"I had one against me up until not so long ago." My grin has yet to leave its place.

"Cassius," she says with eyes pointed up.

"Yes, yes," I ignore, dismissing her irritation and waving her off with my hand. I have no care that she sees through my words. It feels familiar to have her speak as if nothing is different between the two of us. "Fae can sense if creatures have magik, not detect if there are others in an area."

Once more, she peers into the hallway. "Shit. Okay, so we're gonna have to go in her apartment."

"By okkaring?"

"Nah, there's probably wards that'll keep me from doing that. I have to suck it up and knock."

The queen is the first to leave. She wears casual, mortal clothing, similar to what she wore the day amongst the Council of the Coven, dressing me today in similar attire. A dreary, long-sleeved shirt covers my torso. My bottoms, as well, are the unsightly clothing called blue jeans.

She knocks three times. Long moments without so much as a response leave us in silence. Then, the witch, who is the same height as Arabella, answers the door. Her cosmetics have been removed from her face, her ivory skin with a touch of pink shining through.

"What the fuck are you doing here?" she berates with an accent different from both Arabella's and her friends'. Her arms are crossed, and behind her is a screen with sliding pictures blasting music loudly. I've been told by Juliette that these are called televisions, though I do not understand their mechanics–similar to many mortal contraptions.

Arabella remains unfazed. She keeps her eyes directly on the other witch when I ask, "Can we come in?"

Chrissy waves her hand, moving so that we may enter. Her fingers flick to chairs at the table, which pop out for our seating. She walks into another room, excusing herself while telling us to sit.

Her apartment seems just under the size of the king's bedchamber at Nexus. I think I would rather see myself dead than live with my family in something small such as this.

"I don't trust her," I whisper to Arabella.

She scoffs with sarcasm. "And you think I do?"

Nothing in this room shows signs of another living here. There is a spare bedchamber, but it is completely unoccupied. The walls nail with portraits of Chrissy and others, though these are more realistic than portraits that hang in Nexus. There is a rectangular, flat sofa that looks to have no cushion support at all. It sits parallel to the television, with a transparent glass table at knee's height less than a pace away.

Behind me is a counter full of herbs, spices, cauldrons, and transparent jars without a label. I do wonder if such a spread is common for mortals.

"I haven't a clue if it is from my lack of understanding over the Human Lands or the poisons a small length from me, but this residence is quite alarming."

It seems that I am not the only one to take notice of the apartment, for Arabella is darting her eyes at every area, studying every detail carefully while finding amusement in my comment. In a hushed tone, she says, "I don't think Delphi's here, but Esme said that Chrissy has the Stone of Elestial, so, at the very least, we can get that back."

"What if she does no–" I immediately shut my mouth as Chrissy returns to the room. She is not intimidating in the least, but there exists an eerie feeling that coils in her energy.

Arabella narrows her eyes in suspicion. Her head shakes, and a smile of false pretenses grows. "You're still friends with Delphi?"

The witch takes a seat across from Arabella. The two are staring at one another, but neither are outwardly exchanging insults. "Yeah, and you've betrayed your kind while turning another person she loved against her."

Her comment causes me to scoff in laughter. *Adonis cannot possibly be the one she is referring to.*

"How good for you to confess what it is you know," I say. "Now the three of us do not have to pretend you're unaware."

Chrissy rolls her eyes. Her hand summons an object into her hand, and as she presses a button, the pictured screen decreases in volume. "You have five minutes to tell me why you're here, or I'm calling Delphi."

"You know what? Do it. That would actually make this a lot easier," Arabella challenges.

"I would also enjoy speaking again with the witch who captured the heart of my brother while failing to seize power. Not once, but twice."

"Your reputation *does* precede you," Chrissy returns, nearly amused. She curls her fingers into her palm, smiling as I feel my throat constricting to where I cannot breathe.

Arabella flicks her wrist, and as she does, a glass falls from the counter. It pulls Chrissy's attention just long enough for the High Queen to use her magik.

I cannot understand why it is Chrissy who has been trusted with the stone. It takes very little to distract that witch.

"Why are you still friends with Delphi?" Arabella asks. When there is no response, she attempts again by saying, "I know you both had a falling out with the rest of the group. There had to be *some* reason you chose to stay friends with her."

"Some of us know how to keep our friendships."

"Chrissy, please, I'm trying to be nice."

"You're only nice if there's something that benefits you."

I see Arabella's jaw tense, pushing through a spiteful smile as she breathes. "Alright."

The witch ought to know better than to disparage Arabella, though I find it questionable that no punishment has been served. It would be quite easy to hex the woman in front of us, torturing her as the queen had done during our excursions in the past.

Looking between us, Chrissy sneers at Arabella, then turns to me. "How do you know she won't use you until you have nothing left?"

"You're one to talk when Delphi's been using you 'cause of your mom's position," Arabella remarks. Her facade drops, but only when she speaks.

My best and most honest self always remains at her side. However, right now is neither the time for formalities nor kindness.

"I think you are mistaken, madam. Delphi has tricked everyone for her own gain. Especially you, for allowing yourself to be without stronger protection."

Chrissy turns her head around. She concludes later than she should that her warding is already minimal. The magik she's cast around her home does nothing in comparison to what Arabella has learned. It is the same magik that Delphi has acquainted herself with. Someone with adequate knowledge of magik ought to have known that once she allowed us in, her protection faded to nothing.

Arabella outpowers Chrissy significantly.

No, that's not quite right. I do not think the witch has ever once matched the powers of the queen.

"Surely you must realize there was a reason Delphi never taught you the magik she learned." Shadows release from my hands before I am able to think for myself, my silhouette figure drawing towards the brunette. As it stalks near, the lights in the room contrast highly against the smoke of my darkness. When my shadow pushes her against the wall with a light, there are faint reds that reflect in her hair. Colors her blood will be sure to run.

Chrissy squirms with her body pinned to the wall. Her arm lowers into her pocket, fidgeting until she pulls something out. A black metal weapon is clutched in her hand, aimed at Arabella. While I do not recognize it, I worry regardless.

Arabella begins laughing. "You really thought to pull a gun on me?"

"Are you *trying* to get me to shoot you?"

With a face unimpressed, Arabella raises her eyebrows, her challenging posture inciting the wrath of the other witch. "Go ahead. Do it."

She presses her finger to a curved, small section of the object, but nothing comes out. The weapon locks in on itself. Arabella steps to my side, hand closed into a fist with her focus on Chrissy.

"Let her go," Arabella mouths, to which I begrudgingly do.

Chrissy rotates the cylinder with her hand, confounded by what is possibly going wrong. She points the gun to the ground, and while she is preoccupied, Arabella turns her hand, forcing the barrel to aim upwards. She glances one time more at Chrissy, opens her hand, and a loud noise reverberates.

A piece of lead, now stuck into the ceiling, creates a tiny indent. Arabella huffs in laughter from her nose, as if she did not think her dare would be taken. She extends her arm in front of her, using magik to once more trap Chrissy against the wall. "I thought you were smarter than this. Guns are practically useless, remember?"

Summoning knives to her side, Chrissy aims the tips towards the two of us. The front of her palm faces us, and with one flick down, the blades shoot forward.

We duck towards opposite sides, Arabella to the right and me towards the left. I'm breathing heavily, looking in all directions, when I realize Chrissy has used this as an opportunity to escape. She jumps over me but is stopped by my shadow holding her down to a chair.

Once more, a witch has attempted to harm me. Too many instances has a Magik posed a threat to my life.

Perhaps it's time I kept a tally.

To create a safer distance, I back to where the witch was previously standing while Arabella joins my side. She is patting down her clothing, shaking her head as she looks at me.

"We have specific knowledge that has informed us that you are aware of the Stone of Elestial's location," I explain. My shadow's hold wraps tighter around her struggling body, with my thoughts nearly allayed for returning the favor of cruelty to one so close to Delphi. "Tell us, and perhaps there is a chance we will not call for your death when we track Delphi down."

Sure that the stone must be with Chrissy's body, Arabella swiftly moves towards her. She bends down with a hand out, expectantly waiting for what we ask. And as Chrissy's hand reaches toward her legs, instead of giving away what she knows, a solid bar of iron with a sharpened point shoots itself in my direction.

"Cas!" Arabella screams. Her head whips to me and rapidly returns to Chrissy.

The bar wedges into the wall at my side, having narrowly missed piercing deeper into my skin. For endurable moments, I think I am fine. Then I feel the fabric of my clothing sticking to my skin. As I bring my hand to my arm, it soaks with wetness. The fluid dark and warm.

It seems I have foolishly believed to have come out of this unscraped. My head is spinning. I fall back against the wall and into a seated position. The iron in what she has thrown in my direction pains me severely. I will my shadows to join Arabella, but with each attempt, my sight splits in two.

Arabella raises her palm, and suddenly, Chrissy is floating in the air. From my angle, I can see her eyes widen in terror as Arabella, only slightly in my view, grins. Her left hand holds still while her right twists, forcing Chrissy's arms to rotate until I hear something crack.

I've been hit with iron before, but it did not nearly elicit a reaction as strong as this. Something more than the weapon has sliced through me. As I reach into the opening of my shirt, I find a small bag full of the powdered metal. I toss it to the side, compelling myself to return to what is unfolding in front of me.

"Stop, please," Chrissy begs. She's slammed so hard against the wall that a crater of her body is outlined. Her voice yells, but the words are nothing above hoarse shrieks.

The witch *should* have surrendered long ago. Raw desperation for healers seeps through every thought I manage to form, but that same focus is pulled in different directions. The Faerie blood that courses within me will not heal the iron that spreads itself inside my body.

A bath full of spread petals and herbs while enjoying the sweet taste of lasialic and honey would be superb.

"No one can hear you. I made sure of that the second you let us in," Arabella mocks so terrifyingly, I'm sure it is rooted in something I would never wish to provoke. This is a rage I have never before seen from her. She keeps Chrissy levitated as she makes her way into the kitchen with ingredients and different poisons. "You deserve this. For the backstabbing betrayal you did to me with Delphi."

She pulls the dagger from her bag, inserting it into the band of her breeches. Her hand grabs a jar of something, which I cannot see, and saunters with both items until she is in front of the woman about to meet her end.

Chrissy's screams have turned to nearly nothing but sounded exhales. She uses what magik she can against Arabella, but it only knocks her into the furniture that stabilizes her. Running back, Arabella regains her focus, lowering Chrissy with the magik from her hand and plunging the dagger into the witch's stomach.

It is not enough to kill her, though death seems to be the furthest thing from Arabella's goals at this point in time. After one prolonged blink, I hear Arabella scream from something Chrissy has done, though I cannot see it. There is too much throbbing in my arm for me to think.

I try to stand, but as I reach up, I knock a plant off the wooden side table. My hand holds my arm tightly, only making things increasingly more difficult. With even the slightest movement, I feel as if I am carrying out a prophecy set by the spirits against me. Reaching for a bar to bring me up, I realize that it's the same terrible iron that struck me. It burns. Pain heated into my skin.

"We know you have the Stone of Elestial, Chrissy," Arabella barks, the blade pushed deeper into Chrissy's body. "Where is it?"

Then, her hand opens the jar, grabbing a handful of what is inside, and I'm able to see what it is.

Belladonna berries. The poison of increased heart rate and a mind undone.

Chrissy mutters something quietly, but I cannot hear it over the sting of my body or the pounding in my ears.

"*Where, Chrissy?*" Arabella demands.

"My pocket!" she cries.

But Arabella does not spare her. She uses magik to keep Chrissy's mouth open and forces the nearly black berries down her throat.

Juices leak from the witch's mouth, her body suffocating from its toxins. Choking until she regurgitates blood. It goes on for what feels torturously long. Or perhaps that is the iron in me exaggerating.

Arabella goes through Chrissy's pockets, pulls out the Stone of Elestial, and lets the witch fall to the ground. I can only focus on the blood on Arabella's face as she moves to me. When she gets to my side, she lowers to her knees, grunting as she does.

The pain alternates between nagging but bearable and excruciating.

She is fearsome, and beautiful, and I love her.

"Why the fuck would you enable her like that?" She rips open my clothing at the tear of my sleeves, where the iron had slashed through. Her cool hands are a wondrous contrast to the burning and my demise. I can imagine she is worried about me.

I wish she would lie to me now.

"The bar did nothing more than pierce through my skin and drop iron powder into it," I explain as I shudder. I'm also unsure if my words come off as smoothly as I would hope. Her hands are moving around my bleeding skin, and while the cut is not deep, my blood flows down my arm. Her touch stings, but I do not mind in the least.

"Thank the gods you're okay," she breathes out, inspecting every bit of my arm where I had been hit.

I look at her eyes and see there is genuine worry in them. Even angry with me, she wants me saved. I fear the delirium from iron poisoning has effects similar to succumbing to drunkenness. "I'm quite alive. A bit of iron left in my skin, though it's nice to see you care."

Ripping the sleeve completely off, Arabella ties it tightly right above the exposed flesh. She tears another piece from my shirt, pressing it directly on the wound. "This might hurt, so bite down."

She removes her outerwear, handing it to me and waiting as I place the cloth in my mouth. Her hand returns to the wound, eyes closed before breathing in.

In the next moment, I feel particles of iron being removed little by little. It is excruciating. Almost as if the burning sensation that has spread now directs itself into one spot and works as a broken shard reversing from a stabbing. My arm becomes limp, but it is still movable if putting in effort.

It is strenuous to open my eyes from the pain. Her hand clasps into mine, pulling me up as I use her to support myself. She's whimpering, hobbling while hardly able to carry my weight. The weakness from her fight is making it difficult to hold herself up, let alone another.

When pulled to a new destination from her okkaring us, I hear the sound of wood screeching on the floor. She sets me down on a stool. Opens my hand and places a chunk of something into it.

"Eat this," she commands.

As I chew on the gag-worthy piece, I hear the sound of the sink filling water into something, filtering out Arabella's noises.

"And drink this to wash it down," she says, handing me a pitcher to drink. The pain has subsided, and with eyes now open, I am curious as to why she stands on the other side of the table so unbalanced. One of her hands grips the table, the other lower down. "I remember reading somewhere that clay helps with iron poisoning. I think you're fine, but this is in case I couldn't get it all out."

I take in the state of the area, which I only see on rare occasions. We stand in the room dedicated to the healers' craft. There are tables full of different tonics, antidotes, and salves. I see the block of clay, crushed sunflower seeds, and other ingredients on a high-standing table in the middle of the room that Arabella leans her front on.

"You sure you're okay?" she asks, her teeth bared.

"Yes."

A sigh of relief exhales from Arabella. "Okay, cool."

She clutches her sides. Lifting herself onto the table and throwing her right leg over, where a knife is lodged into her thigh.

I'm horrified and scared for her. While she was murdering, while removing the iron from me, her injuries had not halted her.

She slowly removes the weapon, sharp, loud sounds from her throat hissing in pain, with the overflow of bleeding coming to a halt. Tears fall from her eyes as she screams with her mouth shut, while her free hand clamps the table so tight that, as each bit of the blade emerges, I wonder if she will break off a portion.

Frozen in my worry, I can do nothing but stare. Her ability to ruthlessly fight is everything I admire about her, yet it is also my greatest fear. I am so terrified of losing her to her own plans that I cannot think of anything else.

A flicker of my past crashes into my mind. How fortunate I was then to have nothing of value worth losing. And how unfortunate I am now to have everything.

Delphi will pay for what she and her followers have done. Not only for my people, but for my queen.

When she finally gets the weapon free, she drops the knife to her side. Slowly standing, she pulls down her pants to her knees, then sits back on the table. When settled, she spots my panic. "I'm fine. You have to keep the blade in so you don't bleed out. The knife wasn't even that long."

Her hand hovers above the wound to use her magik and speed up her healing process.

"FUCK!" she roars. Magik may not be healing her the same way it had with me. Her hand that grips the table rises and smashes down harshly atop it.

Then she looks at me, heaving in and out.

"Hand me those." She points to a curved needle and a string of clear material.

Promptly, I move to the other side of the table, grabbing what she asks for from the counter of herbs and glass bottles. "What are you meaning to do with these?"

After threading the string through the needle as if she were tailoring clothing, she punctures the sharp object through her skin. "Stitching myself up. The knife she stabbed me with is enchanted, and I'm too weak to use my magik to heal everything perfectly."

"Would you like for me to call the healers?"

With each time she sews together another area of skin, she makes a small sound of pain, which crashes against my ears. "I'm fine. Definitely not doing it right, but-" She huffs out with an exhale, stifling another sound. "Almost done."

The repeat of words is not quite the lie I have been hoping for when she speaks that she is fine.

"I ought to be grateful you know how to remove iron so quickly," I say to distract her. I watch, leaning on the stone behind me while being unable to offer anything for her pain.

Another grunt of suffering vibrates from her throat. She refuses to draw her focus away, whereas I am awaiting the relief of her being healed.

"It was quite impressive on your part. While poison swarmed

inside me as you were busy murdering Chrissy, you appeared like a vengeful goddess of sorts."

"Of sorts," she returns, glancing up at me. "And you were the little king in distress."

It could be due to the simple fact that I am still experiencing the effects of iron embedded into my bloodstream, but a hint of amused joy lights Arabella's eyes when responding.

As she finishes stitching herself up, she uses the knife that was once inside her to cut the thread. She drops it to her side and looks at me in puzzlement. "Why were you so sure I wouldn't leave you for dead?"

"I've never been sure of anything the way I have you." I push myself straight, taking a step until my hand goes through her hair. "Perhaps it is foolish, but I trusted that you would never hate me so much that you'd allow me to die at the hands of another."

She chuckles. Her hand reaches for a rag that she then drenches in the pitcher so that she may wipe the blood from her skin, the other placed on her thigh using magik, which swirls around her leg.

My eyes will not stray from her.

"*I'll always trust you.*"

A twinkle sparkles in her eyes as she pauses to look at me. Smiling. "I think I might know a way for us to meet with Delphi."

"Pray tell, what is that?"

Squeezing out the rag for the last time, she hangs the cloth on the edge of the table. "It's a trick I used on the Fae before. We'll discuss it after I get back."

"*After you get back*? Wheresoever are you off to?" I inquire.

"Chrissy's. I have to make sure her death looks like a suicide. But I'll see the healers as soon as I return." She hops down from the table, pulling her bottoms to her stomach and limping towards the sink. Her hands collect water, rinsing off the blood on her hands, taking another sharp inhale of pain. "Actually, I think I'll need another Magik to help me too."

I make no argument to deter her, not that I could. I believe her well enough that this is something necessary, when her death would alert not only the authorities of humans but the Magikal ones as well. Going along with her would likely lead to the Council of the Coven blaming the Fae for Chrissy's death.

As Arabella shuts off the faucet after splashing water on her face, I go to fetch her a towel. I hear the water from the pitcher being poured down the drain with my back turned, and when I return to her, she is gone.

XXXVI

Dysfunctional Family Drama

Luka

Utter, heart-wrenching anxiety is overtaking my every movement. I have no idea if Ari is safe or if something terrible happened to her. I'm pacing around the same five points in these woods. Others have positioned themselves in their designated areas, leaving me alone and in command of the twenty in my zone who will fight on foot. They talk amongst themselves, whereas I remain in a state of vertigo.

I have to center myself. No good comes from my worry, and these soldiers are depending on me to lead them. That thought alone eases nothing.

We've had no time to gather more Magiks to our side. Some are against the Coven, but those who we have spoken to do not view this as their fight. Seven Magiks, other than my friends, have come to join, though Arabella has assigned them to areas where they can use their magik without physically engaging in the case there is a battle. Roughly half of the Fae army is with us, the other two hundred and fifty guarding Ifaeris.

The urge to rip down one of the many yew trees with my magik crosses my mind. I desperately need an outlet to alleviate my stress.

Precious times with Ari flood back into me. I had no idea then how limited time is. I'm filled with immense dread that no matter how long it was, it feels fleeting in the span of our lives. We've had less than three years together, but there will be many more to come. That's what I have to remind myself of.

"Sir?" a soldier says, interrupting my ruminating thoughts completely and causing me to flinch. "What happens if we do not come out victorious from this?"

"I would find it pathetic that I have trained my entire life to lose to creatures who have just now learned their way around a fight." My focus remains alert to all my surroundings, sensitive to every changing sound.

Others around me turn quiet. Whispers and hushes are traded, but none are loud enough that a fracture in the plan wouldn't be heard.

Water crashing from the rushing river behind the barn can be heard vaguely from the distance. Winds breeze through the trees, rustling the leaves and inviting the smell of florals from the few flowers that have died with the season's end, but it isn't right. It doesn't smell like *her*. There lacks a fresh smell of aloe from her soap or the flowery scents she loves to use on her body. There is none of the high energy that she brings when around others.

Remnants of the way she affects me weave through where my bones connect, seeping through every opening of my brain, fracturing the once narrow-minded man I was meant to be. My lips alone could trace her whole body from memory. Nearly all my thoughts are consumed by her. They always have been, ever since our first conversation at Grayson's birthday.

Running steps come from my side, out of breath gasps leaving the mouth. "Luka," a feminine voice coming from the tiny Fae says. "She's here."

I take off before the Fae tells me exactly where Ari is. The three of us agreed on a spot to meet after she used the Stone of Elestial on Kaileigh to deliver a letter to Delphi. A letter that Ari had written in honor of both herself and Cassius.

Twigs, remains of bones, and other things snap beneath my feet as I move to her. The barn is in my sights, I just have to move faster.

Cassius is already there. His wings are in their resting position, and he has his hand on Ari's shoulder. She inhales loudly, her hand on the red planks that build the structure.

"Fucking Adonis for only bringing me here once. I okkared myself to the top of a godsdamn tree and had to climb down." She stands straighter, taking the back of her hand and wiping it across her forehead before putting on gloves. "If he doesn't die today, I'm gonna kill him."

"Don't say things you do not intend on following through with, Dragon," Cassius says with a laugh, staring at her with a grin.

"Yeah, well, after dropping my blood on this stone, I should at least get a free shot on Adonis."

"He would most decidedly allow that if it meant making amends for his actions," Cassius remarks as a joke.

"We need to get into position," I say, drawing their attention. "We don't have long before Delphi okkars here."

Ari nods, taking my hand and following me back to our position in the woods. "You know what to do, right, Cas?"

His expression shifts smoothly, diminishing from a hardened expression of anticipated hatred against what's to come, into charm. "I ought to think you'd have more faith in me."

The three of us walk together, Cassius remaining positioned in the middle of the field, perfectly equidistant between the barn, the house, and the trees in the forest. Prior to today, the edges surrounding the land that the proprietors own had been warded. I glance around, assessing each stationed position, where each commander focuses towards a common focal point.

Ari and I return to my previous spot with a straight view of the middle, shielding ourselves with a barrier to keep our army from being seen once Delphi arrives.

Nothing is spoken for several minutes. Soldiers behind me squat, sounds coming from their armor and weapons, ranging in different materials from metal, to leather, to magik-incorporated armor made from leaves or other nature.

I hear the troubled breath of Ari, but she says nothing to explain what is running through her mind. Instead, she chortles.

My hand stacks itself over hers, eyes watching the sides of her face harden in her focus. She turns to face me fully, but as her mouth opens to speak, her eyes drift back to Cassius, and ice forms in her eyes.

"I assumed my exchange would be with Ara, but all the better that she sent the Fae king who can't lie," Delphi says. She stands near the entrance of the barn, directly next to the bells hung onto its exterior walls.

Others behind me are crouched down, hidden behind tall shrubs but not so far that they cannot move at a moment's notice. Adonis is two trees away, side pressed to the trunk and his hand openly aimed towards Cassius to project his powers onto him.

Cassius, with his back turned to us, holds a hand behind him, palm flat and keeping us held in place. "Shall I remind you that I have purpose being here as High King?"

"Might *I* remind *you* the last time the two of us made a deal, you tricked me?"

"You had my queen. Had you not been so dull in our exchange, I would have enjoyed it more."

Delphi does her best not to show it, but her pride is wounded.

"You know, Arabella *swore* you were coming to save her. But you never did." She laughs, shoulders rising and falling with each breath. "Or, at least, you took too long to. And little by little, I destroyed any spark she had, until she was nothing more than the useless, obsessive girl that she really is."

Ari lets go of my hand. A cold sweat gathers on my forehead. I believe my breathing to have lost its cycle.

There is a stretching pause between the two in the field as I fight the compelling logic to kill Delphi where she stands. For over a year, I had many confrontations with Delphi, who made Ari feel nothing more than doubtful of herself through passive aggression. I had to sit idly by and watch as my girlfriend inwardly spiraled out of fear of becoming excessive in her need for reassurance. Now I have to watch again, hidden until Cassius signals to attack. It drives impatience from me, and with what Delphi is saying, as I see Ari stiffen at her words, I do not want to kill anyone more.

Delphi whisks her hand, and from behind her, a throng of creatures appears behind the barn and to its sides.

To what I can see, there stands a group of over twenty Magiks, a handful of Fae, creatures that must have come from Gigantia, and animals.

Heads around me begin whipping at each other.

It makes no sense why she would go through all this trouble for a section of land. No. She's come to overtake Ifaeris as a whole.

For months, she must have been steps ahead of us. She never disappeared, never stopped planning her revenge. Instead, she was building an army for herself. This is something that we had expected, but not to this extent.

"I had to be sure you wouldn't try killing me," Delphi says with a calculated smile.

Cassius' hand is steady. Shadows begin creeping their way from his hand and forming into a silhouette at his side. "If you've come to pick a battle with me alone, you have chosen incorrectly. For you see, my queen is the fighter, the anger, the warrior between us. But perhaps you already knew that. I am forever in my queen's debt for the sacrifices she has made for the Fae. While I am well-versed with my tongue, she has a talent for manipulating predicaments in her favor. And if that happens to fall poorly, she takes it by force. I, on the other hand, preen myself on my ability to create a diversion."

A pause. She scans her surroundings by turning in all directions. "What do yo–"

Cassius closes his fist, and our soldiers charge from their respective stations.

With quick response, Delphi's army moves forward, Magiks using their abilities while covered in armor made from what I suspect is iron.

Harpies are clawing their talons into the eyes of Magiks. Blinds them until they have no ability to direct their powers. Other winged animals drop larger stones from their talons.

Too many Magiks that are fighting, both on our side and Delphi's, are untrained in combat. While we have the army of Ifaeris, Delphi has creatures of Gigantia, who are difficult to kill.

I magik earth to shoot from the ground, impaling the body of a Giant who nears a Changeling.

I can sense it.

Delphi's magik is beginning to work against our protection of the Fae.

My friends are scattered, armed with weapons and protected by armor.

A sorcerer approaches me. One I was raised around. He takes a whip from his side. Unravels it and sends it in my direction. The sound is violent but echoes in consistency with everything around us.

He misses. Tries again but is blocked by a protective shield I put up against him.

From my cuirass, I take the two knives, throwing one at him. It strikes directly into his shoulder, though affecting him little. He rips it out, casting it to the side and running headfirst in my direction with a vindictive smile.

With his energy focused on his running, I dodge aside, taking the whip from his hand and quickly wrapping it around his legs. I drag the sorcerer back to me as he claws his hands into the dirt. Step on his back until I wrap the cord tightly around his neck.

He struggles, kicking his feet until I am thrown off balance. He flips up, running away, but I'm quicker. While he regains his breath and raises his hands to hex me, I am already throwing a tomahawk between his two eyes.

Ari's gone off on her own in all this. If she's around any of the guards, around the Aeon twins, or our friends, they'd look out for her. I trust that enough to know they wouldn't let her die. The thought still overtakes me as I stab a Fae.

Armor is clashing.

Feet and hooves are trampling.

I run, chasing behind a shorter witch that aims her magik against Evie, who stays hidden in the house and watches from the window. She has no experience fighting. She is not violent, but stays to protect from the side with weapons mixed alongside potions that act as lethal death when thrown onto another.

The witch goes after her, and I raise her with my magik, levitating her high above the ground before slamming her down. She goes deep into the terrain. So much so that I see the bones of a buried animal. The woman doesn't see me as she tries to climb out. I don't know how she did not die, but that doesn't matter. I lift her again, flinging her into trees that split her body in half.

From the window, I see Evie frozen from watching this all.

Without bothering to check on her, I take off towards the battle and can see nothing but other Fae that are working hard to fight against Magiks, who have an advantage far ahead of them.

Numbness paralyzes me to the ground.

A sorcerer standing at the side of Korine is laughing. The Fae hails jagged rocks from the earth. Knocks me from the back of my head.

"Where's your witch now?" Korine taunts.

I use a rock near me, summon and magik it into a restraint so quickly, the sorcerer doesn't realize until my foot sweeps under him, and he is unmoving.

By the time I'm on my feet, Korine is already out of my sight, abandoning us both.

Constraining him, I bend his body so far back that bones break through his skin. Delphi is more thoughtless than I already assumed her to be for not shielding the Magiks with better armor.

From my side, as I run off, I see Atticus fighting against one of the smaller Giants that has skin nearing a dusty orange.

The Fae wears a gauntlet on both his arms. On it, are three blades. Two curved, with the flat sections facing above and below, the middle blade rising the highest and curving down the same way as a scorpion's tail.

He lunges forward, swinging from the side. It misses. He tries again with the other arm, this one directly going into the Giant's lower abdomen and bringing him down. His enhanced strength lifts the Giant from his ankle, swinging him around and throwing him into an Ogre.

"Behind you!" Atticus yells.

As I turn, a Boggart is raising his weapon to my head.

The creature, though bigger than what they are known to grow to, is still much smaller than me. His eyes are golden, and details of his back are that of a porcupine. The long sword, with extra accessories protruding from its regular blade, swings high, slicing down. But it hits nothing except empty space. He tries again, this time cutting my leg. Just as I lose focus, dropping my stance too low, he plunges the sword through my chest.

The stab should have killed me. Gone right through my body and produced an entry and exit wound.

But it doesn't.

I am perfectly well.

Adonis' Elemental abilities.

The Boggart stands there in confusion, thrusting his weapon in and out of me one more time, but by the time he pulls it through, I loosen his grip, crushing his wrist with magik until he can't hold anything up.

Then he runs.

I hunt the creature, chasing him to the entry of the woods and magiking his organs to burst through his torso, closely resembling nothing more than thin noodles. His drool comes down from the side of his mouth, blood still gurgling inside.

Jumping from beside me, Monty quickly slashes through the throats of two others who side with Delphi.

He stabs a sword right through one's mouth.

An acute pain hits the back of my thigh. It stings with the pain of something sharp, though no creature I can see is close enough to me to hit with this consistency.

A Powrie, the height of my stomach, slashes from all directions. In the distance are five others his size, killing a blond sorcerer that Amber had recruited to our side and wetting their caps with his blood.

From a fallen Fae on the ground, I take his sword, stabbing it through the Powrie. I feel no pity for the creature. Feel little moral guilt for killing any of these creatures that fight against us.

"Luka!" I hear a voice cry. It's Ari, but I can't see her on the ground. I'm rushing to find her, following the direction of her voice.

When I spot her, she is on a horse. The hooves and eyes flame with a fire of neon green, while its tail and mane are a collection of leaves. She grips it tighter as she rises high enough to use her magik, flinging back a group of Delphi's soldiers that surrounds a single Pixie.

The collective is thrown behind me, and at the sound of armor hitting the ground, I realize she has saved me from the Fae sneaking behind with weapons in hand.

I don't know if the gods are real or where souls come from, but she and I are forever tied across all planes of existence.

Five creatures are nearing her. I sprint, running until the handled sickles from my side are unsheathed, and I'm stabbing them through the exact arteries that kill a person. My movements are precise, using a combination of tactical movements and slashing through them with enough power that it cuts deep. One by one, they all go down, whereas I pivot my every movement, taking them on with ease.

Ari stares, mouth agape, with a face of shock. "I- Thank you."

"No need to thank me, love."

Screeches from above draw my attention from her face, and as I turn back, she's charging towards another enemy.

Xavier is mounted, legs tightly gripped on both sides of a griffin's body, scattering down powder with a gloved hand. It draws creatures who fight for Delphi together, and when they're bunched closely enough, he sets land below him ablaze. Some catch on fire, trying to put themselves out and becoming too distracted to fight us.

"General!" Xavier warns, signaling with his arm slamming down through the air.

"Red Drop!" General Callian yells to our army.

Those on our side move away, distance evident enough to warrant suspicion.

A blasting sound of a bomb shakes the land. When I steady myself to assess where it comes from, I see a section of land completely annihilated, along with nearly all of the house.

Bodies scatter. Dead or dragging themselves away from the damage.

A creature with lethal intent comes for me. I could have mistaken her for a witch if I hadn't seen the sharpness of her ears poking through her hair. Her sword is sharp, with other miniature, curved blades along its main one.

She grazes my skin. Moves fast enough to cut the back of my forearm. Her combat skills are impressive, though her agility is superior to her form.

I drop her to her knees with my foot, fracturing her ankle and sabotaging her attacks. Before I'm able to take the sword from her, she sinks her teeth into the same area she had cut me.

It burns, though it does not seem fatal. There must be some form of venom in her bite. My blood is coloring to a shade of purple.

The Fae smiles, clearly satisfied with herself, which leads me behind her. I snap her neck so swiftly that it feels no different from cracking my fingers.

As I turn, I am faced with a brunet sorcerer turning around from his victim. When I see his eyes, the bright shade of emerald, I realize who it is. My cousin–the same whose party introduced me to Delphi–is ripping a knife from a Fae.

He goes still for five seconds, blade still in hand, before he comes towards me. His hands raise to his chest, moving aside all bodies in his path. I'm in such shock that I hardly realize he is fighting alongside Delphi.

Others rush past him, sprinting at me with weapons, but it is no match. I freeze their blood cells, slowing down their movements until they drop to the floor in death. My focus is so pinpointed that I don't notice Harrison until he shoots an iced spike at an animal charging at me.

"As I live and breathe. So you *are* alive," my cousin says, magiking vines from a tree to tie me against it.

Both miss, and, in counter, I send them towards my cousin that comes closer. "You've really decided to align yourself with Delphi, James?"

I target his head, but my magik is blocked by something.

By Delphi protecting him.

His fist, with knuckles covered in brass spikes, sends a punch in my direction. It lands, scraping along my armor but doing no significant damage. Then, he drags the brass to the side of my head, creating a gash that digs into me before puncturing through my lip.

I wrestle with him. Push him off of me.

My cousin is just as agile on his feet as I am. His father trained him just as hard as mine. He summons a sword from the inside of a dead Fae's body to himself before I can. Perforating it through the side of the hardened armor that covers my body, shallowly cutting me many times in several places. James has always been better at his skills than I in terms of handheld weapons.

He uses his magik to take me down. I take my sickles, hold them firmly in my hand, and slice through his side when he superciliously drags me closer to show off his power over me.

The time it takes him to recover is just enough for me to regain a proper stance.

"You and your father assume yourselves so much better than us," he says. "Well, we'll see who was better trained." Again, James brings his sword down.

I duck, dropping the weapons I have and taking a step back to trap his wrist against my chest, using my upper arm to split the bones of his locked arm. Then, I summon a spear to me, using the wooden heel to knock the head of a creature approaching.

Two others begin surrounding me. Spinning the spear, I stab the point through the face of a Fae and whack the shaft into a witch until she is on the ground.

Blood, grunts, and heaved breaths cage around me. I'm elbowing. Punching. Stabbing into multiple beings at once while using every part of the weapon to my advantage.

My magik won't help. No target is in my view long enough to kill them. I have to rely solely on my combat abilities.

Chains from a broken flail cut off my airflow. But whoever is pulling on it isn't strong enough to kill me. I move, take the dagger from my side, and stab it into the creature against my back.

It all happens so fast that it takes prying the knife from near my cousin's shoulder to realize that he's dead. Sometime in this fight, I killed him. His face is bloody. Beaten in.

And with the blood on my fists, he died from my bare hands.

XXXVII

Round Two: Fight

Arabella

The area has become less a battlefield and more a hunting ground. I can't even think about how many creatures I've killed or how none of them were Delphi. There's so much blood on me that I don't think scrubbing for a week straight would get it off. I feel disgusting. I'm completely out of breath, and my legs feel like a combination of jelly and cuts.

A familiar Cyclops is crushing Fatima in her hand. I'm running. Racing to save the Lady of Hearthis inside the largeness of Ramina's hand.

I'm not entirely delusional. I know I'm not as strong as her. I have to work to my strengths.

My fire tries to leave my fingertips, blue flames shooting to the feet of the Cyclops, but it's still weaker than before. My hands warp in a circle, using my magik to force her legs to stick together. It falters her, but only barely. She starts to fall but uses a tree to stabilize her.

Then she spots me. Her attention goes to my face, and in one flick, my body flies into the air and onto the ground. I don't get up on my own. In less than two seconds, I'm dangling by one arm and being held by Ramina's hand. With my arm being the only thing to support the rest of my weight, it feels like my bones are being ripped apart from their ligaments all over again.

It doesn't last too long. It's replaced by something far more terrifying. I'm tossed into the air and grabbed by the same hand.

Stuck, I lay flat to conserve as much space as I can.

I try to think, but the panic in my breath pushes me into accepting my death. I feel the sweat dripping down to every crevice of my body, so with all the energy I can muster, I press my hands into the Cyclops' palm and blast a hex straight through for an opening.

A thunderous roar, loud enough to shake the land, echoes through. Ramina releases Fatima, holding her wrist with the uninjured hand, widening her eyes at the hole.

"You okay?" I shout, reaching an arm down to the Elemental–her height much shorter than mine but still much bigger than a Brownie's.

She nods her head. Her hand reaches to mine, and she's back on her feet as we stare at the flailing Cyclops. "Can you use your magik to help amplify my Elemental powers?"

"I don't think it works like that." I raise my hands, fire already shooting at Ramina, and an idea pops into my mind. If we try what she asks, it would drain my energy completely. "But our powers combined might work."

Fatima turns her head in the same direction as my weakened flames. From what I can see from my peripheral, she's focused on the Cyclops.

Ramina's body cooks, feet charred and crashing into the back section of the barn. My flames are consuming her skin that's already popped from blisters. And as Ramina dies, her eyes are still open.

Jiya and Harrison are fighting off a witch. The Lady of

Windwyrd strikes lightning at the woman, the witch falling to the ground before Harrison freezes the air into spikes and sends them down, plunging right into her head.

A Banshee with pale, white skin is running in my direction. Her screams are so daunting that I'm thrown off. My head throbs, and by the time I refocus, she's at my throat.

My hand immediately reaches for my dagger, but she's too fast. She breaks apart the straps behind me, and my body is armorless. My chest plate has completely fallen to the ground.

I bend, chop, and block, but ultimately, my magik is the only thing defending me from the creature's speed.

I'm not fast enough. I can fight, but not well enough in comparison to our army. Months of training with Kabir pale when fighting against creatures who have lived longer than I have. Let alone when I fight another Magik, the skills I've developed aren't that important at all.

The Banshee is vicious. I thought that they were meant to be more frail in combat, but her speed clearly makes up for her deficiency in strength. She jumps everywhere, knocking me off my feet.

A trident that glows with the color of rusted bronze is pointed directly at my chest. It presses into me while she keeps her foot on my left hand, the other between my legs. Then, she spits on the ground, some saliva hitting the top of my head.

I physically writhe my head in disgust.

Gods, I hate spit.

Reaching towards the top of my boots, my fingers just barely graze the handle of my attached dagger. I bend, stretching my legs into a splits position.

And after another reaching attempt, I have a firm enough grasp on my weapon to wrap my legs around the Banshee's right and stab her calf. As she screams, lifting her foot off my wrist and dropping her weapon, I kick her down.

I push myself up, running far enough so that her weapon can't be launched through me. It only takes her seven seconds to remove the knife and stumble towards me.

My feet dig into the ground, and I direct all that I can into my magik to levitate the creature into the air. She shouts, throws sharp weapons from her side at me, but starts choking when my hands draw closer to each other.

The sight of a tool catches my attention. I keep the Banshee held in the air with one hand and turn the machine on with the other.

I manage to catch a glimmer of horror in her colorless eyes. Not that it matters.

In a swift motion, I throw her. My arms push against the air, and I fling her straight towards the table with multiple blade saws that slice through her.

Behind me, as I turn towards the bloodshed, Gavin has the hair of someone in his hands while he ruthlessly bashes their head against the rock stiff into the ground.

I can see the skull.

Bodies are dropping. Caws from winged creatures screech as they're brought down. I have to duck from too many weapons to harvest enough focus. This battle, there's not nearly as much said between me and those I fight, though it might be due to more of Delphi's followers being better trained than the common fae who sided with Adonis.

And when I turn my head another way, Evie's running from some Fae that looks more like a demonic nightmare than anything. The creature slightly reminds me of what my dad called a Manananggal in order to scare me into sleeping when growing up.

They have wings of a bat with half the body removed, their

intestines hanging as they fly, with long, black hair, messy as a rat's nest, and skin of a decomposing corpse. The only distinct reason I can tell it's a Fae is by their sharp, long ears. But it shouldn't take this form. Not in daylight.

Evie runs, and though I use my magik to hold it still, another sorcerer I notice, who is too far from me, is countering my attack.

I keep my eyes on him and redirect the curse, but by the time I turn back, the Fae has Evie in the air.

I'm sprinting as fast as my feet can take me, pushing past others in battle. I duck under a woman. Flip her from her ankles and pin her onto her back. My hand chokes her from her neck, and as I stand, both hands raise. I use my magik, tearing her body in two.

But I still hear Evie's screams. I watch in horror as one of my best friends has her body slashed into.

"EVIE!" I scream.

The Fae with a narrow, tubular-shaped tongue begins feeding from her body.

My friend, who always knew what to say when I was upset. My friend, who was the first to update me on my ex-friends' whereabouts to keep me from seeing them. My friend, who was the first to confront Grant to his face before we broke up. Dead. I'm heartbroken. Motivated with nothing but the determination to kill.

As if not viewing me as a threat, the Fae looks at me and begins taking off, searching for their next victim. I shoot my fire over and over, but I keep missing. My brain isn't working. Intentions in my mind are too hectic to focus well enough on bringing the creature down.

Keeping my eyes set on the Fae, I follow the direction it flies in. Ahead of me is Theodosia running back behind the barn. Towards the rushing rivers.

She sprints away from the Fae that continues after her. No one is helping her. No one is coming from behind me to save her. She isn't even trained for a battle like this.

So I go towards her. I make a pathway through the barn, taking the trident that still lies on the ground. As I climb up the pile of fallen wood through an opening, I magik the Fae down to the ground.

Theodosia's fallen into the river that violently pulls her downstream. I don't have enough time to kill the Fae the way they deserve. Instead, I rip the wings off with magik. And as they howl in pain, I stab the trident right into where the wings detached.

There's no time to spare. I send my magik to the leaves from a nearby tree, extending them into vines and limbs. It's an estimate that should reach her by the time she's pushed by the current.

Vines wrap securely around her. She pulls on them, climbing up to the land.

"Much appreciated," she says as I approach her. Fear is still lingering on her face. The eye that is the color of mossy waters is tearing up much faster than the one that's the color of hazel.

My breath still hasn't caught up to everything I've done. I think I might pass out. I'm starting to see stars.

"Get somewhere safe," I tell her.

I start towards the barn, where a figure I can just barely see is standing at the entrance. My heart starts beating extremely fast, and I can't even tell why.

"I didn't think Kaileigh liked you enough to give a letter on your behalf," Delphi says with arms crossed.

Her hair's been cut below her shoulders, highlighting her sunken cheekbones. She looks like she's been watching this all from the side, just like she must have been in Hearthis. It seems ludicrous to be conversing with her so calmly like we aren't in the middle of a battle. Like the two of us are both going to make it out of this.

My body tenses up. Suddenly, all my injuries feel like nothing. "You can thank Chrissy giving us the stone for that."

Neither of us have made the first move against the other. I don't think I've breathed much either.

Nobody is around. Everyone is on the field fighting. This is strictly between the two of us.

Delphi, only for half of a second, looks like I said something confusing. She takes one step closer to me. "Chrissy's dead."

"Did you actually think it was a suicide?"

It doesn't take long for her to process. Her eyes narrow, head turning away briefly. It's probably more genuine emotion than she ever actually felt towards me. Her hands summon flames–*my flames*–sending them towards me. I'm barely able to jump aside without it cinching part of my shirt.

"You seem tougher than the last time I saw you. Are you over everything? Completely?"

Nothing comes out. I feel like I physically can't say anything as my stomach twists, with my tongue pressing hard against the roof of my mouth. This must feel similar to what the Fae experience when they try to lie.

Her hand rises again, trying to hex me, which fails against my shield. She tries again, summoning a sword directly towards me. But I use magik to lodge it into fallen wood. I roll down, sending my weaponed necklace around her ankles as I move. The iron doesn't completely subdue her. She isn't a Fae. A small incision into her won't do much.

We go back and forth, sending curses and hexes at each other and countering simultaneously. We've both learned so much restricted magik that our knowledge relatively matches the other. She can't fight physically. Magik is her best chance.

I summon the blades from the saws through the Banshee's body and shoot them towards Delphi, which she breaks in half. They're sent behind her, likely killing–or at least hitting–others.

Then, a plank from behind me slams into my back, and I'm on the ground with my face hitting dirt.

Lack of armor and weapons leave me vulnerable. Even worse, Delphi's magik keeps me stuck to the flooring.

I'm scared, actually terrified, that Delphi will be the one to kill me. If it had been by another creature, I would have accepted that more amicably.

Anyone but her.

My arms are outstretched in front of me, torso unable to lift up. All I can do is move my head. I can see Delphi's shoes as she comes near.

"I told you no one was coming to save you," she says, laughing at the words she repeated constantly when she tortured me.

Something inside me snaps, severing me completely from who I was a year ago.

I close my eyes, and with extreme concentration, I use magik to summon my dagger's blade through my hand. I scream. Cursing while Delphi looks to see what I've done. My voice is giving out from the unending pain. She remains in place, bafflement dropping the magik that binds me long enough to crawl to her and smear my blood on her arm as I pull myself up.

Overconfidence has always been her biggest weakness.

Dislodging my weapon from my hand, I drop it to the ground, using magik to close the wound.

My hands shoot magik towards the chains hung from opposite sides of the ceiling. They wrap around Delphi's arms and raise her. I keep them tight with one hand, magiking two others to attach themselves to the ground and wrap around Delphi's ankles.

I bend to grab my blade. Delphi, eyes flooding to the singular color of scarlet, begins chanting something at a murmuring level.

Dark red specks of sparkle leave her body, but she still can't escape. My blood is on her. I lower my hand, Delphi coming down with it.

Then I stab her. Slicing over and over again in every place she had done to me. I've completely blacked out, unable to force myself to stop. But when I come to, I'm not sure if she's dead or alive.

Delphi is completely spread like a starfish. She's bleeding onto the ground, and I can't help but feel a bit of satisfaction after everything she did to me.

From a chair in the barn, I magik off a wooden leg and hover it over my torturer. Her face holds strong in its hatred.

I drag my hand down, and the stake, pointed at its tip, shoots down Delphi's head. I don't stop until it exits in a new direction from her back.

When the murder weapon returns to my hand, there are bits of her broken-off spine connected to the wood. I flinch at the brutality of it all. That I'm able to do that to my once closest friend.

Confliction as to why it feels weird to kill her tumbles in my mind. I once loved her so much, and until I figured out I was just another option to her, I thought she loved me. I thought that after everything she said about us being meant to be in each other's lives, she'd choose me over our ex-friends.

Shock hits me.

The stake drops from my hand, along with my magik and Delphi's body. She's completely lifeless. Death rings all around.

I rip my dagger from her body, sheathing it to my side. One hobbled step outside the barn, and something plunges through me.

Earth, sharp and formed like stalagmite, has gone straight through my back and out the front of my body. My eyes widen from the actualization. As I turn my head, Korine is standing about fifty feet away, shoulders caving in and out multiple times while smiling wider than Delphi had when she tortured me.

My sight is blurry. Flashes of images tunnel in and out as I blink. The only thing I can register are figures running towards me as I feel the rock extract from my body.

I hear my name, but I can't see anything. My back feels too heavy to hold up.

The next thing I can comprehend is that I'm on the ground. My eyes are closed, but Luka's here somehow. His voice sounds muffled with my head held in his arms. I'm whimpering. I can't breathe without a squeeze seizing my lungs.

"It's okay, love. I've got you."

A gust of wind breezes past me. I'm not breathing anymore. Everything's dark. I can hear Luka's yawp of excruciating agony as he tries to use magik to take away my pain for himself. I can feel my heartbeat slowing in my chest like a malfunctioned time bomb beginning to deteriorate.

Then suddenly, there is nothing at all.

XXXVIII

Ritualistic Prayers

Cassius

Arabella is dead.

Her unmoving body hangs in my arms, confirming this truth in the worst manner possible. I wish to rage and scream, but all I find myself able to do is hold her close with every emotion bottling inside.

Outside, the sun does not shine. It has been covered by stormy snow clouds.

"Esme! Celeste! Maude!" I shout.

My sisters sprint down the stairs, gasping or cursing upon viewing Arabella.

"The throne room," I say. The color in her face is draining, and my stomach is churning, with a heartbeat that races similarly to hands speeding their clapping during a song after its bridge. "We must perform the ritual."

My arms carry Arabella through the doors of the throne room, persevering through anguish and exhaustion up the stairs and behind our thrones. Her clothing is stained with blood, most of which I have no idea belongs to her or another.

We were meant to have a lifetime of arguments and sweet whispers passed in the dark. I was to play the pestering role as she and Luka laughed in the dead of night. At least, that is what I have convinced myself life would be. Nothing could have prepared me for the gut-wrenching feeling that cultivates.

Without my notice, my family, the Wands friend group, and nearly every other person the queen holds close surround me.

I had been a fool during the final moments of battle. Too occupied in distraction when catching the finale of Arabella's murder of Delphi. Wearing an enamored smile in amusement, only to witness Arabella die by the Elemental ability of the Fae I once thought I would spend the infinite of our lives with.

"You cannot be sure this will work," Helena says. Her hand presses to Arabella's forehead.

"I don't care. *We will not lose her.*" My voice has become worn. I can hardly breathe. Especially not when terror has engrossed my very being.

Terror that I am too late. Fear that the lifeless body in my arms will never come back.

I need her. I need her more than the air I breathe.

"Sure what will work? What aren't any of you telling me?" Luka jostles through the crowd that is my family gathered, speaking in a strained, scratchy voice I would not recognize as his.

"The Spiritus ritual," Esme says. A ritual named after the first of our bloodline, who had died and been resurrected by his children a century prior to the war against Magiks. "We're going to try bringing Arabella back to life."

His face hardens as I set Arabella down behind our thrones and onto the made of branches twined together by golden leaves. Though her hair is still braided in two, strands fall loose. I run my finger across her soft lips, tracing the tips along her cheeks covered in blood.

"You're going to do what Delphi did to Luka?" Damien hisses. Anger is riddled in his tone.

Luka shoves away the hands of any who attempt to comfort him. His eyes are bloodshot, face dry from tears.

"There lies no time in explaining this," I respond with a tone grave. An answer can be given at a later time. The ritual must be performed in haste. "You ought to leave anon if you value your life."

"I'm not leaving her," Luka argues. He has been furious with me since I had taken Arabella from his arms.

Grief overtakes me. It is tearing every fragment of my essence from me. Had Arabella not already killed Delphi, I would have had Luka use restricted magik and curse Delphi to bring her to the brink of death, only to have her relive it again each day. If it was something she thought fair enough to treat Arabella with similarly, surely she would deserve such a treatment.

The Aeon twins begin dragging Luka out as he thrashes against them, the three ungraceful. His wrath is of little significance. I would want him here, but if he wishes to live, to have any chance of seeing Arabella alive once more, he must be out of this room.

Xavier, plagued with the wounds and fatigue of battle, shoves Luka aside. "I'm not thrilled about leaving Reaps either, but the ritual sucks the life from anyone not of the Spiritus bloodline if they're in the same room. You can't risk your life for this outcome."

They are the last to leave with a guard, whom I cannot think to recognize the face of, shutting the doors.

"Cassius," Cel calls. They face me with an expression of glumness. "There aren't enough of us."

Since the age of ten, each of us has been taught the history of our ancestors. With the correct amount of us, there is a possibility of resurrecting someone from the dead, but only if it is done within nine minutes of their final breath. Six members of our bloodline are required to complete this ritual. There is no incantation, no words past a vow to summon the spirits and grant us what we ask. We must all join hands, allowing the spirits to drain us of much of our energy.

Even then, it is not guaranteed that the deceased will live.

Adonis comes forward without steadiness, stepping closer to Arabella's body, which I, in no right mind, would ever allow him to do. I had assumed he departed with the others. "I will be the sixth of our blood to revive the queen."

"You do not care for her," I say sharply. "We may have six of the Spiritus bloodline, but all six must care for her."

"She saved me when she had every reason not to. She allowed for me to live in this palace as her guest instead of having me thrown into Phantom Tower. Of course I care for her."

His defiance, though irritating, proves in good faith when I need him most.

My eyes move to the side, peering at our other siblings post my brother's words. "There is still the matter of who is to damn themself in the afterlife."

Hesitation pulsates through all my siblings. Our trade comes at a heavy cost, with burdens and debts owed. One of us must sacrifice our time after crossing the veil.

Before I can volunteer myself, Adonis clears his throat. "It ought to be me."

"No," I snippily respond.

"Cassius–"

"You may help in the ritual, but I refuse to argue with you on this matter."

"I owe her more than whatever awaits me in my death."

A disgruntled huff airs from my nose as I open the circle, allowing for him to join us. "Very well."

"What am I to do?" he asks.

"You have to promise two and a half earthly years. Take Cassius' hand and focus on Arabella's energy. Seek if you can find her spirit, and if you can't, ask that her ancestors search for her." Esme explains this all in a hurry. Her hand grips Cel's, and she takes a deep breath.

Quickly, rather than granting my brother the chance to get the words out, I say, "I vow to any spirits who guide Arabella that I will give two years and six months of my afterlife to serving you."

What has been promised cannot be refuted, and Adonis knows that. When a vow is said, it cannot be unmade unless the other side frees me from the bargain. Though my brother glares, he begrudgingly halts from a response, taking my hand in his.

Atticus looks at me strangely, one hand held in Esme's, the other bare. "What about his other hand? He has none."

"Then grab his shoulder!" Maude snaps.

He turns his head, doing what our sister commands and clamping his hand on Adonis' shoulder tightly.

Our circle, though imperfect, is fully formed around Arabella. I focus on connecting with her, tethering my energy to find her heartbeat as my eyes fall into blackness.

Light is nonexistent where I am, and nothing pulls me in one direction or another. Each breath I take is heavy, choking me with sickening aches of the forgotten souls who have become the dense air of this realm.

"I can't feel anything," Cel says.

Time is running its course. With none of us finding ourselves in luck, I begin panicking more than I already am. We should have longer. Time has most certainly not passed enough for the ritual to render ineffective.

I may be losing myself in all of this.

I am losing her.

Eternal moments pass by. I roam through the empty void, not

once coming across my siblings. I call for her multiple times. My body begins shaking, and then, an unbearable heat touches my body.

The area around me turns blistering, and when I open my eyes, my family is gawking at Arabella. Flames of fire begin consuming her, excess flames jumping away before disappearing into the air. Her body has risen high above the table as her head hangs limp from everything else. Still, I cannot sense a heartbeat. No sign to indicate she is alive.

Even as I think to pull away from my siblings and summon my wings to reach her, I know I cannot without risking breaking the ritual altogether. Doing so may complete her demise.

"Cassius, *she'll only find you*!" Esme emphasizes.

"Live, Arabella." My eyes shut tightly. "Please live."

I pray to every god, every demon, anything that will listen. Hope that the spirits beyond the veil will aid in seeking her soul. I do not care if she hates me, if she would strike me down the second she is brought back and wants nothing to do with me. I just ask that she come back.

She deserves to live.

Arabella's name repeatedly leaves my mouth as I search for her. A sting scrapes down my throat in rounds, with sharp edges slicing through my vocal cords.

"Cas?" Her whispered voice hits my ears as if she is but an embrace away, yet there is also a resonance that sounds similar to echoes in a tunnel, keeping me from something I will never reach.

As I open my eyes, the queen's clothing has been shred through and frayed from fire. She's returned to the table, and our circle has broken. My siblings have dropped to the floor, unconscious. Through all my attempts to contact spirits, I hadn't noticed when Adonis and Cel let go.

From below, roots from the earth shoot through the marble.

They engulf the High Queen into a hollow case, as if she is being preserved.

A burial for the dead.

It startles my bloodline awake and to their feet. Powerless against the lands, we can only watch in awe as she is overtaken by the life of the earth.

Another sound cracks through the room. The flooring from where our thrones sit splits open, and more roots push through, this time with vines. They begin intertwining into the royal chairs, forming the thrones with an added design.

Such power from the lands has not occurred since the first Elementals had come into rulership.

It accepts her. The lands do not reject her ruling, though I think it is perhaps something more. Arabella should not have combusted into flames. The fire should not have turned the colors that match identical to hers if the ritual were reviving an ordinary creature.

Every instance of her using magik in the past managed quite well, save okkaring and her fire abilities. Okkaring can be a difficult skill to perfect if not taught well, but fire should have been just as controllable as the rest of her magik. Her ability to grasp it resembles too closely to external powers of other Elementals.

I laugh as I break energy contact with my siblings. This is far too funny that I never realized the absurdity. She is adopted. Her fire cannot be controlled when her emotional state is unbalanced. Everything begins to make complete sense.

Arabella has the blood of an Elemental.

By all accounts of our history, she would have been my most hated enemy. Her kind is the cause of the decimation of the Fae. Arabella was never meant to be someone in which I love, yet I know nothing else of importance without her. Now that I know she is of two worlds, she is gone, and I remain stagnant in my own wry mirth.

I suppose the very nature of her coming into my life had been an omen in and of itself.

Sensing my epiphany, Cel stares in perplexity while I am laughing so hard that my hand holds onto the wood. "What could you have possibly realized that would cause you to react in such a way?"

"Arabella..." Esme trails off. Her eyes shift from side to side, then return to me as I collect myself together. She has pieced together the information and come to the same conclusion that I have.

Adonis peeks his head up, searching through the room as if he is the only among us who has not grasped the information. "I too am confused."

"She is a Fae, isn't she?" Maude guesses.

With the nodding of my head, Cel goes slack-jawed. "Spirits."

The room is full of nothing more than blinks and wide gazes. I have never wanted my family to say something to ease my mind from its track more. Somehow, I think it would stall my acceptance on the matter.

"We have no idea how long this will take," Esme reminds me after long-standing silence.

It ought not to *need* time at all. Arabella should be alive to tell her tale of her duel with Delphi, but instead, she has not moved. She has not once taken a breath since before I wrapped my arms under her and took her from Luka.

In the stillness, I swear I hear an exchange of air that came from none of my siblings in the room. Some may call it delusion, but I refuse to believe that something as minor as a wound through her body would kill her. Though, I realize I must face the truth that what I hear is dwindled optimism deluding itself. The lands proved this thoroughly when it entombed her into what she is to be buried in.

Atticus puts a hand on my shoulder, his skin and what he

wears covered in grime. "This ritual hasn't been done since the first from our bloodline had died. There's no telling if Arabella will be brought back immediately, or if she will at all."

The answer is not helpful. I understand nothing about what I am to do, nor how to proceed moving forward.

Luka bursts through the door. The ritual is over, and others step outside the room, leaving the two of us.

We stare at each other, both with emotions none other would understand. I grab him into an embrace, the two of us crying into each other's arms as we stand beside the casket that entombs the creature who fought to keep Ifaeris from total destruction.

Our responses are neither poised nor dignified. Words to express the despair both of us feel when looking down have disappeared.

Her heart bleeds for everyone but herself, and now it does not beat at all.

What is coping's purpose if not something to distract us from dealing with the pain at hand?

Wallowing in my sadness keeps me from doing anything of my duties. I am submerged in wine and whatever honeyed desserts we have to keep my mind in a place of happiness.

Under my blanket lies an empty bottle I am sure Arabella would berate me for keeping here. Isa and other healers stay with her in the throne room, tracking any progression or possibility of movement.

Thus far, there has been nothing of note. She has not stirred.

Denial rushes through me. The possibility remains that we had been successful in the ritual, but Arabella has denied returning to her body. This is one which I am too selfish of a bastard to accept. Though, if this becomes the result, I would still owe service to the spirits in my death. Alas, it would be for nothing.

She cannot remain dead.

Because I cannot live without her.

The moment I saw Luka holding Arabella's body, something expelled from me. Power that I never knew I was capable of surged through as I screamed, killing creatures both on our side and Delphi's. Never have my shadows done such a thing.

I wonder what thoughts she might have had at the sight.

She would perhaps stand there for half a moment with eyes widened and a mouth slightly parted. It would be one of the seldom moments I allow myself to feel earnestly smug around her.

There's a tapping at my door, but leaving my bed feels as if it would take far too much effort beyond what I have. Another knock. This time, I throw a chalice at the wood with the intention of deterring whomever is on the other side so that they may leave me to my seclusion.

Rather than granting my wishes, the door opens, and Luka walks through. He strolls in clothing I would equate to sleeping attire, though neither of us have done so. His face has become sunken, more so than mine. I cannot deceive him, nor will I attempt to. That is too tiresome when we both understand each other.

He stands, planted in my room and freshly bathed in our hours apart. Not simply that, but the unspoken between us says more than either of us would care to speak aloud. The two emotions I feel are anger and desolation, which, I suppose, are what Arabella had felt constantly. That serves as a reminder, which hurts me all the more without her presence here.

"How long are we going to wait for her to wake up before we're forced to..." he starts but does not finish. He cuts himself off, unable to get the words out.

"I believe that if, after ten days, there has been no pulse, that would require her burial," I answer reluctantly. Saying the words aloud drops my heart from my chest onto the brutal, unforgiving floor.

She should not have been taken from a life in which she had to constantly fight. The queen should not have to fight to live at all. She ought to spend it living in Ifaeris, though she may have spent the same amount of time in dangerous situations.

Then I think to the sorcerer standing near. If Luka can be brought back by magik, there must exist a spell which can extend his life to the length of ours.

His fingers dance around Arabella's hardcover books, which I have borrowed and kept on my desk after her recommending them. He grabs one, flips it to a page of random, and laughs–perhaps at her messy writing on the open space. It took a long while, but once I was able to decode what her words actually meant, I understood her more.

"Have you come to a decision on if you will stay with us?" I ask. Without Arabella here to keep Luka, he has no reason to continue his role. "Or have you forsworn your title as our seneschal?"

He closes the book, setting it down and taking a seat on my bed. "I will exist entirely on the outskirts if you dismiss me from Nexus, but residing in Ifaeris is a level of security away from the Council. They might search for me when eventually hearing of Delphi's death, and you need the help. That much is obvious to anyone in this palace. The warding may need occasional vetting, but the leaders will die soon enough."

Silence tarries between the two of us. Masks of false personas are put away. I'm unused to the strangeness of mourning. The last I had truly experienced it, I only felt a minuscule amount for my mother. Her death is not comparable to Arabella's. My mother never held care for me, lest it granted her a higher status.

Then, Luka manages out in a solid voice, "Should we begin

drafting a letter to the Council in relation to Delphi's murder against the Fae? We have enough witnesses to testify."

"It would be imprudent to make such a commotion immediately post battle. I think we would fare poorly if war ensues, considering over a quarter of our army is gravely wounded or dead."

"The Council will seek recompense regardless. We should speak with them before another narrative is given."

Advice from him is superior in logic when pitted against mine. I can offer no rebuttal, though it would wage well to assume that neither of us are in the right headspace to be making such gratuitous decisions. It would also be wise to have my court weigh in on the matter.

I haven't the skill set to lead a war if it is declared. But then, I was no murderer before Arabella.

There is unquestionably a consequence in our future for Delphi's death. While I hope that we have longer until the Magikal leaders bring the issue forward, I can only presume such matters will not be worked out without blood spilled.

"She's a Fae," he says. Not to me, but saying the words to fill the air.

"Yes, and what of it?" I wonder if he is possibly upset by this. Arabella shares creature blood from both our worlds. Though I know he holds no prejudice against the Fae, there are many different reasons his shock may be accumulated.

He sighs, eyes wandering around the room in search of something that is not there. "Nothing. I just want her to be happy when she hears this information."

"Well, with Delphi finally eradicated, there is hope yet."

Luka sets himself against my bed. He removes his shoes, sitting adjacent to me and pushing his back against the headboard with his head towards the ceiling. His need for a clearer mind is just as evident as would be mine.

Perhaps I could hire a jester or bard to create gaiety in a way that Arabella would during times such as these.

"With Delphi now dead, along with Korine and Grant, all three of our significant relationships have come to an end," Luka says, huffing in breathy laughter while shaking his head.

"And who, might I ask, is Grant?" I ask with a raised eyebrow.

Times, such as these, when we are able to speak as friends rather than argue as if we are opposing each other, have grown. The sorcerer seemed to like me more than Arabella these past months.

He pushes himself straighter, turning to me with a face expressionless. "I wouldn't expect you to know about him, but the one I killed in Gigantia was Ari's first boyfriend."

"The human?" I snort. I should keep my silence, but it's a bit funny as well. To imagine Arabella taking an ill-suited human as a lover is so implausible, I think that Luka is telling another lie.

He too laughs at the outrageousness of it all. He takes one look at me and laughs again, dropping his head. "Come to think of it, she *did* date a compressed, much uglier variation of you."

"Compressed?"

"He was shorter than Arabella."

In truth, I had not noticed the human as we raced out of the structure. I had been so focused on accounting for all our group, I never caught sight of his likeness. However, the sheer fact that Arabella once took a man shorter than her to bed causes me to laugh harder.

All at once, I am immediately reminded of the man Arabella once told me of. If this is the same mortal, I would very much like to strangle Luka with my shadows. The appalling claim alone brings offense to me. I take a deep breath. "I should resemble nothing of him."

"No, you don't," he replies, slightly amused. He makes no

apology for his humor that shrivels from dryness. "The only thing you two have in common is your similar hair."

"And here I thought Arabella said my humor was horrid."

Our ability to bond has become unlikely to all lately. This fact proves itself when a servant is at my door, shocked at the sight of the two of us. Hours must have gone by, the two of us having spoken more of our interests. Straightaway, the servant asks if I will be dining in my room alone or if Luka will be joining me, to which I send him off.

I should forget my worries, even for a reprieve with good company. But all the worse, I am plagued by Arabella.

Part 5
The
Aftermath

XXXIX

Death's Aftermath

Arabella

Time doesn't exist.

Everything's occurring simultaneously. I feel like I'm living a million lifetimes and experiencing every possible version of my life at once. At one point, I'm being pulled from my earliest childhood memories, the next, I'm here. It's not the same as when Delphi would make me relive my memories. I'm not inside my body living this, more like if I were watching this as an invisible bystander–the same as when she showed me Adonis' 'memory' or hers. Some memories aren't even from my lived experience. There are versions where I don't recognize anything, yet I know it's my life. I'm moving from portal to portal, into other lives I don't realize I'm going into until I arrive in that realm.

One version of me is living a completely mundane life. She's studying for finals in high school and listening to music. Posters hang on her bedroom wall, stress clear on her face, though she tries to ignore it. She has no magik.

Reaching for her bathroom door, I'm then taken to another

one of my lives where I perform for others. I have fame, and fortune, and live in the mansion I dreamt of owning since I was a kid. My awards are displayed on shelves, an attractive, feminine person sleeping next to me on the bed.

I take two steps closer to that version of myself before I'm inside a hospital room. There's a woman on the bed, with a large man holding her hand. The man has a lighter complexion and rounder eyes, with brows trimmed. His nose, while wider and more bulbous than mine, has the same button aspects, though mine is slimmer.

Magik comes from his palms to stabilize the mother, mitigating her pain. She's tanner than the man–Southeast Asian, clearly–my monolid eyes exact to hers, with facial features similar to my foster dad's. Her hair is thick, though perfectly straight. Brown like the trunk of a tree.

Golden specks slip out of her for a faint glimpse, and I catch the points of her ears before they're glamoured back round. Then, the gold disappears. Lights in the room are becoming brighter, with monitors no longer working. The man is using magik to keep the mother from doing something, and as the lights return to their normal brightness, it registers that she's an Elemental Fae with a sorcerer as the father of her child.

This all looks so recent. The technology in this room can't be more than a few decades old.

As the Fae delivers her child, it's a baby girl. She has round ears like her dad's, eyes like her mom's. The area becomes hotter as the baby cries. All in the room, other than the three, are human, hands unable to touch the child without drawing back with a hissing sound.

Quickly, the father takes the child, pacifying her with magik. He looks at her like she's his pride and joy, despite her being born seconds ago. The mother can't see me, but when she looks up, I recognize more and more of the similarities we share, and I realize that she's my mother.

These are my birth parents.

I want to run to them, but I can't. Something under me opens up. I'm falling until I land roughly on the ceramic flooring inside a coat room that I know to be Luka's family estate in New York.

If I'm dead, why can I still feel everything? I try to open the door, but it's locked. My younger self is arguing with Luka. They're repeating the same conversation we had the day that Damien forced us in here until we sorted out what we were to each other.

He thought it would be romantic for the two of us to be in an enclosed space.

Seeing how stubborn I was slaps me in the face. There were times that I unfairly treated Luka by putting him through similar cycles that Grant did with me. I tried so hard to avoid hurting him in that same way that I unintentionally ended up repeating it differently. Opposite reasonings, I know, but the reality check still sobers me.

"You need to tell me you want more, or I need the two of us to be over," Luka says.

Those words hurt me now as much as they did then. I knew by then I loved him, or at least I wanted to. I just didn't know how.

Before I can stay longer, I can feel my body being flung against the door and dragged back. As I flip forward, it's like I'm being sucked into the depths of the ocean. Instead of sea creatures surrounding me, there are reflective flashes. From the corner of my eye, I catch a peek of my twenty-first birthday, with Luka giving me the necklace I rarely take off. At the turn of my head, a view of my adoptive parents playing with me as a young child, my dad holding me high above his head while my mom laughs and tells him to put me down.

Head first, I'm diving to accept whatever next life I'm jumping into. Down, down I go until I land in the throne room. To the day I confessed to Cassius why having feelings for him was so complicated. When I was still putting aside my guilt from mourning Luka. At the time, I couldn't tell how Cassius looked at me, but when watching him from another perspective, he wasn't being sarcastic with his word choice. He looks at me with reverence and absolute adoration. Understanding body language can sometimes be easy to read, depending on the situation and how close I am to the person, but it will always be easier to dissect when I'm not living in the moment.

A tap from behind my shoulder turns me around. Five silhouettes are gathered together. They don't have faces or any distinct features. Rather, the beings are like opaque, holographic versions of Cassius' silhouette shadow.

"Am I dead?" I ask one of them.

One of their hands takes mine, guiding me from the throne room and through an empty void. The only things that light the space are the glow of the silhouettes. I can hear Cassius croakily shouting my name, but he's nowhere to be seen, nor is there any sound which indicates his footsteps.

"Cas?" I say.

"You have a choice, child," one says, though I'm not sure where from without a mouth.

I'm again pulled away as if there were an elastic rope yanking me up. A slow breath comes in and out of my nose, and when I open my eyes, I'm in the throne room again. Except this time, the Disaris family is there. Their hands are joined, my body hovering in the air.

This is the choice. I can choose whether to remain dead or return to my life. Honestly, with this peace after months of being tortured inside my head, I'm not even sure I *want* to return.

But I can feel Cassius' and Luka's energy projecting close to me.

I can see how everyone in this room's faces are squeezed tight and focused. And I *know* these are the people who I want a life with.

Heat consumes my skin. The guides are no longer there. It feels like Fatima's using her Elemental ability on me, and I can't find my breath.

Pushing through the circle of the Fae while my body lowers onto the table, I hold my hand until I am consumed into myself. But everything is still black. And I'm falling again until–

A giant inhale of air enters my lungs as a noise comes from my mouth. I'm panicking. Flailing my body and trying to take in the room as the bright light from the sun blinds me to where I can only keep one eye open.

Even then, I have to squint.

Someone is calming me down. A hand rubs my back, helping me to sit straight as I take in my surroundings. I'm completely alone in here with Vi, who I realize is the one comforting me.

My body feels sticky–balms spread over my ailing skin. The scars from my stabbings are healing, though the one by my dragon tattoo may never fully disappear. I don't mind, but I check to be sure the ones on my inner forearms are there. As soon as my heart relaxes to a more steady rate, I turn to my friend, who holds a cup of tea for me. "What happened?"

"You died," she says. "Korine shot something through you, and your body went down. The next thing we knew, some shadow thing sliced through her body, and she fell to the ground in several pieces. Then it was dark, and a pall of shadows pushed through, and almost everyone fell to the ground to their deaths. There was so much blood." Her words falter through her sentences. It's like she herself is unable to comprehend what went on.

The explanation is overwhelming. It feels like I've been gone for centuries, but my body is also so starved that I don't know what to focus on.

"How long have I been..." I pause. I wonder if I would really be considered dead since I've been living through other realms. It doesn't matter. That's too much to explain right now with the amount of energy I have. "Y'know, dead?"

"Nine days." Her head turns back to me, eyes puffy and nose red. "You regained a heartbeat yesterday, but you've still been unconscious." Another long pause creeps through time as neither of us speak. "You were talking in your sleep."

Her voice is a smooth comfort to my ears. Neither she nor the rest of our friends from England carry accents as thickly posh as someone with their upbringing would typically have. Though, those could have just softened over time.

"Yeah, I used to do that when I got nightmares as a kid," I say. That explains the soreness of my body and the fact it doesn't seem like my mouth has dried while asleep. I drink the tea–maybe tonic– she's given me. When there's enough gone from the cup to where I can maneuver without spilling, I try to leave the bed. At the peeling of the blanket, I realize I've been cleaned somehow and dressed in an oversized shirt and just my underwear. Honestly, I don't know when the healers found time to do this while tending to our injured army. "I should probably get some things settled."

Vi rushes to the edge before I can leave the mattress, putting her arm in front of me. "You're not going anywhere until you finish this."

A noise grumbles from my stomach. My body needs food, which is thankfully laid out on the table in the middle of the room. There's meat, fruit, and a pot full of whatever drink I have in my cup.

"You're alive," she says while facing the door.

"Yeah."

Her arm links into mine as I sit next to her. "I don't know what I would've done if you weren't. What any of us would've done."

In complete honesty, I don't know what I would do without my friends either. Friends have always been my lifeline before I could even consider the possibility of romance. They're my lifeboats on a ship that's constantly on the brink of sinking.

My hand grabs hers, rubbing circles on the back. For once, I'm grateful to be alive. Glad to know I have people in my life that would never abandon me. The love from friendships is incomparable to anything.

"Can I ask you something?"

"Always," she responds.

"When we were in school, and I wasn't able to control my abilities with fire, did you think that was normal? Was there something like that you couldn't control too?"

Hesitation stumps her, her thoughts glass in the stillness. Memories that must date back from not only our time in college but her earlier days. "Not really. If you found it hard to control fire when we were practicing, that would've been one thing, but you could create fire without any being present. Yours had a different color. When you told us about Fae, I wondered if there was a chance you were, but you're so different from them that I just thought it was a coincidence."

More questioning passes inside my head. My entire self-image has changed drastically over something so small, and with my age, I'm already going to start aging slowly. "I think I might be–"

"Part Fae?" she asks, cutting me off. Either she was already told by one of the Disaris family members, or she has clued everything together.

Even so, how would they have known about me being Fae without seeing it themselves? If they had sensed it in me before, they would have said something.

My head nods.

Silence. There's nothing but silence, with neither of us knowing what to say about this revelation. At least, I don't. Vi might just not want to pry.

"I worry about you," she admits, starting something that I'm sure I'll be forced to unpack. Her head is on my shoulder. There could be a number of reasons she says this. Considering the most recent thing to happen to me is dying, it's understandable why she would. "You lose so much of yourself in trying to fix others or problems outside your control that you never have time for yourself."

I don't say anything. I *do* tend to do that. But worse, sometimes I wonder if I'm nothing without my trauma.

"You know, some company reached out and asked if I could design a piece for their new collection," she says, melancholic, with a hint of excitement.

I think she's trying not to overwhelm me.

"Oh my gods, I'm so proud of you!" I respond. "When's the show for your debut into the grand fashion world?"

"Next winter. But I don't think my parents can come." Before I can ask why, she goes on. "They have their business. As usual. They're predicting to close out some big deal by then."

No communication passes again for a brief time as the two of us stew in silence.

"Can you do me a favor and not say anything about me being awake?" I request. I don't feel like facing anyone else for at least a few hours. "I need some time alone to shower and gather my thoughts."

Her eyes stare at me, mouth taking in a deep breath. "Yeah, of course. But you have to promise me you won't put yourself in more danger."

"I think dying is enough for this week," I titter awkwardly.

Vi leaves the room, shutting the door on her way out.

Instead of going to speak with Luka or Cassius, I allow myself time to decompress everything I've been told, okkaring to Lake Mindae, where I do my best head clearing.

I'm surprised those in the palace haven't given me more shit for going around so soon after being dead. I'm certainly not upset by it, but it's suspicious no one's tried to stop me.

Xavier's face is stuffed with a Faerie version of lemon squares, which is overly sweet against my taste buds. The Fae love sugary treats, and while I can concede it's better in some cases, overall, a lot of their meal foods taste nothing like food from the Human Lands.

"Oh, look at me, I'm Reaps running towards another situation that'll get me killed," he mocks in a high-pitched tone and some dragged-out voice to mimic me.

I grab the seashell white fabric of his shirt, ripping the sleeve by pure accident. All this teasing just because I want to go into the hidden Magikal areas to see if anyone knows about Delphi's death. I'm sure *someone* must be concerned as to why no one's heard from her. "I do *not* sound like that."

He laughs, eyes glancing at the tear of his clothing. The strings of the tunic are untied from the neckline, him tying together the sleeve, though I don't think it necessary. The Fae may have just done that out of boredom. "No, but you consented to seeing my impression of you. The only thing I'm missing are the deflecting jokes."

My eyes roll, a chortle of laughter exhaling from my nose. "I'll kill you, I swear to the gods."

"Now, how would it look if a queen murdered her own subject?" he asks with a shaking head. His cocky cadence, while funny, is entirely sure that I would never hurt him.

"Oh, I'll make it look like an accident." My nose scrunches as my face nods with a wide smile. "Just for you."

While flicking a slice of Etherfruite towards me, he forgets I have magik. I stop it before it hits, hovering it up and attempting to catch it in my mouth. But I miss.

"*Aw*, then great stories of the gallant, long-haired Fae may be created, and both you and your other choice in killer lovers can continue your streak of murder," he continues mocking.

"Gallant? Okay, Mister 'I burnt my eyebrows off last year', my record isn't *that* bad," I defend. But when the words finish leaving my mouth, my face reacts to a reflection of how wrong I am. I play with the end of my sleeve, the index of my finger circling around my wrist.

The Fae looks at me, head tilted down in disbelief, with his facial expression rising. "Your latest kill hasn't even been dead for two weeks."

He's got me cornered on that. My finger raises with my mouth opening, only for my lips to immediately close down on each other with the finger curling in and the fist coming to my mouth.

I'm lost in something. Not thought, but my mind isn't entirely here. My brain feels almost empty, and I find it hard to pay attention to anything.

"Reaps," he looks at me, snapping me back, "say something."

"Huh? Wha- why?"

"I just want to make sure you're still the same Reaps that came back," he jests with a wide smile on his face.

I cross my arms, turning my body to him. He's joking, but I wonder if this is an actual concern that anyone else shares. "Is there really any doubt?"

His brows cross. "Yes."

"How's Cas?" I ask, playing with my necklace. Rotating the pendant back and forth around the chain.

Over Xavier's shoulder, he tosses his hair with a confused look pointed at me. "You still haven't spoken to him?"

Cassius and I haven't spoken a word. We've only seen each other once since I woke up, and it was mostly filled with stolen glances. I wanted even then to say something, but I had no idea what.

A few blinks and a look to the floor answer his question. It's too shameful to admit that I'm a coward when it comes to my feelings. "I've only been alive again for a day."

"Part of the reason you're being so irrational is because you repeat the same mistakes I made in my earlier years," he explains with a sigh. He's speaking to me like our age gap is larger than only a few years. "Albeit, with far less affecting me to react as you do, but all the same it results."

"What do you mean?"

Why would he say these things? The two of us are always full of laughter, making jokes and only occasionally talking about feelings, but we rarely get too serious when sharing. It isn't who we are.

"You never allow anyone to get close so they won't hurt you, and in turn, you'll never be let down."

My eyes widen at his callout, along with my jaw dropping. Sometimes, I think we're too similar. It takes a few beats before I'm able to say, "Easier to say this when you're in a relationship with Iris."

He chuckles at my attempt to revert the conversation to him. A smirk is planted on his face when knowing how easily he can recognize my pattern. "So it would be a mistake to assume you didn't do this with Luka either?" I say nothing to defend myself. With Cassius, I've repeated the same defensiveness I had with Luka, if not worse. "The only reason Iris and I even have a relationship is because I saw myself in how you act towards Cassius and realized it's something I needed to change. You're open and trusting with Luka. Learn to do the same with my cousin."

He looks genuinely annoyed with me. It makes my heartbeat the only thing I am conscious of. I have no response to offer, but neither can I drown him out.

"There's more to this world than questioning if Cassius loves you, which he definitely does. If you would just *use your brain*. You're so enveloped in your problems that you refuse to see what's actually happening around you. You owe it to the Fae to stop being so selfish if you're to rule over us."

I refuse to have my feelings hurt by this. Xavier's joking like what he's said isn't hurtful, but he worries when I remain frigid. It's not his fault that he doesn't know what's been going on in my head for months, never mind my whole life. Yet all that's translating is that none of the things I've been through hold any merit for grieving.

"Reaps?" he says slowly. He's studying me as I play with the waistband of my leggings. "I'm sorry. Don't let what I say–"

"No. Just drop it."

A knock at the door is my greatest deterrent. Behind it stands Kabir, with a few papers of varying sizes in his hand.

"What's this?" I ask, pulling myself together enough as I take the stack.

"It was found inside Nemo's drawers when cleaning through his room," he answers. The tone he uses is a mix between mourning for the knight who died in battle and a brief unsureness of whether to hand this to me.

Nemo never really liked me–always making snide comments that Cassius should remove me as queen when he thought I couldn't hear–but I can't possibly guess what of mine he could have taken.

"Thank you," I say, dismissing the Head Guard.

He stalks off down the hall, out the door for training.

I shut the door, Xavier taking the papers from my hand the instant I turn around, slowly moving around while reading the notes. I would think that I should read the notes before the Fae, but he'd probably rip them from my hands anyway.

He's snorting at whatever's written. Laughing like anything on the paper is absurd. "This is almost *sad*."

Hostility that was in the room has left. I'm following right behind him, trying to take back what's mine, but he won't let me.

"I didn't think he had such a way with words." He sits on the sofa, resting his weight on the armrest.

On my desk sits a pair of scissors. "You care a lot about your hair. Would be a shame if someone..." I grab the scissors off the desk, snipping it twice while pumping my brows up a few times.

His face widens in horror. The scissors are snatched from my hands, loosening his grip on the papers. "*Don't you fucking dare.*"

I steal the letters away, reading them on the couch while Xavier hides away my multifunctioning, hair-cutting tool.

Dragon,

I have just finished the book that you speak highly of. We ought to discuss it when you have a chance. Perhaps we can do it over a shared meal and talk of the Fae? You keep to your room so often that I rarely have a chance to see you.

Cas

Dragon,

Do you recall the night you laughed while I thought I would fall prey to death from your valskull concoction? The sky was so clear that I could see many stars glimmering. I had even caught sight of one which flew right past you without your notice. But yet, none of them could engross me the way you had.

I rested by our fountain last eve. Many nights, I sit there musing over my responsibilities that you have forced upon me.

Your decisions as queen continue to prove far superior to what I could have ever thought of. I think, perhaps, you ought to take credit for the decrees I put into action, as many are due to your influence.

Cas

Arabella,

Your presence is here physically, but your mind is absent.

Not a moment passed while you were gone had you left my thoughts. Time and time again, you sit beside me as if everything is well between us, but the moment I dare speak to you on matters regarding something other than our people, you excuse yourself. Some days, I delude myself into believing that perhaps you would come to forgive me, to love me even. Other days, I think that the two of us may have been better off despising each other.

Curse me. I can take whatever loathing you hold, so long as it is directed towards me. I am unkind and a vile creature, yet you see past that. I send you notes of confession when I know you do not wish to speak more than the fewest words in my company.

My mind knows that you want nothing to do with my existence—it has been hammering that very knowledge much longer than now—but it seems my foolish heart refuses to accept that. It would much rather believe there is something there, similar to a sprout left buried under rubble.

My queen, I beg of you.

Yours,
Cas

<del>My darling,</del> Arabella,

I wonder if I am being made to be the point of your cruel jest. Am I a fool writing words only for them to be read by no one? I would like to imagine that you have the decency to have read my last seven missives before throwing them into the fire, whether that be your own or you casting them into the fire in your mind.

Have I done you so wrong that I am not worthy of a response? Of redemption?

Only Yours,
Cassius

The words on the pages are honest and vulnerable, yet I'm breathily laughing. Some of the letters are too ruined from ink and water damage, and I wonder what else Cassius had written. "He's so stupid. I love him."

My eyes nearly pop out, body freezing at what I've just said.

Oh fuck. I love him.

The realization moves me out the door before I'm able to think.

XL

Unholy Library

Arabella

I don't know what I'm doing. Esme has told me that Cassius is in the second library, and now, I'm hastily making my way to him. Only as I pull on the handle do I start to doubt myself. I push through, forcing myself past these scattered thoughts. If I don't go now, I might never bring myself to again.

Cassius sits nonchalantly at the very corner with his back turned. He doesn't look at who it is. His attention is too captured by the book he reads. I don't think he heard me walk in.

In my place, I hesitate again. *Is this a bad idea?*

Before I call his name or even make my presence known, his voice begins carrying. "Whatever you've come for, I'm afraid there is not much left of me to give."

Briskly, I step towards him, twisting my wrist with fingers raised and magiking his chair to face me. He stands while wearing a multitude of emotions. His face seems at ease, but his eyes. They're shattered.

"Delphi is dead. Perhaps your Council will retaliate, but you have fulfilled your promise to bring her to justice," he says. It isn't spoken in a way to push me out, but something is off in the way he says it. As if the words hurt him.

"I'm not leaving. I don't give up that easily." I have too much pride to tell him that it's him I won't give up on. Unsaid words are screaming through the nothingness. All the same, I think he may have guessed it. His mouth curls on one side of his mouth.

He stays in place, but I'm moving fast to get to him. My arms wrap around him tightly, like I'm making up for being apart for infinite time lost. On the initial impact, he goes stiff, with his arms barely touching me and a body tense. We remain like that for seconds until he collapses into me, his hand holding my head as he rests his head on mine. Everything about us since the day we met has held an intense connection.

My hand goes to his loose navy shirt, tugging him down to bring his lips to mine. It tastes of being granted your greatest wish in the most twisted way. I'm on the tips of my toes, and for a passage of time, we mold together.

He pulls back too fast, too soon. Like he's retreating away. In our separation, he looks down, the emotions on his face unchanged. "Don't do this to me," he pleads with a sense of lightness in his tone, though I can sense the ache in his stare. "You may believe I deserve it, but it is unkind. And for once, I want you to have me without feeling disgusted with yourself for desiring such."

All this time, while I was indecisive and spiteful towards him, he had no one else. Yet, he found reasons to believe I wouldn't let him die.

Maybe life is less about our good experiences and more so how we survive. How you touch one soul at a time and change their line of motion. That feeling haunts me whenever I think of me, Luka, and Cassius. Creatures resulted from constant life in misery, forever plagued to mirror each other.

"You found me," is all I can manage.

The High King stares like he's trying to read me in any way he can. He looks at me like what I've said is nonsensical. Before I can think of another thing to say, his lips press deeply onto mine, my nose inhaling in the air he's knocked from my mouth.

"I enjoyed our little role reversal and rescuing you from a scrape for a change." He laughs, kissing me again. Deeper and until I'm out of breath.

I think I've gone delirious.

"I've missed you," he says. "The way you breathe, your touch, the excitement in the way your body reacts when reading a book."

I push him back a bit, enough distance to look at his face. "You watched me read?"

"For one aware of her surroundings when scanning for threats, I'm surprised you never took notice. You become so pulled into their worlds that you giggle, and your feet kick the air–"

"Okay," I say, cutting him off, kissing him so he cannot see my reaction. I'm embarrassed at how well he describes me when I never saw him. And how much he goads me for it. "I get it."

He won't stop staring, amusement at the front line of his nose's exhale. "Others may have a heart open for any to see, but mine is hidden from all but you. Everything that it is, it belongs to you. You are the only one I have no need to wear a disguise around. You are the only one worth loving."

My eyes shut. Exhaling as he sucks the base of my neck. It could be that a million things are roaming through my mind or that every little bit of self-doubt has rendered me so tired I can't filter out logic anymore, but I don't have it in me to keep denying my feelings in place of something bigger. And finally–*finally*–I can say it back.

"I love you."

For a moment, he doesn't react.

My voice is always too loud when it needs to be quiet and too soft when it needs to be heard.

Cassius pulls away, cautious while he strokes my face with his left hand. It's like he doesn't believe I'm real. Like I'm some sort of ghost his hand will go right through. "Perhaps–"

"No," I say to stop him. "Shut the fuck up, and let me say it. I love you." I repeat it many times over with every dragged-out kiss. Everything from the past months, it's all been long forgiven.

He doesn't respond with any outward anger for taking so long to say it. No grudge harbored for my months of denying him. Instead, his mouth is skimming along my neck, weakening me to where I can't move.

"I'm *so* happy you're alive." My words all come out in a breath. I don't have control over what I'm doing with my hands. Or even my body when he moves. I don't want to change anything about him. I love him despite his horrible actions and everything bad I've heard about him.

"How coincidental. I was just sharing that same thought." He presses his lips to me again. This kiss longer. A smirk of teasing gaiety that I cannot stand resides on his face.

"Are you being serious right now? Or are you trying to be funny?"

"What if I am? What will you do to me, my most violent enemy?" He chuckles. His hands roam my body, pinning me against the cool touch of the wall. I can barely focus while his whole mood changes. Not when the heat from his skin brushes mine. When the warmth of his mouth glides around me.

Against my conscious thoughts and actions, my body locks before he can go further. I'm almost afraid to give him access to hurt me, intentional or not. I'm scared for him to see any scars that are left still healing from Delphi. The invisible wounds that remain imprinted on my very psyche and for any way he could use them against me. He wouldn't do that, I know it, but I can't stand the possibility of being used.

"If I have misstepped, please tell me," he worriedly says while backing farther from me. "By no means do I want you to feel pressured to do this. I understand if you are not ready to…"

My head is vibrating, eyes moving faster around the room while I try to come up with some excuse for why everything stopped suddenly feeling pleasurable. I'm breathing, trying multiple times to say something, but no words will come out.

After what feels like an absurdly long time, one of my hands goes to his shirt, my other arm snaking around his neck to pull him down as I rise by standing on the balls of my feet.

Inside me, my feelings are intense. Desire so strong, I think that it may attack. Maybe me, possibly him.

I look at him, smiling. "I just told you to shut up."

His hands unhook each latch of my underbust corset, removing it and taking everything else off my torso. Lips trail down my body–towards my legs–and suddenly, I forget how to think. My mind is taken over by the view of him on his knees, his hands around my hips, and looking up at me.

"If you do not recall how it feels to be touched by me, perhaps you need a reminder." His fingers trail to the band of my leggings, pulling them and my underwear off to leave my whole body bare. Patches that bandage my wounds are visible. I'm not sure if the library has a lock.

From his kisses on my stomach, he travels his mouth from there, to my thighs, and back up. My leg is lifted, thrown over his shoulder as I arch my back, bending my knee for balance. There are no rough touches, only fingers curling straight into me and pumping while his mouth works my clit, tongue flicking and circling.

It feels like I'm being taken to another world.

He wastes no time. He calculates every action.

Then his mouth goes in place of his fingers, moving his tongue in nothing but unrelenting pleasure for an amount of time I can't keep track of.

I can't use anything on the wall to grip onto. I'm just digging my nails into the palms of my hands as Cassius switches between his mouth and fingers inside me. And when he flattens his tongue, I swear he's intent on devouring me like a man with a goal.

Nothing stops him. When I feel myself falling, he simply brings me to the wide table, pushing aside chairs and laying me down. My hips roll against his mouth, breath shuddering as my back arches and my hand goes to his hair. His tongue is breaking away any spell I could possibly ward against him.

The pleasure is too much.

At a stalling pause that I resent, he looks up. His eyes are daring, determined to play this like another one of our contests. And I am entirely set on winning.

"Darling Arabella, you're being so good."

"Cas."

His kisses pepper all around my thighs, and he's chuckling. Cruelness. Callousness. He hasn't stripped a single item of his extravagant clothing, yet he looks more naked than I've ever seen him. "My queen, do you have something to say?"

I could kill him.

But his overconfidence is so much better. It presents a blind spot. His weakness of enjoying seeing me fall to him. Using it to my advantage, I summon his wine bottle placed carefully in the middle against the wall and drink.

Cassius draws his eyes to what I'm doing. He watches as he loses his grasp over me. Watches as I sit myself onto the table and pour the liquid. It drips. From my chin, down the rolls of my stomach.

"You're truly a creature sent as my sweetest torture, aren't you?"

There's no hint of teasing as he holds himself over me. As he licks my body and follows the trail of wine.

Something in his eyes is desperate. His hand goes to my breast, squeezing it as he undoes his pants with the other.

"What do you want me to do?" I know what he wants, but I want to hear him say it.

"Arabella," he whimpers. My name is said in such a confusing way that I don't know if he wants me to stop or continue. He gulps, eyes pleading and breath hitching. "Whatever it is you want to do. I'll take whatever you give me."

"Beg."

XLI

A Studious Sight

Cassius

Lasialic falls down to Arabella's body from her neck. Her body is so wet. Delicious. My tongue follows up from her chest to the source. To her lips. Until I am stealing the wine directly from her mouth. My breeches are down, cock free and in need to be inside her. "*Please.*"

"Not good enough," she says with a face unimpressed.

I take the bottle, placing it in a safe spot as she lays down on her back, and I grind my body onto her. I cannot quite tell if this is my own self-serving thoughts or if it is to be accurate, but at present, she is staring at me as if I created the universe just for her. "My worries for you may have overcrowded my thoughts during the day, but during the most silent hours of no one's wake, I would pleasure myself thinking *of you*. Those thoughts overtook any blatant truth and hatred you would show towards me. Please, Arabella."

"Please, what?"

"Let me inside you."

"You said you were mine," she taunts, pushing me off of her

and onto the floor. Her fingers go to the top section of my shirt, touching my skin with each piece of bronze she unclasps.

"In the past." I attempt to keep from debasing myself further, though I know the point is fruitless as I remove all my clothing, my mouth then wandering lower than her neck.

"Is that still true?"

I can't think of anything to say while my mouth is full of her nipple and the skin of her breast.

Her hand goes under my chin, bringing me up to meet her eyes. "Is it?" Both her eyebrows raise.

A strangled breath. A head nodding as she lowers to the floor. My desire to lie is stronger than it has ever been. To allow a simple word of denial to roll from my tongue. Alas, all that can be said are words of truth.

"Yes."

I do not require her mouth. Right now, all I need is to be inside her cunt. Savoring her as the two of us fall to pleasure. But even that thought falls short as she moves below me.

Pursing her lips, she kisses the slit of my tip and traces her tongue along the veins of my cock while holding her eyes to mine. She waits, tantalizing moments passing before wrapping her mouth around right where her tongue has touched. I ought to demand more, though I am in no position to demonstrate such audacity to defy her.

Whimpers and moans spill from my lips. My legs are trembling, hands gripping the back of her head to steady myself. Deeper, she takes me into her mouth, gagging and using her hand.

My queen enjoys this far too much, though I do not think I am above admitting that I am as well. A hand twists closer to the base of my length, her head bobbing at a fast enough rhythm that I release her head. "You're-" A shuddering breath. "You're taking me so well."

I'm prepared to bargain away anything to be wrapped inside a place in which I am not. She returns to licking my length. Unstopping until my hand grips her hair so harshly she sucks in a harsh sound.

"Don't move," she demands with a voice so angry I fear for what it is she wants from me.

She pushes herself onto the table, parting her legs as I can only stare at her cunt. I want to memorize her. For if this is to be my final time that I am granted closeness, I will find myself able to recall such a sight in the future.

Every bit of her is beautiful. In the clothing she wears, she attempts to make other parts of herself appear hidden, but it's in the curves of her body, her softness, that I want eternity.

"Spread your legs for me, my queen." I stare as she does so, splitting her legs wider for me to see her cunt glistening from her wetness.

As if teasing, she inserts two fingers inside her, pumping in twice, with her gaze on me. Taunting me with what I cannot have. Fucking herself when she is well aware of my ache yearning for her.

I cannot peel my eyes off her. She draws her fingers around her clitoris, and when she throws her head back, I am overtaken by feelings of burning agony.

My imagination bounces from one thought of her to the next. A jolt sparks from my chest, journeying all the way to my mind, lost in the rampaging need to touch the queen. Even the slightest brush will do.

A smirk, wickedly tantalizing, extends wide. "I've touched myself a lot thinking of you, Cas."

My cock throbs as I watch her, though I know she mocks me. Her breath goes rough as her eyes shut. Her physical position shifts, back falling onto the table with her free hand gripping the sides.

"Arabella," I beg, a deep moan grunting from beneath my

lowest levels. I want her in every way. My breaths are trembling, eyes solely focused on her body–from her stomach to her fingers that go in and out of her cunt.

Taking the fingers from inside her, I guide them into my mouth, lapping my tongue until nothing of her taste remains.

"Darling, let me make a mess of you," I purr, gripping her hips. In honest, I would very much like *her* to make a mess of *me*.

I kiss her collarbone, sucking on various areas of her body, lips slowly drifting to her clitoris. My mouth works her cunt while her thighs shake, legs trembling as I taste her. To see her lose herself around me while on my knees is incomparable to any experience I have ever encountered.

Relaxed enjoyment from Arabella halts at the straightening and lifting of her torso. If this is from her need to hold control or she simply does not want for me to go on, I am unsure. Perhaps it is best to allow her to tell me what it is she wants.

With the flowing movement of pulling me towards her, it becomes abundantly clear what she desires.

I sink into her, awaiting to be mocked once more. Anything which mirrors the push and pull of our relationship. When she says nothing, I focus on her breast, flicking my tongue against her nipple and sucking before giving the other its due appreciation.

"You're so warm," I croon as I thrust deeper.

Not once have I forgotten how this felt. Being inside Arabella is something that cannot be so easily forsaken from my memory. At the way she feels around me, no amount of self-pleasure compares to this. Thinking of her body in the most tempting hours would only bring pain when I would finish and realize I was left alone in my bed.

I can feel her cunt squeezing me with each time I pump into her. She's so wet. Perfect enough to move inside her with ease.

"Say my name, Arabella," I rasp gruffly into her ear. "I need to hear you say it."

"Cas, please."

Dangerously close to coming, I must pace myself. Today is not one I would wish to make haste. Her moans sound that of vexation. While she expects me to pleasure her mercilessly, I am delicate with her, still careful with her healing body while also allowing myself this pleasure.

Involuntary things come from my mouth. Beseeching her, curses, cried panting.

As the hardness of the wood presses back against me, I wonder if Arabella is comfortable. My fingers skim her body, lingering at the bruises that I am beside myself over.

"Stop being fucking gentle," she commands. "It looks worse than it is."

"Anything for you." I squeeze my hand around her throat, thrusting harder while she lets out a moan.

She exhales sounds of desire, pleading for more. It is as if I can feel the very planets shifting when I am inside her.

Not an area of exposed skin goes untouched while I make my way to her ear. "I've not been inside you long, yet you're already this worked up?"

She refuses to play into my teasing, only moaning, "*Mmm.*"

"You're so needy. Starved for my cock while you hold control." I'm unsure just how far she will allow me to take this. One single time do I push into her. "I'm a helpless thing at your whim, but you wish me to remind you that it is *my* initials carved into you?"

"Stop joking, or I'm gonna kick you into one of the bookshelves," she reprimands while scratching my back.

I drive deeper into her, connecting my mouth to the base of her neck to suck any remnants of the wine from her skin. "Threaten me again."

She curses out twice with each time my cock leaves and enters her, gasping between each kiss. "I- I fucking hate you."

There is no conviction in her words. Not even *I* can convince myself to believe her words as true. I become completely enamored when she speaks. I am aware of her lying, the untruths that slither from her venomous tongue. And I realize I never needed her to say it. She very much has trouble verbalizing her romantic love the way she would like to. Actions confess what her words cannot.

It does not, however, make her prior declaration any less exhilarating. Arabella chooses the worst things to care for when she chooses to love me, and I am truly fortunate.

"Liar."

She smells of her most wondrous scent. Combined with the smell of books, I may think this is her greatest desire. In contrast, she is mine.

I raise her ankles to my ears, both legs using my shoulders as support.

"How careless of you to forget how horribly you've treated me," I say into her ear as I slow my thrusts. My thumb circles her clitoris, teeth biting her nipple.

The idea of coming inside of her is not lost upon me. My lips are trailing unevenly around her. Beneath me, my legs wobble, hips propelling harder.

"The things I ought to say to you," I coo. I reach behind her, arm stretching towards the wine I would enjoy for myself, perhaps spilling it on my queen and drinking more from her.

She uses her magik to summon the bottle of wine before I am able to grab it. I remove myself from her, pulling her up and pressing my lips to hers, with my hand closer to the glass half full. The two of us switch positions, myself sitting on the table, Arabella settled between my legs. Her hand combs through my hair, tilting my head back and pouring the drink directly into my mouth. "So what, my king? Tell me what you want to say. Go ahead."

Never have I been with someone so sly that they would target my own weaknesses in the bedroom—or library, rather.

The queen pours more wine at my silence, moving the bottle past my mouth and down my body. A smile forms on her face, with eyes narrowing. Then, she is licking my chest, bending towards my cock.

Looking into the bottle, she giggles, drinking what is left before transferring it into my mouth and discarding the bottle to the side. "We're out of wine."

"Are my lips not seducing you enough?" I ask with one eyebrow raised.

"Maybe."

Challenged, I suck on her harshly, marking her and bringing her closer.

"You said I rejected you," she taunts, climbing on the table and moving us farther up it. Wrapping her arms around my neck while lowering me down. "Take it back."

If it allows me to have her, I would freely rescind my words.

It takes everything to keep myself from gripping her and pushing my cock into her. The queen would sooner ruin me before I ever could with her. I still as she grinds her cunt, rocking in agonizingly slow motions.

"Darling," I whisper, pleading as if waving a flag of surrender. Whatever it is she is playing at, she has won.

She moves even slower, her hands playing in mine while her eyes pierce me directly. "Take. It. Back."

Whimpers exchange for the words I am unable to say. And as her hand wraps around my cock, circling the tip around her clitoris, she has taken over me entirely. "I rescind every word you deem hateful against you," I cry. "Please."

Nearly every night have I imagined Arabella remorseful. Apologizing for keeping herself away. Yet such imaginations fade when she is on top of me.

"I love seeing you weak under me," she mocks. A taunt. A remark that reminds me how much I require being around her in any way.

She rides my cock torturously slow. I am nearing insanity as she restricts me from moving my hands around her body, pinning both against the table. If I think it is this that haunts me, my queen will utterly destroy what sense I have left.

"Do you not trust me enough to touch you?" I ask, meeting the roll of her hips by thrusting into her. At that, she moans out half a curse.

"Not even close," she laughs, speeding her motion. With each movement made, her face clenches to keep from appeasing my need to hear her.

I cannot find the will to speak. My jaw becomes slack, breath shallow. A choked sound comes from me when I can barely keep my hands at my side. I need her. To touch her breasts, her waist. Feel her skin.

"Fu- Shit. Cas," she says, releasing my arms at last from her grip. "I need your hands."

Without hesitation, I squeeze her waist with one hand, the other going to her clitoris. Her head throws back, and all I can think about is fucking her until a new day rises. There is something so intoxicating about her.

On both sides of me, her hands fall, pushing against the table. Perhaps her knees are too pressured from the wood, and if it allows me to have her close, both provide delight to me. I pull her body onto mine as she continues gliding up and down my length.

She is done doing what it is she demands of me. My fingers stop just as she begins to tighten around me, that same hand taking hers and dragging it down between our bodies. "Touch yourself."

Her face hardens, but I do not allow her to think twice. My feet press against the table, pumping into her while she speedily moves her fingers.

"Cas. Fucking. *Fuck*." She comes apart, dropping onto me while my thrusting continues.

"*Arabella*." My voice fills the air. I have had her too many times and held in my need to come for too long. I gulp, releasing inside of her as her name leaving my lips echoes against the walls.

Peeling off of me, the two of us lay close, her resting half of her body on mine. When our bodies connect, I swear that I understand what it means to feel souls intertwining.

"I love you," she says, breathing onto my skin, my fingers outlining the black crystal heart that inks the back nape of her neck.

"I've dreamt you said that once. It filled me with ecstasy, and even though I knew I was dreaming, I wished to never wake."

"You told Korine you thought Magiks deserved to die," she manages with a strangled voice.

Most Magiks. I so badly want to remind her of my exact wording. Instead, I push myself up with my weight on my arms to look down on her. "Not you. Never you. And by any matter, you are not just of them."

Her lips clamp tightly against each other. "So Delphi's dead?"

"By your own magik."

Seeing Arabella is indescribable. I am in awe of her presence, and this very sight of her holds me in a daze. She loves me, and I almost think that I am imagining it. That I will wake up in my bed and it will have been another elaborate dream of my mind's creation.

"Shall I leave?" I ask.

"Never."

"I've seen you broken before, but for nine days, I thought

you dead. And I thought, perhaps, I died with you." I take a deep breath, focusing my gaze on her flushed face and hair a mess. I have no care for how desperate I sound. "My devotion is to you. You are who I love."

"I'm sorry. I'm *so* fucking sorry," she confesses, holding me close. "I wanted you dead for your betrayal, and I... I couldn't forgive myself if I loved another person who hurt me. I wasn't able to understand myself. But you didn't deserve all the shit I did."

An intense effect more entrancing than sweets and lasialic overcomes me. While assuming we would remain no more than co-rulers, I had learned just how much one could miss another while living under the same palace as them. Although her skin is pressed to mine, there stays traces of that same feeling.

My hand goes to her cheek, bringing her close enough to kiss. "You've chosen to stay."

"I think that's a horrible idea," our seneschal says, cutting the queen off. The sentiment is one I agree with wholly. For Arabella to even suggest personally speaking to the Council of the Coven with a common fae by her side so soon after being killed by Delphi is a plan impulsive.

If even I think such a thing, it only proves a need for her to recuperate. If she presses further on demands to the Council on revisiting our treaty, it will bring about the issue of Magiks killed.

Lateness of afternoon is beginning to play with my head. Perhaps it is the tiredness from an empty stomach or boredom from the dull talk of politics, but I want the issue done with.

We must still earn back the trust of the common fae and bridge the gap between them and the Elementals. Many continue to despise Arabella and Luka, despite the two fighting alongside the Fae. Against their kind. Regardless of what evidence is shown, many will not waver on their opinions.

"The Fae have lost many as a result of your kind so long ago," I remind them. "Our battle against Delphi has lessened our population to an even smaller amount. They will not be swayed so easily to speak to your Council, even if it is to prove the effects of Delphi's crimes. The common fae hardly take up their issues to the lower courts' rulers."

Arabella moves her lips around as she exhales. She tucks the longest locks of her hair behind her ears, propping her legs to take up the whole of the sofa and clicking her tongue on the roof of her mouth multiple times. "Fine, but shouldn't the common fae feel more comfortable speaking to the younger Elementals? With Theodosia being a ruler and Harrison somewhat helping his mothers, I'd think the common fae would feel less timid bringing up their problems to them."

"Gideon and his group of friends should be sufficient enough to hold from another revolution," Luka says when unbuttoning the top button of his taupe long-sleeved shirt. "But it's still too soon to say that it has worked. At the very least, the common fae don't want us all dead."

I'm rather pleased that Arabella has taken to confiding her plans with us, instead of sneaking around to go about things on her own. The ruffles of my sleeve have become sticky from honey. It bothers me not, but Arabella cannot stop staring at it in disgust.

"Perhaps we can discuss another matter," I announce in hopes of changing the subject before the two decide to campaign publicly in favor of the crown. Both sets of eyes point in my direction. "What are we to do of Arabella being half Fae?"

The High Queen peers at me. The three of us have yet to discuss the matter as a trio. "There's not much to talk about. I'm the queen. Half Magik, half Fae."

"Yes, but you are the first of your kind to live. We know not of the things you can do," I expand. I am certain there is nothing which concerns myself largely, but she is now more potentially dangerous than others once thought her.

"That we know of," she interjects, taking a sip of water from the table. When rubbing her eyes, she rests her head on the chair's arm. "There's no way that throughout all of history, there hasn't been *some* child born of both Fae and Magik."

"Well, you are the first in history that has been known to be both Magik and Elemental *and* survive," Luka clarifies. With his research as seneschal, he knows more of documented records than I have been taught. "I imagine that when word inevitably gets out about you being an Elemental, the common fae will become more concerned about your rulership."

This topic touches on the very thing I would have hoped Luka's logic could deny. Knowledge of Arabella's blood is a danger if word were to spread outside of Nexus. As a witch, she is already considered a danger to the Fae, as a queen, even more so. When piling on being an Elemental, she is now the exact creature which caused a near extinction of our people.

Arabella sighs with a smile falsely planted. "As long as we can stop the Fae from going against us before the Council, I'm pretty sure we can find ways to bring the common fae to our side."

"And how do you suppose we do that?" I ask. These paths of decisions are only my fault to blame. It was I, after all, who had chosen her as my queen and Luka to rule alongside me. I had assumed, though, that by appointing them to such positions, it would mean being free from worry of responsibilities rather than creating worry for them.

"Like Luka said, we already have Gideon and his friends. And Maude can glamour her appearance to trick even a Fae..." she rambles, silent without completing her thought. I know not of what she means to do with these connecting truths, though it may be that Luka does, as he nods at her words.

"Arabella?" I call after a long silence, with my hand reaching to hers. There is a look on her that isn't quite right. She has gone still, a distance in her stare growing further with each stretching moment. "You're okay. You're here with us."

She shakes her head, dropping her feet from the sofa onto the floor with her focus on neither of us. "It's not that. It's Delphi."

My eyebrows come together in confusion. I look at Luka, then back to her, searching for an answer, but I'm given none. "She is no longer here to torment you. Her body has been burned, and nothing is left."

"I know that." The sound is just above a whisper. "I just- I don't know. It's weird."

"Delphi wasn't a good person," Luka reminds her.

Another breath shakes from her. I fear the possibilities she will do to avoid this, throwing herself into something else instead.

While playing with the paint of her nails, she scratches off the color from one entirely. "I know. And I know I'm not exactly sad about her dying, but something still feels off, you know? I think maybe we were too fucked up to ever properly care about each other."

It pains me that she ails herself with the decisions that Delphi has enacted, which have effectively ruined both her and my people's lives. She assumes that if she had made some choices of better mind, it would have resulted in a different outcome, which simply isn't true.

"Maybe it'll just stick with me forev- *Oh hell no.*" She jumps from where she is sitting, legs lifting off the ground and staring directly at one spot on the floor. "Someone kill that thing."

On the floor crawls an iridescent spider, glowing with colors of green, orange, and blue. It scurries around the ground, undoubtedly more afraid of Arabella than she is of it, yet it is she cowering in fear on the cushions.

Her reaction causes me to become hysterical from laughter. I'm choking on wine as I vow to myself never to forget this. It is nearly the exact reaction I'm sure many Fae have when meeting Arabella.

"You're a terrifying witch that murdered many, and you're afraid of a small spider?" I laugh harder with an arm around my stomach. My head falls back at the thought of this being the single time that she has allowed someone other than herself to be the brave one.

I am given a deathly glare from my High Queen as Luka returns with toilet tissue in hand, bending towards the insect. "Yeah!" she pules. "*Now kill it*!"

With a final glance at the fearsome queen cowering, Luka chuckles, slightly shaking his head while squashing the bug, throwing it in the waste as I dismiss us for the day into lighter things that bring more merriment. Food being the first matter.

XLII

Family Yule

Luka

After a long morning of rescheduling meetings and delegating my responsibilities to Damita for the rest of the day, I am nearly free. It's not something that I would particularly choose–trusting my tasks onto someone else, but it will be worth it. The snow from the outside covers all of the grounds of the Nexus estate, leaving all the guards, knights, and workers in layered attire. Two guards stand at the front with smiles of neutrality. As they open the doors for me, the inside is empty, with the servants occasionally passing me towards one of the empty offices, which has turned into a gathering room.

One more thing is still on my agenda for the day before Cassius and I can whisk Ari away from her duties of the day to allow a day of rest.

A feminine creature, who I have never seen in the palace, walks down the hall through the foyer. The Fae shakes her head, twirling her hands around while waving hello to me.

The glamour of the Fae's appearance drops with each step,

changing from white hair and glowing eyes that shade golden, to her natural state of a tall woman with bright blue eyes and a rounder body. It's perfect in timing. She is my last bit I need to have taken care of before I settle for the day.

"Maude," I call.

She pivots towards me. Her face is gleaming with a glow of fresh pampering, blonde curls tied into a bun. "Hey, Luka! Did you need something of me?"

During the conversation between Ari, Cassius, and myself, Maude had been decided to be the spy for the court. Her Elemental ability shifts her appearance so that even the other Fae cannot decipher the difference between her glamour and their reality. And with that power, she can uncover things we cannot. With Gideon as her boyfriend, the two can blend in when traveling between other courts. Per our agreement with Gideon's friends, that group will work to our advantage, persuading other common fae into respecting the crown enough not to revolt. It may be a slow endeavor, but it will likely have long-lasting effects rather than forcing the common fae into submission.

"May I speak with you in my office?" I ask.

We walk together towards the west wing. Step into my office, where I shut the door, using silencing magik around the room to keep from anyone listening in. "You can deceive other Fae with your glamour, correct?"

"*Mm-hmm*," the princess hums, her face curious. She takes a seat on the cushioned, mulberry daybed, throwing her feet on the table of arfvedsonite. "What about it?"

"Can you explain the point of Fae glamouring themselves when you can see through the fact they are glamoured?"

This is not something the two of us will typically speak of. Our conversations extend primarily to the duties of the crown, less so to anything else. While the purpose of my question involves the request of Ari and Cassius, right now, it seems no different than the two of us making surface-level talk.

"Fae can see through each other's glamour in the sense that we know they have cast it because of the golden shimmer around them, but not knowing exactly what it is," she explains.

Apparently, their glamour holds very similar to the way in which we can see that magik has been used, but not the magik that is being cast. Nor do we have the ability to see an outlining of magik when changing our appearance with a potion.

After seconds of confusion resting on her face, she asks, "Why do you ask this anyway?"

"Since Gideon works with his friends on convincing the common fae of the crown caring for their issues, we will require your abilities." I sit, sifting through the papers messily spread on my desk with pens, which hold no ink, needing to be thrown away. If Maude is to agree, while she is of the Disaris family, Gideon would also be included under working for the crown, meaning he would need to sign paperwork agreeing to his title.

The two of them together can move through the lands without the common fae worrying about speaking poorly of the crown and receiving punishment. They would have the ability to collect other information, us sending Maude to other areas of creatures if needed.

"How exactly would I be useful?" she laughs. "By glamouring myself or someone else?" Maude has never enjoyed the demands of being a princess. It's why she has chosen a romantic partner who is so disagreeable with what her father would have preferred her with. By agreeing to be the spy of the court, she is allowed to detach herself from the demanding image of being a princess.

"You can glamour Gideon and yourself. You don't have to interfere with common fae who disparage the ruling, but report back any information you deem worthy from your spying."

"Gideon will be with me too?" she asks, taking the paper from my hands that states the specificity of his duties to the crown. On it are contractual obligations that extend beyond spying.

Having Gideon work as a diplomat, serving as communication between the crown and the common fae, removes the additional responsibility from Ari and Cassius. We can focus on the overall of ruling instead of managing over minuscule things.

I nod.

She is stunned. Her eyes are widened with the blue reappearing with each blink. She swallows something in her throat, the debate in her head appearing on her externally.

Quickly, I understand the significance of this. She is being offered something that her father never allowed her. Cassius once told me of Maude hiding her relationship from their parents, sneaking off and shamefully seeing Gideon only at night, but with this, she is given the chance to explore life without her title.

"If it means I can have freedom from this palace with him and do what it is I want, I will, of course, be the spy for the court," she says cheerily.

"Discuss it with Gideon first, and return the signed paper to me."

With the wave of my hand, the magik silencing the room from the world around us comes down, and the door unlocks. Maude stands, exiting while I now have a day fully set on distracting my girlfriend.

Convincing Ari not to shower and instead wear comfortable clothing before eating dinner was a strenuous effort to navigate around without revealing anything. I had to emphasize the importance of eating together with Cassius' family today, forcing her to keep from bathing herself. The two of us had known that the moment she showered, our plans would be ruined.

From the other room, Cassius yells out, "Did you steal my kohl, Dragon? I cannot find it."

"You think I'd take it? Something that goes on your eyes. And use it on... mine? That's unsanitary." Her voice is filled with dismay, saying this while she slips her arms through her pink sweatshirt that is sizes too large for her body.

"You steal most of our blanket at night. Why would this be any different?" Cassius comes from the bathroom, wearing nothing but the same lounging pants as mine. He watches Ari as her head pops from the clothing. Ari stares at him, flicking her head between the two of us.

I take her into my arms, carrying her towards the bed, with her feet grazing the floor. Ours and ours alone have added a designed fabric flooring. It hadn't needed to be done, but while we dragged Ari around to keep her preoccupied, Cassius had the bedroom changed for her preference.

Both the king and I take her in with our lips. He claims her neck while I take her thighs, Ari giggling and squirming under us.

"I don't get it," she says. Using her strength, she sits up, crossing her legs with one foot under her thigh, the opposite atop the other. "Why exactly are you putting on makeup if we're in pajamas?"

"That discussion's unimportant," Cassius replies with a grin. He rises from the bed and strolls to the connected room, leisurely searching the closet for a duration long enough to last the next minutes needed before taking Ari downstairs.

She climbs on top of me, lips tangled with mine while running her hand through my hair. When I kiss her, I can feel in my bones an electrifying feeling of gratitude.

I'm pushed down, her body on mine with her fingers playing

with my shirt. For seconds, her hands rest on my chest. A few breaths later, they move lower.

"What's Cas doing?" she asks, her eyes gazing into me.

"You can ask yourself," Cassius says while crossing the room towards us. In his hand is a black box with two knobs on both sides of the splitting opening in the middle. Near the edges, gold frames it. He looks at me, subtly sliding over a ring box while Ari is distracted opening the box after detaching herself from me.

Inside is a necklace. The pendant is a tiny stone, nearly clear but with colors of greens, reds, and oranges reflecting–more visible when you angle it differently. Silver wraps the stone, the bail looping with multiple wires in the same shape the top section of a treble clef does.

"I missed your birthday," he says.

"So you got me something," she responds, laughing, "half a year later?"

Rubbing the back of his neck, he smiles with his focus directed on any place but Ari. It takes him four seconds before he looks back. "Well, I wanted to get you a gift, and Luka said he would hit me until I could not think again if I bought you something from somewhere as lowly as a chain store, so I had this handcrafted."

Ari slips her hand between the necklace and the cushion of the box. Her thumb rubs the stone, eyes blinking with a look of suspicion. "This isn't the Stone of Elestial, right?"

The king doesn't speak. He smiles instead, confirming it for her.

"Cas, you can't just turn one of the world's most powerful objects into a necklace for me," she reprimands with wariness in her tone. "I can't have this. I won't ever win the Fae's trust if I do, especially not with everything that happened. And what if I use it on one of you by accident?"

"The stone is useless now," Cassius says, cutting Ari off before she speaks herself into a monologue. "And regardless, you do not need it to command me."

I can't help but watch with a grin as Ari's face grows with curiosity. She tries to piece the information together, and I can see as it processes in her mind.

Right as she is about to speak, she glances at Cassius. He removes the necklace from its holding and clasps it around her neck, the piece layering well with the one I had given her, the chain from the newest necklace shorter than her onyx one.

My hand goes around her waist, bringing her closer as I breathe her in. "After some research done, we learned that it was created by a Magik and had to be destroyed with one. When you died with the stone in your pocket, the magik of control it once possessed was broken."

Not thinking too much of it, she cocks her head to the side. She knows the two of us wouldn't lie to her. Cassius is unable to, and I would not for something such as this. If I were to lie to her about the stone, it would outweigh protecting her.

"Oh," she says, holding a pause of unsureness. "Okay."

"Love," I call, summoning out a bag from under the bed while my hand reveals the gift from the two of us, "you have two more things to open before we go downstairs."

She turns to me with her head angled up, blinking with darting glances around the room. Her hand goes to mine, taking the box of satin from me. Any question she must have concocted in her mind must have dissipated and redirected to the item. "What's this?"

"A present for Yule."

With all the busyness of planning a battle against Delphi and the scare of losing Ari, the holiday had become buried in the back of our minds. Those in the palace may have ensconced themselves into a regular routine, but the three of us have yet to settle into a state of tranquility.

Unwrapping the box, she finds a ring with an iolite sunstone as the centerpiece gem. The band is silver, with four tiny pieces of smoky quartz surrounding each side of the gem on the band.

"Is that an inscription?" she asks when inspecting the jewelry. Her eyes view it as if it is the most valuable thing in existence, but to me, nothing is more valuable than her.

"Our names," Cassius answers, pressing his lips on her hand as she puts the ring on the fourth finger of her right hand.

Ari kisses him, throwing her arms around his neck before doing the same to me. She returns to staring at her hand, eyes fixated on her new piece of jewelry.

From my other hand, I give her the paper bag, the inside filled with highlighters, sticky tabs, pens, and other stationery for her book annotations. There is a look of wonder when being handed another gift, but when tearing the tissue paper to uncover what is hers, her eyes go wide. Gleams with excitement.

Wholly captivated by her smile, I am held still. When she smiles, the world stops in its place. The axis tilts in her favor, her cheeks growing to their widest size while the fuller skin under her chin becomes more evident.

I catch my heart calming into peace every single time.

"What's going on downstairs?" she asks after kissing us, calling to attention that I had mistakenly given away the surprise.

I would much rather stay here, in the room locked with my girlfriend naked, or reorganize my desk, but that is not what is planned for the evening.

Cassius grabs his casual shirt from the chair, putting it on before reaching for Ari's hand. "Yule is important to your kind, so we had something orchestrated."

I've never cared much for the holiday, but a call for celebration is glaringly obvious. So much has revolved around death that perhaps a gathering of livelihood would cheer the mood.

A guard opens one of the doors, everyone greeting us as we walk in. All are wearing clothing that you would to bed or if you had no plans to see the public for a whole day.

Everything in the room is filled with the liking of others. Cultural foods prepared by the chefs and Grayson—as well as meats, sweets, and cheeses the Fae enjoy—are placed decoratively by other servants. In a bowl is fruit salad that is already being served into Dyana's cup, while Isa eats pomegranate seeds. There is a tray filled with other fruits, such as lychee, blackberries, rambutan, and, of course, Etherfruite.

Heady smells overpower the room. Not one scent is more dominant than the other. I realize instantly, despite Esme catering and planning this party with my ideas in mind, this may be too extravagant.

"Where's the rest of your family?" Ari asks Dyana as we approach her.

"Well, Helena didn't want to interrupt us, so she got food earlier. Atticus is with his wife and son, Maude's with Gideon, and Celeste is on a date with Damita," she responds, counting on her fingers all of her family members who have declined to come tonight. "Oh, and this is from Celeste too." She takes something from her pocket—an unwrapped, silver hair pin with leaves as decoration. If straightened, it is the length of a hair stick, built with metal and edges sharp enough to stab through, though I don't think it would be able to hold Ari's short hair now.

After pinning the side of her hair, Ari looks at me, silently questioning if she has placed it correctly or if she has somehow ruined her appearance. With the slight tilt of her head, I have learned to read the questions she asks without saying a word.

I take the accessory from her, carefully repinning it so that no strays tangle in a lump. My hand goes inside hers as she stares at the two Aeon sisters, taking a sip of the pop in her hand before thanking the women for delivering the present.

"Please tell me how you managed to get Cassius in something so... mortal," Isa says. She spills jelly onto the gray T-shirt she wears, wiping it with a cloth and dabbing water on it to remove the possibility of it staining. It is a failed effort. The red continues to show through.

Laughing, Ari continues walking around the table, filling her plate with the dim sum laid out. "Honestly, I didn't even know about this party, so I could *not* tell you."

"A long, convincing, and seemingly endless, persuading conversation," Esme answers.

Cassius looks at Ari without her noticing, grinning to himself. He wanders off, joining some of his family towards the more comfortable couches that Damien and Violette had earlier magiked the appearance of from the once elegant sofas.

"You're already packing food?" Ari questions while noticing the sisters wrapping their food on a plate.

Dyana sucks a breath in while looking at her sister. She is jittery when running her fingers through her hair to tuck behind her ears. "We just came to drop Celeste's gift off for you. Isa still has to help the healers tend to the wounded from the battle, and I have other matters I must attend to."

There's something entirely unforthcoming about her.

Whether thinking nothing of it or letting what Dyana said go just for tonight, Ari doesn't question her. She finishes filling her plate, sitting with some of the Fae in another area while I join our friends.

As we eat, Adonis, Vi, and Damien are talking amongst themselves, while Juli and Grayson discuss how they should go about asking Ari if Grayson can move into hers and Juli's shared house permanently. A house which was bought by my mother so that the women would not be burdened by rent from the previous owners.

Music plays from a speaker behind us, with the Fae in the room laughing as Cassius finds himself in the acquaintance of technology while lowering the volume.

"If the chefs weren't royally employed, I would've yelled at them," Grayson says, pouting while stuffing a piece of garlic bread into his mouth. He stares at the spaghetti on his plate, grimacing at the sight. It's the kind of expression that someone makes if personally offended. I don't put it past the man to believe an inanimate plate has struck a vendetta against his honor.

"What did they do?" Juli groans. She twirls her fork around the pasta, her boyfriend prodding what's on his plate.

The folding chair Grayson is sitting on, brought by Damien, is slowly breaking, one side uneven from the other legs. He rocks it back and forth, taking long to acknowledge his girlfriend's question. After half a minute, he sharply lifts his head, looking at Juli. "They snapped the noodles in half before boiling it. How can you not tell?"

Grayson and his superstitions.

"It's not *my* fault I don't like most shellfish," Ari says to Cassius as they near us. "The texture's just-" Her body shakes, a disgusted, closed-mouth moan joining it.

"Gods, your taste in food is shit," Gray says, interjecting himself into their conversation. "Actually, your taste in... *well, everything* isn't very good."

"Is that why I decided to keep you as a friend?" Ari replies playfully.

The remaining bodies in the room gather around in a poorly formed circle, the Fae bringing the wrapped presents that had been neatly stacked in the corner. Different gifts are exchanged–candles, personalized lights, clothing, most things that are one of a kind. On any other day, the Wands could buy the other something we find interesting, but birthdays and Yules are the agreed-upon occasions that gifts will be original, whether they be something personally made or commissioned to be designed.

Adonis is opening his present, tearing apart the wrapping of the box. "What gift could you have possibly gotten me? Is it our father apologizing?" He asks in jocund laughter. "Or better yet, have you perhaps found another way to impale more *fucking* iron into me? If the answer to that is yes, how generous that you have wrapped it this time."

While the Fae do not celebrate Yule the way in which our group does, they participate by handing presents related to the interests of their chosen person. Cassius too has gifted my friends bracelets infused with magik of their glamour, which allows them to alter their appearances without potions needed. A gift I'm more than sure they will abuse.

The last gift is given to Ari from the Aeon twins. Monty hands Ari a large bag, which is poorly wrapped. She digs through it, throwing the four boxes inside each other behind her while on her knees. This goes on for over a minute until she reaches the last box and pulls out a decorated one. Ari glares at the twins, Xavier in a fit of snickering, Monty smiling after a snort.

Finally, she opens the smallest box to find a vial made from gold and glass, a ruby on one flat surface near the top. Filled inside is the same shade as the lipstick she wears as signature.

"Poison?"

"Lip paint," Monty says. "Though if you want, it can be drained and filled with poison."

"It also works as a dagger," Xavier says excitedly. He twists the sealed top part of the vial that unscrews the lip wand clockwise, a blade coming from the bottom. It is sharp on all edges, the applicator lip screw transforming into the hilt of the weapon.

"The two of us combined our weaponry craftsmanship, along with magik and glamour to make this. Personally, I *wanted* to get you a pet cockatrice, but Monty didn't think my clever idea was a good choice."

I give him a look.

"Adonis came up with the idea," Esme says, returning the subject to the present and reminding them of that fact.

"Adi, this was literally the coolest thing you could have ever thought of!" Ari remarks with giddy, though I think that of all the things he has come up with in the past, this is far from his best idea. In this case, however, it is *for* Ari rather than to be used against her. She glances around the room, guilt showing on her face. "I didn't get any of you anything. If you give me another day, I could buy a few things."

"Ara, you're our queen. And you killed Delphi," Esme reassures. "That's enough."

"Plus, you randomly get us things all the time. And the Fae do not take or accept gifts for free," Monty says, though that is dependent on whether the Fae likes the gifter or not. "This is for you."

"Yeah, that's not enough for me," Grayson interjects with the insinuating face of someone who spews purposeful nonsense. "I'd like unlimited access to your vault of jewels."

Just as I predicted. An inane statement.

Next to Grayson, Juli elbows him. She takes Ari's wine glass from the table, inspecting the drink and bringing it to her mouth.

"Juliette, what are you drinking?" Esme asks her from across the table.

Juli's cheeks already flushing, Esme puts down her plate with ensaymada on it, quickly rushing over to take the wine away. She glances over at her family, all of whom are looking at each other with light worry. Giggles erupt from Juli's mouth, eyes solely directed at

Grayson. She becomes overly affectionate with him, rubbing his arm and planting kisses on his skin.

"What's so great about this wine anyway?" Grayson asks with doubt.

"Trust me, Gray, their alcohol works differently. It hits faster and makes you a little more..." Ari trails off, making a noise and cocking her head down before she takes Juli's glass from Esme, drinking its contents.

Doubt again clouds Grayson's judgment, assuming himself to be unaffected. He walks over to the table separate from the food, where there are two bottles full of lasialic. "You're just saying that because you're the baby of the Wands."

"A little of their Faerie wine wouldn't kill us," Violette says, joining Grayson at the table and pouring herself a glass of the wine.

The Fae are already mocking the rest of us before we've had the chance to taste the lasialic. Many times, I have been advised by Cassius to be wary when drinking this, which, until now, strayed me away from the wine. Alcohol has never particularly been a vice I partake in, other than on social occasions. My fear of not having control over my mind and actions due to an outside force is too great.

My friends begin drinking, overindulging themselves to prove a point. While I take smaller, controlled sips from the wine, they take gulps.

The lasialic acts quickly. My body starts heating with thoughts that I should not commit in front of this group of people forming. This is nothing like alcohol I've had before. There are effects I feel which are more or less the same as from alcohol I have had, but this boosts the intensity of my emotions to a much higher extent. I look around at the others of my group, and I realize I seem to be the only one of us to have control over myself. The wine has been taken from their hands, and they have instead been given water, which they reluctantly drink. As quickly as the energy from the alcohol comes into my system, it leaves just as fast, but that could perhaps be due to the little I've consumed.

Ari has removed her sweatshirt in the middle of all our friends' experimentation. She is sitting next to Xavier while continuing to drink the wine that affects her with less severity than it does the rest of us. Though she cannot consume as much as the other Fae, she does not stop from drinking either.

Cassius glances over at Ari and Xavier, clearing his throat to grab their attention, but neither pay him any mind. Nor does anyone in the room. Nearly everyone is drunk or caught up in their own conversations.

Xavier and Ari are watching something on her phone, the two laughing at whatever it is. When they finish, she takes another shot from the table in the corner. Her face, reddening from the alcohol, focuses between Cassius and myself before walking and sitting next to me, her head on my shoulder.

From the singular chair that Cassius sits on, he switches to the armrest of the sofa, placing his hand between her thighs in a manner that earns a grumble of disturbance.

"You three are gross," Xavier says, a forced face of revulsion following. None in the room seem to care, but then, he is being so dramatic that I would think others know better than to lean into his act.

"Says you," Ari returns while rolling her eyes, drinking the glass of water I hand to her. "The amount of times I've had to see you and Iris acting coupley is too many to count."

The Fae snorts at the hypocrisy. It pulls some from their conversations, watching the two go at each other the way that siblings would. Perhaps the same many of them in the room already have with each other. "Such brevity from the disgusting activities you participate in. You aren't discreet, and it makes me sick to know the things you do," he speeds through.

"Are you a child? Get a hold of yourself," I say. Ari, continuing to lean into their banter, puts her hand over mine and guides it to her other thigh, which seems to disgust the Fae further. It is not sexual in her intention. She instead assumes this as a joke. "We are adults partaking in common, grown proclivities."

Xavier's mouth hangs open in shock. Others in the room look at me from the sides of their eyes with eyebrows knitted together in surprise that I would respond this way. In the distance, Esme shivers while setting down a sesame ball.

"What a devious set of words to form a sentence. A choice of wording that truly makes me want to vomit." The long-haired Fae drops the food from his hand onto his plate on the table, moving to a new spot and unable to look us in the eyes. "Congratulations. You've activated my gag reflex without touching me."

I shoot a scathing glare, while Ari nears tears from laughing at his delivery of what I assume he thinks to be a joke.

Esme chuckles at his comment, sitting on the floor across from us. She throws a roll of bread at the twin's face, the crumbs tumbling from his hair. "Someone really ought to put cloth in your mouth."

"I thought you said they speak normally," Violette says to Ari. While our friends have alternated their time spent here, none have stayed long enough to know the speech patterns of those in the palace.

"They do," Ari replies while looking to Xavier, who is shining a smile of feigned innocence. "Mostly."

"Xavier also *mostly* takes on irritating Cassius and Luka as a secondary role to his main one here," Esme mocks with a toothy grin.

"They're just jealous 'cause they'll *never* have what Reaps and I have," he brags. He pumps his eyebrows at Ari, acting as though he would be the heartbroken one if she were to reject him.

"What you *have* is a title due to your friendship with the queen," Cassius says, taking another drink from his chalice.

He and I converse as everyone groups off to their enjoyment. We speak about our agreement on the music, which neither of us particularly care for, being played. While we do not have much in common, I appreciate the ways in which he knows to keep me steady, specifically during the days when I was more outwardly anxious than he had been. I am more cynical than he, though we share a similar trait of charming others in our favor. The simplicity of our friendship goes beyond what I can understand.

With the little amount of sobering up that has been done amongst the room, it has now reverted into nothing but incoherent ramblings. Others take shot after shot, glass after glass of either peppermint liqueurs or the lasialic. In the middle of the room are bodies dancing with each other, drinking their weight as the Fae wine works through their system. My friends are inseparable, with even the slightest pull away from their respective partners causing squabbles. All of them but Xavier, who looks identical to waving a noodle after it has been boiled.

I never thought something like this possible after the stressful months that have passed.

The music is paused by Damien. Him saying, "This is for Vi, my sweetlove, who requested this."

"No one requested this," Violette shouts back before a slow, rhythm and blues love song begins playing.

Damien sings along, loudly and terribly but dancing well for someone inebriated. He uses the smoothness of the floor to spin himself, sliding closer and farther away from Vi, missing several lines of the song as he does so. Then, out of pure pity, Esme and

Grayson join in as a substitution for the siblings that he doesn't have. Both of whom are just loudly speaking along to the music.

His performance is excruciating. But when it finally ends, Juli, Ari, and Vi purposefully sing the following song incorrectly, falling into wheezing laughter. I can hear as they summarize the events of what has happened in the past thirty seconds, only to lose their breath from cackling, repeating this cycle for minutes.

When the three return their focus to the music, Ari bangs her head a few times before spinning in a circle, continuing until she is failing to stay upright. Cassius has joined the others in the room, merrily dancing with them. I go to hold her, wrapping my arms around her until her head stops moving. Her eyes stare at the beauty of the palace that she knows inside and out, with a smile of an open mouth.

She pats my arms, forcing me to release her as she walks towards the table of food. After one bite into the fried chicken, she puts it onto a plate that sits too closely to the table's edge. I force a glass of water into her hands, staring at her until she drinks it.

"Let's go outside," Ari suggests, struggling to walk linearly to her phone and shut off the music.

Others in the room say nothing and instead begin exiting towards the hall and out the door to the back entrance of Nexus.

Ari trips over her foot. She tumbles into the table, sending the plate she kept too close to the edge to the floor and shattering.

"*Ay, hala!*" Vi shouts immediately.

Heads turn to the sound, eyes in the room going to Ari, servants already rushing over to pick up the glass.

"*Ouuu,*" the rest in our friend group taunt in song simultaneously. They sound similar to children who mock a classmate when called on by the teacher to face repercussions. They continue with childish threats, uttering different phrases that would only frighten someone in primary school.

I do not join in.

Ari covers her mouth with her hand, a laugh unsuccessfully attempting to be stifled. She bursts into laughter from her drunken state, knocking into my side as her body rotates in different directions.

Perhaps I should have stopped her from consuming alcohol two drinks ago.

Adonis, standing next to Cassius in front of us, says, "An odd sight to see killers among your friends act instantly like younglings."

"Brother, you too were laughing at something immature not too many days ago," Esme teases. Her tone is light-hearted, eyebrow cocked in his direction and awaiting him to challenge her. "I would keep from making jokes that put you at the expense of exposing yourself."

He, of course, cannot lie to her, leaving him with only an excuse he deems acceptable, shocked if only by his sister's word choice while a light glint of a smile forms on his face. Rather than defending himself, he raises a glass in her direction before drinking it.

The lot of us walk outside into the fresh air of night, everyone wearing layers to keep warm, Esme leaving for the Human Lands to spend time with the woman she loves.

Once reaching the bottom step, Grayson shoves us aside, vomiting the food he overate and alcohol, which he was warned against drinking so much of. His hand grips the protrusion of the rail, breath heaving between each hurl. Somehow, when leaving his mouth, the glow and sparkle from the lasialic is still there.

The three witches have all gone into the snow that covers the grass. Ari pushes Juliette, jumping with every few steps. I hear the collective laughter of the women as they lay down in the grass. Ari holds a hand from Vi and Juli, lying in between them.

The breeze of the winter chills the air colder than it already is.

White from the snow is the only thing bright around us, illuminated by the lighting from the foyer.

"Fuck you mean you put it–" Ari's boisterous voice says while laughing, her voice carrying, words cut off. The rest of their conversation cannot be heard, especially not with vomit rocketing out of Grayson's mouth.

Damien is laughing, nearing tears from his enjoyment. He mocks our friend mercilessly, all while Grayson glares at him between vomiting.

The Fae are watching them. They mutter snide comments between the others, laughing alongside Damien.

"In fairness, Esme warned you not to drink Fae wine," Adonis reminds Grayson. It's condescending but said in a tone that most Fae find funny.

"Stay long enough, and you will see just how often some in this palace will do the exact thing you tell them not to," Cassius comments. He guides himself towards the servant holding more wine. For some time, he remains there while amusing himself with what surrounds him.

The twins are cheering Grayson on, placing bets on how many more times the sorcerer will try insisting he can go back to drinking after he's done. A bet which Damien and Cassius participate in.

From the periphery of my vision, I see Vi take one more shot from a tiny bottle that Ari had stashed in her pocket. From what I assume is Vi finishing the bottle, I see it tossed to the side right before she jerks herself up and begins the action that Grayson has just finished. Juli pulls herself up to sit in her wheelchair, rubbing Vi's back while Ari holds her hair.

"Someone get drinks with electrolytes," Ari yells, collecting the miniature bottle from the ground.

At her command, knights for her and Cassius leave their station to grab both what she asks for and water. The rest of us go towards the snow, Damien helping Violette inside and ensuring that she stays awake until she is sober enough that she does not risk choking on vomit in her sleep.

A laugh passes through Cassius as the group sits on the steps. Ari falls into silence, resting her head on his shoulder while my thumb rubs around her inner thighs.

Now more than ever, I understand that duties I have set high on priorities mean nothing when presented next to time spent with those you care for. And sometimes, I wonder if I deserve moments like this.

XLIII
Tag, You're It

Arabella

A child Goblin sits on the stairs as I walk through the palace. He has hands drumming at a fast tempo, but without another person there, I don't really know what he could be excited about. Only two servants have children younger than fifteen, and I know for certain this kid is younger than that. He turns his head back as I approach him, the little tuft of hair he has moving with the wind.

"Queen Arabella!" the child greets with a wide smile. He's running up the stairs with open arms, crashing into me with a hug. From the color of his yellow eyes, where the whites of mine would be, as well as the silver of his iris, I grasp that it's Arwan. He's giddily shaking my arm with our connected hands, dragging me down the steps.

"Arwan!" I greet. I try to keep up, but his youthful speed is faster than mine. "What are you doing here?"

"The king found my mother and sent for me. He promised, remember?"

Honestly, I assumed that Cassius had forgotten about finding his mom. I thought she'd be backlogged to the furthest part of his mind with everything he had to take care of in my absence.

"Why do you always look so scared or angry?" Arwan asks with a quizzical face, releasing my hand. *"Are you angry?"*

"No, of course not," I reply.

He continues to carry a carefree attitude while also being somewhat knowledgeable that something within the lands is wrong. However, he is still far too young to be told the atrocities that lurk beyond a minor cut. His mind still blames himself for his mother's disappearance without knowing the lengths to which she has gone to protest the Elementals' ruling. All for the better treatment of the Fae. All for Arwan's future.

I won't take that kind of innocence from him.

The Goblin shrugs, beckoning his fingers to me with a flat palm. "Come here! I need to show you something!"

As I approach him, he cannot contain his giggling, his face beaming with excitement. When I get close enough, his hands quickly ball into fists, hitting me at my lower stomach in uneven beats as if he were a younger family member. Each hit made comes with a grunting sound of exertion, the child laughing at my fake reactions.

His hits become harder, not significantly enough to cause pain, but it's definitely going to bruise. He pulls my clothing, pinching me hard as I pick him up before softly plopping him into the snow.

Arwan crawls around me, latching himself onto my leg and pulling it as if he's trying to bring me down. And when I play into falling from his tug, he jumps up victoriously, dancing in an almost silly fashion. He moves with attempted cartwheels and knees hitting the snow while chanting multiple times that he's strong.

From Phantom Tower, a Fae, skin blushed like a queen conch shell, walks alongside Kabir. She's wearing the suppression cuffs without the chains, smiling in our direction. Midway through a spin,

Arwan catches sight of the woman, running to her immediately. He's screaming for his mother, tears falling from the woman's eyes, and when he is close enough to her, she immediately picks him up, her tail wrapping around him.

Kabir says something to her, which I can't make out. He holds a smiling Arwan back as he removes the cuffs.

The Fae continues sobbing while holding her child in her arms again, lingering for so long that I sit on the stairs to wait for Kabir. For minutes, I watch until one of our carriages pulls to the snowed-on stone pavement. Another guard opens the door for the three, saying something about departing for Enthar.

As they leave, Arwan waves at me through the window of the carriage. He even sticks his head out, continuing his goodbye until I can no longer see him.

"Are you not cold wearing that in this weather?" Kabir asks as he treks in leather shoes from the snow onto the stairs. He nearly slips but grabs the rail before he can. A sound from the back of my throat comes through, earning a glare from my Head Guard.

"I didn't mean to be outside today until I saw Arwan."

He's right though. I'm freezing in this skirt. It was fine in the palace during the court gathering, but now I'm shivering, with my arms colder than my legs.

"Did you wait all that time for me?" he questions in a mocking manner.

"I wanted to see why a kid was sitting on the palace's steps," I answer as the guard sits.

The grounds look so different in winter compared to summer. It's nice, but the clothing I own definitely needs some adjusting. At worst, I'll get sick from the biting weather.

Next to me, the guard ties his hair, wearing a shirt that has fabric as thin as mine, though his is a long sleeve. I don't get how he's unbothered with such little layers, but it could be due to the possibility Fae can withstand cold better than mortals.

Behind us, servants are preparing for lunch and discussing what meal would be better served. I'm so busy eavesdropping for anything interesting that Kabir has to call my name to snap my attention to his words.

"Huh? Sorry, what?"

He shakes his head. "Were you planning on training with me today? I don't recall us scheduling anything."

"Yeah, I'd rather not have you kick my ass today." I'm only partially joking, but my body is so sore, I don't think I could handle being tossed onto the ground. "I'll just use the dummy."

"You are choosing to fight against a training stand that cannot fight back or predict your next move?" He snorts, continuing his teasing.

"*Wow*. Attacking me with words instead of your Fae strength."

"And the stabbing of your words can often be more lethal than your daggers."

I roll my eyes. He's the guard I have the best relationship with. Probably the only one I trust to keep sparring with without going too easy on me. For a short period, it's so quiet, I swear I can hear the sounds of horses in the stables from the far distance. Then, he turns to me with crossed arms. "Are you decided on what to do with the traitors of the crown?"

That had actually been the purpose of the meeting that has so recently adjourned.

"I'll gather them soon, but Cas, Luka, and I agreed if the traitors *do* want to make up for their wrongdoings, they have to live without their loved ones for eight months outside of Phantom Tower. They can't make contact with them or use any Fae abilities, like glamouring and okkaring, so they'll understand the severity of hearing nothing from their family."

Humming with a short sound, Kabir rolls the sleeves of his shirt, standing up with a hand extended to pull me from where I sit. The two of us walk into the palace, towards the training room where he's meant to do a quick session with the other guards before they eat. "This was your idea?"

"Little bit mine, little bit Cas', *definitely* a lot of input from Luka."

"How will you be sure this will atone?"

"Magik will wrap chains around their hearts. They'll feel constant friction in their chest until the time is up. And if they break their agreement, it'll kill them. If they succeed, they'll be exonerated."

"They'll be pardoned?" he guesses with a brow of suspicion raised.

I huff a singular breath of laughter. "Technically."

Other guards pass us, entering the room to stretch. Some remove layers of their clothing, leaving many bare-chested or in sports bras, light gleaming against their skin. A few pair up to practice their punches or forms while waiting.

Kabir isn't exactly smiling, but something that looks like dazzlement is on his face. "There are still many things for you to sort through, aren't there?"

"Yeah, but hopefully by assigning roles and jobs, it'll make things simpler for us."

That's still a hope I'm clinging to. I have so much to attend to that the thoughts give me a headache. Most of the things that have been created by Cas, Luka, and me should have been done by our court. The primary duties of the High King and Queen are more centered around approving or denying a proposition, yet here we are trying to take on every issue. Most of which, Cassius constantly reminds me, do not fall under our responsibilities.

Of course I know that logically. The two of us are more symbolic than anything. But if I don't worry about things, I fear that no one else will.

I love Ifaeris at night. Sometimes, I'll go out onto a balcony just to look at the sky. The beauty of the lands contrasts heavily with the twinkle of the stars, Will-o'-the-wisps, and fireflies in the quiet of this time. Hearing the winds rustle through the trees and viewing the lights from the palace grounds make me think of serenity. When left alone to my thoughts, with the current security that I have, I find it easier to sleep. I never thought it possible to find myself being enticed by nature, but none of this is ordinary. Even the color of some waters runs impossible shades. It may be the same sky that humans look up at, but the exposure to things far beyond their limited experience is something I don't take for granted. Here, I get to experience a different kind of life.

"It's so pretty. The stars, and the sky, and the moon," I say at hearing the doors behind me open, with the conversation between Cassius and Luka carrying over from our room. They're standing next to me, but I don't bother to drag my eyes to them.

"Quite," Cassius' voice says.

"Absolutely," Luka says, nearly in unison.

My head turns to my side, twisting in both directions. "You're not even looking."

"I've studied the stars for years, my love," Luka returns. "I'd like to study you tonight."

I'm guided into the bedroom, Luka's arm around my waist, Cassius' around my shoulder. We've stopped–standing right at the round desk closest to the main sofa with our slippers off and the two chuckling.

"You think this is funny?" I ask.

"Oh, this is no laughing matter," Cassius says. Yet his face is still insinuating, and he is near laughter himself.

"In fact," Luka starts while smirking, "it's amusing. That you would find someone to love you the way I would."

They're coming closer. Watching me. When they look at me, lust floods their gazes, and everything in the world begins fading away.

Cassius taunts me with a hand inching towards my breast. "It seems she has a specific taste."

"It's flattering," Luka comments while pushing my hair aside, gliding his lips down my neck.

"Devastating," the Fae purrs into my ear. He grabs my face, lowering down to me, with his other arm slipping behind my back. And he's kissing me. Lingering on my lips as I feel his mouth widen into a smile.

I can hear Luka's pants unzip behind us.

"Should we see just how similar we are to her in the bedroom?" he asks with a flash of a faint smirk as I turn to him.

Wanting them endlessly is like a sickness. Too fast does my hitched breath expose my desire. My fingers creep towards the belt of my robe, dropping it. Before the fabric hits the floor, the inky lingerie I wear is gawked at. I allow them to stare for measly seconds before pulling the ribbon, undoing the bow and freeing my breasts from being pushed together.

I've worn nightgowns and forms of lingerie around Luka, but not something this obscene. Neither of them say anything, and I feel more conscious than before.

My hand is pulled by Cassius, leading us to one of our wider chairs. His fingers trace around the lace underbust, and I feel a pull as Luka rips through the back of my lingerie, breaking the clasp that holds the thin fabric together, the two sections of fabric flowing to my side.

"Don't ruin this," I scold, though I say it in a half-hearted moan as Cassius bites on my nipple, exhilaration overcoming the feeling of my apprehensiveness. Luka's hand spreads, widening my stance. "It was-" I inhale sharply. The moment his two fingers stroke my clit, my head throws back onto his shoulders. "Expensive."

"You say this as if I am meant to care," Cassius teases in an overly confident manner. He quickly shucks off the Aegean blue poet shirt. It seems pointless when half the thing is already cut into his torso. Then goes the rest of his clothing.

The hardness of Luka's cock presses against my back, and when I feel his body against mine, I realize he's naked. His breath breezes against my ear, teeth nipping into my skin as he continues grinding himself behind me.

They're in sync.

Too in sync with each other.

I want to do so many things that my mind can't even begin to focus on where to start—on who to start with. If that's even my decision to make.

A sharp pain stings my ass. My neck is gripped by Cassius, with his tongue inside my mouth. The panties I wish I never wore are torn apart by Luka, making it a complete waste of money.

"Do you remember our safe word, Dragon?" Cassius asks, his arms around my waist and positioning me over him on the chair.

I don't say anything. Just nod my head furiously.

"Say it properly, love. Tell us you want us to fuck you," Luka says, kneading my nipples.

I'd think that I'm losing control, but that would imply I actually had any in the first place.

"Please," I beg while Cassius moves my hips to slide my body along the underside of his cock. "I want you to fuck me."

"That's it," Cassius encourages. "Show us how good you are."

It's nearly embarrassing how sickly abiding I am to whatever it is that they demand of me. But gods, I'm willing to do it for the slightest bit of words that come from their mouths. I'm moving along his length, him no longer doing any work to guide me. Pre-cum leaks from his tip, grazing my clit each time I come back to it.

Still, he refuses to take me.

It's frustrating. Worse when I try to put him inside me, and his hand smacks harshly on my ass.

"You've denied me for months, but you think you deserve me fulfilling your filthy desires so soon?" he taunts, caressing my neck on one side, his lips on the other.

I'm debating committing regicide from his words alone. Part of me wants to remind him that *he* had been the one begging to be inside me not long ago. But I can't think straight when Luka's hand cups my chin, opening my mouth for him to fuck.

His hand puts light pressure on my head as my cheeks hollow. While trying to pleasure both men at once, moving my body and mouth in differing ways, I think I've forgotten how to breathe. I'm forgetting myself in their sounds that praise me. I raise my hand closer to Luka's length, but it's batted away, giving me no command over touching him the way I want.

"*Spirits, Arabella,*" Cassius whines. The neediness snaps my drive faster, sinking more of my weight onto him. I can feel the arrogance he enjoys when pleasuring me seeping into my mind. His nails dig into my back, dragging lines harsh enough to be evident even if someone were to look from a distance. "*Keep doing that.*"

The cock inside my mouth retracts, and in that same moment, my hands that grip the back of the chair release. My skin is sucked on by Cassius, fingers dancing around a nipple when swapping between palming and pinching my breast.

I'm aching so badly that I begin moving my fingers towards my clit. An action cut short once my hand touches my lower stomach, and Cassius grabs my wrist, making a sound, his voice gruff. "Were you hoping to find your own release?"

My breath shudders with a fear of answering. "Yes."

"That's too bad," Luka chuckles, now behind me.

"We take care of you tonight, my queen," Cassius says, his smile malicious on my skin.

When the comfort of his breath is around me, the soothe of his touch, I think that it's nice when it's not me tending to everyone.

It's nice *being* the one cared for.

One of my hands goes to his hair, tangling my fingers so deeply in his curls that I'm not sure if they'll ever become unknotted. Maybe I don't want them to be. I want both of them to dominate every essence of my being.

Moans from Cassius are becoming breathier, audible whining joining them. Gods, his face is so breathtaking. There's adoration present that erases every plan I had to kill him.

And kneeling next to us is Luka, the sorcerer perfectly crafted in the universe's favor, working my other breast. He squeezes it hard enough that I arch my back, pushing my hips closer to Cassius. And for a flickering second, I feel the tip of Cassius' cock nudging my entrance.

Did I just whimper?

Cassius picks up his rhythm, continuing until his mouth on my nipple clamps down with his body tensing. He hugs me close as he thrusts upwards, my movements continuing while strangled whines of pleasure erupt from him as he orgasms.

And without thinking of my actions, I shift myself to his thigh, circling my body to feel something–*anything*–to stimulate my clit.

"I think she deserves an opportunity to come, wouldn't you say, Cassius?" Luka says.

He nods while keeping his eyes on me. Release is all over his stomach. "I suppose she has earned something."

Both look at me like there's no one else they could ever desire more.

I'm taken by Luka towards the bed. It's huge. So wide that it would fit well over two of his body's length across, with maybe a foot longer than his height in length. Swirls made from the root design pattern frame the bed as an archway. It's built out past the pillows, with leaves extending from different areas, though I'm unsure if they're real or glamoured for decorative effect.

Cassius is standing, leaning down to sloppily press his mouth around the back of my shoulders. He grinds his body against mine, holding me closer to him, Luka in front to trap me between them. I don't know what to focus on. It's all so quick. My lips are on Cassius' one moment, then Luka's the next.

Their kisses are mind-shattering. World-ending.

"Look at me, darling," Cassius commands, and when I do, turning my head towards his, his lips go to mine.

The lingerie I wear is ripped apart completely by Luka's hands before he throws it to the side. Then, I'm scooped up. Carried and placed onto the mattress.

"Don't be quiet," Cassius croons.

"That's up to you."

He flicks my nipple, and my whole body crumbles, my legs spreading wide as his head lowers. Both thighs are seized by his fingers, shaking them with the squeeze of each hand while his mouth touches my skin in teasing.

"Press these together for me, won't you, love?" Luka says, hands pushing together my breasts. He kneels, hovering over me and drizzling oil onto my body. Straddling himself to place his length between the cleavage of my chest.

My heartbeat speeds up.

Under his breath, Luka curses, feverishly sliding his cock between my breasts. Head thrown back with a mouth seemingly open from my view.

In all ways possible, I'm being satisfied. Cassius doesn't care about my squirming, slapping or putting his lips to my thighs each time my legs begin closing in. I need something to pull at, but with Luka thrusting himself, Cassius so far down, and the requirement of me holding my body together, I have no options.

I already miss the taste of their lips.

Pressure from Luka's cock is incredibly debilitating for my attention. His hand holds my neck, the other latching onto one of the branches of the frame for dear life. I can hear how close he is from his breathing alone.

"*Fuck,*" I manage out in an exhaled breath, the sound shaky.

"You sound so pretty when you're desperate," Cassius mocks. His thumb moves faster, chuckling as my legs quiver. "So desperate for us."

The combination of his fingers with the sensation of Luka's sliding becomes so overwhelming, I feel myself come. I'm trying to be as quiet as I can, refusing to satisfy either of them. Though, when Cassius' mouth goes to my clit, my sight becomes full of black stars.

Luka's thrusts become sharper, efforts driving him at an uneven pace until his cum falls onto my skin. All around my neck and trailing a line down the center of my chest.

Less than eight seconds pass of me staring up at the ceiling, with both men having stepped away from the bed. Two of my fingers leave my mouth, tasting Luka's cum on my tongue.

A body shifts the area of the mattress next to me. Cassius, at my side, cups my face to bring our lips together. He lets me bring him down, the Fae grinding against my body as the two of us shift around.

Complete delirium is running through me.

Ire flickers into my senses as he rips away, giving no explanation as to why he exits off the edge of the mattress. I'm lost, staring while he beckons for me to come to him.

Our lips collide when we meet, kissing until we drown in each other. I move my hands methodically around his body, dragging my tongue lower, and though I don't know my own strategy to target his desires, I know there is one. Once I get to his cock, I wrap my mouth around it, solely focusing on his tip while my hand strokes his length.

But he doesn't let me do this for as long as I'd like. His hand goes to my wrist, smiling as Luka moves in his place.

I have no time to think. He's guiding me up the bed and onto my back, kissing down my body, dropping to kiss my lower stomach. My inner thighs.

His mouth sucks on my skin, biting into areas that are too close to the marks that Cassius has made. I can't understand it. How I know the exact feel of both their touches but am still just as shocked as if it were the first time.

My hips immediately lift at his tongue swirling around my clit. At his head burying to take me hungrily.

He alternates between his fingers pumping in me and exchanging them to spear in his tongue, never ignoring my clit. "Do you like it when I do this?"

"Yes. Keep–*fuck*–going." I reach for his hair, sifting through what I can grip onto. My breath has become both heavy and stuttering, words coming out as barely-formed sounds. He makes a noise of appeasement as I involuntarily jerk around him, clenching my thighs closer to his head.

The way Luka gazes up at me with a fueled face of longing is sensualistic in itself. I want to indulge in this forever.

"You can do better than that, love," he encourages while grabbing around my calves, pressing my legs into the mattress.

Then, he shifts my body, diving into me with ardor. I'm completely weak as his mouth explores me. He's moving his hand in lazy circles around my skin, tongue flicking my clit in ways that tighten my fist into his hair.

I'm trembling. Little screams and gasps climb their way from my vocal cords.

Less time than I'd care to admit passes before I'm coming around him. My hands reach behind me, one gripping the silky case of a pillow, a branch inside the other.

I don't even know how lost I am in pleasure before I feel Luka putting an arm around my body, moving me to my side. His mouth is on mine, the two of us kissing while–at the same time–he thrusts himself into me.

Heat from his skin burns into mine. Pushing himself deeper and deeper until I'm unsure where he and I separate. His lips are a distraction, his hand my own masochistic torture of pleasure.

Hints of mint are still present on his tongue.

"Scream for me, Blossom," he whispers with a smooth voice into my ear, his movements rocking harder into me. His mouth falls lower, eliciting something from me that only he and Cassius can. I know it. They know it. And in a quick movement, Luka drops his arm from holding my leg, grabbing me until our bodies are closer. He smacks my ass before clawing his nails in, skimming up to my breast to squeeze it tight.

It's at that when I can't bite my tongue any longer.

"Did you enjoy tasting yourself on me?" I speak into his skin, marking his neck as mine.

"I'm going to fuck that attitude out of you."

His movements become faster. Frenzied.

The look in his eyes is feral. I feel seconds pass, our eyes staring, before he's swallowing my cries with his mouth. The drawn-out way he pumps into me is no different than bliss found in a jacuzzi on a cold winter's day.

He breathes out in a moan as his fingers twine through my hair. "I can feel how much you like this, Blossom."

Nibbling my ear, Luka brings my attention to Cassius. He's sitting on a chair, looking at me while openly thrusting his cock into his hand. His body leans forward at a slight slant but still lolled. Even then, he finds delight at the sight right in front of him.

"He's looking at–" I pant, cut off by Luka thrusting into me mid-sentence.

"Were you expecting him to do nothing this whole time?" he mocks into my ear, momentarily pausing. I look at Luka, tilting my attention to him with eyes wider than they should be. "Don't look at me. Look at Cassius. Watch as he doesn't take his eyes from you."

Cassius' posture is lax. And it isn't simply lust I feel when I gaze at him. It's a craving for wanting him closer. For him to be near enough so I can touch him myself.

I keep my focus on Cassius, my eyes narrowing. They scan his body from top, to bottom, back up, grinning at him as his hand works faster.

If this is what it means to be worshiped, I now understand the adoration which created temples to be made in the gods' honor.

"My eyes are here, darling," Cassius taunts, pulling my chin up with his shadows.

Fuck me.

The sound of my name falling from my lover's lips brings another curse from me. Slow tears roll down my face as I lose focus.

"Do you think he's jealous?" Luka groans into my ear, touching my body in every way that will get a reaction. Something inside me twirls with satisfaction at knowing that *I* am the only one my lovers will behave this way around. "Do you think he envies the way you clench around me? How he only watches while I have you to myself? Selfish of me, don't you think?"

Wordlessly, I use my arm to hold my leg, rolling fully onto my back while still fixated on the Fae shooting his hips up. My brain is scattered.

"What do you want?" Luka rasps with his mouth so close to mine that I can breathe him in.

"B- Bot–" I can't get out what I need as he rubs my clit.

Air heats along my skin as he breathes, bringing his face from my neck to kiss me. "Speak up, love."

"I want both of you. In me. *Now*," I force out. I make a keening noise against my will. A beseeching sound that begs him to continue pleasuring my clit. I swear I'm deconstructing. An orgasm is building from inside me. While he moves to my neck, something oiled touches my ass. It's not a finger, but it also has a sensation of an uncanny object. I feel it touching between my cheeks, inserting itself.

My head whips to the side. Cassius' shadow is plunging in and out, slowly stretching me in a way both enjoyable and intense. Neither have said a word about it, though the look on their face shines with satisfaction.

"What are you doing?" I ask, curious but not alarmed.

Cassius, with his hand continuing to stroke himself even as he strolls to us, answers. "Preparing for what you've requested. Luka's already had the fortune of being inside your cunt. It's only fair that I am invited."

Everything pauses, my lovers looking at each other with faces that look to be conspiring.

Such looming threats to my body.

"Up," Luka orders before I kiss him roughly. He gasps for air at the parting of our lips, withdrawing his cock before his hand. "I want you up."

Cassius lays himself flat on his back, and I lean myself over him, ensnaring his body between my legs. The strands of his curls fall freely onto the pillow as he pushes into me, worthless sounds passing from his mouth while I rock my body.

"Would you watch me?" Cassius asks suggestively when I'm unable to hold contact with his eyes glittering up. "Oh Arabella, do not feign shyness now. Despite the times you looked at me with hatred, you would watch me."

I'd hate to admit he's right. Any time, even when I couldn't stand to be in the same room as him, I was still *looking at him*. I would observe his every move, mostly to make sure he wouldn't bring about a horrible decision to our kingdom, but that too, while in denial, I knew then wasn't the only reason.

I sway my hips back and forth, grinning as he takes a gulp, when a curious idea pops into my head. I slide one hand up, squeezing it around his throat the same way he has done many times to me.

"Arabella," he grits out, back arching, cock throbbing.

Then, I'm brought down by Luka pushing me onto the king's chest, Cassius clearly not upset at all, with hands wrapping around my back to plunge harder into me. He's going faster, my lips playing along the nape of his neck.

The sound of something being squeezed pokes my attention, liquid warming my skin as my Luka pumps his fingers into my ass. I love the feeling of warming lube. Despite the oil in the corner, Luka uses something to make this more enjoyable.

I can feel the head of his cock pressed against me while Cassius drives himself up.

"Is this what you want?" Luka asks, voice direct and silky.

Anxiety barrels through me like if I were being run over. Luka's about to fuck my ass. We've only done this on two occasions. When it was just the two of us and not a third party present.

"Are you planning to break me, my love?" I tease. I want this, but I can feel how tense my body goes at his cock slowly slipping into my ass. "Are you going to fuck yourself inside me until I collapse?"

He doesn't confirm or deny. Instead, the blond grips his hand on my waist, pushing himself in deeper. The feeling forms a different pleasure than when he is inside another part of me. Different, but still feeling as if we belong connected at all times. Three puzzle pieces fitting perfectly. His strokes are gentle, but I don't know if my body can take this much.

"Breathe for me, Ari," Luka comforts, tone dulcet, with a quick peck to the side of my head.

His hold is tight around my hips, his magik working my clit as if it were a mouth sucking around it. I don't care about the sounds I make or that I can't somehow kiss two people at once.

They're here. With me.

My name from Cassius' voice opens my eyes only for a slight second. His movement inside me stops, fingers lightly skimming around the hair crest of my dragon tattoo, making a clicking sound with his tongue. "I think you would find it wise not to let me repeat myself, my queen."

I'm confused. Trying to remember what it is he's talking about.

"Eyes on us, love," Luka says while moving a hand from my waist to my throat. "If your lips are not on mine, you look at Cassius. Don't shut your eyes."

But I do. I'm in too much ecstasy to focus. My vision is barely there. All I see is the blackness from the inside of my lids. My body feels like it's being set on fire, with the hottest part being my clit. It's better than anything I've ever experienced in my life.

"Beg for it," Cassius demands. It sounds more of something for himself than what he can force from me, though a hint of dominance is in his actions. "Beg for the two of us to fill you."

It's happening faster than I can keep up with. The multiple

penetration with a pressure on my clit is building an orgasm quicker than the previous times.

"*Gods please*," I cry out as their actions resume. "I needa feel-" A sharp breath cuts me off from going on. Resisting them is pointless. I'm desperate. "*Fuck*. I needa feel you come in me."

Grunts from Luka coincide with him digging the tips of his fingers into my skin–his and Cassius' a small space apart. "Love. Gods, you're perfect."

He fucks me in timed movements, thrusting a few more times as Cassius slows. I feel Luka's cock exit, with cum shooting onto my skin multiple times before he sinks his length back into me in one erratic thrust and continues pumping.

Through this, his magik doesn't yield around my clit. And the High King under me refuses to neglect my breasts as he stills. "How does it feel to have your pathetic moans give away your true thoughts on our control? Tell us how terribly you want us."

An impending explosion coils in my stomach as the two thrust into me, my head dropping, hips shifting back. I can't stop my body from clamping tighter, switching between their names while coming.

Cassius' hips buck erratically, no set pace as his movements speed up with his panting–my name cut off midway by a whimpering sound. I feel him pulsing inside me, his cum spilling.

Having the four hands on my body, it feels like an anchor to ground me back into reality. In the chaos that is the world falling around me, they are my solace. They're the gravity that keeps me pulled down from spiraling. I feel like I can finally breathe. I'm so lightheaded that I realize holding in everything for months has bigger ramifications than I thought them to.

We are to each other what nature is to existence. Everchanging. Growing. But each needing the other to survive.

To live a life without them in it would be equal to the oceans without the moon. Tides will decrease, and though the water still remains, everything that inhabits it will wither away.

As Luka pulls out and I lift myself off Cassius, I'm completely wasted away. The three of us lay side by side, faces flushed while catching our breaths like we're learning how to take in air for the first time. My body is sore, mouth unable to say anything even if I were to try. So I simply bask in the pleasantness that is a comfortable silence of affection.

XLIV

Heads Will Roll

Arabella

I wake up sandwiched between Luka and Cassius. Caging me. They're relaxed, somehow calmly wrapping themselves around my body. I'm surprised I'm managing to wake up at all. But I really have to pee.

My body's naked. Freezing at the contact of my skin touching the toilet. Somehow, I was convinced to sleep without any clothes, my exhaustion *absolutely* working in their favor. The only incentive I had motivating me to move last night was that if I didn't take another shower, I'd be completely covered in their cum. There's also the fact that we needed to change the sheets.

"Arabella," Cassius' morning voice grumbles from the other room as I wash my hands. I hear him patting around the bed.

"Bathroom." I throw a robe around me, walking into the closet to pick something to wear today. It's the first time we're meeting with common fae to settle a dispute after Delphi.

Apparently, the Lady of Aquatius couldn't be bothered to solve it.

Luka sneaks up on me, reaching over my head to grab himself a button-down. His naked body presses into the silk of my robe, pulling the sleeve down to kiss my shoulder. He's grinning when turning me around before he presses his lips onto mine. "Good morning, love."

"Can we not put this off for a longer time?" Cassius complains. He moves behind me, his hands going towards the front of what I wear, skimming around until they find themselves touching my bare skin. "Let the kingdom believe that I've corrupted you with my lack of ambition."

I worm myself out of the two, going towards the dress I've decided on wearing today. It's the newest creation from the tailors, with straps like vines twining themselves along limbs of branches, cinched at the waist with a basque waistline, everything black. "We can't ignore our jobs just 'cause *someone* doesn't feel like doing anything before noon."

The High King groans, stalking to our other closet with hair tousled to pick something I'm sure will be just as dramatic as he is.

Cassius is leaning his head on the back of the throne. He appears more frustrated by the repetitiveness of the conversation than anything. "Can the two of you get on with the issue at hand, rather than arguing over who deserves to reside where?"

"I beg you to consider that, after the Fae's betrayal and disappearance, he should not be granted back his property," the smaller Fae with dragonfly wings and antennas says.

"But, Your Majesty, you must understand," the Fae, who looks like a tree, protests, his voice cracking, head angling down sharply when Cassius brings his attention to the man. "This land has been my family's for centuries. He cannot just stake claim over it after living there with no one's knowledge just because he presumed me dead."

Glancing at me with amused eyes while I play with the leaves and flowers on the skirt of my dress, Cassius grins. I'm just as uncaring over this debacle as he is. It has an easy solution, and I don't know why it's taken so long for this to end.

"Very well. The two of you bore me. If it is a home you want, might you settle this in a different manner?" Cassius suggests. His tone is just as smooth as the ornate trimming of his clothing.

"What shall we do?" the one with wings asks. "A battle of sorts? Perhaps a competition is in order."

The Fae next to me looks delighted at the offer. He becomes interested in the matter, pushing himself straight. His face appears fascinated, with ideas that I can tell are going in and out of his brain as he stews in silence. If I didn't like him so much, I'd probably be more annoyed.

"Prince Atticus has plenty of areas available to be occupied," I tell them before Cassius chimes in with something less civil.

The king doesn't contradict me. He's smiling in support of what I say. "Come forth." He points to the tree creature Fae, beckoning him with his finger. "Your ownership over your land is a reminder that the crown offers you kindness despite your betrayal. Now go. Before we determine neither of you deserve charity."

Both bow when making their exit. One mutters something of anger, and though I can't hear it, Cassius seems to find it funny.

The prisoners who have sworn to do right and remedy their crimes have already been released–the Fae who demanded his land back being proof of this–but something is still unaccounted for. Murdering some who are so well-known in the Magikal community directly puts a target on my friends' backs. They're in danger.

Besides me, Cassius, Luka, and two of our knights, the only

ones in the room are the rest of the Wands after being escorted in at the leave of the two Fae.

"The king and I have decided to offer something," I announce. It doesn't sound right coming from me to them.

As my friends approach the thrones, I don't know how exactly to word that they're better off staying here where the wards protect them. I would do anything to keep them happy and safe, but to take away their choice wouldn't be fair of me to demand.

"To the most trusted Magiks, you have helped in keeping our kingdom safe. For this, Ifaeris will always be open to you if you so choose," Cassius declares for me, though some of the witches that this extends to aren't here. He stands there with the curve of his mouth to the side. A little too proud of himself. "Your work with us makes you just as much a part of our court as you are our friends. May the chain of the relationships never break."

Our decisions are much more eloquent when coming from his mouth than mine. It's hard to believe that this is the same Fae who thought Ifaeris wasn't worth ruling over. His eyes go to me, and I feel something churning in my stomach. Something feels wrong.

The doors burst open. Flung by magik. At the far end, standing directly in the middle, a witch carrying a small woven basket directs her focus on me. My heart begins rushing exceedingly fast. Quicker with each step she takes towards us.

I don't recognize her, but Damien does. He steps in front of Vi with his hands raised, magik already holding the woman firmly in place. "Executive Quinn, to what do we owe the pleasure?"

The thin-haired witch mutters something in a language I think may be German, but I'm not entirely sure. Her face has been lifted, and she has lips so plump, it looks like she's had an allergic reaction to something she's eaten.

"Your thoughts and commentary should be kept to yourself," Luka says. His voice is cold. Deadly. He's already holding one of the weapons that we keep hidden behind the thrones, presenting himself more lethal. "I would have thought you'd know better than to speak so poorly of a ruler of another land."

Cassius too raises his hands. After what he did on the battlefield, I'm not sure what else his shadows are capable of doing.

"It's fascinating to meet the witch who killed my poor excuse of a daughter," Quinn says, tongue clicking against the roof of her mouth. "Especially now that I can see your physical capabilities."

Snorting, I stare at the witch. She insults her daughter, but instead of being upset about her death, she compliments how I murdered her. I don't even know if it was *her* daughter I killed.

"Well, at least I killed her fast," I reply to replace the fact I don't understand what she means.

"She was insulting you, love," Luka says. His stance looks prepared to kill her for this.

The High King next to me looks provoked, his brows raised.

"Oh. I didn't think she would go for looks." I pause, trying to hold back the comment I've already thought of. But it's already coming out as my head cocks to her. "Not with that asymmetrical face."

Based on the vain look of horror, her reaction reminds me exactly who her daughter is. It wasn't her on the battlefield. Reyna's told me that in order to prove the Fae's vengeance to the Coven executives–validating that the Fae still hold a grudge against Magiks–the Council would seek out executives' children who had begun questioning their leadership and have them killed. Quinn's daughter was the first to die to further the propaganda.

"Why are you here?" I demand. My posture is so bad that even with the corsets, I slouch. I hunch my shoulders too much in a relaxed state, so I force myself to temporarily sit straighter to present myself as more of the queen that's expected.

My hand skims toward my thigh holster, which keeps my dagger sheathed. Fingers part the slit of the dress to reveal to the witch that many of us in the room are armed with weaponry.

"I was sent here by the Council," she answers with a smile I find questionable, "to deliver a gift for Yule." She glances at the king before turning to me. "And to see if Nicki's son was lying when telling us Arabella had died. It looks like he left before ensuring that she was."

"Yes, well, in a right turn of events, Arabella is alive," Cassius explains, shrugging, with the shoulder area of his black jerkin rising with him. The puffs from the sleeves of his cream shirt become wider as he moves the cuffs from his wrist to the middle of his forearms. "If not for Arabella taking matters into her own hands, Delphi would have killed more of the Fae."

"You speak highly of Miss Huǒ, who, may I remind you, snaked her way into queenship."

"You cannot snake your way to a crown when it is rightfully earned," he retorts. He doesn't break eye contact with the Coven executive. "I love her, and her cunning nature is what made her the queen. It is much more simple than you are making it to be."

Luka takes two steps down, his glare focused. "Executive, you use bold words when speaking about Arabella, yet you are a supercilious witch who holds power simply because the Council has assigned you a duty." He pauses, letting the insult settle before continuing. "The Council leaders are the ones who killed your daughter and your husband. What do you think I will do to you if you touch Arabella?"

The ambiguous candor in his threats makes him terrifying, but something in Quinn doesn't look intimidated. She sets the basket down, pulling out what's in it. And, for a second, I don't believe what I see. The curls of black and eyes that can only be attributed to the Disaris bloodline are what stop my breathing.

"Nobody move," I command loudly, stopping the knights

and my friends before they can get to her with a hand up, running down to the bodiless Fae myself. I'm still in denial, even as I can see Adonis' lifeless eyes staring directly back at me. From the swelling of his face, the little bump on the bridge of his nose is accentuated.

"He begged Leader Hilton to spare your kingdom. He even offered himself if it would save from any further blood spilled." She speaks without empathy. Says this as if she isn't holding a bloody head in her hands. "After that, he confessed to everything he and Delphi did. So the Council doesn't care too much about what happened to her. She killed herself by learning magik she couldn't handle."

We gave Adonis the freedom to roam whenever he wanted after he earned our trust, but I wouldn't have thought he would go to the Council.

"You admit your leaders have acknowledged what Delphi has done," Cassius interjects. "Then what reason have they thought it right to kill my brother?"

"The Fae had to die for the death of a Council leader's son, whom you killed in battle," Quinn answers. "And as an addition, if the Fae do not want to engage in war, the Council has requested that if Arabella is still alive, she return with me as compensation for the other Magiks whose lives were taken."

Awareness forces its way through me as the executive stares expectantly in my direction. "You seriously think I'm going with you?"

Others of the royal family have gathered in the room. They stare between Quinn and me, waiting until I give them a signal to do something. At their gazes dropping to Adonis, they do their best to hide their initial shock, but the widening of their eyes may reveal it.

My hand pushes through the air, pinning the witch down on her back and causing Adonis' head to drop from her hand. It rolls, but not more than half a rotation. I send my dagger to hover right above her throat, the edge's point slightly poking into her neck.

"You do not scare us," she says, unmoving and still.

"Your words say that," Luka starts, "but the way your arm is shaking, your inability to hold eye contact with any of us, and the fact your bottom lip is quivering suggest otherwise."

Quinn becomes more rigid, uttering nothing in response. I think carefully, going through every option and repercussions for any outcome. To murder her after so many had died, especially someone the Council has sent, would be too suspicious. It could be exactly what they're hoping for. If she dies while coming to negotiate, despite Adonis, it would confirm any false narratives already spread.

"I'm not killing her," I decidedly proclaim.

She goes uneasy at my stance. Her body is rigid while suspended in distrust. "You're not?"

"No. You're going to deliver a message for me." My fingers squeeze together, right hand closing in a cupping position as if I were choking her. The witch begins turning purple, suffocating without air entering her lungs. "And I'm not one to mail body parts."

Then, I take in one breath, controlling myself enough to loosen my magik that binds her. She gasps for air, tears running down as she stands. I can't kill her. Not if I want her to relay something for me.

"Tell the Council that I spared you. Beg them to reconsider whatever else they have planned against us." Against my better judgment, I release her. If I were to use magik to ensure that she follows through, it would make it less truthful to the Council. They already refuse to search for evidence if it doesn't work in their preconceived decisions, executing to preserve secrets that they and the executives keep from the public.

"You ought to leave before my queen changes her mind and has you murdered where you stand," Cassius remarks, smiling and amused. "If you defy what she demands, I'm sure she will ensure you are the first we have killed."

Nodding furiously, she okkars away.

Gavin goes to pick up Adonis' head to have it concealed until a decision is reached on what to do with it. It's similar to what they did with Elliot, except this time, Cassius and I will be the ones determining his burial.

"What does this mean?" Grayson asks.

"It means the Fae and Magiks may be at war once again," Dyana answers.

Cassius orders everyone out, and as the room empties, my lovers and I make our way towards the steps. I seat myself between the front legs of my throne, my head placing itself on Luka's shoulder, while Cassius has his arm hooked in my right, with our fingers locked.

My mind whirls with the danger and death that's sure to follow. The two beside me are saying something about the Wands going to the wards, but I'm barely listening. Too concerned with going over the endless possibilities of what we're up against.

There's no real way to deny the act that's already been done.

Our peace with the Coven is uncertain.

And it's our responsibility to make sure they don't finish what the ancestors started.

Arabella's Diary Entries

Following this page are a few entries from Arabella's diary that she kept in Gigantia.

~ I've been in here 3 weeks (I think) and there's not much light. No clock. No way for me to tell how long it's really been. Adonis was ~~dumb~~ kind enough to give me a notebook and a pen. Maybe I can kill myself with it? They let me shower once a week. I think I'm going crazy

~ Writing in this is the only thing that makes me feel real. It reminds me that I'm alive and not in one of those mind games Delphi likes to torture me with. I keep wondering if anyone's looking for me. If they even care enough or bother to try. Most days I wonder why the universe allows me to wake up every day

~ I found a piece of glass today. I think if I slice myself enough, I'll be able to tell if Delphi is in my mind or not. How did the one person who I used to vent to on a daily basis become the same one to throw it back in my face? How did we go from unconditional support to unfiltered hatred?

Anyway, I can't stand what my body looks like, and I'm starting to think I should throw up whenever I eat, but I don't know who I'm trying to impress. All I really know is I don't think I deserve to be loved. And it's so pointless to think that because I know I'm just being irrational. But, I feel like if Cas and Luka ARE coming for me, they deserve to be with someone who looks prettier than I am.

~ What did I do to deserve this? Any of this? Maybe I was just destined to live a life of absolute misery. GODS please just let me die

I feel like I'm ranting about the same four things over and over, but I can't help it. What else am I supposed to talk about? I need some outlet or I might as well die.

Honestly, maybe Delphi's getting to me because all I can think of myself is worthlessness. It's such a fucked up thing to even think, but if no one wants me, not even the man who abused me, what hope is there for the ones that I think love me? I wonder if the reason (besides keeping me from escaping) that I have chains on is to keep me from using my magik and committing suicide.

Why am I self aware enough of my own emotions to shut them down but still cry about them? I try being tough and acting like what Delphi does to me isn't that bad, but I know she sees through it. I don't think I'm that convincing when I'm bleeding from my sides and screaming for my life. It's kinda funny she manipulates my reality now just as much as she did when we were friends. Plus, sometimes I think she's right about me. I wasn't the best in our friendship, but even then, I don't think it warrants this??

I don't bother keeping track of how long I've been here anymore. Everything blends together and honestly with the amount of my warped reality I'm put under, I don't think time matters. I just wish I knew what Delphi wanted from me.

~ Delphi didn't torture me that long today. The limit of holding my pee is really being tested

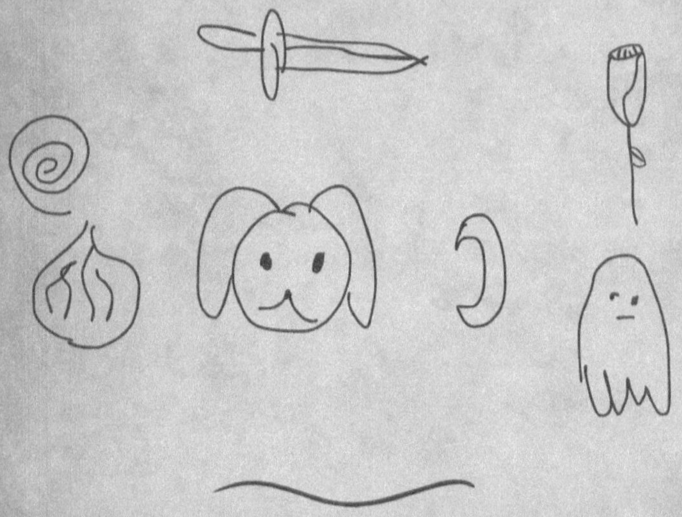

~ Gods I'm so replaceable. As much as I think people have love for me, I feel like if Delphi killed me, my friends and family would be sad, but it's not like they won't move on. I'm replaceable enough

North America
North Atlantic Ocean
Ifaeris
South America
South Atlantic Ocean
Pacific Ocean
Searuck

Arctic Ocean
Europe
Asia
Magik Cove
Pacific Ocean
Indian Ocean
Africa
Australia
Gigantia
Antarctica

ACKNOWLEDGMENTS

I can't even begin to explain how much book 2 of the Elements of Magik trilogy has changed my writing style. So much happened while drafting this book. At one point, I was at an anime convention with my friends, and while they went clubbing one night, I literally stayed in just to write smut. And then there were other times when I cried about this book, either from stress or because of how much it has moved on from Elemental Ruin. Continuing to build this world and the characters has been fun and challenging at the same time, but I still worried about how book two would wind up being perceived. In the end, I am so proud of it.

To my wonderful friends in the writing and book community whom I have met while on this journey, I appreciate you so much. From writing sprints, to motivation, to just being here to talk with me through something, I am grateful for all of you. To Congregation, I love you. The lot of you have literally heard me say the most insane things when drafting and have *seen* the routes that Elements have gone. And to Alexandra, Alex 1, Pearla, and everyone who has ever helped me with my indecisiveness, I'm unbelievably glad that your sleep schedules are as bad as mine (or you're awake for work by the time I'm going to sleep). Thank you for helping me improve as a writer and caring as much about Elements as I do. Honestly, I could go on and on about everyone I'm grateful for and the reason, but then this would be *way* too many pages.

Mars, Bia, and Yans, the three who have known me since sandbox days, thank you for putting up with my rantings about this book. Thank you for allowing me to not shut up about this. Thank you for your unending support and patience with me being down bad for these characters.

Of course, I can't write these acknowledgments without thanking my book team. Thank you to both my editors, Quinn and Jude, for helping me and answering all my questions. Thank you for aiding where I lack (horrendously) in grammar. I'm grateful for your comments and your yelling at my choices.

I know that Magikal Reckoning may have been a shock to some people. The book deals with heavy topics, and I thought it was really important to show how mental health issues can manifest in very different ways. If you have ever dealt with things similar, remember that it's okay to ask for help when you need it. And I truly hope that none of you ever dealt with (or will deal with) your ex-girlfriend becoming hellbent on destroying you. Thank you for reading my book, and thank you for reading this!

About the Author

Alx Chan Yee is a college graduate born and raised in California. She's gone from loving fantasy since a young age, to writing her own characters that are full of whimsy and strength. At nearly all times, you will find her talking about fictional characters, whether from movies, shows, or books.

She can be found on:

Instagram: @bookmarkalx
Tiktok: @bookmarkalx
Twitter: @bookmarkalx
Website: www.alxwritesbooks.com

www.ingramcontent.com/pod-product-compliance
Lightning Source LLC
Chambersburg PA
CBHW022008300726
48970CB00003B/791